HER HUSBAND

HER HUSBAND

by Luigi Pirandello

Translated and with an Afterword

by Martha King and Mary Ann Frese Witt

DUKE UNIVERSITY PRESS

DURHAM AND LONDON

2000

Printed in the United States of America on acid-free paper ∞

Library of Congress Cataloging-in-Publication Data

appear on the last printed page of this book.

CONTENTS

ACKNOWLEDGMENTS

We are indebted to several people who have generously offered us their time, suggestions, and encouragement in the fascinating but sometimes frustrating endeavor to translate Pirandello. After we had started on the project, we learned from Daniela Bini that Eric Bentley was interested in finding a translator for *Suo marito*. He was more than generous to us with his time, encouragement, enthusiasm, and help. He read the entire manuscript carefully, raising important questions, pointing out stylistic problems, and offering suggestions. Indeed, without Eric Bentley's work, the present translation would be a very different product.

Others have left their mark on this translation by helping us to understand a sometimes obscure Italian term and thus to find its English equivalent. We are grateful to Alberto Malfitano, Domenico Frezza, Donatella Spinelli, and Ronald Witt for their help in this area. In Florence, Gloria Anzilotti was always willing to help work out puzzling passages. We also thank Alexander DeGrand, who suggested important changes in the Afterword. Our editor, J. Reynolds Smith, made incisive and useful remarks on both the translation and the Afterword. Our copyeditor, Estelle Silbermann, read the manuscript with great care and precision, making several suggestions and changes.

Martha Witt Santalucia not only read the entire translation, improving it with several acute observations: she brought us together in the first place. We would like to dedicate our translation to her.

HER HUSBAND

1 ✳ THE BANQUET

1

Attilio Raceni, publisher for four years of the women's (not feminist) magazine *The Muses*, woke up late that morning in a bad mood.

Under the eyes of innumerable young Italian women writers—poets, novelists, and short-story writers (even some playwrights)—watching him from photographs arranged in various groupings on the walls, all with faces composed in a particular attitude of vivacious or sentimental charm, he got out of bed—oh, dear, in his night shirt, naturally, but a long one, long enough to reach his ankles, fortunately. Slipping into house shoes, he went to open the window.

Attilio Raceni was little aware of what he did in the privacy of his home, so if someone had said to him: "You just did this and this," he would have objected, red as a beet.

"Me? Not true! Impossible."

And yet, there he is: sitting in his night shirt at the foot of his bed, with two fingers tenaciously tugging at a hair deeply embedded in his right nostril. And he rolls his eyes and wrinkles his nose and purses his lips in the sharp pain of that obstinate pinching until all at once he opens his mouth and his nostrils dilate for the sudden explosion of a couple of sneezes.

"Two hundred and forty!" he then says. "Thirty times eight, two hundred and forty."

Because while Attilio Raceni was tugging at that nose hair, he was absorbed in reckoning that if thirty guests paid eight lire each they might expect champagne, or at least some modest (that is, local) sparkling wine for the toasts.

In attending to his routine personal care, even if he had looked up he wouldn't have noticed the images of those writers, for the most part spinsters, although most of them tried to demonstrate in their writing that they were experienced in the ways of the world. Therefore, he wouldn't have noticed that those sentimental ladies seemed distressed at the sight of their nice director doing certain unpleasant things (however natural), out of unconscious habit, and that they were smiling about it rather superciliously.

Having recently turned thirty, Attilio Raceni had not yet lost his youthful appearance. The pale languor of his face, his curly mustache, his velvety almond-shaped eyes, his raven forelock, gave him the air of a troubadour.

He was basically satisfied with the regard he enjoyed as director of that women's (not feminist) magazine, *The Muses*, although it cost him considerable financial sacrifice. But from childhood he had been devoted to women's literature, because his "mamma," Teresa Raceni Villardi, had been a noted poetess, and in "Mamma's" house many women writers had gathered, some now dead, others now very old, upon whose knees he could almost say he had been raised. And their endless fondling and caresses had almost left an indelible patina on him. It seemed as if those light, delicate, experienced female hands, stroking and smoothing, had shaped him into that ambiguous, artificial beauty forever. He often moistened his lips, bent over smiling to listen, held his chest high, turned his head, patted his hair like a woman. Once a friend had jokingly touched his chest: "Do you have them?"

Breasts! The schmuck! He had turned bright red.

Left an orphan with a small income, the first thing he did was quit the university, and in order to give himself a profession, he founded *The Muses*. It ate into his inheritance, but gave him enough to live modestly and devote all his time to the magazine. With the subscriptions he had diligently garnered, he had assured its continuation, which, aside from the worries, no longer cost him anything: just as the numerous women collaborators cost him nothing, since they were never paid for their writing.

This morning he did not even have the time to regret the hairs his raven forelock left in the comb after a hasty styling. He had so much to do!

At ten he had to be at Via Sistina, at the home of Dora Barmis, the *prima musa* of *The Muses*, the very knowledgeable adviser on the beauty, natural charm, and morals of Italian signore and signorine. He had to get together with her to plan the banquet, the fraternal literary *agape*, that he wanted to give for the young and already very celebrated writer Silvia Roncella. Only recently she had come from Taranto with her husband to settle in Rome, "responding to Glory's first call, after the triumphant reception unanimously given by critics and public for her latest novel, *House of Dwarves*," as he had written in the last issue of *The Muses*.

From his desk he took a bunch of papers dealing with the banquet, gave a final glance in the mirror almost as if to say good-bye to himself, and left.

2

A confused outcry in the distance, a flurry of people racing toward Piazza Venezia. On Via San Marco an alarmed Attilio Raceni approached an overweight merchant of aluminum kitchenware who was huffing and puffing as he hurriedly pulled down the metal barrier over his shop windows and asked him politely: "Please, what is it?"

"Uh . . . they say . . . I don't know," the man grunted in reply without turning.

A street sweeper, sitting quietly on the shaft of his cart with a broom on his shoulder like a flag, one arm on its handle as counterbalance, took his pipe from his mouth, spat, and said in Roman dialect: "They're trying it again."

Attilio Raceni turned and looked at him as though in pity. "A demonstration? Why?"

3

"Uhm!"

"Dogs!" shouted the potbellied merchant, purple-faced and panting as he straightened up.

Under the cart a hairless old dog with half-closed, runny eyes was stretched out, more placid than the street sweeper. At the merchant's "Dogs!" he barely raised his head off his paws without opening his eyes, only wiggling his ears a little sorrowfully. Were they talking to him? He waited for a kick. The kick didn't come. Then they weren't talking to him. He settled down to sleep again.

The Roman street sweeper observed: "They've done with their meeting."

"And they want to kick in the windows," the other one added. "You hear? You hear?"

A cacophony of whistles rose from the next piazza and right after that a shout that reached the heavens.

The chaos there must be awful.

"There's a police barricade, no one can get through." Without moving from the shaft, the placid street sweeper sang out after the people who were rushing by, and he spat again.

Attilio Raceni hurried off in a huff. Fine thing if he couldn't get through! All these obstacles now, as if the worries, cares, and annoyances plaguing him since he got the idea of that banquet weren't enough. Now all he needed was the rabble in the streets demanding some new right, and the tremendous April weather didn't help things: the fiery warmth of the spring sun was inebriating!

At Piazza Venezia Attilio Raceni's face dropped as though an inner string had suddenly let go. Struck by the violent spectacle before him, he stood open-mouthed.

The piazza swarmed with people. The soldiers' barrier was at the head of Via del Plebiscito and the Corso. Many demonstrators had climbed onto a waiting trolley and were yelling at the top of their lungs.

"Death to the traitors."

"Death!"

"Down with the minister."

"Down!"

In a fit of spite toward these dregs of humanity, and not about to take it quietly, Attilio Raceni got the desperate idea of elbowing his way quickly right across the piazza. If he managed that, he would plead with the officer guarding the Corso to please let him pass. He wouldn't refuse him. But suddenly from the middle of the piazza: "*Beep, beep, beep.*"

The trumpet. The first blare. A crushing confusion: many, roughed up in the rioting, wanted to run away, but they were so crammed and squeezed together they could only struggle angrily, while the most overwrought ruffians tried to force their way through the crowd, or rather, push ahead of the others among the ever more tempestuous whistles and shouts.

"To Palazzo Braschiiii!"

"Go! Go ahead!"

"Break through the barriers!"

And again the trumpet blared.

Suddenly, without knowing how it happened, Attilio Raceni, choking, crushed, gasping like a fish, found himself bounced back to Trajan's Forum in the middle of the fleeing and delirious crowd. Trajan's Column seemed to be teetering. Where was it safe? Which direction to take? It seemed to him that the greater part of the crowd was moving up a street northeast of the Forum, Magnanapoli, so he bolted like a deer up Via Tre Cannelle. But even there he stumbled onto soldiers blocking off Via Nazionale.

"No passing here!"

"Listen, please, I must. . . ."

A furious push from behind broke off Attilio Raceni's explanation, causing his nose to squirt on the face of the officer, who repulsed him fiercely with blows to his stomach. But another very violent shove hurled him against the soldiers who caved in at the onslaught. A tremendous discharge of rifles roared from the piazza. And Attilio Raceni, in the terror-crazed crowd, was lost in the middle of the cavalry that appeared suddenly from heaven knows where, perhaps from Piazza

Pilota. Away, away with the others, away at full speed, he, Attilio Raceni, followed by the cavalry, Attilio Raceni, director of the women's (not feminist) magazine *The Muses*.

Out of breath, he stopped at the entrance to Via Quattro Fontane.

"Cowards! Riffraff! Scoundrels!" he shouted through his teeth, turning into that street, almost crying with anger, pale, shaken, trembling all over. He touched his ribs, his hips, and tried to straighten his clothes, to remove every trace of the violence suffered in the humiliating rout.

"Cowards! Scoundrels!" and he turned to look behind him, afraid someone might have seen him in that condition, and he rubbed his quivering neck with his fist. And there, to be sure, was a little old man standing at a window taking it all in with his mouth open, toothless, scratching his short yellowish beard with pleasure. Attilio Raceni wrinkled his nose and was just about to hurl some insults at that blockhead, but he looked down, snorted, and turned again to look toward Via Nazionale. To regain his lost sense of dignity, he would have liked to throw himself into the fray again, to grab those rascals one by one and grind them under his feet, to knock that crowd around that had unexpectedly assaulted him so savagely and had made him suffer the disgrace of turning tail, the shame of his fear and flight, the derision of that old imbecile. . . . Ah, beasts, beasts, beasts! How triumphantly they rose up on their hind legs, shouting and lurching, about to snatch up the sop of those charlatan organizers!

This image pleased him, and comforted him somewhat. But, looking down at his hands . . . Oh, God, the papers, where were the papers he had taken with him when he left home? The guest list . . . the acceptances? They had been torn from his hands, or he had lost them in the crush. How could he remember everyone he had invited? Those who had accepted or excused themselves from participating in the banquet? And among the acceptances, one dear to him, really precious, one that he had wanted to show Signora Barmis and then get framed to hang in his room: the one from Maurizio Gueli, the Maestro, sent from Monteporzio, handwritten. . . . That one lost as well! Ah, Gueli's autograph, there, trampled under the filthy feet of those brutes. . . . Attilio Raceni felt all worked up again. How disgusting to be living in times of such horrid barbarity masquerading as civility!

With the proud bearing and mien of an indignant eagle, he was already on Via Sistina near the descent of Via Capo le Case. Dora Barmis lived there alone in four small, dark rooms with low ceilings.

3

Dora Barmis enjoyed letting everyone think she was extremely poor, however many her cosmetics, galas, and charmingly capricious gowns. The little sitting room that also served as a writing room, the alcove, the dining room, and entry hall were, like the owner, strangely but certainly not at all poorly outfitted.

Separated for years from a husband no one had ever known, dark and agile, with eyes lightly touched up, her voice a little hoarse, she clearly declared her knowledge of life with her looks and smiles, with every movement of her body. She knew the throbs of heart and nerves, the art of pleasing, of awakening, of arousing the most refined and vehement male desires that made her laugh loudly when she saw them flame in the eyes of the man she was talking to. But she laughed even louder at seeing certain eyes grow dreamy as if from the promise of a lasting sentiment.

Attilio Raceni found her in the little sitting room near a small nickel-plated iron desk decorated with arabesques. She was engrossed in reading, wearing a low-necked Japanese gown.

"Poor Attilio! Poor Attilio!" she said after roaring with laughter at his account of the disagreeable adventure. "Sit down. What can I give you to soothe your troubled spirit?"

She looked at him with a kindly mocking air, winking an eye and cocking her head on her provocative bare neck.

"Nothing? Nothing at all? Anyway, you know? You look nice this way . . . a bit untidy. I've always told you, darling: a *nuance* of brutality would do wonders! Too languid and . . . must I say it? Your elegance has been for some time a little . . . a little *démodée*. For example, I don't like the gesture you made just now as you sat down."

"What gesture?" asked Raceni, who didn't know he had made one.

"Pulling your lapels this way and that . . . And put that hand down! Always in your hair. We know it's beautiful!"

"Please, Dora!" Raceni snorted. "I'm frazzled!"

Dora Barmis broke into laughter again, placing her hands on the desk and leaning backward. "The banquet?" Then she said, "Are you serious? While my proletarian brothers are protesting . . ."

"Don't joke, please, or I'm leaving!" Raceni threatened.

Dora Barmis got to her feet. "But I'm serious, darling! I wouldn't worry myself so much if I were you. Silvia Roncella . . . but first of all tell me what she's like! I'm dying of curiosity to meet her. She's not receiving yet?"

"Uh, no. Poor things just found a house a few days ago. You'll see her at the banquet."

"Give me a light," Dora said, "and then answer me frankly."

She lit her cigarette, bending over and leaning her face toward the match held by Raceni; then, in a cloud of smoke, she asked: "Are you in love with her?"

"Are you crazy?" Raceni fired back. "Don't make me angry."

"A little plain, then?" Signora Barmis observed.

Raceni did not reply. He crossed one leg over the other; he looked up at the ceiling; he closed his eyes.

"Oh, no, darling!" Signora Barmis exclaimed. "We'll get nothing done like that. You came to me for help. First you have to satisfy my curiosity."

"Well, I'm sorry!" Raceni snorted again, relaxing somewhat. "Those are some questions you're asking!"

"I understand," Signora Barmis said. "It's either one thing or the other: either you truly are in love or she must be really ugly, as they say in Milan. Come on now, tell me: how does she dress? Badly, without a doubt!"

"Rather badly. Inexperienced, you understand."

"I see, I see," repeated Signora Barmis. "Shall we say a ruffled duckling?"

She opened her mouth, wrinkled her nose, and pretended to laugh, with her throat.

"Wait," she went over to him. "You're losing your pin. My goodness, how have you knotted this tie?"

"Oh," Raceni began. "With all that . . ."

He stopped. Dora's face was too close. Concentrating on his tie, she felt herself being watched. When she finished she gave him a little tap on his nose, and with an indefinable smile: "Well, then?" she asked him. "We were saying . . . ah, Signora Roncella! You don't like duckling? Little monkey, then."

"You're wrong," retorted Raceni. "She's pretty enough, I assure you. Not striking, perhaps; but her eyes are exceptional!"

"Dark?"

"No, blue, intense, very gentle. And a sad smile, intelligent. She must be very very nice, that's all."

Dora Barmis attacked: "Nice you said? Nice? Go on! The person who wrote *House of Dwarves* can't be nice, I assure you."

"And yet . . ." Raceni said.

"I assure you!" Dora repeated. "That woman goes well armed, you can be certain!"

Raceni smiled.

"She must have a character sharp as a knife," continued Signora Barmis. "And tell me, is it true she has a hairy wart here, on her lip?"

"A wart?"

"Hairy, here."

"I never noticed one. But no, who told you that?"

"I imagined it. As far as I'm concerned, Roncella must have a hairy wart on her lip. I always seem to see it when I read her things. And tell me: her husband? What's her husband like?"

"Just drop it!" Raceni replied impatiently. "He's not for you."

"Thank you very much!" Dora said. "I want to know what he's like. I imagine him rotund. . . . Rotund, isn't he? For heaven's sake, tell me he's rotund, blond, ruddy, and . . . not mean."

"All right: that's the way he'll be, if it makes you happy. Now, please, can't we be serious?"

"About the banquet?" Signora Barmis asked again. "Listen, darling: Silvia Roncella is no longer for us. Your little dove has flown too too

9

high. She has crossed the Alps and the sea and will go to make herself a nest far far away, with many golden straws, in the great literary journals of France, Germany, and England. . . . How can you expect her to lay any more little blue eggs, even if very tiny ones, like this . . . on the altar of our poor *Muses?*"

"What eggs! What eggs!" Raceni said, shaking himself. "Not dove eggs, not an ostrich egg. Signora Roncella won't write for any magazine again. She's devoting herself entirely to the theater."

"To the theater? Really?" exclaimed Signora Barmis, her curiosity aroused.

"Not to act!" Raceni said. "That would be the last straw! To write."

"For the theater?"

"Yes. Because her husband . . ."

"Right! Her husband . . . what's his name?"

"Boggiolo."

"Yes, yes. I remember. Boggiolo. And he writes, too."

"Hardly! He's at the Notary Public Office."

"A notary? Oh, dear! A notary?"

"In a record office. A fine young man. Stop it, please. I want to finish with this business of the banquet as quickly as possible. I had a guest list, and those dogs . . . But let's see if we can reconstruct it. You write. By the way, did you know that Gueli has accepted? It's the clearest proof he really admires Signora Roncella, as they say."

Dora Barmis was absorbed in thought; then she said: "I don't understand. . . . Gueli . . . he seems so different. . . ."

"Let's not argue," Raceni cut her off. "Write: Maurizio Gueli."

"I'll add in parenthesis, if you don't mind, *Signora Frezzi permitting.* Next?"

"Senator Borghi."

"Has he accepted?"

"Good heavens. He'll be presiding! He published *House of Dwarves* in his literary review. Write: Donna Francesca Lampugnani."

"My lovely president, yes, yes," Signora Barmis said as she wrote. "Dear, dear, dear . . ."

"Donna Maria Rosa Bornè-Laturzi," Raceni continued to dictate.

"Oh, God!" snorted Dora Barmis. "That virtuous little guinea hen?"

"And decorative," Raceni said. "Write: Filiberto Litti."

"Very good! It gets better and better!" Signora Barmis approved. "Archaeology next to antiquity! Tell me, Raceni: we're having this banquet in the ruins of the Forum?"

"By the way!" exclaimed Raceni. "We still have to decide where to have it. Where would you suggest?"

"But with these guests . . ."

"Oh, God, no, I say again, let's be serious! I was thinking of the Caffè di Roma."

"In the evening? No! It's spring. We need to have it during the day, in a beautiful place, outside. . . Wait: at the Castello di Costantino. That's it. Delightful. In the glassed-in hall, with the whole countryside in view . . . the Albani mountains . . . the Castelli romani . . . and then, opposite, the Palatine . . . Yes, yes, there . . . it's enchanting! Without a doubt!"

"I'm for the Castello di Costantino," Raceni said. "Let's go there tomorrow to make the arrangements. I think we'll be about thirty. Listen, Giustino has been particularly insistent. . . ."

"Who is Giustino?"

"Her husband, I told you, Giustino Boggiolo. He's insisting on the press. He would like a lot of journalists. I invited Lampini. . . ."

"Ah, Ciceroncino, bravo!"

"And I think another four or five, I don't know: Bardozzi, Centanni, Federici, and . . . what's his name? the one who writes for the *Capitale*. . . ."

"Mola?"

"Mola. Write it down. We need some others who are a little more . . . a little more . . . With Gueli coming, you understand. For example, Casimiro Luna."

"Wait a minute," Signora Barmis said, "if Donna Francesca Lampugnani comes, it won't be difficult to get Betti."

"But Betti gave *The House of Dwarves* a bad review. Have you seen it?" Raceni asked.

"What does that matter? It's even better. Invite him! I'll speak to Donna Francesca. As for Miro Luna, I hope to bring him along with me."

"You'll make Boggiolo happy, really happy! Now write down the Honorable Carpi, and that little cripple . . . the poet . . ."

"Zago, yes! Poor little dear! What beautiful poems he writes. I love him, don't you know? Look at his portrait there. I made him give it to me. Doesn't he look like Leopardi with glasses?"

"Faustino Toronti," Raceni continued dictating. "And Jacono . . ."

"No!" shouted Dora Barmis, throwing down her pen. "You've invited that dreadful Neapolitan Raimondo Jacono? Then I'm not coming!"

"Calm down. I had to," Raceni replied regretfully. "He was with Zago. . . . If I invited one I had to invite the other."

"Well, then, I insist on Flavia Morlacchi," Signora Barmis said. "There: Fla-vi-a Morlacchi. Flavia's not her real name. Her name's Gaetana, Gaetana."

"That's what Jacono says!" smiled Raceni. "After the tiff."

"Tiff?" Signora Barmis replied. "But they beat each other with sticks, darling! They spat in each other's faces, the watchmen came running. . . ."

Signora Barmis and Raceni reread the list, taking their time over this or that name, as if honing their list to a fine point on a grinder as they sharpened their tongues, which hardly needed it. Finally, a large fly quietly sleeping on a door woke up and zoomed in to make a third in the conversation. Dora reacted with terror—more than disgust, real terror. First she grabbed Raceni, holding him tight, her fragrant hair beneath his chin; then she ran to the alcove, shouting to Raceni behind the door that she wouldn't come back in the room until he chased the fly out the window or killed the *horrible beast*.

"I'll leave you there and be on my way," Raceni said calmly, taking the new list from the desk.

"No, Raceni, for heaven's sake!" Dora entreated from the other side.

"Well, open the door then!"

"There, I opened it, but you . . . Oh! what are you doing?"

"One kiss," said Raceni, his foot holding the door open the crack allowed by Dora. "Just one . . ."

"What's got into you?" she shouted, straining to close the door again.

"Just a little one," he insisted. "I've practically come from a war. . . . A tiny reward, from there, come on . . . just one!"

"The fly might come in. Oh, dear, Raceni!"

"Well, do it quickly!"

Through the crack in the door their two mouths met and the opening gradually widened, when they heard the newsboy's cry in the street outside: "*Third edition! Four dead and twenty wounded! Clash with the military! Assault on Palazzo Braschiiii! Bloodshed on Piazza Navonaaaa!*"

Attilio Raceni withdrew from the kiss, ashen: "Did you hear? Four dead. For God's sake! Don't they have anything to do? And I could have been there smack in the middle. . . ."

4

It had already struck twelve and only five of the thirty guests who should be coming to the banquet at Castello di Costantino had arrived. These five secretly regretted their punctuality, fearing it might make them seem overanxious or too accommodating.

First to come had been Flavia Morlacchi, poet, novelist, and playwright. After the other four arrived they left her alone, standing to one side. They were the old professor of archaeology and forgotten poet Filiberto Litti; the short-story writer from Piacenza, Faustino Toronti, affected and chaste; the overweight Neapolitan novelist Raimondo Jacono, and the Venetian poet Cosimo Zago, rickety and lame in one foot. All five stood on the terrace in front of the glassed-in hall.

Filiberto Litti was tall, thin, wooden, with a large white mustache and a smudge of hair between his lower lip and chin, and a pair of enormous fleshy, purple ears. He was speaking, stammering a little, about the ruins there on the Palatine (as if they belonged to him) with Faustino Toronti, also elderly, but less obviously so with his hair combed over his ears and dyed mustache. Raimondo Jacono, his back to Signora Morlacchi, was compassionately watching Zago admire the cool green countryside there before them on that sweet April day.

The poor fellow had just arrived at the terrace railing, still wearing an old overcoat green with age that billowed around his neck. He placed a large-knuckled hand on the decorative top of the railing, his fingernails pink and deformed by the continual pressure on his crutch. Now, his sorrowful eyes closed behind his glasses, he repeated, as though he had never in his life enjoyed such a feast of light and color: "How enchanting! How intoxicating, this sun! What a view!"

"Yes, indeed," ruminated Jacono. "Very beautiful. Marvelous. A pity that . . ."

"Those mountains over there, aerial . . . almost fragile . . . Are they still the Albani?"

"Apennines or Albani, don't faint! You can ask Professor Litti over there. He's an archaeologist."

"And . . . and, excuse me, what do the mountains have to do with . . . with archaeology?" Litti asked a little resentfully.

"Professor, what are you saying!" exclaimed the Neapolitan. "Monuments of nature, of the most venerable antiquity. It's a shame that . . . I was saying . . . It's twelve-thirty, my oh my! I'm hungry."

Signora Morlacchi grimaced in disgust from where she stood. She seethed in silence as she pretended to be enchanted by the marvelous landscape. The Apennines or the Albani? She didn't know either, but why was the name important? No one understood "azure" poetry better than she. And she asked herself if the word for the Roman burial niche, columbarium . . . the austere columbarium, wouldn't successfully capture the image of those Palatine ruins: blind eyes, shadowy eyes of the fierce and glorious ghost of ancient Rome, still vainly gazing there from the hill on the spectacle of the green bewitching life of this April from a far distant time.

Of this April from a far distant time . . .

Nice line! Dreamlike . . .

And she lowered her large, heavy eyelids over her gloomy, pale eyes, like those of a dying goat. There. She had managed to pluck the flower

14

of a beautiful image from nature and history. Because of this she no longer regretted having lowered herself to honor Silvia Roncella, so much younger than herself, almost a beginner still, uncultured, totally unpoetic.

While thinking such thoughts, with a gesture of disdain, she turned her pale, coarse, worn face, with violently contrasting thick painted lips, toward those four, who were paying no attention to her. She straightened her back and lifted a hand overloaded with rings to lightly pat the strawlike fringe on her forehead.

Perhaps Zago was also pondering a poem, pinching the bristly black hairs under his lip. But in order to create he first needed to know many things. However, he no longer wanted to ask anything of that Neapolitan who, before such a spectacle as that, said he was hungry.

Coming in with his customary hop and skip was the young journalist Tito Lampini — Ciceroncino, as they called him, also the author of a small volume of poems. Skinny, with a lean, almost bald head on a swanlike neck, protected by a button-on collar at least eight inches high.

Signora Morlacchi waylaid him in a shrill voice: "What kind of treatment is this, Lampini? They said it was at noon; in a moment it will be one; no one is here. . . ."

Lampini bowed, opened his arms, turned smiling to the other four, and said: "Excuse me, but what do I have to do with it, Signora?"

"I know you have nothing to do with it," Signora Morlacchi continued. "But at least Raceni, as organizer of the banquet . . ."

"Yes, as the . . . archae . . . archaeo-logician." Lampini concluded his word play shyly, hand over his mouth, looking at the archaeologist, Professor Litti.

"Yes, all right. But he should be here, it seems to me. It's not very pleasant, that's all."

"You're right, it's unpleasant. yes! But I don't know, I have nothing to do with it. I'm a guest like you, Signora. Will you excuse me?" And with a hasty bow, Lampini went to shake hands with Litti, Toronti, Jacono. He didn't know Zago.

"I came in a carriage, afraid of being late," he announced. "But others are coming. I saw Donna Francesca Lampugnani and Betti, and also Signora Barmis with Casimiro Luna coming up the hill."

He looked in the glassed-in hall where the long table was already set, decorated with flowers and a spiral of ivy snaking round. Then he turned again to Signora Morlacchi, sorry that she was by herself, and said: "But Signora, excuse me, why . . ."

Raimondo Jacono interrupted him in time: "Tell us, Lampini, you always keep up with the latest: have you seen Signora Roncella?"

"No. It's not true that I always keep up with the latest. I haven't yet had the pleasure and honor."

And Lampini, bowing a third time, sent a kind smile Morlacchi's way.

"Very young?" asked Filiberto Litti, bending and looking surreptitiously at one of his very long, false-looking mustaches that seemed stuck to his wooden face.

"Twenty-four years old, they say," Faustino Toronti replied.

"Does she also write poetry?" Litti asked, looking down at his other mustache.

"No, thank your stars!" Jacono shouted. "Professor, do you want to kill us off? Another poetess in Italy? Tell us, tell us, Lampini, and the husband?"

"Yes, the husband. Yes," said Lampini. "He came to the office last week to get a copy of the newspaper with Betti's article about *The House of Dwarves.*"

"What's his name?"

"The husband's? I don't know."

"I think I understood Bóggiolo," Toronti said. "Or Boggiòlo. Something like that."

"A little plump, nice looking enough," added Lampini. "Gold-rimmed glasses. Short, square, blond beard. And he must have beautiful penmanship. You can tell it from his mustache."

The four men laughed. Signora Morlacchi also smiled from afar in spite of herself.

16

They came onto the terrace, heaving a great sigh of relief—Marchesa Donna Francesca Lampugnani, tall, stately, as though she carried on her magnificent bosom a card with the title President of the Ladies' Culture Club, and her handsome knight-errant, Riccardo Betti. In his rather dreamy expression, in his half-smiles under his sparse very blond mustache and in his gestures and dress, just as in his prose and articles, he affected the dignity, the moderation, the correctness, the manners of the . . . no, *du vrai monde*.

Betti, just as Casimiro Luna, had come only to accommodate Donna Francesca, who, in her position as President of the Ladies' Culture Club, could not miss that banquet. They belonged to another intellectual climate, the cream of journalism; they would never condescend to attend a gathering of literati. Betti made it very clear. On the other hand, Casimiro Luna, of a more jovial nature, erupted noisily onto the terrace with Dora Barmis. Passing through the entrance, he had made crude remarks about the large keyhole of the Castello di Costantino and of the enormous cardboard key put there for a joke. She laughed, pretending to be scandalized, and appealed to the Marchesa for help, and then, in her Italian that she wanted to seem French at all costs:

"You are abominable," she protested, "absolutely abominable, Luna! What is this continual, odious *persiflage?*"

After this outburst she alone among the four new arrivals approached Signora Morlacchi and dragged her forcibly into the group, not wanting to miss any of "terrible" Luna's other suggestive remarks.

Litti (continuing to tug on each side of that mustache and then stretch his neck as if he could never get his head arranged well enough on his body) watched those people, listened to their fickle chatter, and soon felt his large fleshy ears burning. He was thinking that they all lived in Rome just as they would in any other modern city, and that Rome's new population was composed of false, fatuous, vain people like them. What did they know about Rome? Three or four rhetorical commonplaces. What vision did they have of it? The Corso, the Pincio, cafés, salons, theaters, editorial offices . . . They were like the new streets and houses that had broadened the city only materially, disfiguring it. When the circle of walls was smaller, Rome's greatness roamed across the frontiers of the world. Now that the circle had widened . . . there it was, the new Rome. And Filiberto Litti stretched his neck.

In the meanwhile several others had arrived: nuisances who began to get in the way of the waiters carrying in the food to two or three couples, outsiders eating in the glassed-in dining room.

Among these young people (more or less with full heads of hair, aspirants to glory, unpaid collaborators of the innumerable literary periodicals of the peninsula) were three young women, evidently students of literature: two with glasses, sickly looking and taciturn; the third, on the other hand, was very vivacious, with red hair cut in a masculine style, a lively little freckled face, with variegated gray eyes that seemed to sparkle with malice. She laughed boisterously, bobbing around with laughter that provoked a grimace halfway between disdain and pity in a serious elderly man wandering amid such careless youth. He was Mario Puglia, who in former times had sung with a certain forced enthusiasm and vulgar passion. Now he felt he was already history. He sang no more. However, he had kept his long hair, which rained dandruff on the lapels of his military overcoat, and he sported a stately paunch.

Casimiro Luna, who had been watching him for a while, frowning, sighed at a certain point and said quietly: "Gentlemen, look at Puglia. Who knows where he left his guitar . . ."

"Cariolin! Cariolin!" several people shouted at that moment, making way for a perfumed, elegant little man who seemed to have been made and set on his feet as a joke, with twenty long hairs combed over his bald head, two violets in his buttonhole, and a monocle.

Smiling and bowing, Momo Cariolin saluted everyone with both bejeweled hands and ran to kiss the hand of Donna Francesca Lampugnani. He knew everyone. He could not resist bowing low, kissing the women's hands, and telling jokes in Venetian dialect. He went everywhere, to all the important salons, to all the editorial offices, and was given a hearty welcome everywhere—no one knew why. He represented nothing, but his presence nevertheless managed to give a

18

certain class to gatherings, banquets, meetings—perhaps because of his impeccable, ingratiating manners, perhaps because of that certain diplomatic air of his.

The old poetess Donna Maria Rosa Bornè-Laturzi was accompanied by the Honorable Silvestro Carpi and the Lombard novelist Carlino Sanna, who was passing through Rome. As a poet, Bornè-Laturzi (according to Casimiro Luna) was an excellent mother. She adamantly believed that poetry, and art in general, was no excuse for loose morals. For this reason she did not speak to Signora Barmis or Signora Morlacchi—she spoke only to Marchesa Lampugnani because she was a marchesa and club president, Filiberto Litti because he was an archaeologist, and she let her hand be kissed by Cariolin, because Cariolin kissed only the hands of real nobility.

In the meantime several groups had formed, but the conversation languished because each person was concerned only about himself, and this concern impeded thought. Each one repeated what someone else, making a great effort, had managed to say about the weather or the landscape. Tito Lampini, for instance, hopped from one group to another, smilingly repeating, with one hand over his mouth, some turn of phrase that seemed pleasing to him, gleaned here and there, but that he passed off as his own.

Each one made silent, more or less bitter, criticisms of the other. Each one would have liked to talk about himself, about his latest publication, but no one dared give the other this satisfaction. Two even spoke in a low voice about what a third one there, close by, had written, and they spoke ill of it. When the latter came closer, they immediately changed the subject and smiled at him.

There were the miserably bored and the rowdy, like Luna. And the former envied the latter. Not out of respect, but because they knew that in the end such brashness triumphed. They would have happily imitated them, but being timid and in order not to admit this timidity to themselves, they preferred to believe that the seriousness of their intentions kept them from doing otherwise.

A blondish man with blue eyeglasses disconcerted everyone, so emaciated he seemed barely alive, with long hair, a long neck, scrawny, stiff and tall as a processional statue. Over his frock coat he wore a gray mantelet. He bent his head this way and that and his fingers nervously worked his cuticles. He was obviously a foreigner: Swedish or Norwegian. No one knew him, no one knew who he was, and everyone looked at him with amazement and disgust.

Noticing the attention he was attracting, he smiled and seemed to say ceremoniously to all: "Brothers, we are all dying!"

That walking skeleton was a real indecency among so much vanity. Where in the world had Raceni dug him up? Whatever had given him the idea of inviting him to the banquet?

"I'm leaving!" Luna declared. "I can't eat opposite that grasshopper."

But stopped by Signora Barmis, who wanted to know—*honestly, please*—what he thought of Roncella, he didn't leave.

"A great deal, my friend! I've never read a line."

"That's a mistake," said Donna Francesca Lampugnani, smiling. "I assure you, Luna, that's a mistake."

"M . . . me neither," Litti added. "But . . . it seems to me that all this su . . . sudden fame . . . At least from what I've heard . . ."

"Yes," said Betti, tugging at his cuffs with a certain courtly nonchalance. "She is a bit lacking in form, that's the thing."

"Terribly ignorant!" Raimondo Jacono burst out.

"Well," Casimiro Luna then said, "perhaps that's why I love her."

Carlino Sanna, the Lombard novelist passing through Rome, put a smile on his grim, goatish face, letting the monocle fall from his eye. He passed a hand through his thick grizzly hair and said softly: "But, really, to give her a banquet? Doesn't it seem to you . . . doesn't it seem just a bit too much?"

"A banquet . . . Dear me, what's so bad about it?" asked Donna Francesca Lampugnani.

"We are promoting her glory!" Jacono snorted again.

"Ah!" All spoke in unison.

An inspired Jacono went on: "Excuse me, excuse me, it will be in all the newspapers."

"So?" Dora Barmis said, opening her arms and shrugging.

From that spark of chitchat the conversation caught fire. Everyone began to talk about Signora Roncella, as though they only now remembered why they were there. No one admitted being an unqualified admirer. Here and there someone recognized . . . yes, some good qualities, such as an unusually clear, strange penetration of life through a too close, perhaps myopic, attention to detail . . . and some kind of new and distinctive spirit in the poetic descriptions, and an unusual narrative quality. But it seemed to everyone that too much had been made of *House of Dwarves*. Admittedly a good novel . . . perhaps. Affirmation of an unusual talent, without a doubt, but not the masterpiece of humor it had been proclaimed. Anyway, it was strange that a young woman could write it who up to now had lived almost totally without worldly experience down there in Taranto. There was imagination and also thought: little literature, but life, life.

"Has she been married long?"

"For one or two years, they say."

Suddenly all the discussions were interrupted. On the terrace were the Honorable Senator Romualdo Borghi, Minister of Public Instruction, director of *Vita Italiana,* and Maurizio Gueli, the famous writer, the Maestro. For ten years neither friends' entreaties nor editors' lucrative offers had been able to make him break his silence.

Everyone moved aside to let them pass. The two did not go well together: Borghi was short, stocky, long haired, with a gossipy old servant's flat, leathery face; Gueli was tall, vigorous, with a still youthful air despite his white hair that contrasted strongly with the high color of his austere, masculine face.

With the presence of Gueli and Borghi, the banquet now assumed great importance.

Not a few were surprised that the Maestro had come to personally affirm his esteem of Roncella, which he had already declared to some. He was known to be very affable and friendly to young people, but his presence at the banquet seemed overly generous, and many suffered from envy, realizing that this would almost officially consecrate Silvia Roncella today. Others felt more cheerful. Gueli's appearance validated their presence also.

But why hadn't Raceni come yet? It was really shameful! Keeping everyone waiting like that; and Gueli and Borghi mixed with the others, without anyone to receive them. . . .

"Here they are! Here they are!" Lampini, who had gone down to check, ran in to announce.

"Raceni's here?"

"Yes, with Signora Roncella and her husband. Here they are!"

Everyone turned with lively curiosity toward the terrace entrance.

A very pale Silvia Roncella appeared on Raceni's arm, her face troubled by inner agitation. Among the guests who moved aside to let them pass, there immediately spread a flurry of whispered comments: "That one?" "Short!" "No, not too . . ." "Badly dressed." "Beautiful eyes!" "God, what a hat!" "Poor thing, she's uncomfortable!" "Skinny!" "She's not saying a word." "Why not? She's pretty when she smiles." "Very shy." "But look at her eyes: she's not bashful!" "Pretty enough, isn't she?" "It seems impossible!" "If she were well dressed . . . hair done . . ." "You can't really say she's beautiful." "She's so awkward!" "She doesn't seem . . ." "What compliments from Borghi!" "Get an umbrella! All that spit." "What's Gueli saying to her?" "But her husband, ladies and gentlemen! Look at her husband!" "Where is he? Where is he?" "There, next to Gueli . . . look at him! Look at him!"

In evening dress. Giustino Boggiolo had come in white tie and tails. Shining, almost like enameled porcelain; gold-rimmed eyeglasses; fan-shaped beard; and a well-trimmed, brown mustache. Close-cropped dark hair.

What was he doing there, between Borghi and Gueli, Lampugnani and Luna? Attilio Raceni drew him away and then called to Signora Barmis.

"Here, I'm turning him over to you, Dora. Giustino Boggiolo, her husband. Dora Barmis. I'm going to see what's going on in the kitchen. Meanwhile, please take your places."

And Attilio Raceni, with satisfaction in his beautiful dark and languid troubadour eyes, smoothing his raven hair, made his way through the crowd that wanted to know the reason for the delay.

"She felt a little ill. But it's nothing, it passed. Be seated, everyone, be seated! Take your places."

"You're a Knight of the Republic, aren't you?" asked Dora Barmis as she offered her arm to Giustino Boggiolo.

"Yes, actually . . ."

"Officially?"

"No, not yet. I don't really care about it, you see? It's useful at the office."

"You are the luckiest man on earth!" Signora Barmis exclaimed impulsively, squeezing his arm.

Giustino Boggiolo turned red, smiled: "Me?"

"You, you, you! I envy you! I'd like to be a man and be you, understand? To have your wife! How delightful she is! How pretty! Don't you just gobble her up with kisses? Tell me, don't you just gobble her up with kisses? And she must be very, very nice, isn't she?"

"Yes . . . really . . ." stammered Giustino Boggiolo again, bewildered, dazed, confused.

"And you must do everything to make her happy. A sacred obligation. You'll be in hot water with me if you don't make her happy! Look at me! Why did you come in tails?"

"But . . . I thought . . ."

"Hush! It's out of place. Don't do it again! Luna! Luna!" Signora Barmis called out.

Casimiro Luna hurried over.

"This is Cavalier Giustino Boggiolo, her husband."

"Ah, very good," replied Luna, bowing slightly. "Congratulations."

"Very glad to meet you, thank you. I've wanted so much to meet you," Boggiolo hastened to say. "Excuse me, you . . ."

"Give me your arm!" Doris Barmis shouted. "Don't run away. You're my responsibility."

"Yes, Signora, thank you," replied Boggiolo, smiling; then turning back to Luna he continued: "You write for the *Corriere di Milano*, don't you? I know the *Corriere* pays well. . . ."

"Ah," said Luna. "So-so . . . fairly well . . ."

"Yes, so I've heard," insisted Boggiolo. "I asked you because the *Corriere* has asked Silvia for a novel. But we may not accept because, really, in Italy . . . in Italy it's not profitable, that's all. But in France . . . and in

23

Germany, too, you know? The magazine *Grundbau* gave me two thousand five hundred marks for *House of Dwarves*."

"Good for you!" exclaimed Luna.

"Yes, sir, in advance, and you know? Paying her, in addition to the translator," added Giustino Boggiolo. "I don't know how much. . . . Schweizer-Sidler . . . good, good . . . she translates well. I've heard that in Italy the theater is more profitable. Because, you know? at first I didn't understand a thing about literature. Now, little by little, a certain amount of experience . . . You have to keep your eyes open, especially when making contracts. To Silvia, for example . . ."

"Hurry, hurry, sit down!" Dora Barmis interrupted him hastily. "Everyone is taking his place! Will you sit next to us, Luna?"

"Of course!" he said.

"Please, may I," pleaded Giustino Boggiolo. "There's Signor Lifjeld over there, who's translating *House of Dwarves* into Swedish. Please . . . I need to have a word with him."

And so, leaving Signora Barmis's arm, he went over to the blondish, gaunt, scrawny statue whose macabre appearance disconcerted everyone.

"Hurry!" Signora Barmis hissed after him.

Silvia Roncella had already taken her place between Maurizio Gueli and Senator Romualdo Borghi. Attilio Raceni had given a lot of thought to the seating arrangement, so that when he saw Casimiro Luna sitting in a corner by Signora Barmis, who had left the seat next to herself empty for Boggiolo, he ran over to advise him that that was not his seat, confound it! Come on, come on, next to Marchesa Lampugnani.

"No, thank you, Raceni," Luna said to him. "Please let me sit here. We have her husband with us."

As if she had understood, Silvia Roncella turned to look for Giustino. That long searching look around the table and then around the hall itself seemed a painful effort, interrupted at a certain point by the sight of someone dear to her to whom she gave a sad, sweet smile. It was an elderly woman who had come in the carriage with her, to whom no one paid any attention, hidden away in a corner, since Raceni had forgotten about introducing her, at least to those near her at the table, as he had promised. The elderly woman, who wore a blond wig low on her forehead and whose face was heavily powdered, made a short energetic gesture with her hand to Signora Roncella, as if to say: "Chin up!" Silvia Roncella smiled sadly, barely nodding her head. Then she turned to Gueli, who had said something to her.

Giustino Boggiolo, coming back into the glassed-in hall with the Swede, went up to Raceni, who had taken Luna's place next to Lampugnani, and quietly told him that the very learned Lifjeld, professor of psychology at the University of Upsala, had nowhere to sit. Raceni gave him his place at once, introducing him to Lampugnani on one side and Donna Maria Bornè-Laturzi on the other. This was the result of the loss of the first guest list: the table was set for thirty, and there were thirty-five guests! Never mind. He, Raceni, would make the best of it and sit in some corner.

"Listen," Giustino Boggiolo added very softly, pulling Raceni by the sleeve and furtively handing him a small scrap of rolled-up paper. "Here is the title of Silvia's play. It would be nice if Senator Borghi would mention it when he makes the toast. What do you say? You can take care of it."

The waiters came in at a fast clip with the first course. It was very late and the prospect of food provoked a religious silence in everyone.

Maurizio Gueli noticed it, turned to look at the Palatine ruins, and smiled. Then he bent toward Silvia Roncella and said quietly: "Look, Signora Silvia. You'll see that at a certain point the ancient Romans will come out to watch us, with satisfaction."

5

Do they really come out?

Certainly none of the guests would notice. The reality of the banquet, a not very well cooked reality, to tell the truth, and not abundant or varied, the reality of the present with its secret rivalries that flower on the lips of the various guests in false smiles and poisonous compliments, with badly concealed jealousies that pull here and there in subdued backbiting, with the unsatisfied ambitions and fatuous illusions and aspirations that find no way to reveal themselves, this reality held all those restless souls captive by the effort that the pretense and defense cost each one. Like snails that, unable or unwilling to withdraw into their shells, wrap themselves in their slime and from that unproductive iridescent foam stretch out their prudent tentacles, they fried the others in their gossip, maliciously raising hints of cuckoldry from time to time.

Who among all these people could think about the ruins of the Palatine and imagine the souls of the ancient Romans gazing with satisfaction upon that modern symposium? Only Maurizio Gueli. In one of his better-known books, *Favole di Roma*, Gueli had collected and fused (discovering the most hidden analogies) the lives and most representative figures of the three Romes. His profound and characteristic philosophical humor was more accessible in this book than in some of his others. In *Favole di Roma* the harsh and pitiless criticism—desperately skeptical and yet clear and flowering with all the grace of his style— was most successfully joined to his bizarre creative fantasy. Had he not in this book called Cicero to defend before the Senate (a Senate no longer only Roman) the prefect of a Sicilian province, a prevaricator, a very amusing clerical prefect of our times?

Now who did Gueli see looking down from the Palatine ruins in their long flapping white togas to greet all these ephemeral literati banqueting in the glassed-in hall of the Castello di Costantino? Gueli who felt fate's cruel mockery of Rome, mitered by the popes with tiara and cross, crowned with a Piedmontese crown by the diverse peoples of Italy.

Perhaps he saw many senators there advising Romualdo Borghi, their venerable colleague, not to let himself be too overcome by temptation, and to eat only meat for the sake of his country's literature, since he had been diabetic for many years. And next . . . next all of Rome's poets and prose writers: the playwrights, lyricists, historians, writers of epics and short stories. All of them? Not all. Not Virgil, in fact, or

Tacitus; Plautus and Catullus and Horace, yes; Lucretius, no. Propertius, yes. And certainly the one who more than all the others made signs of wanting to participate in that banquet, not because he supposed it worth his while, but to make fun of it, as he had already done with a famous supper in Cuma.[1]

Maurizio Gueli wiped his lips with his napkin to conceal a smile. Oh, if only he could stand up and say to that table: "Ladies and gentlemen, please make way for Petronius Arbiter who wants to come in."

Silvia Roncella, in the meanwhile, in order not to feel the embarrassment of so many eyes fixed on her, had turned her gaze and thoughts to the green fields in the distance, to the blades of grass growing there, to the leaves shining there, and to the birds for whom the happy season was beginning, to the lizards dozing in the first warmth of the sun, to the black rows of ants that she had stopped to watch so many times, absorbed. That humble, tenuous, transient life, without a shadow of ambition, always had the power to move her by its vulnerability. It takes so little for a bird to die. A farmhand passes and tramples those blades of grass with his hobnailed boots, tramples a multitude of ants. To pick out one ant from the many and follow it for a bit, becoming one with such a small creature amid the coming and going of the others. To pick out one blade of grass from many and tremble with it at every slight breeze. Then to look away, and afterward to search again for *that* blade of grass, *that* small ant among the many: to be unable to find either one again, losing a part of one's soul there with them, forever.

A sudden silence interrupted Silvia Roncella's daydream. Beside her, Romualdo Borghi had stood up. She looked at her husband who made a sign for her to rise immediately. She stood, perturbed, with her eyes lowered. But what was happening over there, in the corner where her husband was sitting?

Giustino Boggiolo also wanted to get to his feet, and Dora Barmis ineffectively tugged at the tails of his evening coat. "Get down! Stay seated! What do you have to do with this? Sit down."

1 A reference to Trimalchius's banquet in Petronius's *Satyricon*.

Nothing doing! Stiffly upright, Giustino Boggiolo in tails wanted to be toasted also by Borghi, as the husband. And there was no way to make him sit down.

"Kind ladies, my dear gentlemen!" Borghi began, chin on chest, brow contracted, eyes closed.

("Silence! He's talking to himself," Casimiro whispered.)

"It is a beautiful and memorable occasion for us to be able to welcome this fine young woman on the threshold of a new life, already on her way to glory."

"Very good," exclaimed two or three.

Eyes shining, Giustino Boggiolo looked around and noticed with pleasure that three of the journalists were taking notes. Then he looked at Raceni to ask him if he had given Borghi the title of Silvia's play written on the paper he handed him before sitting at the table. But Raceni was absorbed in listening to the toast and didn't turn around. Giustino Boggiolo began to fret inwardly.

"What will Rome say," Borghi went on, raising his head and trying to open his eyes, *"what will Rome say, the immortal soul of Rome, to the soul of this young woman? It seems, oh, ladies and gentlemen, that the greatness of Rome loves the severe majesty of History more than the imaginative caprices of art. In the* "First Decade of Livy," *oh, ladies and gentlemen, is Rome's epic. Its tragedy is in the* "Annals of Tacitus." (Good! Bravo! Bravissimo!)

Giustino Boggiolo bowed, with his eyes fixed on Raceni, who still had not turned. Signora Barmis tugged at his tails.

"History is Rome's voice, and this voice overwhelms any individual voice. . . ."

Oh, now Raceni was turning, nodding his head in approval. Giustino Boggiolo made a sign to him with his eyes starting out of his head from the intense effort to attract his attention.

"But, on the other hand, oh, ladies and gentlemen, "Julius Caesar"? "Coriolanus"? "Antony and Cleopatra"? *The great Roman plays of Shakespeare . . ."*

"That piece of paper I gave you." Giustino Boggiolo's fingers spoke, opening and closing in a frenzy, since Raceni still did not understand and was looking at him as though dumbfounded.

Applause broke out and Giustino Boggiolo bowed mechanically.

"Excuse me, are you Shakespeare?" Dora Barmis asked him under her breath.

"Me? No. What does Shakespeare have to do with it?"

"We don't know, either," Casimiro Luna said to him. "But sit down, sit down. Heaven only knows how long this magnificent toast will go on!"

". . . *for all the vicissitudes, oh, ladies and gentlemen, of an infinite evolution!* (Good! Bravo! Benissimo!) *Now the turmoil of the new life needs a new voice, a voice that . . .*"

Finally! Raceni understood; he searched his vest pockets. Yes, here it is, the piece of paper. "This?" "Yes, yes." "But, why now? To whom?" "To Borghi!" "How?" "You forgot. Too late now." But never mind, Boggiolo should relax; he would give the title to the journalists . . . afterward, yes afterward . . .

All this discourse took place in a flurry of gestures from one end of the table to the other.

A new burst of applause. Borghi turned to touch his glass to Silvia Roncella's. The toast was over, to the great relief of everyone. The dinner guests rose, each with a glass in hand and hurried over to the guest of honor.

"I'll toast with you. . . . It's the same thing!" Dora Barmis said to Giustino Boggiolo.

"Sì, Signora, thank you!" he replied, giddy with irritation. "Good heavens, everything's ruined!"

"Did I do something?" asked Signora Barmis.

"No, Signora. Raceni . . . I gave him the title of the thing . . . the play and . . . and . . . and nothing. He stuck it in his pocket and forgot all about it! You just don't do these things! The senator, so kind . . . Uh, excuse me, Signora, the journalists over there are calling me. . . . Thank you, Raceni! The play's title? You are Signor Mola, aren't you? Yes, of the *Capitale*, I know. Thank you, a great pleasure . . . Her husband, yes,

29

sir. In four acts, the play. The title? *The New Colony*. You're Centanni? A great pleasure. Her husband, yes, sir. *The New Colony*, certainly, in four acts . . . It's already been translated into French, you know? Desroches translated it, yes, sir. You are Federici? A great pleasure. Her husband, yes, sir. In fact, look, if you would be kind enough to add that . . ."

"Boggiolo! Boggiolo!" Raceni came running.

"What is it?"

"Come . . . Your wife is feeling a little under the weather again. Better to leave, you know!"

"Ah," Boggiolo said sadly to the journalists, raising his eyebrows and throwing his arms wide. In this way he let it be known what kind of illness his little wife had and off he went.

"You're a scoundrel!" Dora Barmis said to him shortly afterward, frowning, and giving his arms a squeeze. "She needs quiet, understand? Quiet! Now go! Go! But don't forget to come see me soon. Then I'll give you a good scolding, you rascal!"

And she threatened him with her hand while he, bowing and smiling at everyone, red, confused, happy, left the terrace with his wife and Raceni.

2 ✳ SCHOOL FOR GREATNESS

1

The furniture in the small study was—if not shoddy, certainly very nondescript, bought haphazardly on the installment plan. Yet the room was furnished with a brand new rug and two new curtains at the door that gave the impression no one was in there.

But he was there, Ippolito Onorio Roncella: there, still as the curtains, as that little table in front of the ugly divan, still as the two squat bookcases and the three overstuffed chairs. With sleepy eyes he looked at these objects and thought that he, too, might just as well be made of wood. Really. And just as worm-infested. He sat at the small desk with his back to the single square little window that was rather unnecessarily covered by a thin curtain, since it overlooked the courtyard from which little light entered anyway.

At a certain point it seemed like the whole study shook. Nothing to be concerned about. Ippolito Onorio Roncella had moved.

In order not to disturb his full, very beautiful gray and curly beard that he washed, combed, sprayed with cologne in the grooming he gave it each morning, patting it with his curved palm, he had flipped the ribbon on his military *bersagliere's* hat (which he never removed) onto his chest with a movement of his head and began to slowly stroke it. Just like a baby stroking his mother's breast, so he, smoking, needed to stroke something, and not wanting to touch his beard, stroked the ribbon on his *bersagliere's* hat instead.

In the quiet gray morning gloom, in the grave silence that was like time's grim shadow, Ippolito Onorio Roncella felt the life of everything near and far almost suspended in the stillness of dismal, somber, and resigned anticipation. And it seemed to him that this silence, a shadow of time, crossed the boundaries of the present and slowly sank into the past, into the history of Rome, into the remote history of men who had worked and struggled so hard, always with the hope of achieving something, and what was the result? It was this: to be able to consider as he did — when all was said and done — that this quiet stroking of the ribbon of his *bersagliere's* hat was equal to any other endeavor highly esteemed by humanity.

"*What are you doing?*" The damned old parrot from the silence of the courtyard screeched the question from time to time in a hoarse voice and grating tone: the parrot of Signora Ely Faciolli, who lived next door.

"What are you doing?" that wise old signora would ask the stupid bird hourly.

"*What are you doing?*" the parrot would reply each time. Then, on its own, it seemed to repeat the question all day long to the inhabitants of the apartment building.

Each one responded in his own way, with a snort, depending on the kind or difficulty of his own activity. Everyone with little courtesy. Most impolite of all was Ippolito Onorio Roncella, who had nothing more to do after three years of enforced retirement because — without the slightest intention to offend (he could swear to it) — he had told off his superior.

For more than fifty years he had worked with his head. Fine head, his. Full of thoughts, one more delightful than the other. Now that was all over. Now he devoted himself exclusively to nature's three kingdoms, represented by his hair and beard (vegetable), by his teeth (mineral), and by all the other parts of his old carcass (animal). The latter and the mineral kingdoms were somewhat ravaged by age; however, the vegetable kingdom still gave him great satisfaction. For that reason he, who had always done everything with care and wanted it to appear so, would point to his beard and gravely reply, "Gardening," when anyone asked him—like that parrot: "Signor Ippolito, what are you doing?"

He knew he had a bitter inner enemy: a rebellious rascal who couldn't keep from spitting the truth in everyone's face as a wild watermelon squirts its purgative juice. Not to offend, of course, but to put things in order.

"You're an ass. I've got your number. Don't speak about it again."

"This is stupid. I've got your number. Don't speak about it again."

That enemy inside him loved things to be dispatched in short order. A put-down and that was that. Thank goodness that for some time he had managed to lull it to sleep a little with poison, smoking that long-stemmed pipe from morning to night while stroking the ribbon on his *bersagliere's* hat. From time to time, however, terrible coughing fits warned him that his enemy was rebelling against the poisoning. Then Signor Ippolito, choking, purple in the face, eyes popping, would pound his fists, kick his feet, twist and turn, struggling madly to conquer, to tame, the rebel. In vain the doctor told him that his psyche had nothing to do with it, but that the cough came from his poisoned bronchi, and that he should quit smoking or not smoke so much if he didn't want to get something worse.

"My dear sir," Signor Ippolito had replied, "consider my scales! On one side all the weight of old age. On the other I have only my pipe. If I take that away there's nothing to balance the scales. What's left? What can I do if I don't smoke?"

And so he continued to smoke.

Dismissed from a job unworthy of him at the local school office for that explicit and impartial judgment he made of his boss, he hadn't returned to his home town Taranto, where, after his brother's death, he had no living relatives. Instead, he had stayed on in Rome with his small pension to help his niece, Silvia Roncella, who had come to Rome about three months ago with her husband. But he already regretted it. And how!

He especially couldn't stand that new nephew of his, Giustino Boggiolo. For many reasons, but most of all because he was oppressive. Like sultry weather. What is sultriness? Low-lying stagnation, a dull light. Well, then. His new nephew toiled slowly when it came to making light, the most vexing light in the biosphere: he talked too much, he explained the most obvious and most mundane things, as if only he could see them and that without his illumination others wouldn't be able to see them. What a strain, how exhausting to hear him talk! Signor Ippolito at first would huff and puff softly two and three times in order not to offend him. Finally, when he couldn't take it anymore, he would snort loudly and even clap his hands to extinguish all that useless light and make the air fresh and breathable.

As for Silvia, he knew that from the time she was a child she had this little vice of scribbling; and that she had published four or five books and maybe more, but he really never expected that she would come to literary Rome already famous. And just the day before some other crazy scribblers like her had even given her a banquet. Nevertheless, Silvia was not basically bad. No. In fact, the poor thing didn't seem at all like someone sick in the head. She had, she really had a kind of talent, that little woman. And in many ways the two of them were alike. Naturally! The same blood . . . the same Roncella way of thinking.

Signor Ippolito closed his eyes and nodded his head, very slowly, so as to not disturb his beard.

He had made a special study of that infernal machine, a kind of filtered pump that put the brain in communication with the heart and drew ideas from feelings, or, as he said, drew out the concentrated extract, the sublimated corrosive of logical deductions.

Famous pumpers and filterers, the Roncella family. All of them, from time immemorial!

But no one up to now, to tell the truth, had thought of setting himself up in the poison business professionally like that girl now seemed to want to do, that blessed child, Silvia.

Signor Ippolito couldn't stand women who wore glasses, walked like soldiers, were employed as postal workers, telegraph and telephone workers, or who aspired to electoral offices. Who knows what tomorrow will bring? Next they'll want to be senators and even army officers.

He would have liked Giustino to keep his wife from writing, or if he couldn't stop her (because Silvia really didn't seem the type to let herself be imposed on by her husband), at least not encourage her, for heaven's sake! Encourage her? More than encourage her. He was by her side from morning to night, prodding her, urging her, stimulating that damned obsession in every way. Instead of asking her if she had straightened up the house, had supervised the maid's cleaning or cooking, or even if she had had a nice walk at the Villa Borghese, he would ask her if and what she had written during the day while he was at the office, how many pages, how many lines, how many words. . . . Really! Because he even counted the words that his wife had scrawled, as if he had to send them off by telegraph. And look there: he had bought a secondhand typewriter, and every evening after dinner until midnight or one o'clock, he played on that little piano in order to have ready, retyped, the *material*—as he called it—to send to the newspapers, magazines, editors, translators with whom he was in active correspondence. And there was the shelf with cubbyholes for scripts, copies of letters. . . . Bookkeeper to the nth degree, impeccable! Because the poison was beginning to sell. Ah, yes indeed! Even outside Italy . . . It's only right! Don't they sell tobacco? And what are words? Smoke. And what is smoke? Nicotine. Poison.

Signor Ippolito couldn't take much more of this family life. He had been very patient for three months, but he could already see the day was not far off when he wouldn't be able to stand it anymore and would tell off that young man. Not to offend him, of course, but to get things straight, as was his way. Speak his mind and that would be the end of it. Then maybe he would go live by himself.

"May I come in?" just then a soft little woman's voice asked. Signor Ippolito recognized it immediately as belonging to old Signora Faciolli (or the "Lombard," as he called her), owner of the parrot and the apartment house.

"Come in, come in," he muttered without moving.

2

This was the same old lady who had accompanied Silvia to the banquet the day before. Every morning from eight to nine she came to give Giustino Boggiolo English lessons.

Free of charge these lessons, naturally. Just as Signora Ely Faciolli, the landlady, always granted free use of her own parlor if her dear tenant Boggiolo needed to receive some literary figure.

The old signora was worm-eaten, too. Not so much by the solitary worm of literature as by the termite of history and the moth of erudition. She was attentive to Giustino Boggiolo, making a continual and insistent fuss after Giustino allowed her a glimpse of the mirage of an editor in the distance, and perhaps even a translator (German, of course) for her voluminous unpublished work: *On the Last Lombard Dynasty and on the Origins of the Popes' Temporal Power* (with unpublished documents), in which she clearly demonstrated how the unfortunate family of the last Lombard kings had not completely died out after Desiderius's imprisonment or with Adelchi's exile to Constantinople, but instead how the family had returned to Italy, hiding behind a false name in a corner of this classical land (Italy) to save it from the ire of the Carolingians, and there continued to live on for a very long time.

Signora Ely's mother had been English, as could still be seen by the blond color of the curly wig her daughter wore over her forehead. She had never married because she had been too sharply critical as a young woman, paying too much attention to the slightly crooked nose of this suitor, or to the fat fingers of that one. Regretting, too late, such fastidiousness, she was now all honey around men. But she wasn't dangerous. Yes, she wore that little wig over her forehead and built up her eyelashes with mascara a little, but only in order not to frighten the mirror too much and to induce a small smile of compassion. That was enough.

"Good morning, Signor Ippolito," she said, entering with many bows and squeezing a smile from her eyes and little mouth. She need not have bothered since Roncella had solemnly lowered his eyes to avoid looking at her.

"Good morning to you, Signora," he replied. "I'll keep my hat on as usual and not get up. All right? Make yourself at home. . . ."

"Certainly, thank you . . . don't get up, for heaven's sake!" Signora Ely hastened to say, holding out her hands full of newspapers. "Is Signor Boggiolo still in bed? I came in a hurry because I read here . . . Oh, if you only knew how many many nice things the newspapers say about yesterday's banquet, Signor Ippolito! They report Senator Borghi's magnificent toast! They announce Signora Silvia's play with the greatest anticipation! Signor Giustino will be so happy!"

"It's raining, isn't it?"

"What did you say?"

"It's not raining? I thought it was raining," Signor Ippolito grumbled, turning toward the window.

Signora Ely was accustomed to Signor Ippolito's habit of giving brusque turns to the conversation. Nevertheless it left her a bit bewildered this time. Then she understood and rallied quickly: "No, no. But perhaps it will. It's cloudy. So beautiful yesterday, and today. Oh, yesterday, yesterday, a day that will never be . . . A day . . . What did you say?"

"Gifts," shouted Signor Ippolito. "Gifts, I say, from Our Eternal Father, my dear Signora, freely given for men's happiness. How are the English lessons going?"

"Ah, very well, indeed!" the old woman exclaimed. "Signor Boggiolo shows an aptitude for learning languages, an aptitude that never before . . . He's already mastered French fairly well and he'll speak English well in four or five months (oh, even sooner!). Then we'll begin German."

"German, too?"

"Oh, yes . . . he has to! It's so useful, you know?"

"For the Lombards?"

"You're always joking about my Lombards, you naughty man!" said Signora Ely, gracefully threatening him with a finger. "It will help him

37

read the contracts, to know who to trust with the translations, and also to keep abreast of literary trends, to read the articles and criticism in the newspapers . . ."

"But Adelchi, Adelchi," bellowed Signor Ippolito. "How's this business with Adelchi going? Is it really true?"

"True? But there's a tombstone, didn't I tell you? I discovered it in the little church of San Eustachio at Catino near Farfa by a fortunate coincidence, around seven months ago while I was on vacation. Believe me, Signor Ippolito, King Adelchi did not die in Calabria as Gregorovius says."

"Died in a canteen?"

"At Catino! Irrefutable evidence. The tombstone says: *Loparius et judex Hubertus.*"

"Well, here's Giustino!" Signor Ippolito interrupted, rubbing his hands together. "I recognize his footsteps."

And very speedily he puffed out five or six large mouthfuls of smoke.

He knew his nephew couldn't stand him to be there at the desk. Actually, he had his own room, the best in the apartment, where no one would disturb him. But he preferred to stay here and fill the little cubbyhole with smoke.

("Olympus Cloudmaker!" he snickered to himself.)

Boggiolo did not smoke. Every morning when he appeared in the doorway he would close his eyes and wave away the smoke, blow and cough. Signor Ippolito would pretend not to notice. In fact, he would draw more smoke into his mouth, just as he was doing now, and let it waft thickly in the air without puffing.

However, that smoke was no more intolerable to Giustino Boggiolo than the way his uncle-in-law looked at him. That look seemed to him almost a sticky substance that impeded not only his actions but also his thoughts. And he had so much to do there in that room in the few hours his office left him free! In the meantime he'd have to have the English lesson in the dining room, as though he had no study.

However, that morning he had something to tell Signora Faciolli in secret and he couldn't do it in the small dining room next to the bedroom where Silvia stayed until late. Therefore he summoned his courage and, greeting his uncle with an uncustomary smile, asked him to have the goodness to leave him alone with Signora Ely for a moment.

Signor Ippolito frowned. "What's that in your hand?" he asked.

"A piece of bread," was Giustino's reply. "Why? I use it to clean my tie."

He took off his tie, the kind that's already knotted, and showed how he rubbed the bread over it.

Signor Ippolito nodded approval. He got up and seemed about to say something else but stopped himself. Head back, he puffed smoke first one way and then the other, and, making the ribbon on his hat swing, he went out.

The first thing Giustino, puffing and blowing, did was to throw open the window, and he angrily tossed out the piece of bread.

"Have you seen the papers?" Signora Faciolli asked him immediately, taking little hopping steps, sprightly and happy as a little sparrow.

"Yes, Signora, I went out to get them," answered Giustino sulkily. "You brought them, too? Thank you. I still have many more to buy. I must send a lot away. But did you see what a mishmash . . . what a muddle these journalists . . . ?"

"It seemed to me that . . ." ventured Signora Ely.

"No, Signora, I'm sorry!" interrupted Boggiolo. "When they don't know something, they shouldn't talk about it, or, if they want to say something they can first ask someone who knows something about it. As if I weren't there! I was there, confound it, ready to give all the explanations, make all the clarifications. . . . Why pull things out of a hat? For example, *Lifield* here . . . no, where is it? In the *Tribuna* . . . has become a German editor! And then, look: *Delosche* . . . here, *Deloche* instead of Desroches. I'm sorry . . . I'm really sorry. I have to send the papers to him, too, in France, and . . ."

"How are you, and how is Signora Silvia?" asked Signora Faciolli, in an effort to play another tune.

It played worse than the previous one.

"Don't ask!" blustered Giustino, turning his back and tossing the papers on the desk. "Bad night."

"Perhaps the excitement . . ." she attempted an excuse.

"What do you mean, excitement!" Boggiolo reacted in irritation. "That woman . . . excited? The Heavenly Father couldn't budge that blessed woman. So many people there for her, the cream of the crop, you understand? Gueli, Borghi . . . do you think that made her happy? Not at all! You saw how I had to drag her there, didn't you? And I swear to goodness, Signora, that this banquet came along on its own. What I mean is that it was Raceni's idea, and his alone. I had nothing whatever to do with it. Anyway, I think it turned out well."

"Very well! Of course!" Signora Ely immediately agreed. "There'll never be anything like it again!"

"Well, according to her she made a bad impression," Giustino said with a shrug of his shoulders.

"Who?" shouted Signora Faciolli, clapping her hands. "Signora Silvia? Oh, for heaven's sake!"

"Yes! But she laughs when she says it." Boggiolo continued, "She says it means nothing to her. Now do we socialize with the others or not? I do what I can . . . but she has to help. I'm not the writer; she is. When something works, why shouldn't we do all we can to see that it works as well as possible?"

"Certainly!" Signora Ely agreed once more, completely convinced.

"That's what I say," Giustino continued. "Yes, Silvia may have talent. She may know how to write, but believe me there are things she doesn't understand. And I'm not talking about inexperience, mind you. Two books tossed away like that before she married me, without a contract. Incredible! As soon as I can I'll do everything possible to reclaim them—I'll do everything in my power for her books. I don't have so many illusions now. Yes, the novel is selling, but we aren't in England or even France. Now she's written a play. She let herself be talked into it and wrote it right away, I have to say, in two months. I'm no expert. . . . Senator Borghi read it and says that . . . yes, he couldn't predict the outcome, because it's something . . . I don't know how he put it . . . classical, it seems to me. . . . Yes, classical and new. Now I say, if we hit it big, if we do well in the theater, you understand, my dear Signora, it could make our fortune."

"Oh, certainly! Oh, certainly!" exclaimed Signora Ely.

"But we have to be ready," he added angrily, clasping his hands together. "There's anticipation, curiosity. . . . After this banquet. I could see they liked her."

"Very much!" seconded Faciolli.

"Look," Giustino continued. "Marchesa Lampugnani has invited her to her home. I've heard she is one of the important ladies. That other one has also invited her, the one who has a much sought-after salon. . . . What's her name? Signora Bornè-Laturzi. Silvia has to go, doesn't she? To be seen. Many journalists and drama critics go there. She needs to see them, talk to them, let them know her, appreciate her. Well, you can imagine how much trouble it will be to convince her!"

"Maybe it's because," Signora Ely risked, feeling uncomfortable, "maybe it's because of her . . . condition?"

"Not at all!" Giustino Boggiolo disagreed at once. "For two or three months more it won't show. She'll be very presentable! I told her I'd have a beautiful dress made. . . . In fact, that is exactly what I wanted to ask you, Signora Ely: if you know a good dressmaker who wouldn't be too pretentious, too frivolous. That is, because . . . wait, excuse me, and then if you would help me pick out this dress and . . . and also persuade, yes, persuade Silvia that, for heaven's sake, she should listen to reason and do what she needs to do! The play will open toward the middle of October."

"Oh, so late?"

"It's late, I agree. But I really don't mind this delay, you know? The ground isn't well enough prepared yet, I know so few people, and then the timing won't be right in a few weeks. The real problem is Silvia, and Silvia is still so difficult. We have around six months ahead of us to prepare and put all these things right and other things, too. Now, I'd like to make a little plan. There's no need of it for me, but for Silvia. It gets my goat, believe me, that she should be the biggest obstacle. It's

41

not that she rebels against my suggestions, but she won't make any effort to play her part, to make the kind of impression she should, in other words, to overcome her own character. . . ."

"Bashful . . . yes!"

"What did you say?"

"She's too bashful, I said."

"Bashful? That's what it's called? I didn't know. She lacks know-how. Bashful, yes, the word sounds right. She just needs a little basic, every-day instruction. I've noticed that . . . I don't know . . . there's something like an . . . an understanding among so many that . . . I don't know . . . they pick something out of the air . . . just say a name . . . the name . . . wait, what is it? . . . of that English poet who lived on Piazza di Spagna, who died young . . ."

"Keats! Keats!" Signora Ely shouted.

"Keezi, yes . . . that one! As soon as they say *Keezi* . . . they've said it all, they understand each other. Or if they say . . . I don't know . . . the name of a foreign artist . . . There are four or five names they all know, and they don't even need to talk . . . a smile . . . a look . . . and they make a great impression, a great impression! You are so well edu-cated, Signora Ely, could you do me this favor? Help me to help Silvia a little."

And why not? Signora Ely happily promises she will do everything she can, and the best she can. She knows a dressmaker, and as for the dress—a nice black dress, a shiny material, all right?—it has to be made in such a way that gradually . . .

"Naturally!"

"Yes, it can be done."

"Naturally in three . . . four months . . . Shall we go tomorrow to buy it together?"

That settled, Giustino pulled out some albums from a desk drawer and grumbled: "Look, four today!"

A serious business, these albums. They rained down from every di-rection on his wife. Admirers who, directly or through Raceni, or even through Senator Borghi, asked for a thought, a quotation, or a simple autograph to be written in them.

Silvia would waste a lot of time attending to each one. It's true that she didn't have much to do right now, considering her condition. But she kept occupied with some little piece of work or another in order not to be completely idle and to answer the small requests of various newspapers.

Giustino Boggiolo was saddled with the bother of those albums: he wrote in them instead of his wife. No one would be the wiser because he knew how to imitate Silvia's handwriting and signature exactly. He copied excerpts from her already published books; or rather, in order not to have to leaf through them every time to find one, he had copied some into a notebook, and had even inserted some thought of his own here and there. Yes, some thought of his own that could pass among the many . . . At times he was tempted to secretly make some tiny little change in the quotations from his wife's work. Reading articles in the newspapers by refined writers (as, for example, Betti, who had found so much to laugh about in Silvia's prose), he had noticed that (who knows why) they capitalized certain letters. And so he too found something capitalizable in Silvia's thoughts every once in a while, such as *life, death,* etc. There, a nice *L,* a magnificent *D!* If you can make a better impression with such little effort . . .

He skimmed through the notebook and, with the help of Signora Ely, chose four thoughts.

"This one . . . Listen to this! '*We always say: Do what you should! But our inner Duty often affects those around us. What is Duty for us can be harmful to others. Therefore do what you must, but know what you are doing.*' "

"Stupendous!" exclaimed Signora Ely.

"It's mine," said Giustino.

And he transcribed it into one of those albums following Signora Ely's dictation. "Duty" with a capital letter, twice. He rubbed his hands and then looked at his watch. "Ugh, I have to be in the office in twenty minutes. *Lectio brevis,* this morning."

They sat, teacher and student, at the desk.

"Why do I do all this?" Giustino sighed. "Tell me."

He opened the English grammar and handed it to Signora Ely.

43

"Negative form," he began to recite with his eyes closed. "Present tense: *I do not go, thou dost not go, he does not go.*"

3

Thus began Silvia Roncella's school for greatness: head maestro, her husband; temporary assistant, Ely Faciolli.

She submitted to it with admirable resignation.

She had always shrunk from looking deep into her soul. On some rare occasions when she tried it for an instant she almost feared going insane.

Entering into herself meant stripping her soul of all the usual pretenses and seeing life in a dry, frightening nudity. Like seeing that dear, good Signora Ely Faciolli without her blond wig, without makeup, nude. God, no, poor Signora Ely!

Then was that truth? No, not even that. Truth: a mirror that by itself sees nothing, and in which each person looks at himself, as he believes he is, as he imagines himself to be.

Well, then, she had a horror of that mirror where the image of her own soul, stripped of every necessary pretense, must also necessarily appear to her deprived of every glimmer of reason.

Many times when she couldn't sleep, and while her husband and maestro was sleeping peacefully beside her, she would be suddenly attacked in the silence by a strange, unexpected terror that cut her breathing short and made her heart pound! What was very clear in the context of her daily existence would be rent in a second, allowing her to glimpse a very different reality, deprived of sense and purpose, when suspended in the night and in the emptiness of her soul. It was a horrible reality in its impassive and mysterious rawness in which all the ordinary fictitious connections of feelings and images separated and disintegrated.

Right at that terrible moment she would feel she was dying. She would feel all the horror of death and with a supreme effort would try to reestablish the ordinary awareness of things, to reconnect ideas, to feel alive again. But she no longer had faith in that ordinary awareness, in those reconnected ideas, in that usual feeling of life, since she now knew they were illusions to enable one to live, and that underneath there was something else that cannot be seen except at the expense of dying or going insane.

For many days everything seemed different; nothing stimulated her desire anymore. In fact, nothing in life seemed desirable anymore. Time stood before her empty, gloomy, and somber, and everything in it, as though dumbfounded, waited for decay and death.

Often, as she meditated, she would arbitrarily fix her gaze on an object and closely observe it in detail, as though that object were of particular interest to her. At first her observation was merely mechanical: her physical eyes stared and concentrated on that object alone, as if to ward off every distraction and to help her mental eye in the meditation. But gradually that object would begin to take over. It would begin to live by itself, as though suddenly becoming conscious of all the details she had discovered, and it would detach itself from all connection with her and with things around it.

For fear of being besieged again by that different, horrible reality that lived beyond ordinary sight, almost outside the pattern of human reason, perhaps without any suspicion of human self-deception or with a condescending sympathy for it, she would immediately avert her gaze, but without being able to focus on any other object. She felt the horror of the sight. It seemed to her that her eyes could pierce everything. She closed them and anxiously searched her heart for any kind of help in reassembling the shattered fiction. However, in that unfamiliar confusion her heart withered. Nothing like the machine Zio Ippolito spoke of! She was unable to draw any idea from that deep dark feeling: she didn't know how to reflect, or rather, she had never allowed herself to do so.

As a child she had witnessed painful scenes between her father and her mother, who had been a saintly woman entirely devoted to religious practices. She remembered her mother's look as she pressed her rosary to her heart when her husband ridiculed her for her faith in God and for her lengthy prayers. She remembered the spasmodic contortion

45

of her mother's face, almost as if by shutting her eyes she could shut out her husband's blasphemies. Poor Mamma! And with what effort and tears she would then stretch out her arms to her little girl and draw her to her breast and stop her ears. Then just as soon as her father's back was turned, her mother would have her kneel with hands joined and repeat a prayer to God that He might pardon that man whose honesty and goodness were surely a sign that he had Him in His heart and just didn't want to acknowledge it outwardly! Yes, those were her mother's words. How many times after her mother's death had she repeated them! To have God in her heart and not want to acknowledge it outwardly. As a child she had always gone to church with her mother, and after her death had continued to go alone every Sunday. But hadn't the same thing happened to her that had happened to her father? Did she really acknowledge God outwardly? She followed religious practices externally, like so many others. But what did she have inside? Like her father, a deep and dark feeling, a dread, the same that both had discerned in the other's eyes when they stood over her dying mother's bed. Now, of course, she tried to believe. But wasn't God perhaps a supreme fiction created by this deep, dark feeling to calm itself? Everything, absolutely everything, was a fictional contrivance that you mustn't tear apart, which you had to believe—not out of hypocrisy, but out of necessity—if you didn't want to die or go crazy. But how could you believe, knowing it a pretense? Alas, without a purpose what sense did life have? Animals lived just to exist, but human beings couldn't and didn't know how to. Human beings had to live, not just to exist but for something fictitious, illusory, that gave meaning and value to their lives.

Back in Taranto the look of ordinary things, familiar to her from birth and becoming part of her daily life almost unconsciously, had never disturbed her very much, although she had discovered so many marvelous things hidden from others, shadows and lights that the others had never noticed. She would have liked to stay down there near her sea, in the house where she was born and grew up, where she could still see (but with the strange impression that it was someone else) another *self* that she struggled to recognize. She seemed to see herself from such a distance with another's eyes and perceive herself as . . . she didn't know how to put it . . . different . . . curious. . . . And that girl down there wrote? She had been able to write so many things? How? Why? Who had taught her? How could those things have occurred to her? She had read only a few books, and in none of them had she ever found a passage, an idea that had the vaguest resemblance to anything that had come to her to write, spontaneously, out of the blue. Perhaps she shouldn't have written such things? Was it a mistake to write about them like that? She, or rather the girl down there, didn't know. It would never have occurred to her to publish them if her father hadn't discovered them and ripped them from her hands. At first she had been ashamed. She was afraid of seeming strange when she wasn't at all. She knew how to do all the other things well enough: to cook, sew, look after the house, and she spoke so sensibly, then. . . . Oh, like all the other girls in town . . . However, there was something inside her, a crazy sprite that didn't appear, because she herself didn't want to hear its voice or follow its pranks, except at some leisurely moment during the day or in the evening before going to bed.

More than satisfaction at seeing her first book favorably received and warmly praised, she had felt a great confusion, an anguish, a befuddling consternation. Would she know how to write as before? When no longer writing only for herself? The thought of praise occurred to her and disturbed her; it came between her and the things she wanted to describe or portray. For about a year she hadn't touched her pen. Then . . . oh, how she had rediscovered that little demon of hers grown and how wicked, malicious, discontented it had become. It had become such a bad demon that it almost frightened her, because now it wanted to talk loudly when it shouldn't, and laugh at certain things that she, like the others in the daily business of living, would like to consider serious. Her inner battle had begun at that time. Then she met Giustino.

It was clear that her husband didn't understand her, or rather, didn't understand that part of herself that, in order not to appear different

47

from others, she kept locked inside, that she herself didn't want to investigate or penetrate in depth. If some day this part got the upper hand in her where would it drag her? At first, when Giustino (though without understanding) had begun to urge her and force her to work, enticed by an unexpected source of revenue, she had been pleased, but really more for him than for herself. However, she would have liked him to stop there, and above all—after the stir caused by her novel *House of Dwarves*—not to have schemed and planned to come to Rome.

When she left Taranto, she had the impression that she was lost, and that it would take a tremendous effort to find herself again in such a vastly different life. How would she do it? She didn't understand herself yet, and didn't want to. She would have to talk, to be on exhibit . . . to say what? She was ignorant of everything. What was deliberately provincial, primitive, homely in her had rebelled, especially when the first signs of pregnancy appeared. How she had suffered during that banquet, on display as if at a fair! She had appeared to herself like a badly assembled windup mechanism. For fear that she might go off any moment she held herself in with all her strength. But then the thought that inside this automaton the germ of a life was growing for which she would soon have such tremendous responsibility had given her sharp pangs of remorse and had made the spectacle of that fatuous and foolish vanity unbearable.

Once the bewilderment and confusion of the first days had passed she had begun to walk around Rome with Zio Ippolito. What nice conversations they had had! What delightful explanations her uncle had given her! It had been a great comfort having him in Rome with her.

It was enough merely to utter this name—Rome—for many to feel obligated to express their admiration and enthusiasm. Yes, she had also admired it, but with a constant feeling of sadness. She had admired the solitary villas guarded by cypresses, the silent gardens on the Celio and Aventino hills, the tragic solemnity of the ruins and of certain ancient roads like the Appian Way, the clear freshness of the Tiber. She had little interest in what men had done and said to shore up their greatness in their own eyes. And Rome . . . yes, was also a large prison where the more exaggerated the prisoners' talk and gestures, the smaller and clumsier they appeared.

She still sought refuge in the most humble occupations, applying herself to the most modest and simple, almost elemental, things. She knew she couldn't say what she would wish, what she was thinking, because that same wish and thought often made no sense even to her, if she reflected a little.

To keep Giustino from sulking, she forced herself to be cheerful, to strike a certain attitude, to maintain a certain humor. She read, she read a lot, but among the many books only Gueli's were able to interest her greatly. There was a man who must have an inner demon similar to hers but was much more learned!

It wasn't enough for Giustino that she read. He also wanted her to feel comfortable speaking French and to practice it with Signora Ely Faciolli, who knew many languages, and to go to museums and galleries of ancient and modern art with her in order to be able to speak about such things if the occasion arose. He also wanted her to take more interest in her appearance and even to do her hair better, for goodness sake!

Sometimes she started laughing in front of the mirror. She was fascinated by her reflection. Oh, why did she have to be like this, with this face, this body? She would raise her hand unconsciously, and the gesture would remain there suspended in the air. It seemed strange that it was she who had performed that gesture. *She watched herself live.* With that suspended gesture she resembled a statue of an ancient orator she had seen (she didn't know who he was) as she went up the steps of the Quirinal one day from Via Dataria. That orator, with a rolled parchment in one hand and the other hand outstretched in a solemn gesture, seemed astonished that he had remained there as stone for so many centuries, suspended in that attitude before all those people going up and down those steps. What a strange impression it had made on her! She had been in Rome only a few days. One February noon. Pale sun on the wet gray stones of the deserted Quirinal piazza. Only the sentry and a carabiniere at the Royal Palace door. (Perhaps at that time of day the king was yawning inside his palace.) Under the obelisk, among the great prancing horses, the fountain murmured. And, as though the encircling silence had suddenly spread into the distance, she had the impression that the incessant roar was her own sea. She turned: on the cordon in front of the palace she saw a chipper sparrow hopping around on the stone pavement, shaking its little head. Did it also feel a strange emptiness in that silence, like a mysterious pause in time and life, and, looking on it in fear, want reassurance?

She was very familiar with this sudden and fortunately brief and silent sinking into the mysterious abyss. However, the impression of awful dizziness lasted a long time, in conflict with the stability of things (so misleading): ambitious and yet paltry appearances. The small, everyday life wandering among these appearances then seemed unreal to her, like a magic lantern show. Why give them importance? Why treat them with respect, that respect, that importance that Giustino wanted?

And yet, one has to live. . . . Yes, she realized that he, her husband, was basically right and she was wrong to be that way. She must now do as he did. And she decided to do as he wished and let herself be led, conquering her distaste and making herself appear to favor what he had done and was doing for her.

Poor Giustino! So economical and moderate. The expense of putting her on display didn't even bother him. . . . That beautiful dress he had secretly bought and had altered for her! And now she had to go to Marchesa Lampugnani's house against her will, squarely against her will? Yes, yes, she would go. Like a mannequin in that beautiful new dress: a mannequin not very presentable, not very . . . slender right now, but never mind! If he really believed it necessary, she was ready to go.

"When?"

Overjoyed at seeing her so compliant, Giustino told her that they would go the next evening.

"But wait," he added. "I don't want you to be embarrassed. I know there are so many little formalities, so many . . . Yes, they are probably

50

even foolish, as you think, but it's good to know them, my dear. I'll find out. To tell the truth I don't have much faith in Signora Ely for these things."

And that evening after leaving the office, Giustino Boggiolo went off to make the visit he had promised Dora Barmis.

<h1 style="text-align:center">4</h1>

Propped against the chest in the entry hall, a crutch. On the crutch, a felt hat. The double doors leading into the parlor were closed, and in the dim anteroom a yellowish green light was diffused through the checkered paper on the glass panels.

"No, no, no. I told you no. Stop it!" He heard the angry shouts from inside.

The maid, coming to open the door, was a little uncertain after this outburst whether it was the right moment to announce the new visitor.

"Is this a bad time?" Giustino asked timidly.

The maid shrugged her shoulders, then took heart and after knocking on the glass panel, she opened it: "There is a gentleman. . . ."

"Boggiolo," Giustino prompted in a low voice.

"Ah, you Boggiolo? How nice! Come in, come in," exclaimed Dora Barmis, inclining her head and quickly forcing a smile to replace the scornful, spiteful expression on her flushed face.

Giustino Boggiolo entered a little flustered and nodded to Cosimo Zago, who, downcast and very pale, was getting up. Bowing his large disheveled head, he leaned painfully against the back of a chair.

"I'm going. Good-bye," he said in a voice he hoped sounded calm.

"Addio," Dora replied at once, contemptuously, without looking at him; and she turned to smile at Giustino. "Sit down, sit down, Boggiolo. How good of you . . . About time, eh?"

As soon as Zago, limping badly, was gone, she threw herself into a chair and, arms in the air, sighed deeply: "I can't take anymore! Ah, my dear friend, how people can make you regret having a little heart! But if a poor unfortunate man comes to tell you: 'I'm ugly . . . I'm crippled . . .' what can you say? 'No, dear: why? Then just think how Nature has compensated you with other gifts.' It's the truth! You know what beautiful poetry that poor man can make. I tell everyone. I even told him. I've published it. But now he makes me regret it. *C'est toujours ainsi!* Because I'm a woman, you see? But I told him *tout bonnemont,* you can believe that. Just like a colleague . . . I'm a woman because . . . because I'm not a man, for God's sake! But I don't often even think about being a woman, and that's the truth! I completely forget about it. You know how I'm reminded of it? By the way some men look at me. . . . Oh, God! I burst out laughing. Yes, of course! I say to myself. I really am a woman. They love me. Ha, ha, ha. And now, what can I do, dear Boggiolo, I'm old now, aren't I? Come on, for heaven's sake! Give me a compliment, tell me I'm not old."

"There's no need to say it," Giustino said, blushing and lowering his eyes.

Dora Barmis burst out laughing in her usual way, wrinkling her nose: "Darling! Are you embarrassed? But no, come on! Will you have some tea? Vermouth? Here!"

She offered him the box of cigarettes with one hand and with the other pressed the button of the electric bell situated under a shelf loaded with books, knickknacks, statuettes, and photographs.

"Thank you, I don't smoke," Giustino said.

Dora placed the cigarettes on the bottom shelf of a small, round coffee table in front of the divan. The maid entered.

"Bring the vermouth. For me, tea. Bring it here, Nina. I'll pour myself."

The maid returned shortly with the tea, the vermouth, and sweet rolls in a silver-plated bowl. Dora poured the vermouth and said: "Now that I think of it there's something else you should be ashamed of, silly boy! Pay attention, because I'm serious now."

"What should I be ashamed of?" asked Giustino, who had already caught her drift. So much so that a foolish smile took shape under his mustache.

"Nature has given you a treasure, Boggiolo!" Signora Barmis said in a threatening and admonishing tone, wagging a finger. "Have a *fon-*

dant. . . . Your wife doesn't belong just to you. Your rights, darling, must be limited. If it won't make your wife unhappy, you should even . . . Tell me, is your wife jealous of you?"

"Of course not," Giustino replied. "Anyway, I can't say, because . . ."

"You've never given her the slightest reason," Dora finished his sentence. "You really are a good boy. That's obvious. Perhaps *too* good. Huh? Tell the truth. No, you must spare her, Boggiolo. Besides . . . men give a bad name to the thing." She bent the middle and ring finger of one hand to make the sign of the cuckold. "But a woman with any spirit doesn't give a hoot: women have their peccadilloes, too. Look at me! Why don't you look at me? Do I seem very peculiar? Oh, fine, just like that! You laugh? Certainly, darling, being a good boy is not enough when one has the good fortune of having a wife like yours. Do you know the poetess Bertolè-Viazzi? She didn't come to the banquet because, poor woman . . ."

"She is, also?" Giustino Boggiolo asked piteously.

"Eh . . . but much more serious!" Dora exclaimed. "She has a really awful husband!"

Giustino shrugged his shoulders and sighed with a sad smile. "On the other hand . . ."

"What do you mean, the other hand!" Dora Barmis exploded. "In certain cases a husband has to be considerate and think that . . . Look, for four or five years Bertolè has worked on a poem—very beautiful, I assure you, interwoven with memories of her courageous family: her grandfather was a real patriot, exiled to London, then a soldier with Garibaldi. Her father died at Bezzecca in the War of Independence. Well, then, to think that she already had a gestation like that in her head, a poem I tell you, a poem! And then to see the poor woman simultaneously oppressed, pulled down for another reason. No, no, believe me, it's just one of many, a cruel oppression! Either one thing or the other!"

"I see," said Giustino, distressed. "But do you think she's a little annoyed with me, too? However, Silvia won't be doing anything all this time."

"And it will be precious time lost!" exclaimed Dora.

"You're telling me?" continued Giustino. "Everything lost and nothing earned. A growing family . . . and who knows how many expenses and cares and worries. Then, the separation. Because we'll have to send the boy or girl to a wet nurse, near its grandmother."

"To Taranto?"

"No, not to Taranto. Silvia's mother died years ago. To my mother at Cargiore."

"Cargiore?" asked Dora, stretching out on the divan. "Where is Cargiore?"

"In Piedmont. Oh, a small village with just a few houses, near Turin."

"Because you're Piedmontese, aren't you?" asked Signora Barmis, wrapping herself in cigarette smoke. "I can tell by your accent. And how did you ever meet Silvia?"

"Well," said Giustino, "they sent me down to Taranto after the Notarial Archives competition."

"Oh, poor dear!"

"A year and a half of exile, believe me. Luckily Silvia's father was my boss."

"At the Archives?"

"Chief Archivist, yes indeed. Oh, it was a good job because of him. He took a liking to me immediately."

"And you, you rascal, you fell in love with his literary daughter?"

"Yes, out of necessity," smiled Giustino.

"Why 'necessity'?" Dora asked, startled.

"I say out of necessity because . . . going there every day . . . A poor young man there alone . . . She couldn't know what was going on. I had always lived with my mamma, poor little old woman. I was used to her taking care of me. The Honorable Datti promised that he would soon have me called to Rome, to the archives of the Council of State. Yes, Datti! But could my mother have gone there with me? I had to take a wife. By necessity. But I didn't fall in love with Silvia because she was a literary celebrity, you know? I wasn't even thinking about literature then. Yes, I knew that Silvia had published two books. But that didn't mean anything to me. . . . I'm going on too much!"

54

"No, no, tell me, tell me," Dora encouraged. "This is such fun."

"But there's not much to tell," Giustino said. "When I went to her house for the first time I expected to find . . . I don't know, a flighty young woman. But just the opposite! Simple, shy . . . but you've already seen her."

"What a dear! Yes, what a dear!" Dora exclaimed.

"Her father, my father-in-law, was a good soul, also."

"Oh, did her father die too?"

"Yes, indeed, suddenly, barely a month after our wedding. Poor man, he was such a fanatic! But it's understandable: she was his only child. He was so proud of her. He gave all his employees at the office her books and the newspaper articles about them. That was the first time I'd read them, too, and so . . ."

"An official duty, eh?" Signora Barmis asked with a laugh.

"Just imagine," Giustino replied. "However, her father's enthusiasm really bothered Silvia, and she wouldn't let him talk about her books around her. Very quiet, not ostentatious, even in the way she dressed, you know? She took care of the house, did everything. After we were married, she even made me laugh. . . ."

"When you wanted to cry?"

"No, I'm saying she made me laugh because she confessed what she called her secret vice: writing. She said I had to respect it, but in exchange I would never know when she wrote or how she managed to write between household duties."

"Dear girl! And you?"

"I promised. But then, a few months after the wedding—honestly! —a check for three hundred marks arrived from Germany for the translation rights. Silvia hadn't expected it either, imagine! She was so happy that those books of hers had a value that she didn't even suspect. Ignorant, inexperienced, she had agreed to the request for the translation of *Stormy Petrel* (her second volume of short stories) without expecting anything."

"And what did you do then?"

"Well, you can imagine what an eye-opener that was! Other requests came from journals, from newspapers. Silvia admitted she had many other short stories in a drawer, and the outline for a novel . . . *House of Dwarves*. . . . Free? What do you mean, free? Why? Isn't it work? And shouldn't work earn money? Writers don't know how to assert themselves when it comes to this part. It takes someone who knows about these things and takes care of them. Look, as soon as I understood there was something to be gotten out of them, I went about it in a proper, orderly way. I wrote a friend of mine who owns a bookstore in Turin to get information about the book trade and corresponded with several editors of journals and newspapers who had praised Silvia's books. I even wrote to Raceni, I remember."

"I remember that, too!" Dora exclaimed, smiling.

"Raceni is so kind!" Giustino continued. "And then I studied the law concerning literary property, of course! And also the Bern treaty on authors' rights . . . Ah, literature is a battlefield, my dear lady, where one fights bald-faced exploitation by the press and editors. In the early days they even exploited me! I negotiated blindly, you know. . . . But then, seeing how things worked . . . Silvia was alarmed by the conditions I made, but when she saw my demands were accepted and when I showed her the money, she was pleased. . . . Oh, naturally! But, you know, I can say I earned the money, because she never knew how to get anything out of her work."

"What a prize you are, Boggiolo!" Dora said, bending over for a closer look at him.

"I'm not saying that," Giustino replied, "but I know how to make a deal. I work at it. I really am grateful to my friends, to Raceni, for example, who has been so kind to my wife from the beginning. To you, too."

"But no! Me? What have I done?" Dora protested vigorously.

"You, too, dear lady, you too," Giustino repeated. "Along with Raceni, so kind. And Senator Borghi?"

"Ah, he has been the godfather of Silvia Roncella's fame!" said Dora.

"Yes, Signora, yes, Signora . . . exactly," confirmed Boggiolo. "And I owe my coming to Rome to him also, did you know that? We didn't need the problems of a pregnancy right now. . . ."

"You see?" exclaimed Dora. "And she'll suffer tremendously when she has to be separated from her baby!"

"But!" said Boggiolo, "having to work . . ."

"It's very sad!" sighed Signora Barmis. "A child! . . . It must be terrible to see yourself, feel yourself a mother! I would die of joy and fright! Dear, dear, dear, don't let me think about it."

She leaped to her feet, as though spring-propelled, and went to find the light switch next to the door. Then she turned and said in a different voice: "Or do we want to stay like this? Don't you like it? *Dämmerung* . . . The sorrow of the dying day makes me sad, but it's also a good thing. Good and bad, for me. Often I become a worse person, thinking in this dim light. It breaks my heart and makes me envious of other people's homes, of every home different from this one."

"But it's so beautiful here," Giustino said, looking around.

"I mean, so alone . . ." Dora explained, "so sad . . . I hate you all—you men, understand? Because it would be so much easier for you to be good, and you aren't, and you brag about it. Oh, how many men I've heard laugh about their treachery, Boggiolo. And while listening to them I've laughed, too. But afterward, thinking it over alone, at this time of day, how often I've so wanted . . . to kill! Oh, well, let's have the light. It'll be better!"

She turned the switch and greeted the light with a deep sigh. She had actually grown pale and tears veiled her heavily made-up eyes.

"You can be sure I'm not talking about you," she added with a sad smile as she came back to sit down. "You're a good man, I can see. Do you want to be my good friend?"

"Very much!" Giustino was quick to respond, a bit unsettled.

"Give me your hand," Dora continued. "Really good? For a long time I've looked for someone who would be a brother to me. . . ."

And she squeezed his hand.

"Yes, Signora . . ."

"One I can talk freely to . . ."

And she gave a harder squeeze.

"Yes, Signora . . ."

"Ah, if you only knew how painful it is to feel all alone, alone in my soul, understand? Because my body . . . Oh, they only look at my body, how I'm made. . . . My hips, breast, mouth . . . But they don't look into my eyes because they are ashamed. And I want them to look into my eyes, my eyes. . . ."

She continued squeezing his hand.

"Yes, Signora," Giustino repeated, looking her in the eyes, confused and blushing.

"Because my soul is in my eyes, my soul that looks for another soul to confide in and say it's not true that we don't believe in goodness, that we are not honest when we laugh at everything, when we become cynical in order to appear experienced, Boggiolo! Boggiolo!"

"What should I do?" Giustino Boggiolo asked, bewildered, upset, in a pitiful state clutched by that frail and yet so strong and nervous hand.

Dora Barmis fell into a fit of laughter.

"No, I'm serious!" Giustino said with conviction, trying to recover his balance. "If I can do anything for you, just ask me, Signora! You want a friend? I am here, I mean it."

"Thank you, thank you," Dora replied, drawing herself up. "Excuse me for laughing. I believe you. You are too . . . Oh, God . . . Do you know that the muscles for laughing don't obey the will but certain unconscious emotions? I'm not used to goodness like yours. I've taken some hard knocks; and in my dealings with unscrupulous men, I too . . . unfortunately . . . I don't want to hurt you! Your goodness might be destroyed. Others would be malicious in any case. And yes, I, too, talking about it with others, you know? I'm capable of laughing about being so honest with you today. . . . That's enough! Let's stop kidding ourselves. Do you know who asked me about your wife? The Marchesa Lampugnani. You've been invited and you haven't gone yet."

"Yes, Signora. Tomorrow evening, without fail," said Giustino Boggiolo. "Silvia hasn't been able. In fact, that's why I came here. Will you be there at the Marchesa's tomorrow evening?"

"Yes, yes," answered Dora. "Marchesa Lampugnani is so kind and so interested in your wife. She really wants to see her. You keep her too secluded."

"I?" exclaimed Giustino. "Not I, Signora. In fact, I would like . . . But Silvia is still a little . . . I don't know how to put it."

"Don't ruin her!" shouted Dora. "Leave her like she is, for heaven's sake! Don't force her."

"No, that's just it," said Giustino. "Just so we'll know what to do. Just imagine. . . . Do many go to the Marchesa's?"

"Oh, the usual people," Signora Barmis replied. "Maybe Gueli will also be there tomorrow evening, Signora Frezzi permitting, of course."

"Signora Frezzi? Who is she?" asked Giustino.

"A terrible woman, darling," responded Signora Barmis. "She keeps Maurizio Gueli totally under her control."

"Oh, Gueli doesn't have a wife?"

"He has Signora Frezzi, which is the same thing, or rather, worse. Poor Gueli! There is quite a story behind it all. But never mind. Does your wife like music?"

"I think so," answered Giustino, uneasily. "I really don't know. She's heard so little . . . there, at Taranto. Why, do they play much music at the Marchesa's?"

"Yes, sometimes. The cellist Begler comes and improvises a quartet with Milani, Cordova, and Furlini."

"Ah, yes," sighed Giustino. "A little knowledge of music . . . the difficult kind . . . is really necessary today. . . . Wagner . . ."

"There are no Wagner quartets!" exclaimed Dora. "Tchaikovsky, Dvořák . . . and then, you know, Glazunov, Mahler, Raff."

"Ah, yes," Giustino sighed again. "So many things one should know."

"Not really! It's quite enough to know how to pronounce their names, dear Boggiolo!" said Dora, laughing. "Don't worry about it. If I didn't have to protect my professional reputation, I would write a book called *The Fair* or *The Bazaar of Knowledge*. Suggest it to your wife, Boggiolo. I'm serious! I could give her all the dates and descriptions and documents. A list of those difficult names . . . then a little art history. Any little digest will do . . . some Hellenism, or rather, pre-Hellenism, Mycenaean art, and so forth. A little Nietzsche, a little Bergson, a few lectures, and get accustomed to taking tea, dear Boggiolo. You don't take it and that is a mistake. Taking tea for the first time makes one begin to understand many things! Do you want to try?"

"But I've already taken tea," said Giustino.

"And you still didn't understand?"

"I prefer coffee."

"Darling! Anyway, don't say that! Tea, tea, you must get used to tea, Boggiolo! You will come in white tie and tails tomorrow evening to the Marchesa's. Men in tails, women . . . no, some even come without *décolleté*."

"That's what I wanted to ask you," said Giustino. "Because Silvia . . ."

"Naturally!" interrupted Dora, laughing loudly. "She needn't come *décolleté* in her condition; that goes without saying. Is that clear?"

When Giustino Boggiolo left Dora Barmis's house shortly after, his head was whirling like a windmill.

For a while now, when around the different literary personalities, he had observed and studied how they managed to make a certain impression: their pose of greatness. But it all seemed totally without substance. The fickleness of fame worried him. It looked to him like one of those suspended silvery plumes on a thistle that the slightest breeze carries off. Fashion could, from one moment to another, send Silvia's name to the seven heavens or throw it to earth, lost in a dark corner.

He suspected that Dora Barmis had been making fun of him, but that didn't keep him from admiring the woman's exuberant spirit. Ah, how much easier his job would be if Silvia had a little of that spirit, those ways, that self-control. He had lacked it himself up to now! He realized that, and he recognized Signora Barmis almost had a right to mock him. That didn't matter. It had been a lesson, after all. He had to accept instruction and direction, even at the cost of suffering some small humiliations in the beginning. He had his eye on his goal.

And as though gathering the fruit of those first instructions, he returned home that evening with three new books for his wife to read:

1. a brief illustrated compendium of art history;

2. a French book about Nietzsche;

3. an Italian book about Richard Wagner.

3 ✸ MISTRESS RONCELLA:
TWO ACCOUCHEMENTS

1

The young maid from Abruzzi, who always laughed when she saw that *bersagliere* hat on Signor Ippolito's head, entered the study to announce the arrival of a foreign gentleman who wished to speak with Signor Giustino.

"At the office!"

"If the signora could receive him, he says."

"Horse feathers, you know the signora is . . ." He described with his hands how she was, then added: "Let him come in. He can talk to me."

The maid went out as she had entered, laughing. Signor Ippolito mumbled to himself, rubbing his hands together: "I'll take care of him myself."

A moment later there entered a very blond gentleman with a pink face like a plump child and cheerful, expressive blue eyes.

Ippolito Onorio Roncella made an elaborate pretense of removing his hat.

"Please, sit down. Here, here, in the armchair. May I keep my hat on? I might catch cold."

Ippolito took the card that the gentleman, with a mixture of uncertainty and bewilderment, handed him and read: c. NATHAN CROWELL.

"English?"

"No, sir, American," answered Crowell, almost carving the syllables as he pronounced them. "Correspondent for the American journal *The Nation*, New York. Signor Bòggiolo . . ."

"Excuse me, it's Boggiolo."

"Ah! Boggiolo, thank you. Signor—Boggiolo—granted—interview—about—new—great—work—great—Italian—writer—Silvia—Roncella," Crowell stammered in Italian.

"For this morning?" asked Signor Ippolito, hands outstretched. (Oh, how irritating that foreigner's telegraphic style and difficult pronunciation were!)

Mr. Crowell stood up and took a small notebook from his pocket, showing him a page with the penciled note: *Mr. Boggiolo, Thursday, 23 (morning).*

"Very good. I don't understand, but go ahead," Signor Ippolito said. "Have a seat. My *nipote*, as you see, is not here."

"Ni-pote?"

"Yes, sir. Giustino Boggiolo, my *ni-po-te* . . . *Nipote*, understand? That would be . . . *nepos* in Latin; *neveu* in French. I don't know what it is in English . . . do you understand Italian?"

"*Sì, poco,*" Mr. Crowell replied, more bewildered and uncertain than ever.

"That's good," continued Signor Ippolito. "But in the meantime, *nipote*, eh? Actually I don't understand him either. Never mind. Look, there's been a hitch."

Signor Crowell squirmed a little in his chair, as if hurt by certain words he didn't think he deserved.

"I'll explain," Signor Ippolito said, squirming a bit also. "Giustino has gone to the office . . . *uffi-uf-fi-cio,* to the *ufficio,* yes, sir, the Notary Public Office. He's gone to ask permission—again! and he'll lose his job, I keep telling him!—permission to take leave because we had a fine consolation yesterday."

At this pronouncement Mr. Crowell was perplexed at first, and then suddenly he had a gleeful reaction as the light finally dawned.

"*Conciolescione?*" he repeated with his eyes full of tears. "Really, a *conciolescione?*"

This time it was Signor Ippolito who was caught off guard.

"No, no!" he said irritably. "What do you think I said? We received a

62

telegram from Cargiore announcing that Signora Velia Boggiolo, that would be Giustino's mother, is arriving today. It's nothing to celebrate because she's coming to help Silvia, my niece, who finally . . . we're almost at the end. In a few days a boy or a girl. And let's hope it's a boy because if it's a girl, she'll start writing, God help us, my dear sir! Did you understand?"

"I'll bet he didn't understand a damn thing!" he grumbled to himself, looking at him.

Mr. Crowell smiled.

Then Signor Ippolito smiled back at Mr. Crowell. And so, both smiling, they looked at each other for a while. What a fine thing, eh? Oh, to be sure . . .

Now the conversation had to start over from the beginning.

"It seems to me that your Italian is sort of . . . sketchy, that's it," Signor Ippolito said in a friendly manner. "*Scusi, part . . . par-to-ri-re . . .*"

"Oh, *sì, partorire, benissimo,*" Crowell affirmed.

"May God be praised!" exclaimed Roncella. "Now, my niece . . ."

"A great work? A play?"

"No, sir. A child. A flesh and blood child. Ugh, how difficult it is for you to understand certain things! I'm trying to be polite. The play is about to be born. The rehearsals started yesterday at the theater. Maybe the two will be born at the same time, play and child. Two parts . . . that is, parts, plural of part . . . and parts in the sense of . . . of . . . parturitions. Understand?"

Mr. Crowell became very serious, sat up straight, turned pale, and said: "*Molto interessante.*"

And taking another notebook from his pocket, Mr. Crowell hurriedly wrote: *Mrs. Roncella two accouchements.*

"But believe me, this is nothing." Ippolito Onorio Roncella continued, relieved and happy, "There's something else! Do you think my niece Silvia deserves so much attention? I don't say she doesn't. She might be a great writer. But there's someone much greater in this house than she, and one who deserves to be taken much more seriously by the international press."

"Really? Here? In this house?" Mr. Crowell asked, his eyes open wide.

"Yes, sir," answered Signor Roncella. "Not me, of course! Her husband, Silvia's husband."

"Mister Boggiolo?"

"If you want to call him Boggiolo, go ahead, but I've told you his name is Boggiolo. Immeasurably greater. Look, Silvia herself, my niece, realizes that she would be nothing, or very little, without him."

"*Molto interessante,*" Mr. Crowell repeated with the same air as before, but turning a little paler.

Ippolito Onorio Roncella: "Yes, sir. If you wanted me to, I could talk about him until tomorrow morning. And you would thank me."

"Well, yes, many thanks, Signore," Mr. Crowell said, rising and bowing several times.

"No, I was saying," Signor Ippolito continued, "—sit down, for heaven's sake! You would thank me, as I was saying, because your . . . what do you call it? interview, yes, interview . . . your interview would turn out much more . . . more . . . tasty, shall we say, than if you just write about Silvia's play. I can't give you much help because literature is not my business, and I've never read a line of my niece's work. Out of principle, you know? And to keep a certain healthy balance in the family. My nephew reads a good deal! And he reads only her work. . . . By the way, is it true that writers are paid by the word in America?"

Mr. Crowell hastened to assent, and he added that every word of the best-known writers was usually paid as much as one lira, even two, and as much as two lire and fifty centesimi, in American currency.

"*Gesù! Gesù!*" exclaimed Signor Ippolito. "Suppose I write 'oh!,' for example. I get two lire and fifty? Now the Americans must never write *quasi* or *già*: they must always write *quasi quasi* or *già già*. . . . Now I understand why that poor boy . . . Ah, it must be agony for him to count all the words his wife scrawls for him and think how much they would earn in America. That's why he keeps saying Italy is a country of ragamuffins and illiterates. . . . My dear sir, words are much cheaper here in Italy. In fact, you could say that words are the only thing that is cheap. That's why we don't do much but talk."

Who knows where Signor Ippolito might have taken this discussion that morning if Giustino Boggiolo hadn't suddenly turned up to save the innocent victim from his clutches.

Giustino couldn't breathe: face burning and stinging with perspiration, he turned a ferocious eye on the uncle and then, in broken English, asked Mr. Crowell to excuse his tardiness and begged him please to postpone the interview until that evening, because now he was in a great hurry. He had to go to the station to get his mother, then go to the Valle Theater for the play rehearsal, then . . .

"But I was just helping out!" Signor Ippolito said to him.

"You could at least do me the kindness of not interfering in this business," Giustino couldn't keep from saying. "Pardon me, but it seems you do it on purpose."

He turned again to the American and asked him to wait a moment. He wanted to see how his wife was and then they could leave together.

"He'll lose his job, he'll lose his job, as true as God's word," Signor Ippolito repeated, happily rubbing his hands together as soon as Giustino left the room. "He lost his head and now he'll lose his job."

Mr. Crowell smiled at him.

At the office Giustino really had quarreled with his boss, who hadn't wanted to excuse his absence that morning, since he had received permission not to return to the office in the afternoon several days in a row so he could attend rehearsals.

"Too much," his boss had told him, "too much, my dear Roncello!"

"*Roncello?*" Giustino had exclaimed.

He was unaware that all his colleagues called him that almost automatically now.

"Boggiolo, of course . . . excuse me, Boggiolo," the head of the office had immediately corrected himself. "I addressed you by the name of your distinguished wife. Anyway, it seems natural."

"Why?"

"Don't take it badly, but let me talk to you like a father. It seems you do everything, Boggiolo, for . . . yes, you put your wife's interests first. You could be a good employee, diligent, intelligent . . . but must I say it? You do too . . . too much for your wife."

"My wife is Silvia Roncella," Giustino murmured.

And the boss: "So? My wife is Donna Rosolina Caruso! That's not a good reason for my not doing my duty here. This morning you can go. But think over what I've told you."

Leaving Mr. Crowell at the foot of the stairs, Giustino Boggiolo, very annoyed by all the small and vulgar vexations on the eve of the great battle, almost ran to the station. But even so he held a book open before his eyes—his English grammar.

Once he had climbed up the hill past the church of Santa Susanna, he put the book under his arm, looked at his watch, took a lira from his vest pocket and put it in a wallet he kept in the back pocket of his trousers. Then he took out a notebook and wrote in pencil: *Carriage to station . . . L. 1,00.*

He had earned it. In five minutes he would reach the station in time for the train from Turin. True, he was a little overheated and out of breath, but . . . a lira is a lira.

If anyone were silly enough to accuse him of stinginess, he would let him leaf through his notebook, where there was clear proof not only of his splendid intentions, but also of his generosity of feeling and nobility of thought, of the breadth of his vision, as well as his (deplorable) inclination to spend.

In fact, he jotted down in that notebook all the money he would have spent if he were not so judicious. Those figures represented daily inner struggles with himself, painful cavils, endless indecisions, and the most astute calculations of opportunities: public subscriptions, benefits for local and national calamities in which, with the most ingenious subterfuges and without casting a bad light on himself, he had *not* participated. Elegant little hats for his wife for thirty-five, forty lire each that he had *not* bought. Theater tickets for twenty lire for extraordinary performances that he had *not* attended. And then . . . how many daily expenses were written there as proof of his good intentions!

Hadn't he seen, for example, on his way to and from the office a poor blind man who truly inspired his pity? He, before anyone else passing by, would be moved to pity. He would stop at a distance to consider the unfortunate man's poverty and say to himself: "Who wouldn't give him two *soldini?*"

Often he would actually take them out of the wallet in his waistcoat and be just about to go over and give them to him when first one thought and then another, and then so many distressing thoughts all together, made him raise his eyebrows, take a deep breath, lower his hand, and slowly put the coins in the wallet in his trouser pocket. Then, with a sigh, he would write in his notebook: *Alms, o lire, 10 centesimi.* Because a kind heart is one thing, money another. A kind heart is tyrannical, money more so. Then, too, it is more painful not to give than to give when one cannot afford it.

Yes, yes, his family was beginning to grow, alas, and who bore the burden of it? Well, then, rather than having satisfaction on that day, he had had a kindly desire, a generous intention. As an honorable gentleman he could not allow himself to give in to the impulse to aid human misery.

2

For more than four years he hadn't seen his mother, that is, since they had transferred him to Taranto. How many things had happened in those four years, and how changed he felt now that the imminent arrival of his mother reminded him of his former life with her, of the humble and saintly affection rigorously maintained, of the simple life he had been torn from, because of so many unforeseen events!

That quiet, solitary life amid the snows and green meadows singing with water, among the chestnut trees of his Cargiore watched over by the perennial rumbling of the Sangone River. Those affections, those thoughts he would soon embrace again in his mother, but with an uneasy conscience.

When he married Silvia he had hidden from his mother the fact that she was a writer. Instead, he had written lengthy letters about her qualities that his mother could better accept. All true, however. But that was exactly why the uneasiness he now felt was all the more prickly, because it was he who had encouraged his wife to neglect those good qualities, and if Silvia's book was now making the leap to the stage, it was he who had pushed it. His mother would realize it when she saw Silvia, forlorn and in need only of maternal care, unmindful of anything not directly concerned with her pitiful condition. He, instead, would be at the theater with the actors, busily involved with the concerns of opening night.

It's true he was no longer a boy. By now he should be able to manage his own affairs. Besides, he saw nothing wrong in what he was doing. But because he had always been a good son, obedient and submissive to his good mamma's way of thinking and feeling, he was troubled by the thought of her disapproval, of doing anything to displease her. It bothered him even more to think that the saintly little old woman, traveling such a distance to be a loving help to her daughter-in-law, would in no way show her disapproval or express the slightest criticism.

Many people were also waiting for the Turin train, already late. To divert himself from these troublesome thoughts, he walked up and down the platform, forcing himself to read the English grammar, but at every train whistle he turned or stopped.

The arrival of the train was finally announced. The considerable crowd watched as it entered the station puffing noisily. The first windows opened. People ran in various states of anxiety from one carriage to the other.

"There she is!" Giustino said, growing cheerful, and he threw himself into the crowd in order to get to one of the last second-class carriages, from which appeared the bewildered head of a pale old woman dressed in black. "Mamma! Mamma!"

She turned, raised a hand, and smiled at him with her black, intense eyes whose vivacity contrasted with the paleness of a face already withered by the years.

The joy of seeing her son again was a refuge for little Signora Velia from the confusion that had oppressed her during the long journey, and from the many new impressions colliding tumultuously in her tired mind, closed and limited by the endless years of the same routine in her sheltered, monotonous life.

As though dazed, she responded to her son in monosyllables. Among so many people and such confusion, he seemed different to her; even the sound of his voice, his expression, his whole appearance seemed changed. And Giustino had the same impression of his mother. They both felt as if something between them had loosened, separated: the natural intimacy that had once kept them from seeing each other as they saw each other now, no longer one being, but two, not different, but separate. And hadn't he in fact been nurtured far from her—his mother was thinking—by a life she knew nothing about? And didn't he now have another woman at his side whom she didn't know and who surely had to be dearer to him than *she* was? But when his mother was finally alone with him in the carriage and saw that the luggage and bundle she had brought with her were safe, she felt relieved and comforted.

"How is your wife?" she then asked, revealing in the tone of her voice and expression that she was in awe of her.

"She's anxious to see you," Giustino replied. "She suffers a lot. . . ."

"Oh, poor thing . . ." Signora Velia sighed, closing her eyes. "I'm afraid there is little . . . little I can do . . . because maybe for her . . . I won't be . . ."

"What do you mean!" Giustino interrupted. "Get those notions out of your head, Mamma! You'll see how good she is."

"I'm sure she is, I know she is," Signora Velia said quickly. "I'm talking about myself. . . ."

"Because you imagine that someone who writes," added Giustino, "naturally has to be pretentious? Vain? Not at all! You'll see. In fact, she is too . . . too modest . . . That's what is driving me crazy! And then, in her condition . . . Come on, Mammina, she's just like you, you know? No different."

The old woman nodded her head in assent. Those words wounded her heart. She was the mother, and another woman, now, for her son was *like her, no different*. But she agreed. She agreed with a nod of her head.

"I do everything!" continued Giustino. "I make the deals. Besides in Rome, oh, my dear Mamma . . . it's impossible! Everything's twice the price . . . you can't even imagine! And if I didn't help out in every possible way . . . She works at home. I make her work pay outside."

"And . . . it pays?" his mother timidly asked, trying to shield the glare from her eyes.

"Because I'm the one who makes it pay!" answered Giustino. "My work, no doubt about it! It's me . . . all my work . . . What she does . . . yes, nothing, it would be like nothing . . . because the thing . . . literature, understand? is something that . . . you can do or not do, according to the day. Today you get an idea, you know how to write, so you write it. What does it cost you? Nothing! Literature is nothing in itself. It produces nothing, it wouldn't pay if it weren't . . . if it weren't . . . yes, if it weren't for me, that's all there is to it! I do everything. And if she's known now all over Italy . . ."

"Bravo, bravo." Signora Velia attempted to interrupt him. Then she ventured: "Is she known in our parts, too?"

"Even outside Italy!" exclaimed Giustino. "I have dealings with France! With France, Germany, Spain. Now I'm starting to deal with England! See? I'm studying English. But England is serious business! Take last year. How much? Eight thousand five hundred forty-five lire. Between the original and translations. More, with the translations."

"So much!" exclaimed Signora Velia, falling back in amazement.

"That's nothing!" Giustino laughed scornfully. "You make me laugh. If you knew how much they earn in America, in England! Five hundred lire, like nothing. But this year, who knows!"

Instead of toning things down, he now felt compelled to exaggerate out of irritation at what he pretended to himself was his mother's lack of savvy, though it really came from his inner discomfort, his remorse.

His mother looked at him and immediately lowered her eyes.

Oh, my, how her poor son had become involved with his wife's activity! What earnings he dreamed of! He hadn't asked anything about their town, just barely asked about her health and if she'd had a good trip. She sighed and said, as though returning from a long distance: "Graziella sends her greetings, you know?"

"Good, good!" Giustino exclaimed. "Is my old nurse well?"

"She's starting to lose her memory, like me," was his mother's reply. "But, you know, she's dependable. Prever also sends his best."

"Still crazy?" asked Giustino.

"As always," the old woman said with a smile.

"Does he still want to marry you?"

Signora Velia waved a hand, as if to brush away a fly. She smiled and repeated: "Crazy . . . crazy . . . Did you know we already have snow at Cargiore? Snow on Roccia Vrè and Rubinett!"

"If all goes well," said Giustino, "after the baby comes, maybe Silvia will go to Cargiore and be with you for a few months."

"Up there, with the snow?" his mother asked with concern.

"She'll like it. She's never seen snow," exclaimed Giustino. "I may have to go away on business. . . . We'll talk more about this later. You'll see how soon you'll get along with Silvia. Poor thing, she was raised without a mother."

3

It happened as he had predicted.

From the first moment she saw her, Signora Velia read in Silvia's sorrowful eyes the desire to be loved like a daughter, and Silvia read in the mother's eyes the fear and pain of feeling that with nothing more than her simple affection, she wasn't up to the task her son had assigned her. Immediately the mother hastened to satisfy that desire in Silvia and Silvia to remove that fear in the mother.

"I imagined you just as you are!" Silvia said with her eyes full of affectionate and tender reverence. "It's strange! . . . I feel I've always known you."

"There's nothing here!" replied Signora Velia, tapping her forehead. "But in my heart, yes, daughter, as much as you want."

71

"Hurrah for the simple things of life!" exclaimed Signor Ippolito, relieved finally to find a nice little old-fashioned woman. "Heart, heart, yes, well said, Signora! It takes heart and damn the head! You're the mamma, perform a miracle! Take the bellows out of your son's hands!"

"The bellows?" asked Signora Velia, puzzled, and looking at Giustino's hands.

"Yes, Signora, the bellows," replied Signor Ippolito. "A bellows he sticks in the ear of this poor girl, and blows and blows and blows till her head is this big!"

"Poor Giustino!" said Silvia with a smile, turning to her mother-in-law. "Pay no attention to him."

Giustino snickered like a snail in the fire.

"Go on! The woman understands me!" continued Uncle Ippolito. "It's lucky, my dear signora, that this little fool doesn't fly into the air! She, too, has heart, and it's solid, you know? If she didn't at this time . . . Her brain would sail like a ball . . . into the clouds . . . if there wasn't a little ballast in the boat of her heart. I don't write, don't worry, but I speak well when I get started. And my niece steals my images. All tomfoolery!"

With a shrug he went to smoke in the study.

"A bit cuckoo, but a good man," Silvia said to reassure the startled old woman. "He can't stand for Giustino . . ."

"I've already told Mamma!" he interrupted in annoyance. "I do everything. He smokes, and I think about earning money! After all, we're in Rome. Listen, Silvia: let Mamma rest now—we'll eat later. I have to dash off to the rehearsal. You know every minute is precious. Oh, yes, by the way, I meant to tell you that Signora Carmi . . ."

"Oh, dear, no, Giustino!" Silvia begged. "Don't tell me anything today, for pity's sake!"

"Eight! nine! ten!" exploded Giustino, finally losing his patience. "All on my back! Well, all right . . . I have to tell you, my dear! You can get over all your aggravation in one fell swoop, by receiving Signora Carmi."

"But how can I, in my condition?" Silvia asked. "Tell him, Mamma . . ."

"What does Mamma know about it!" exclaimed Giustino, more irritated than ever. "What is she? Isn't Signora Carmi a woman like you? She has a husband and children, too. An actress . . . Of course! If the play is to be performed it must have actresses! You can't go to the theater to help with the rehearsals. So I go: I have taken care of everything. But you should understand that if she wants to clarify something about her role, she has to ask you. But you won't receive her—you won't even talk to me about it! What can I do?"

"Later, later," Silvia said, to end the discussion. "Let me think about Mamma now."

Giustino rushed off in a fury.

He was so occupied with the imminent battle that he hadn't noticed his wife's aggravation every time he turned to the subject of the play.

Really bad timing that *The New Colony* had to be staged just while Silvia was in this condition. Giustino had miscalculated the months: he had figured that his wife would be free by October, but instead . . .

The Carmi-Revelli Company, engaging the Valle for just that month, was especially relying on *The New Colony,* which had been hot news for several months.

Claudio Revelli, director and actor, heartily detested Italian drama, as did all his fellow directors and actors. But during these months of preparation, helped by all of those who, to his satisfaction, had begun to enjoy it, Giustino Boggiolo was able to make such a fuss around that play that its opening was now awaited as a great artistic event, and promised to bring in almost as much profit as a vulgar little Parisian farce. Therefore, Revelli thought he could give in this once to the ardent and eager wishes of his associate and leading lady of the company, Signora Laura Carmi, who displayed a passionate predilection for Italian playwrights, as well as a deep dislike for all the scheduling concerns. She didn't want to hear about postponing the first performance of the play until November in Naples, because by doing so they might lose their priority in the theater at Rome. Another company, now performing in Bologna and waiting for the go-ahead from Rome to present their play, might take their place immediately, and after the reactions of the audience in Bologna, bring a newly revised play to Rome in December.

Therefore, Giustino really couldn't spare his wife these worries.

Silvia had suffered a great deal during the summer. Signora Ely Faciolli had begged her to take a vacation with her at Catino, near Farfa. She had sent several affectionate letters and postcards from there, inviting Silvia to join her. Not only did Silvia not want to move from Rome, but she did not even want to leave the house, feeling disgusted, and even ashamed, of her unsightliness, almost seeing it as a sordid and cruel mockery of nature.

"You are right, child!" Uncle Ippolito said to her. "Nature is a lot kinder to hens. An egg and maternal warmth."

"Oh, really!" grumbled Giustino. "A human chick has to be born, in fact . . ."

"But from the she-ass, dear boy! Should a human being be born from a she-ass? Do you think it's nice to treat a woman like an ass?"

Silvia smiled wanly. Thank goodness her uncle was in the house. His sporadic rockets shook her out of her torpor, from the stupidity into which she felt she had fallen.

Under the weight of such an oppressive reality, she felt a deep disgust these days with everything in the art field that is essentially, like life itself, banal. Even her own work seemed false and disgusting to her — work so often violated by life's sudden eruptions, as if by gusts of wind and impetuous waves. Eruptions that sometimes worked against the logic of her concept.

And the play?

She forced herself not to think about it so as not to upset herself. But from time to time the rawness of certain scenes gripped her and left her breathless. That play now seemed monstrous to her.

She had imagined a very fertile little island in the Ionian Sea, once a penal colony, abandoned after a disastrous earthquake that had reduced the little city there to a pile of rubble. After the few survivors cleared out, it had remained deserted for years, probably destined to disappear one day into the sea. That is the play's setting.

A first colony of sailors from Otranto, rough and primitive, has secretly gone to settle in the ruins in spite of the terrible threat of another earthquake that hangs over the island. They live there outside all law, almost outside time. Only one woman is with them, Spera, a woman with a doubtful past, but now honored like a queen, venerated like a saint, and ferociously protected by the man who brought her, a certain Currao, who has become the leader of the colony for that reason alone. But Currao is also the strongest, and because of his power over everyone, keeps the woman to himself, who in that new life has become another person. She has returned to her natural state of goodness, looks after the fires, comforts and cares for everyone, and has given Currao a son that he adores.

But, one day, one of those sailors, Currao's most ardent rival, whom Currao surprised and subdued in the act of raping Spera, disappears from the island. Perhaps he threw himself into the sea on a plank. Perhaps he swam to a ship passing in the distance.

Sometime later a new colony disembarks on the island, led by the runaway. However, the other sailors bring their own women, mothers, wives, daughters, and sisters. When the men of the first colony under Currao's command see this, they stop fighting the newcomers. Currao is isolated, suddenly bereft of his power. Spera immediately appears to all of them to be what she was before. But she is not as sorry for herself as she is for Currao. She can tell that he who was at first so proud of her is now ashamed, and she bears his contempt quietly. In the end Spera realizes that Currao, in order to hold up his head and keep the respect of the others, is thinking of leaving her. Some young sailors, the same men who had in vain yearned for her so ardently, come to tell her mockingly that he no longer cares for her because he has taken up with Mita, the daughter of an old sailor, Padron Dodo, who serves as the head of the new colony. When Spera hears this, she takes their son, hoping in this way to have a hold over the man who has spurned her. But old Padron Dodo will not agree to the marriage unless Currao brings the boy with him. Spera pleads, begs, turns to the others to intervene. No one pays any attention to her. Then she goes to plead with the old man and the bride, but they insist her son should remain with his father. Mita assures her that the boy will be well cared for. Spera, desperately wanting to keep her son, and wanting to break the heart of the man who abandoned her, embraces her child in a mad, screaming rage, and in that terrible embrace suffocates him. Stones fall after that scream, and others fall lugubriously in the horrible silence following the crime. Other screams are heard in the distance. Spera lives on top of a hill, in the ruins of a house that had collapsed at the time of the first disaster. Now she wonders if she didn't make those stones fall with her scream of horror. No, no, it's the earth! It's the earth! She jumps to her feet. Everyone is shrieking, overcome by terror, some flee, saved from disaster. The earth has opened up! The earth has caved in! Spera hears herself calling her son's name with heartrending cries from the side of the hill; she staggers about with the others, leans over to look down, horrified, and into the clamor coming from below, she shouts:

"Did it open under your feet? Did it half-swallow you? Your son? Because of you I killed him with my own hands. Die, die and be damned to hell!"

What impression would this play make? Silvia closed her eyes and saw the theater and the audience flash before her and was terrified. No! No! She had written it for herself! When she wrote it she wasn't thinking about the audience that would now see, hear, judge it. She had seen those characters and scenes on paper as she had written them down, translating her inner vision with the utmost fidelity. How would they make the leap from paper to the stage? With what voice? What gestures? What impression would those live words and real actions make on the boards, in front of the cardboard scenery in a fictitious and artificial reality?

"Come see," Giustino had advised her. "You don't even need to go on the stage. You can watch the rehearsals from the orchestra or a box near the stage. No one is better suited to judge, advise, or suggest than you."

Silvia was tempted to go, but then, about to leave, had felt her strength and spirit weaken. She was afraid that the excessive emotion would harm that other being living in her womb. How could she appear in that condition? How could she talk to the actors? No, no, it would be torture.

"At least tell me, how are they doing?" she asked her husband. "Do you think they understand their roles?"

Giustino, returning from the rehearsals, eyes bright and face red as though slapped, would snort, raise his hands angrily: "They don't understand a thing!"

Giustino was dejected. That dark stage impregnated with mildew and damp dust, those stagehands hammering on the canvas, nailing together the scenery for the evening's performance, all the gossip and pettiness and laziness and indifference of the actors clustered around in groups, that prompter in the prompt box in his skullcap, the script before him full of cuts and additions, the director, always surly and impolite, sitting near the prompt box, that man sitting at the little table who copied down the parts, and the property man working among the large boxes, sweating and puffing, were the cause of the cruel disappointment exasperating him.

He had photographs of the sailors and inhabitants of Terra d'Otranto sent from Taranto to use as models for the costumes, as well as dresses, shawls, and caps. For the most part, the costumes made a big hit. But some stupid minor actress had declared she didn't want to disguise herself in those rags. Revelli wanted to skimp on all the "savage" (as he put it) outdoor sets. And Laura Carmi, the leading lady, feigned indignation. Only Signora Carmi was a little bit of comfort to Giustino: she had wanted to read *Stormy Petrel* and *House of Dwarves* to better prepare herself, as she said, for acting her part. And she said she was enthusiastic about the part of Spera: she would make a "creation" of it! But she still didn't know a word of her part. She would walk past the prompt box and mechanically repeat, like all the others, the lines that the prompter gave her, shouting and giving directions according to the script. Only the character actor Adolfo Grimi was beginning to give some shape to his role as the old Padron Dodo and Revelli to that of Currao. But to Giustino it seemed that they both overdid it somewhat. Grimi performed his part like a baritone. Giustino took him

77

aside and politely pointed it out, but he couldn't risk it with Revelli, so he just stewed inwardly. He would have liked to ask different actors how they would make this gesture, how they would utter that phrase.

At the third and fourth rehearsals, Revelli, piqued by Signora Carmi's showy enthusiasm, had begun to rudely interrupt everyone from time to time. Many times he would interrupt for no good reason, just when Giustino thought everything was going well and the scene had begun to warm up and assume a life of its own, gradually triumphing over the actors' indifference and moving them to add feeling to their voice and gestures. Signora Grassi, for example, who played the role of Mita, had almost started to cry because of one of Revelli's rude remarks. Confound it! He could at least be a little nicer with the women! Giustino did his utmost to console her.

He didn't notice that several actors on the stage, especially Grimi, were making fun of him. They even went so far as to ask him to recite the most difficult lines of the play, when Revelli wasn't there.

"How would you say this? And how this? Let's hear it."

Right away! he would say. He knew very well he would speak badly. He didn't take the applause and shouts of admiration of those scatterbrains seriously, but at least he could show them his wife's intentions in writing those . . . what did they call them? Oh, yes, lines . . . those lines.

He tried to inspire them in every way, to make them friendly collaborators for a supreme and crucial undertaking. It seemed to him that some actors were a little apprehensive about the boldness of certain scenes and the passionate violence of certain situations. To tell the truth, he wasn't comfortable about several points, and sometimes he, too, was seized by apprehension when he looked out at the theater from the stage. All those rows of seats placed out there, as though waiting, the orderly tiers of boxes, all those dark spaces, those shadowy, menacing mouths encircling the theater. And then the ramshackle backstage, the backdrops pulled halfway up, the disorder on the stage in that humid and dusty half-light, the extraneous conversations of the actors, who would finish rehearsing some scene and then not listen to their companions rehearse, Revelli's anger, and the prompter's annoying voice all disconcerted him, upset him, kept him from formulating a clear idea of how the performance would be after a few evenings.

Laura Carmi came to shake him out of these sudden despondencies.

"Well, Boggiolo? Aren't we happy?"

"My dear signora . . ." sighed Giustino, opening his arms, breathing in with pleasure the perfume of the very elegant actress with the provocative figure and voluptuous expression—even though her face was almost totally artificial, her eyes lengthened, her eyelids darkened, her lips reddened, and beneath all the makeup the signs of age and tiredness were plain to see.

"Chin up, darling! It will be a success, you'll see!"

"Do you think so?"

"Without a doubt! Novelty, power, poetry: it has everything! And it's not *theater*," she added with a grimace of disgust. "Neither characters, style, nor action *qui sentent le 'théâtre.'* Do you understand?"

Giustino was comforted.

"Listen, Signora Carmi: you have to do me a favor. You have to let me hear Spera's scream in the last act, when she strangles her son."

"Oh, that's impossible, my darling! That has to come at the time. Are you joking? It would tear my throat. And besides, if I hear it once, even from myself, that's it! I'd imitate myself at the performance. It would come out cold. No, no! It has to come naturally. Oh, that sublime embrace! The rage of love and hate at the same time. Spera, you see? almost wants to bring into herself, into her own breast, the child they want to tear from her arms, and she strangles him! You'll see! You'll hear!"

"Will it be your son?" Giustino asked her, overjoyed.

"No, I'll strangle Grimi's son," was Signora Carmi's reply. "For your information, dear Boggiolo, my son will never set foot on the stage. Never! Never!"

When the rehearsal was over, Giustino Boggiolo ran to newspaper editorial offices to find Lampini, Ciceroncino at one office and Centanni or Federici or Mola at others. He had struck up friendships with them and through them had made the acquaintance of almost all the so-called "militant" journalists in the capital, the nonacademic literary critics. Even these, it's true, openly had their fun with him, but he didn't take it badly; he had his sights on another target. Casimiro Luna had heard that at the Notary Public Office they had changed his name. A mean thing to do! Names should be respected, not distorted! And he had taken up a collection with his colleagues to give Boggiolo a hundred calling cards printed with the words:

GIUSTINO RONCELLA

né Boggiolo

All right, fine. But in the meantime he had gotten a brilliant article out of Casimiro Luna about all of his wife's works and had managed to have the papers emphasize the public's eager anticipation for the new play, *The New Colony*, exciting curiosity with "interviews" and "gossip."

He came home evenings dead tired and beside himself. His old mother no longer recognized him. But by now he was in no shape to notice either her surprise or Uncle Ippolito's mocking air, just as he wasn't aware of the agitation he was causing his wife. He told her about the outcome of the rehearsals and what he said in the editorial offices.

"Signora Carmi is great! And you should see that little Grassi in the role of Mita: adorable! Posters for the first performances are already up. This evening they begin taking reservations. It's a real event, you know? They say the most important theater critics are coming from Milan, Turin, Florence, Naples, and Bologna."

The evening before opening night he returned home as though intoxicated. He brought three bits of news: two luminous as the sun; the other dark, slimy, and poisonous as a snake. The theater was sold out for three nights; the dress rehearsal had gone admirably; the best-known journalists and some literary figures who had seen it were all amazed, openmouthed. Except that Betti, Riccardo Betti, that affected, cold imbecile, had dared to say that *The New Colony* "was *Medea* translated into Tarentino dialect."

"*Medea?*" asked Silvia, totally baffled.

She knew nothing, nothing at all, about the famous witch of Colchis. Yes, she had read that name somewhere, but she had no idea who Medea was or what she had done.

"I told him! I told him!" shouted Giustino. "I couldn't stop myself. Maybe I shouldn't have said it. In fact, Signora Barmis, who was there, didn't want me to say anything. Medea? Euripides? Out of curiosity, tomorrow morning, as soon as Signora Faciolli arrives from Catino, have her lend you this blessed *Medea*. They say it's a tragedy of . . . of . . . something . . . I said it a moment ago. Study them, study these blessed Greek things, Myce . . . I don't know what they're called . . . Mycenaeans . . . study them! It's the fashion today! Do you realize that a phrase tossed out like *Medea translated into Tarentino dialect* can destroy you? That has to stop! There are so many imbeciles who don't know anything, less than I do! Now I know them. Ah, yes, now I know them!"

Signora Velia, very worried about Silvia's condition these last days, lovingly insisted she leave the house after supper with her husband. It was already late and no one would see them. A slow walk would do her good. She shouldn't have stayed in so much all this time.

Silvia let herself be talked into it. But when Giustino, at a street corner in the light of a flickering yellowish street lamp, pointed out the poster of the Valle Theater, with the title of the play, her name, and the list of characters in large letters and, emblazoned underneath, *A New Play,* she felt faint. She grew dizzy and leaned her cold, pale forehead on his shoulder: "What if I die?" she murmured.

4

Giustino Boggiolo arrived late at the theater, distraught and almost feverish, this time in a carriage.

As far as the little Piazza of Sant'Eustachio, the road was blocked by carriages with impatient drivers trying to get through. In order not to get stuck in line, Giustino paid the driver and slipped between the carriages and crowd of pedestrians. On the run-down facade of the theater the large electric lamps vibrated and hummed, almost as if participating in the frenzy of that extraordinary evening.

Attilio Raceni was standing in the doorway. "Well?"

81

"Don't ask!" panted Giustino, with a desperate gesture. "It's her time. Labor pains. I left her with labor pains!"

"Good heavens!" Raceni said. "It was to be expected. . . . The excitement . . ."

"Like hell!" replied Giustino, fiercely exasperated, rolling his eyes and trying to get to the box office ahead of those crowding around to buy tickets.

He rose on tiptoes to see the announcement in the box office window: *Sold Out.*

In his hurry a man bumped into him. "Pardon me. . . ."

"That's all right. But, you know, it's useless, I tell you. There are no more seats. Sold out. Come back tomorrow evening. There'll be another performance."

"Come on, Boggiolo!" Raceni called to him. "Better to let them see you on the stage."

"Two . . . four . . . one . . . two . . . one . . . three . . ." the ushers in festive livery shouted as they took the tickets at the entrance.

"But where can all these people find seats?" asked Giustino, on pins and needles. "How many tickets have they given away? I should have been here earlier. . . . But luck's against us! And I'm worried, really worried, believe me. I have an awful feeling. . . ."

"Don't talk like that!" Raceni urged.

"About Silvia, I'm talking about Silvia!" Giustino explained. "Not about the play. I left her in a bad way, believe me. And then, look, all these people . . . where will they sit? They'll be uncomfortable, impatient, unruly. . . . When they pay for something, they want to enjoy themselves. . . . But they can come the second night, for heaven's sake! There will be other performances. . . . Let's go."

The whole theater buzzed in noisy confusion, like a gigantic beehive. How to satisfy the hunger for pleasure, the curiosity, the tastes, the expectations of all these people gathered together and thereby lifted to a more expansive, warmer, more united level of life than usual?

As he looked from the entrance to the orchestra seats, Giustino became anxiously aware of the swarm of spectators. His face, ordinarily ruddy, had now become purple.

On the stage, barely lit by a few electric lights shining behind the backdrop, the stagehands and the property man gave the last touches to the scene while, with mournful mewing, the small orchestra tuned up. The stage director rushed around, with the bell in his hand, ready to give the signal to the actors.

Some of the actors were ready. Little Grassi was dressed as Mita and Grimi as Padron Dodo, with a gray, short false beard, his face blackened like a pepper-cured ham, horrible to see up close. His sailor's cap was folded over one ear, his trousers were rolled up, and he wore a flesh-colored sweater. Both were talking with Tito Lampini, who was in tails, and with Centanni and Mola. As soon as they saw Giustino and Raceni, they come over to greet them boisterously.

"Here he is!" shouted Grimi, arms outstretched. "Well, how's it going?"

"A full house!" exclaimed Centanni.

"Happy, eh?" added Mola.

"Wonderful!" Signora Grassi said, shaking his hand vigorously.

Lampini asked: "Your wife? . . ."

"Not well, not well at all . . ." Giustino began.

But Raceni, opening his eyes wide, made a rapid gesture with his head. Giustino understood, lowered his eyes, and said: "They must understand that . . . she can't be too . . . well."

"But she'll be fine! She'll be just fine! Very fine, indeed!" Grimi said in his mellow voice, tossing his head and grinning.

"Come on, Lampini," Centanni said. "The customary good wish: *Break a leg!*"

"Where's Signora Carmi?" Giustino asked.

"In her dressing room," Signora Grassi answered.

Through the curtain came the incessant din from the large hall. The rumble of a thousand voices near and far mixed with doors banging, keys screeching, and feet shuffling. The sea in the backdrop and Grimi dressed like a sailor gave Giustino the impression that there was a large wharf there with many steamers ready to depart. His ears suddenly started ringing and his mind went completely blank.

"Let's look at the audience!" Raceni said, taking him by the arm and

83

drawing him to the peephole in the curtain. "Don't let it get out, for heaven's sake!" Then he added softly, ". . . that your wife is about to deliver."

"I understand, I understand," replied Giustino, who felt his legs go numb so near the footlights. "Listen, Raceni, you have to do me the favor of running to my house at the end of every act . . ."

"But of course!" interrupted Raceni. "You don't have to tell me."

"For Silvia, I mean," added Giustino, "so I'll know how she is. She'll understand you can't tell her anything. Ah, what a terrible coincidence! Thank goodness I had the foresight to ask my mother to come! And her uncle's with her. And I've also asked poor Signora Faciolli to give up the performance tonight she wanted to see so badly."

Putting an eye to the peephole, he was amazed as he looked down first at the orchestra seats, then around the boxes, and finally up at the galleries swarming with heads. They were restless and impatient up there. They shouted, clapped their hands, stamped their feet. A furiously ringing bell startled Giustino.

"It's nothing!" Raceni said to calm him. "It's a signal for the orchestra."

Then the little orchestra began tuning up.

All the boxes were unusually crowded and there wasn't an empty place in the orchestra, and what a throng in the small standing room area! Giustino felt burned by the hot breeze from the bright theater, by the tremendous spectacle of such an expectant multitude. The innumerable eyes wounded him, pierced him. All those restless glittering eyes made the crowd terrible and monstrous. He sought out a familiar face there in the stalls. Ah, there was Luna looking up at the boxes and nodding his head with a smile. . . . And over there was Betti looking through binoculars. Who knows how many times by now he had repeated that phrase in his lordly, offhand way: "Medea translated into Tarentino dialect."

Imbecile! He looked again at the boxes and, following Raceni's directions, looked for Gueli in the first tier, Donna Francesca Lampugnani and Signora Bornè-Laturzi in the second. But he could spot none of them. He swelled with pride now, thinking that the full theater was

84

already a splendid and magnificent spectacle in itself. And it all was due to him: his wife's reputation and fame was his work, the fruit of his constant, tireless efforts. The author, the real author of it all, was himself!

"Boggiolo! Boggiolo!"

He turned. A radiant Dora Barmis stood before him. "Really splendid! I've never seen a theater like this! A magician, you are a magician, Boggiolo! Truly magnificent, à ne voir que les dehors. And what a miracle. Did you see? Livia Frezzi came! They say she's terribly jealous of your wife."

"Of my wife?" Giustino exclaimed in surprise. "Why?"

He was so infatuated with himself at that moment that if Signora Barmis had said that Gueli's friend and every woman in the theater was wild about him, he would have understood and easily believed it. But his wife . . . "What does my wife have to do with it? Livia Frezzi jealous of Silvia? Why?"

"Does it bother you?" said Signora Barmis. "Who knows how many other women will soon be jealous of Silvia Roncella! What a shame she isn't here! How is she? How is she?"

Giustino didn't have time to answer her. The bells were ringing. Dora Barmis squeezed his hand and ran off. Raceni dragged him behind the scenes to the right.

The curtain went up, and Giustino Boggiolo felt as if his soul was being exposed and that the suddenly silent multitude was prepared for the fierce enjoyment of his torture, his unspeakable suffering, almost a drawing and quartering, but with something shameful about it, as if he had been stripped naked. As if at any moment, through some unexpected false move, he might appear terribly ridiculous and disgusting.

He knew the whole play inside out, each actor's part from the first line to the last. Involuntarily he nearly repeated them aloud, while, almost as though reacting to continual electrical shocks, he would suddenly turn this way or that with his eyes gleaming, cheeks aflame, tormented by the actors' slow delivery of every line—on purpose, it seemed to him, to prolong his agony, as though they were enjoying it.

At a certain point Raceni kindly tried to tear him away, to lead him to the dressing room of Revelli, who had not yet made his entrance, but he couldn't get him to move.

Gradually, as the play progressed, a weird compulsion, a frightful fascination froze Giustino in his tracks, like the sight of something monstrous. The play that his wife had written, that he had memorized word for word, that he had almost gestated, was detaching itself from him. From everyone. It was rising, rising over the crowd like a paper balloon that he might have brought there on this gala evening, that he had for a long time and with trembling care inflated by holding it over the flames issuing from him. Then he had lit the wick. It was detaching itself from him, it was liberating itself. Palpitating and luminous, it rose, rose to the sky, pulling with it his whole lurching soul and almost ripping away his vital organs, his heart, his breath, in the anxious fear that a puff of air, a blast of wind would hurl against it and it would burn, devoured there in the sky by the very fire he had lit.

But where was the crowd's reaction to that ascent?

The hideous thing was this terrible silence the play was passing through. It alone was living there, by itself and for itself, suspending, or rather, absorbing, the life of everyone, tearing words from his mouth, and with the words, his breath. And that life whose extraordinary independence he now felt, that life one moment floating calm and powerful, the next quick and frantic amid such silence, aroused his dismay and horror, mixed with increasing resentment. Almost as if the play, delighting in itself, delighting in living for itself and for itself alone, scorned the pleasure of others, prevented others from showing their pleasure. It was as if it had assumed a too prominent and serious part, disregarding and diminishing the infinite care he had given it up to now, until it made his concerns appear ineffectual and ridiculous, compromising those material interests that were his greatest concern. If no applause broke out . . . if everyone sat like that until the end, hesitant and stupefied . . . But what was that? What happened? Soon the first act would be over. . . . No applause whatever . . . Not one sign of approval . . . Nothing! He thought he was going crazy. . . . He opened and closed his hands, dug his nails into his palms, scratched his forehead that was burning and yet damp with cold sweat. He stared at Raceni's transformed face, totally absorbed in the play, and he seemed to read there his same dismay. . . . No, a different dismay, almost astonishment . . . Perhaps the same kind that held all the spectators . . . For a moment he was afraid that the play was an atrocious, horrid thing never before created, and that at any moment a fierce insurrection would break out among the indignant, offended spectators. Ah, that silence was truly terrible! What was it? What was it? Were they disturbed? Were they entertained? No one was breathing. . . . The actors' shouts in the last scene were echoing on stage. There, now the curtain was falling. . . .

After an endless moment of agonizing suspense, Giustino felt that he alone, there by the footlights, with his anxiety, with his longing, with all his soul, in a tremendous, supreme effort, tore the applause from the theater, the first applause: dry, labored, like the crackle of dry twigs, of burned stubble, then a burst of flame, a fire: loud, hot, long, clamorous, deafening. . . . And then he felt his whole body relax, almost falling in a faint, drowning in the frenzied roar that went on and on, incessantly growing and endless. . . .

Raceni held him in his arms, sobbing against his chest, while the actors went to the footlights four, five, times toward the eruption out there. . . . He sobbed, laughed and sobbed, and trembled with joy. From Raceni's arms he fell into Signora Carmi's, and then Revelli's, and then Grimi's. Grimi imprinted the colors of his makeup on Boggiolo's lips, on the end of his nose, on his cheeks, because in an emotional outburst he was determined to kiss him at any cost, in spite of the fact that Boggiolo, knowing what a mess it would make, tried to fend him off. With his smeared face he continued to fall into the arms of the journalists and everyone he knew who rushed onstage to congratulate him. He could do no less. He was so exhausted, done in, finished—it was the only way he could find relief. And now he abandoned himself to everyone almost automatically. He would have fallen into the arms of the firemen, stagehands, scene changers, if Signora Barmis hadn't finally come to divert him from that comic and pitiful gesture by giving him a good shake and leading him to Signora Carmi's dressing room to make him wash his face. Raceni had slipped out to get news of his wife.

In the aisles, in the boxes, there was shouting, excitement, turmoil. The entire audience, for three quarters of an hour enthralled by the powerful fascination of this new and extraordinary creation, so alive from start to finish with a quick, violent life that gave no respite, flashing with unexpected spirit, seemed to be liberated from their enchantment by that frantic, interminable applause. Now everyone felt an overpowering joy, an absolute certainty that that life, which in its innovative spirit and expression showed such a diamond-hard strength, could never be shattered by differences of opinion, because now every judgment, as in reality itself, would seem necessary, controlled, and made logical by the inevitability of the action.

This was exactly what constituted the miracle of art, a miracle in which they participated this evening almost with trepidation. It did not seem to come from a writer's premeditated concept, but from the uncertain, unpredictable action born minute by minute in the clash of savage passions, in the freedom of a life unhampered by laws or even by time, in the arbitrary choices of so many wills that overpowered each other in turn, of so many beings left to themselves who acted in the full independence of their nature, that is, *against* whatever end the author might have intended.

Many people, among those most excited and yet no less worried that their impression might not accord with the judgment of competent critics, searched the orchestra and boxes to read the faces of drama critics from the most widely circulated newspapers. Critics from other cities were pointed out and carefully scrutinized. Eyes were especially fixed on a box in the first tier: the box of Zeta, the terror of all actors and playwrights who came to face the judgment of the Roman audience.

Zeta was in animated conversation with two other critics, Devicis from Milan and Corica from Naples. Did he approve? Disapprove? And of what? The play or the actors' interpretation? Another critic entered the box. Who was he? Oh, Fongia from Turin . . . How he was laughing! And then he was pretending to cry, leaning first on Corica's chest and then on Devicis'. Why? Zeta jumped to his feet with a furious gesture of indignation and shouted something that made the other three burst out laughing. In the nearby box, a gloomy, dark woman, with deeply circled green eyes and a very dignified, somber manner, got up and went to sit in the corner of the box. While in the back a gentleman with gray hair . . . ah, Gueli, Gueli! Maurizio Gueli! leaned out to look into the critics' box.

"Pardon me, Maestro," Zeta said to him, "and pardon me, Signora. But this is very unfortunate, Maestro! This is the ruin of that poor girl! If you are fond of Signora Roncella . . ."

"I? For heaven's sake!" said Gueli, and his angry face drew back, looking into his lady friend's eyes.

With the flicker of a cutting laugh on her dark lips, and narrowing her eyes almost as if to dim their green flashes, she bowed her head several times toward the journalist and said: "Oh, very . . . very fond . . ."

"Signora, with reason!" the other exclaimed. "Silvia Roncella is the true daughter of Maurizio Gueli! I say it, I have said it, and I will say it. This is a great thing, my dear lady! A great thing! Signora Roncella is great! But who will save her from her husband?"

Livia Frezzi smiled as before and said: "Don't worry. . . . She'll have help . . . paternal, of course."

Shortly after this conversation between boxes and while the curtain was going up on the second act, Maurizio Gueli and Livia Frezzi left the theater as two people unable to restrain their clashing passions any further might leave to avoid making an obscene and scandalous spectacle of themselves. They were about to enter their carriage when another one arrived, and Attilio Raceni dismounted in a great flurry.

"Ah, Maestro, what misfortune!"

"What is it?" Gueli asked in a voice that he hoped appeared calm.

"She's dying . . . she's dying . . . she's dying . . . Signora Roncella, perhaps right now. . . . I left her . . . to come get her husband. . . ."

And without a word to Signora Frezzi, Raceni dashed into the theater. Passing by the orchestra entrance he heard a high rumble of applause. In a twinkling he leaped on stage and found himself in the midst of a ruckus. Giustino Boggiolo, now elated, in fact nearly crazed with joy, was being pulled along by the lapels of his jacket by the actors. He shouted and wriggled free so he could get to the footlights — he himself — in the place of his wife, to thank the audience that had still not tired of calling for the author.

4 ✸ AFTER THE TRIUMPH

1

A crowd was milling around the train station. The newspapers had spread the word that Silvia Roncella, miraculously escaping death at the precise moment of her supreme triumph, was at last in a condition to bear the stress of a long journey. Still convalescent, she was leaving that morning to recoup her strength and health in Piedmont, her husband's native village. Journalists, literati, and admirers had run to the station to see and greet her. They were all jammed in front of the waiting room door, since her doctor, who would go with her as far as Turin, wouldn't allow too many people to crowd around her.

"Cargiore? Where's Cargiore?"

"Uhm! Near Turin, they say."

"It will be cold there!"

"Of course!"

Those who went in to shake her hand and congratulate her anyway, in spite of her doctor's protests and her husband's entreaties, couldn't make themselves move aside so others could come in. And even if they moved away a little from the bench where she was sitting between her mother-in-law and the nurse, they stayed in the room intently observing her every movement, expression, smile. Those outside tapped on the window, called out, made gestures of impatience and irritation: those inside pretended not to understand; in fact, some appeared to enjoy showing their impudence to the point of looking at that display of impatience and irritation with scornful, mocking smiles.

The reception of the play, *The New Colony*, had really been extraordinary, a triumph. News of the author's death had spread like wildfire through the theater that night, at the end of the second act, when the whole audience was enthralled, fascinated by the enormous and powerful originality of the play. That rumor had given rise to such a strange and solemn demonstration of both mourning and enthusiasm that even after two months, anyone who had had the good fortune to be there still felt a shiver of emotion. Affirming the triumph of life in that work of art, the raving, shouting, entreating, sobbing audience seemed that evening to want to defeat death itself. At the end of the performance, the excited audience had remained in the theater for a long time, almost as though waiting for death to release its sacred prey to glory and restore her to life. And when an exultant Laura Carmi had burst onto the stage to announce that the playwright was not yet dead, a delirious shout went up as though for a supernatural victory.

The next morning all the newspapers put out extra editions to describe that memorable evening. Immediately, the word spread throughout Italy, making every town impatient to see the play and to have more news of the writer and of the state of her health, as well as more information about her work.

It was enough to look at Giustino Boggiolo to get an idea of the magnitude of the event and of the feverish curiosity spreading like wildfire. It was he who seemed to have narrowly escaped the jaws of death, not his wife.

That evening it was Attilio Raceni who had tearfully dragged Boggiolo away from the stage to take him home. Raceni had to tear him from the arms of the actors, who had seized him by the chest, by the shoulders, by his lapels to keep him from taking a bow, to keep him from rushing to the footlights in the place of his wife, wildly intoxicated as he was by the thunderous applause that broke out at the beginning of the second act, at the moment of the landing of the new colony, just when the men of the first colony had stopped fighting at the sight of the women, leaving Currao on his own.

Why hadn't he gone mad at the sight of the tragic turmoil there at home, with those three doctors bent over his bleeding, shrieking wife, tormenting and butchering her exposed body?

Anyone else would have gone mad, bouncing like that from one violent, terrible emotion to its opposite, no less violent and terrible. Not he! Instead, soon after he entered the house, Giustino had been obliged to find, and had succeeded in finding, the superhuman strength to keep his head in the face of the cruel impudence of the journalists who had run from the theater as soon as the first news of her death had begun to circulate among the audience. And while his wife's shrieks and long, horrendous howls came from the other room, he had been able to respond to all the questions asked of him (though those shrieks and howls tore at his heart), and to give out information and news, and even go rummaging through boxes to find a photograph of his wife to give to the editors of the more prestigious newspapers for use in the morning extra editions.

In the meantime, for good or ill, she was liberated from her burden: she had done what she had to do. There it was, that dear, pink, delicate little thing in the nurse's arms, and Silvia was going off to rest and recover in peace and inactivity. While he . . . already, before everything else, certainly before that little thing there, had given birth to a giant! A giant that now, at once, wanted to start taking great strides through all Italy, through Europe, even through America, to reap laurels, to pile up money, and it was up to him to follow it with sack in hand; up to him, already exhausted, worn out by the pains of its gigantic birth.

For Giustino Boggiolo, in truth, the giant wasn't the play written by his wife. The giant was the success of which he alone was the author. Of course! If it hadn't been for him, if he hadn't performed miracles over all those months of preparation, all these people wouldn't be running here to the station now to pay their respects to his wife, to congratulate her, to wish her *buon viaggio!*

"Please, please . . . Quiet down. Didn't you hear the doctor? And besides, look at all the others waiting outside. Yes, thank you, thank you . . . Please, for heaven's sake . . . Take turns, take turns, the doctor says. . . . Thank you, please, for heaven's sake," he turned here and there, with his hands outstretched, in an attempt to keep them away from his wife as much as possible, to manage even this performance in such a laudable way that the evening papers would speak of it as another event. "Thank you, oh, please, for heaven's sake . . . Oh, Signora Marchesa, how kind . . . Yes, yes, go on, thank you. . . . Come on in, come on, Zago. I'll let you shake her hand and then be off, please. Make room, please, ladies and gentlemen. . . . Thank you, thank you . . . Oh, Signora Barmis, Signora Barmis, help me, for goodness sake. . . . Look, Raceni, if Senator Borghi comes . . . Make room, make room, please. . . . Yes, she's leaving without seeing her play even once. . . . What did you say? Ah, yes . . . unfortunately, yes, not even once, not even a rehearsal . . . Oh, what can she do? She has to leave, because I . . . Thank you, Centanni! . . . She has to leave. . . . Ciao, Mola, ciao! And don't forget, you know? . . . She has to leave, because . . . What did you say? Yes, indeed, that is Signora Carmi, the leading lady. . . . Played Spera, yes, indeed! Because I . . . never mind, just never mind. . . . Don't talk about it, don't talk about it, don't talk about it. . . . In Naples, Bologna, Florence, Milan, Turin, Venice . . . I don't know how to be everywhere at once . . . seven, seven companies on tour, yes, indeed . . ."

And so, a word to this or that person, to leave everyone happy. Glances and knowing smiles to the journalists, handing out all that information almost as though by chance, and saying this or that name loudly on purpose so the journalists would take note.

Ashen, with bloodless lips, dilated nostrils, enormous eyes, hair loose, Silvia Roncella looked small and miserable in the center of all that activity. More than dumbfounded, she looked lost. Her face was a study in uncertainty—nervous tics and grimaces that betrayed strenuous efforts of concentration, as though she didn't always believe what she was seeing and was wondering what she was supposed to do, what they wanted from her, now that she was about to leave with her baby. As though all those people, all that confusion might harm her baby, just as they were upsetting her.

This struggle plainly said: "Why? Why? So this triumph is true, really true?"

She seemed afraid to believe it was real, or perhaps she was suddenly seized by the suspicion that everything had been orchestrated, a plot hatched by her husband, who bustled around so busily, a grandiose, overbearing act—that was it—for which she ought to feel more shame than abhorrence, as an affront to her maternity and the atrocious suffering it had cost her, an invasion, a violence to her quiet, modest ways. An intrusion not only tiresome but also uncalled for because she had done nothing to draw so many people there: she had to leave, and that was all there was to it, with the nurse and the little one and her mother-in-law, poor dear, confused old woman, and Uncle Ippolito, who was making such a sacrifice to move up there with her instead of her husband, and to keep her company in her mother-in-law's house. This was just a little family trip, to be made with all the proper precautions, with consideration for her infirmity.

If the triumph was real, it only meant bother, oppression, nightmare for her at that moment. But maybe . . . yes, just maybe, later, as soon as she had recovered her strength . . . if it was true . . . who knows!

Something like an enormous, stinging ferocity rose from the depths of her soul, upsetting, disturbing, wrenching affections and feelings. It was the demon, that wild demon that she felt inside her, that had always frightened her. She had always struggled to keep it from grabbing and dragging her heavens knows where, far from the love and care in which she took comfort and felt secure.

Ah, her husband did everything, everything to fling her into its grasp! Did the idea never occur to him that if she . . . ?

No, no. In opposition to her demon, another more terrible specter reared up inside her now: the specter of death. It had touched her, so recently touched her; and she knew how it felt: icy, dark, and hard. That jarring impact! Ah, that jolt! Beneath her soft flesh, beneath the fervent flow of blood, that wallop against the bones of her skeleton, against her inner frame! Death had struck her with the little feet of her baby boy, who wanted to live by killing her. Her death and her baby's life rose up to face the enticing demon of glory: a bloody, brutal, shameful foulness, and that rosy dawn wrapped in its blankets, that delicate and tender purity, flesh of her flesh, blood of her blood.

Buffeted like that in the exhaustion of convalescence, flung from one emotion to another, Silvia Roncella turned to her baby between one greeting and another, then she gave the hands of the old woman sitting next to her a rapid, encouraging squeeze, and here and there she replied with a cold and almost hostile expression to the good wishes and congratulations of a journalist or writer, as if to say to them: "This is not very important to me, you know? I nearly died!" In response to some other words of congratulation or good wishes, her expression would clear, her eyes would shine and she would smile.

"She's marvelous! Marvelous! Naive, unaffected, enchanting! Fresh as spring!" Signora Barmis couldn't stop exclaiming to the cluster of actors who had come, along with so many others, to see and meet the playwright for the first time.

In order not to seem peevish, the actors nodded their heads. They had all come certain of a warm reception, a suitable reception, if not exactly as the main creators of such a success, at least as her most effective collaborators, not easy to replace or surpass! Instead, they had been greeted like all the others, and the high spirits they came with had immediately drooped and cooled.

"Yes, she doesn't feel well," Grimi observed, making faces with baritone gravity. "It's obvious she's suffering, just look at her! I tell you that poor little woman is suffering. . . ."

"What strength for such a little woman!" Signora Carmi said, biting her lip. "Who would have said? I imagined her quite different!"

"Really? Not me! No! No! She's just as I thought," declared Signora Barmis. "But if you look closely . . ."

"Yes, of course, in her eyes . . ." Signora Carmi assented at once. "There! There! There's something in her eyes. . . . Certain flashes, yes, yes . . . Because the greatness of her art is . . . I don't know . . . in flashes, isn't it? Doesn't it seem to you? Sudden, unexpected . . . in certain brusque intervals that shake and stun you. We are used to only one tone, that's it. To those that tell us: life is this, this, and this; to others that tell us: it's this other, this other, and this other. Isn't that right? Signora Roncella paints one side, too, but then she suddenly switches and shows the other side. That's the way it seems to me!"

Sucking her satisfaction like a piece of candy at having spoken so

96

well, Signora Carmi looked around as though to receive the applause of the entire room, or at the very least signs of unanimous agreement in order to avenge herself with true superiority for Roncella's coldness and ingratitude. But she got no support even from her own group, because her stage companions realized as surely as Signora Barmis did that she had spoken to be heard by the others more than by them, and by Roncella most of all. Only two people hidden in a corner, Signora Ely Faciolli and Cosimo Zago leaning on his crutch, nodded approval. And Laura Carmi scornfully ignored them as though they had insulted her.

Suddenly a lively, curious commotion spread through the room. Removing their hats and bowing, many hurriedly stepped aside to let a man through. Evidently the unexpected presence of so many people had caused him, more than annoyance or embarrassment, a true and profound anxiety, almost a combination of anger, irritation, and shame, an anxiety everyone noticed and that could not be entirely explained by the obvious disdain that man showed upon finding himself grazing with the herd.

Something else must be behind it, and something else there was. Dora Barmis whispered into Raceni's ear with fierce joy: "He's afraid the journalists will mention his name this evening! And I'm sure they will! And they'll put it on the first page, with his name first! Who knows, my dear, where he told Signora Frezzi he was going. And here he is. He came here. . . . And this evening Livia Frezzi will read the newspapers. She'll read his name first, and imagine the scene she'll make! Crazy jealous, I've already told you! Crazy jealous. But to be honest, with good reason, it seems. . . . For me, anyway, there's no doubt about it!"

"Be quiet!" Raceni said aloud. "What are you saying! He could be her father!"

"*Bambino!*" Barmis then exclaimed with a smile of commiseration.

"Frezzi will be jealous! You know it, but I don't," Raceni insisted.

Signora Barmis held up her hands: "But all Rome knows it, for God's sake!"

"All right. What does that mean?" Raceni continued excitedly. "It's

unlikely she's both jealous *and crazy!* She's probably only crazy. . . .
But on the opening night he left after the first act. All the gossips saw
it as proof that he didn't like the play!"

"For another reason, darling, he left for another reason!" Signora
Barmis said in a singsong voice.

"Thank you. I know! But which reason?" asked Raceni. "Because
he's in love with Silvia Roncella? You make me laugh if you say that.
It makes no sense! He left because of Frezzi, I agree! But what does
that mean? Everyone knows he's that woman's slave! And that woman
nags him! And he'd do anything to keep peace with her!"

"So he comes here?" Signora Barmis asked shrewdly.

"Certainly! He comes here! Certainly!" Raceni replied with irritation. "Because he knows how his leaving the theater would be viewed
by the gossips, and he's coming to make up for it. He's upset, of course!
He didn't expect all these people. He's afraid that this evening she, like
you and all the others, will gossip about his coming. But heavens! If
it were otherwise, either he wouldn't have come or he wouldn't be so
upset. That's obvious!"

"*Bambino!*" Signora Barmis repeated.

She had to stop there because Signora Roncella was getting ready
to leave the waiting room, between Maurizio Gueli and Senator Romualdo Borghi, with her husband clearing the way, to go take her seat on
the train.

Every man took off his hat, and hurrahs were heard along with a
long burst of applause; and Giustino Boggiolo, already prepared and
waiting, looking here and there, smiling, beaming, with eyes shining
and cheeks aglow, bowed in gratitude many times, instead of his wife.

Left alone in the room behind the glass door, sobbing into her perfumed hankie, was Signora Ely Faciolli, forgotten and inconsolable.
Cautiously glancing sideways with his large rumpled head, the cripple
Cosimo Zago hopped with his crutch to the place on the sofa where a
short time ago Signora Roncella had been sitting. He picked up a little
feather that had fallen from her boa and stuck it in his pocket just in
time to miss being seen by the Neapolitan novelist, Raimondo Jacono,
who was crossing the room to leave, snorting with disgust.

"Oh, it's you? What are you doing? You look like a lost dog. . . . Do you hear the shouting? The hosannas! She's the saint of the day! Fools, worse than her husband! Cheer up, my boy! It's the easiest thing in the world, you see. . . . She took Medea and remade her into a ragamuffin from Taranto; take Ulysses and remake him into a Venetian gondolier. A triumph! Believe me! And see how rich you'll get that way. My heavens! Two, three hundred thousand lire, like nothing! Dance, woman, dance while fortune plays!"

2

Returning home in the carriage with Signora Ely Faciolli (the poor thing couldn't take her hankie from her eyes, but not so much now out of sadness for Silvia's leaving as to hide the damage her long and desperate weeping had done to her makeup), Giustino Boggiolo shrugged, wrinkled his nose, fumed as though he might be angry with her. But no, poor Signora Ely, no. She had nothing to do with it.

Three minutes before the train left, Giustino was beset with a new problem. As if he didn't have enough of them! Almost like a piece of paper, a rag, a clinging weed that sticks to the foot of a runner concentrating on the race in a crowded track. Senator Borghi, talking to Silvia through the train window, had asked her for nothing less than the script of *The New Colony* to publish in his review. Luckily he had been able to intervene in time to tell Borghi why that would not be possible. Already three of the best editors had made very lucrative offers and he was holding off all three, fearing that publication of the book might somewhat lessen the public's curiosity in those cities waiting with feverish impatience to see the play. Then in its place, Borghi had made Silvia promise a story—a long one—for his literary review, *Vita Italiana*.

"Excuse me, on what conditions?" Giustino said, as if the senator-director and onetime minister were sitting beside him, and not that disconsolate Signora Ely, who really couldn't expose her eyes or converse in the state she was in. "What conditions? We have to see, we have to come to an understanding, then. . . . The days of *House of the Dwarves* have passed. What was enough for a dwarf, my dear signora—let's be

99

realistic—isn't enough for a giant. Gratitude, yes! But gratitude . . . gratitude above all shouldn't be exploited. What do you think?"

Signora Ely nodded approval several times behind her hankie, and Giustino went on: "In my hometown, anyone exploiting gratitude would not only lose everyone's esteem, but would be seen the same as . . . no, what am I saying? worse! seen as worse than someone who cruelly refused to lend a helping hand. Look, I'll keep that as a good thought for the first album the senator sends me. Rather, I'll make a note of it. So he can read it. . . ."

He took out his notebook and jotted down the thought.

"Believe me, if I don't write things down . . . Ah, my dear signora, my dear signora! I should have a hundred heads, a hundred, but that wouldn't be enough! When I think of all I have to do, I get dizzy! Now I'm going to go to the office and ask for six months' leave. I can't ask for less. And if they don't agree to it? You tell me. . . . If they don't agree to it? It will be a serious business. I'll be forced to . . . to . . . What did you say?"

Signora Ely said something into her hankie, something she didn't want to repeat or indicate by gestures—she only twitched her shoulder slightly. And then Giustino said: "But, you see, against my will . . . You'll see that they'll force me to leave my job! And then they'll begin saying—uh, I'm sure of it!—that I live off my wife. Me! Off my wife! As if my wife, without me . . . A laughing matter, that's all there is to it! It's obvious: look at her there, going on a holiday. And who stays here to work, to make war? It's a war, you know? A real honest-to-goodness war . . . The battle has begun! Seven armies and a hundred cities! If I can just hold out. . . . And the office! If I lose my job tomorrow, whose fault will it be? I'll lose it because of her. . . . Ah, well, better not to think about it!"

So many things were on his mind that only by venting his feelings for a few moments could he forget the strain he was under. Nevertheless, just before reaching his house he couldn't help thinking about Senator Borghi's asinine request. It had upset him so, particularly because the senator should have come to him instead of his wife. But, then, for Christ's sake! a little consideration! The poor little woman was going away to get well, to rest. If she wanted to think about something at Cargiore, it would be a new play, by heaven! Not some frivolous waste of time that earned nothing. A little consideration, for Christ's sake!

As soon as they reached home—pow! another obstacle, another inconvenience, another reason to be annoyed. But this one rather more serious.

He found a lanky young fellow in the studio, with a forest of wild curly hair, a Van Dyke beard curving over his chin, mustache standing at attention, an old green silk kerchief at his neck that perhaps hid the lack of a shirt. A black jacket out at the elbows left his bony wrists exposed and made his arms and hands seem out of proportion. Boggiolo found him installed like the lord of the manor in the midst of an exhibition of twenty-five pastels placed around the room, on straight chairs, on armchairs, on the desk, everywhere: twenty-five pastels depicting final scenes of *The New Colony.*

"Well, pardon me . . . pardon me . . . pardon me . . ." Giustino Boggiolo began saying as he entered, flustered and ill at ease with all those things cluttering the room. "Pardon me, but who are you?"

"I?" said the young man smiling with a triumphant air. "Who am I? Nino Pirino. I am Nino Pirino, painterino, Tarentino. Therefore compatriotino of Silvia Roncella. You're her husband, aren't you? Pleased to meet you! I've done these things here and I've come to show them to Silvia Roncella, my illustrious compatriot."

"And where is she?" ventured Giustino.

The young man looked at him, bewildered. "Where is who? What?"

"My dear sir, she is gone!"

"Gone?"

"For heaven's sake, all Rome knows it! All Rome was at the station, and you don't know! I don't have much time, pardon me. . . . But, wait a minute. . . . Pardon me, these are scenes from *The New Colony,* if I'm not mistaken?"

"Yes, sir."

"And *The New Colony* belongs to everyone? You take the scenes and
. . . appropriate them to yourself. . . . How? With what right?"

"I? What are you saying? Not at all!" said the young man. "I am an
artist! I have seen and . . ."

"No, sir!" exclaimed Giustino with feeling. "What have you seen?
You have seen my wife's *The New Colony*. . . ."

"Yes, sir."

"And this is a deserted island, isn't it?"

"Yes, sir."

"Where did you ever see it? Does this island exist in reality, on a
map? You can't have seen it!"

The young man actually believed the whole thing a joke, and he was
ready to laugh about it. But as it was turning out to be so different from
what he expected, the laugh congealed on his lips. More bewildered
than ever, he said:

"With my own eyes? No, certainly not with my own eyes! I haven't
seen it. But I imagined it!"

"You? No, sir!" Giustino pressed ahead. "My wife! My wife imagined it, not you! And if my wife had not imagined it, I tell you, you
wouldn't have had a thing to paint! The ownership . . ."

At this point Nino Pirino succeeded in letting out the laughter that
had been building up inside him for a while.

"The ownership? Oh, yes? Of that island? Oh, great! Oh, fine! Oh,
wonderful! You want to be the sole owner of that island? The owner of
an island that doesn't exist?"

Giustino Boggiolo, feeling himself the butt of a joke, shook with
anger and shouted: "Oh, it doesn't exist? You say it doesn't exist? It
exists, it exists, it exists, yes, sir! I'll show you it exists!"

"The island?"

"The ownership! My literary property rights! My rights, my rights
exist. And you'll see if I don't know how to validate them! That's why
I'm here! Everyone is used to infringing on these rights that come from
the sacrosanct law of the State, by heaven! But, I repeat, I'm here now,
and I'll show you!"

"All right . . . but, look . . . yes, sir . . . calm down, look . . ." the young man said, distressed at seeing him so furious. "Look, I . . . I didn't want to usurp any rights, any property. . . . If it makes you so mad . . . but I'm ready to leave all my pastels here and go away. I'll give them to you and go away. . . . I had just wanted to please, to honor my fellow townswoman. . . . Yes, I also wanted to ask her to . . . to . . . help me with the prestige of her name, because I believe I'm worth some help. . . . They're beautiful, aren't they? My pastels are worth a glance at least. . . . Not bad. I'll give them to you and go away."

Giustino Boggiolo suddenly felt disarmed and ashamed in the face of that ragamuffin's generosity.

"No, not at all . . . thank you . . . excuse me . . . I was speaking of, I was arguing for the . . . her . . . my . . . rights, the ownership, that's all. Believe me it's serious business . . . as if it didn't exist. . . . There's constant piracy in the literary world. . . . I'm riled up, aren't I? But because, look . . . these days I . . . I . . . I . . . get riled up easily. I'm dead tired of it all, and there's nothing worse than being tired! I have to keep all sides covered, my dear sir. I have to protect my interests. You can understand that."

"Certainly! Naturally!" exclaimed Nino Pirino, taking a conciliatory tone. "But, listen . . . Please don't get mad again. Listen . . . do you think I can't make a painting, let's say, of Manzoni's *The Betrothed*? I read *The Betrothed*, I get an idea for the scene . . . can't I paint it?"

Giustino Boggiolo concentrated with great effort, smoothing his fan-shaped mustache with two fingers as he pondered: "Oh," he finally said, "I really wouldn't know. . . . Perhaps, dealing with the work of a dead author, already in the public domain for some time . . . I don't know. I need to study the question. In any event, your case is different. Look! The fact remains that if tomorrow a musician asks my permission to put *The New Colony* to music, I'll tell him that because I'm already negotiating with two of the best composers, and having the libretto done by others, he must pay me what I ask, and that's not chicken feed, you know? Now, if I'm not mistaken, your case is the same. What applies to the musician for music applies to you for painting."

"Really . . . I see. . . ." Nino Pirino began, stroking his goatee, but then, suddenly, reconsidering: "Not at all! You're wrong, you know! Look . . . that's a different case! The musician has to pay because he uses the text for his opera, but if he doesn't use it, if he expresses in music his impressions, his feelings aroused by your wife's play, in a symphony or whatever, he won't have to pay, don't you see? You can be sure of that; he won't have to pay anything!"

Giustino Boggiolo parried with his hands as though to ward off danger or a threat of it.

"I'm speaking academically," the young man hastened to add. "I've already told you why I came, and, I repeat, I'll be happy to leave my pastels here."

That gave Giustino an idea. Sooner or later the play would be published. They could make an expensive, illustrated edition, with color reproductions of those twenty-five pastels. . . . The book wouldn't go through many hands, so he could keep that painter from profiting from his wife's work. And it would also take care of the painter's request for moral and material help, because the publisher would compensate him adequately for those pastels.

Nino Pirino was enthusiastic about the idea and almost kissed the hands of his benefactor, who in the meanwhile had had another brain storm. He signaled for the young man to hold on while he brought it all out into the light.

"Here it is. A preface by Gueli . . . And so all the gossips that go around cackling that Gueli didn't like the play . . . Do you know he came this morning to pay his respects to my wife at the station? But they can also say (I know them so well!) that he came out of mere courtesy. If Gueli writes the preface . . . Wonderful, yes, yes, wonderful. I'll go there today just as soon as I leave the office. But see how many worries I have, and how much more you've given me to do now? I don't have much time! I have to leave for Bologna tonight. Never mind. . . . I'll take care of everything. Leave your pastels here. I promise that as soon as I go to Milan . . . What is your address?"

Nino Pirino squeezed his elbows into his waist and drew up his chest, ill at ease: "Well . . . when . . . will you be going to Milan?"

"I don't know," Boggiolo said. "In two or three months at the most."

"Well, then," smiled Pirino, "it's pointless to give you my address. In three months I could have changed it at least eight times. Nino Pirino, General Delivery: that's how you can write me."

3

When Giustino Boggiolo came back home later (barely leaving time to hurriedly pack his suitcase), he was so tired, and in such a stupefied condition, that even stones would have taken pity. But he gave himself no pity.

As soon as he entered the shadowy gloom of the studio, he found himself, without knowing how or why, in the arms and against the breast of a woman who gently caressed his cheek with a warm perfumed hand and said to him in a sweet, maternal voice: "Poor man . . . poor man . . . I know! . . . Keep this up and you'll destroy yourself, darling! . . . Oh, poor man . . . poor man . . ."

And without the slightest clue as to why Dora Barmis was here in his house, in the dark, or how she could have known that because of his troubles, because of the unpleasant encounters, and because of his tremendous tiredness, he had an overwhelming need for solace and rest, he let himself be stroked like a baby.

Perhaps he had come into the study raving and complaining.

He really couldn't take it anymore! At the office his boss had listened to him with his ears cocked like a dog's, and he had sworn he would no longer be able to call himself Gennaro Ricoglia if he didn't wholeheartedly deny his request for six months' leave. After that, in Gueli's house . . . Oh, Lord, what had happened at Gueli's house? . . . He didn't know how to reconstruct it. . . . Had he dreamed it? But why? Hadn't Gueli gone to the station that morning? He must have gone mad. . . . One of them was loony. . . . But perhaps in the middle of all that giddy confusion, something happened that he hadn't noticed, and that was the reason why he couldn't understand anything now, not even why Signora Barmis was here. . . . Perhaps it was right and natural for her to be here . . . and that compassionate and affectionate comfort was also appropriate, and—yes—deserved . . . but now . . . now enough of that.

And he started to move away. Dora stopped him by pressing his head against her breast: "No, why? Wait. . . ."

"I must . . . the . . . the suitcases . . ." Giustino stammered.

"No! What are you saying!" Dora's voice spoke to him. "You want to leave in this state? You can't, darling, you can't!"

Giustino resisted the pressure of that hand. By now that comfort was beginning to seem too much and a little odd, even though he knew that Signora Barmis often forgot she was a woman.

"But . . . but why? . . ." he continued to stammer, "without . . . without a light here? What has Signora Ely's maid done?"

"The light? I didn't want it," Dora said. "They brought it. Here, here, sit with me here. It's nice in the dark . . . here. . . ."

"And the suitcases? Who's going to pack for me?" asked Giustino, miserably.

"Do you have to leave?"

"My dear signora . . ."

"And if I keep you from going?"

In the dark Giustino felt his arm squeezed tightly. More than ever bewildered, upset, trembling, he repeated: "My dear signora . . ."

"You idiot!" she broke out with a quivering, convulsive laugh, taking him by the other arm and shaking him. "Stupid! Stupid! What are you doing? Don't you see? It's stupid . . . yes, stupid, your wanting to leave like this. . . . Where are your suitcases? They'll be in your bedroom. Where's your bedroom? Come on, let's go, I'll help you!"

Giustino felt he was being coerced. He was reluctant, lost, stammering: "But . . . but if . . . if they don't bring us a light . . ."

A strident laugh at this moment rent the darkness and seemed to shake the whole silent house.

By now Giustino was accustomed to Signora Barmis's sudden bursts of mad hilarity. Dealing with her was always like skating on thin ice, never knowing how he should interpret certain actions, certain looks, certain smiles, certain words. At that moment, yes, it really seemed obvious that . . . but what if he were mistaken? And then . . . Forget it! Aside from the state he was in . . . Forget it! That would definitely be wrong, something he couldn't do.

With this knowledge of his incorruptible conjugal honesty, he found the courage to resolutely and with a certain contempt light a match.

Another, more strident, wilder laugh seized and contorted Signora Barmis at the sight of him with that match burning between his fingers.

"What's the matter?" Giustino asked angrily. "In the dark . . . surely . . ."

It took some time before Dora recovered from that convulsive laughter. She composed herself and wiped away her tears. In the meanwhile he lit a candle he had found on the desk after brushing aside three of Pirino's pastels.

"Ah, twenty years! Twenty years! Twenty years!" Dora shuddered finally. "Men, you know? To me they are toothpicks! Here, between the teeth, clean, and toss away! Stupid! Stupid! Stupid! The soul, then, the soul, the soul . . . Where is the soul? God! God! My, how good it is to breathe. . . . Tell me, Boggiolo: according to you, where is it? Inside or out? I'm talking about the soul! Inside or outside us? Everything depends on it! You say inside? I say outside. The soul is outside, darling; the soul is everything in the world; and once dead we will be nothing anymore, darling, nothing, nothing more. . . . Go ahead with the light! To the suitcases at once . . . I'll help you. . . . Seriously!"

"You're too kind," Giustino said quietly, flabbergasted, moving ahead with the candle toward the bedroom.

As soon as she entered, Dora looked at the double bed and looked around at the other more than modest furniture under the low roof: "Ah, here . . ." she said. "Yes, well . . . That nice odor of home, family, the provinces . . . Yes, yes . . . well . . . lucky you, darling! May it always be so! But you must hurry. When does the race start? Oh, right away . . . Hurry, hurry, without losing any more time . . ."

And into the two bags open on the bed she quickly and skillfully packed the items that Giustino took from the drawer and handed her.

While doing so: "Do you know why I came? I wanted to warn you that Signora Carmi . . . all the actors of the company, but especially Signora Carmi, are furious, my dear!"

"Why?" asked Giustino, stopping.

"Your wife, darling, didn't you notice?" Dora responded, signaling with her hand for him to keep going. "Your wife . . . perhaps, poor thing, because she's still . . . she received them very very badly."

Giustino, swallowing bitterly, nodded his head several times to signify that he had noticed and had been pained.

"Amends must be made!" continued Signora Barmis. "As soon as you join the company in Naples after Bologna . . . That's it, Signora Carmi wants to get revenge at all costs. You absolutely have to help her get revenge."

"Me? How?" Giustino asked, again confused.

"Oh, dear!" Signora Barmis exclaimed, hugging her shoulders. "Don't expect me to teach you how. You are so difficult. . . . But when a woman wants to get revenge on another woman . . . Look, a woman can be good to a man, especially if he is like a devoted child. . . . But to another woman she can be wicked, my dear, capable of anything then if she feels she has been insulted or treated rudely. And envy! If only you knew how much envy there is between women, and how mean it makes them! You're a nice, good young man, a very good man . . . enormously kind, I know. But if you want to look after your own interests, you must . . . you must force yourself . . . even to be a little wild. . . . Besides, you will be away from your wife for several months, won't you? Now you don't expect me to believe . . ."

"No, no, believe me, my dear signora!" Giustino exclaimed. "I don't think about it! I don't even have time to think about it! As far as I'm concerned, I'm a married man, and that's that!"

"Are you her possession?"

"It's over! I don't think about it anymore! All other women are the same as men to me; I don't see any difference anymore. My wife is enough woman for me. Maybe for women it's different . . . but for men, at least for me . . . A man has so many other things to think about. . . . Imagine if I, with so many worries, so much to do . . ."

"Oh, dear, I know! But I'm telling you for your own sake, can't you understand that?" Signora Barmis went on, bending over the suitcases, trying hard to keep from laughing. "If you want to look after your interests, dear . . . It may be fine for you, but you have to deal with women — actresses, journalists. . . . And if you don't do what they want? If you don't follow them in their inclinations, even if naughty? Right! If these women envy your wife? If they want revenge . . . understand? I'm telling you for your own good. . . . These are necessities, darling, why do you want to make so much out of them? Life's necessities! Come on, they're packed. Close them up and let's get on our way at once. I'll go to the station with you."

In the carriage she took his hand instinctively; suddenly she remembered and was about to let it go, but then . . . since it was already there. . . . Giustino did not object. He was thinking about what had happened at Gueli's house.

"You explain it. I don't understand," he said to Dora. "I went to Gueli's . . ."

"To his house?" asked Dora, and immediately she exclaimed: "Oh, God, what have you done?"

"Why?" questioned Giustino. "I went to . . . to ask him a favor. . . . All right. Would you believe it? He received me as if we had never met. . . ."

"Was Signora Frezzi there?" asked Signora Barmis.

"Yes, she was . . ."

"Well, then, why are you surprised?" Dora said. "You don't know?"

"But, I don't get it!" Giustino went on. "I'm dumbfounded! To pretend not to remember being at the station that morning . . ."

"You said that, too, in Signora Frezzi's presence?" Dora burst out laughing. "Poor Gueli, poor Gueli! What you have done, dear Boggiolo!"

"Why?" Giustino asked again. "Excuse me, but I can't imagine . . ."

"You! We're starting all over from the beginning!" exclaimed Signora Barmis. "You want to reckon without the woman! You've got to get that out of your head. . . . You want a favor from Gueli, who has a warm feeling for your wife? My dear, you have to try to court her enemy a little. Who knows!"

"Her as well?"

"Livia Frezzi's not ugly, for goodness sakes! She's not young anymore . . . but . . ."

"Don't say it even as a joke," said Giustino.

"But I'm really serious, darling, dead serious," Dora retorted. "You have to change your tune! Like this you'll get nowhere. . . ."

And until the train gave a shuddering start, Dora Barmis continued to hammer on that nail: "Remember . . . Signora Carmi! Signora Carmi! Help her get revenge. . . . Patience . . . darling . . . Good-bye! . . . Be strong . . . for your own good . . . Be tough. . . . Good-bye, darling, good luck! Good-bye! Good-bye!"

4

Where was she?

Yes, over there, beyond the meadow, beside the path, the old church dedicated to the Virgin of the Rising Star rose out of the grassy clearing. It had a tall bell tower with an octagonal cusp, mullioned windows, and a clock that bore a rather odd motto for a church: TO EACH HIS OWN. Next to the church was the white rectory with the deserted garden, and beyond that a little walled cemetery.

At dawn the sound of bells over those neglected tombs.

No, perhaps not the bells, but their echo penetrated those tombs, making the dead shiver with anxious desire.

Oh, women of the scattered hamlets, women of Villareto and Galleana, women of Rufinera and Pian del Viermo, women of Brando and Fornello, go away so that your ancient, devout grandmothers may attend this dawn mass alone just this once. And let their old parish priest officiate, who has also lain buried for so many years, and who perhaps when the mass is finished, before going back to rest underground, will linger to look through the gate at the solitary garden of the priest's house, to see if the new priest is taking as good care of it as he did.

No . . . Where was she? Where was she?

By now she knew so many places and their names, places even far from Cargiore. She had been on Roccia Corba, on Braida hill, to view the entire immense Valsusa. She knew that the lane beyond the church descended through chestnut and oak woods to Giaveno, where she had also been, going down that strange Via della Buffa, wide and hollowed out, singing with water running down the center. She knew it was the sound of the Sangone River that she always heard, whose frenzy kept her from sleeping at night with the image of all that water running forever. She knew that further down, the Sangonetto made its noisy way into the Indritto valley; she had stood on the rocks in the middle of that thunderous roar to see it: a good part of the water separated into canals that were harnessed for various purposes. Up there noisy, free, swirling, foaming, unrestrained, down below in the canals placid, tamed, subjugated to man's industry.

She had visited all the hamlets around Cargiore, their stumplike houses scattered among the chestnut, alder, poplar trees, and she knew their names. She knew that the church to the east, far, far in the distance, high on the hills, was the Basilica of Superga. She knew the names of the surrounding mountains, already covered with snow: Luzer and Uja and the Costa del Pagliajo and the Cugno dell' Alpet, Brunello and Roccia Vrè. That one opposite, at twelve o'clock, was Bocciarda mountain, and the Rubinett beyond that.

She knew everything. Mamma (Madama Velia, as they called her here), and Graziella, and that dear Signor Martino Prever, Mamma's suitor, had already told her about everything. Yes, everything. But she . . . where was she? Where was she?

Her eyes felt full of a vague, unnatural splendor, in her ears was a continual musical wave that was both voice and light in which her soul rocked serenely with an extraordinary weightlessness, provided she was not so indiscreet as to want to understand that voice or gaze at the light.

Was the silence of those green hills really as full of throbbing life as it seemed? Pricked, almost pierced at intervals by long, thin, high-pitched animal squeals, by sharp threads of sound, by crickets? Was that everlasting throbbing the laughter of all those streams running through deep, dark ravines, puddles, torrents in the shade of the low alder trees, blessed brooks rushing downward in frothy garrulous cascades after watering a meadow, to do good elsewhere, in another field awaiting them, where it seems that the very leaves call for them, joyful and sparkling?

No, no, she saw everything—people, places, and things—suffused in a vaporous dreamlike air, making even the closest things seem far away and unreal.

At times, it is true, that dreamlike quality would suddenly be shattered, and then certain details would fling themselves before her eyes, transformed in their bare reality. Disturbed, stunned by that cold, hard, impassible, inanimate stupidity that assaulted her so violently, she would close her eyes and press her hands hard against her temples. Was it really like that? No, perhaps it wasn't! Perhaps, others saw it differently . . . if they even saw it! And that dreamlike quality would fall back in place.

One evening Mamma had retired to her room with a headache. Silvia went with Graziella to see how she was. In the clean, modest little room, a single votive light burned on a table below an old ivory crucifix, but the full moon filled the room with its soft white light. As soon as Graziella entered the room, she went to look out the window at the green meadow flooded with light. Suddenly she sighed:

"What a moon, Madama! My goodness, it seems like daytime. . . ."

Mamma then asked her to open the shutter.

Oh, what amazing, sublime enchantment! In what dream had those tall poplars risen up from the meadows that the moon flooded with limpid silence? And to Silvia that silence seemed to be founded in time immemorial, and she thought of nights long ago, watched over by the moon like this, and all that peace surrounding her then acquired a mysterious meaning. Far away in the valley, the Sangone continued to rumble, a gloomy admonition. Out there, close by, a curious intermittent screeching.

"What's that screeching, Graziella?" Mamma asked.

And Graziella, gazing out the window at the clear night, had replied happily: "A farmer. He's cutting hay under the moon. He's sharpening his scythe."

Where had Graziella spoken from? To Silvia it seemed she had spoken from the Moon.

A short time later, from a distant group of houses, women's voices were raised in sweet song. And Graziella, still almost as though speaking from the Moon, announced: "They're singing at Rufinera. . . ."

Silvia couldn't utter a sound.

Since she left Rome, and while on the journey, many new images had tumultuously invaded her mind, from which the shadow of death had barely faded. She was dismayed to notice an irreparable separation from all her former life. She could no longer speak or communicate with the others, with all those who wanted to continue to have the same relations with her as before. She felt totally cut off by that separation. She no longer felt she belonged to herself.

What was bound to happen had happened. Was it perhaps because up here, where they had taken her, she missed those humble, familiar things around her, things that she had clung to before and in which she used to take refuge? She felt lost up here, and her demon had taken advantage of it. He caused a kind of deafening drunkenness that made her delirious, flushed, and stupefied, since he transformed everything with that dreamlike fog. But sometimes he pierced through the fog in such a way that she suddenly saw the stupidity of everything. He was terribly spiteful: he took pleasure in revealing the stupidity of everything she held most dear and sacred, and he had no respect even for her baby or her motherhood! He suggested to her that both of these would no longer be stupid if she, through him, made a beautiful creation out of them. He also told her that those things were like everything else, and that she was born only for creating, and not for materially producing stupid things, or for being caught up and losing herself in them.

What was there, in the valley of the Indritto? Channeled water — a good, obedient housewife — and free, rumbling, foaming water. She had to be the latter and stop being the former.

Now the hour was striking. What did the tower clock say? TO EACH HIS OWN.

Soon the eternal snow will come,
houses and meadows will all be white,
the roof, the bell tower of that country church,
where now, at dawn, like sheep from a pen,
the peasant women exit through two gates,
their bridegrooms at their sides.
They have thought about death and the soul
(nearby is the cemetery lined with crosses);
now life reclaims them, they speak loudly,
happy to hear their own voices
in the fresh holiday air,
amid the fast-flowing streams,
amid the meadows greening around them.

Just like that! TO EACH HIS OWN. How could that be! Never before
had she written a line of poetry! She didn't even know how to go about
it. . . . How was it possible? But she had done it! Just as they had sung
inside her. . . . Not the lines, the things.

Things really were singing inside her, and everything was transfig-
ured, suddenly revealing incredible new facets. And she was reveling
in nearly sublime joy.

Those clouds and mountains . . . Often the mountains seemed like
great stone clouds, and the clouds like black, heavy, somber mountains of air. The clouds over those mountains were a busy lot! At times
they attacked them with thunder and lightning; then, languid, gentle,
they draped over them caressingly. But the mountains, their blue faces
in the sky, absorbed in the mystery of the remote ages within them,
seemed indifferent both to the furies and the languor. Never mind
women and clouds! The mountains were fond of snow.

And that meadow up there, at this time of year, covered with daisies?
Was she dreaming it? Or had the earth wanted to tease the sky, making the ground white with flowers before it was white with snow? No,
no. In certain deep, humid recesses of the woods, flowers were still
blooming, and she had almost felt a strange religious awe of such hid-

den life. . . . Ah, man, who takes everything from the earth and believes everything is made for him! Even this life? No. Here the absolute lord was a large buzzing hornet that stopped to drink voraciously from the tender, delicate flower chalices that bowed beneath him. And the brutality of that brown roaring beast, velvety and gold-striped, was as offensive as something obscene. It almost gloated over the way those tremulous, fragile bell flowers submitted to its assault, and then remained quivering slightly on their stems after the insect, satisfied though still greedy, went leisurely on its way.

On returning to the quiet little house, she felt uncomfortable not to be, or at least not to seem to be, what she had once been to her dear old mother-in-law. Perhaps because she had never been able to keep herself, compose herself, mold herself into a solid and stable concept, she had always nervously sensed the extraordinary, disorderly restlessness of her inner being and had often rejected it in astonishment, immediately, like a shameful thing. She had surprised so many unconscious, spontaneous movements of both her mind and body, strange, odd, almost like those of a darting, incorrigible animal. She had always been somewhat afraid of herself, as well as curious, almost suspecting that an alien inside her was making her do things she wasn't aware of or didn't want to do: grimaces, even inappropriate gestures, and other worrisome things neither of heaven nor earth, but yes! horrible, sometimes really incredible things that filled her with shock and horror. She! She so anxious not to take up too much space or call attention to herself, or even to have the bother of many eyes on her! Now she hoped her mother-in-law would not notice in her eyes the laughter she felt quivering inside her when in the little dining room she found that good, innocuous Signor Martino Prever knitting his hairy eyebrows, puffed up with grim ferocity, jealous as a tiger of Uncle Ippolito, who seemed to thoroughly enjoy irritating him by continuing his customary habit of quietly stroking the ribbon on his *bersagliere* hat and smoking his long pipe from morning to evening.

"Monsù" (as a gentleman is addressed in the Piedmont dialect) Prever was also a nice-looking elderly gentleman, with a beard even longer than Uncle Ippolito's (but untended and unruly), and with the clear blue eyes of a boy in spite of his frequent attempts to make them appear ferocious. On his head there was always a white linen cap, with a large leather visor. Though very well off, he sought only the company of more humble folk and secretly helped them. He had also built and supported a children's preschool.

He owned a beautiful little house at Cargiore, and on top of Braida hill in Valgioje, a great solitary villa, where beyond chestnut, beech, and birch trees spread the wide, magnificent, blue-veiled Valsusa. In compensation for the many benefices it had received, the little town of Cargiore had not reelected him mayor, and perhaps for that reason he avoided the company of the few so-called well-bred people. Nevertheless he never left town, not even in wintertime.

There was a reason, and everyone in Cargiore knew it: that persistent, stubborn love for "Madama" Velia Boggiolo. Poor Monsù Martino couldn't exist without seeing that "madamina" of his. Everyone in Cargiore knew Madama Velia, and no one spoke badly of her, even knowing that Monsù Martino spent almost every day in her home.

He would have liked to marry her, but she didn't want to, and she didn't want to because . . . My goodness, it would be pointless now at their age. Get married just for the fun of it? Didn't he stay there in her house all day like the master? Well, then! That should be enough for him. . . . Money? Everyone knew that as Prever had no relatives anywhere, all he had, except perhaps for some little legacy for the servants, would one day go to Madama Velia just the same, if he died first.

It was a kind of fascination, a mysterious attraction that Monsù Martino had felt late in life for that little woman, who always stayed quietly, humbly, and timidly in her place. Signor Martino might be late, but a brother of his had been too early and too violent, so that one day, knowing she was already engaged, he very quietly, poor boy, killed himself.

More than forty years had passed, and Madama Velia still felt a sorrow, if not remorse, in her heart because of it; and for that reason also perhaps, though sometimes feeling somewhat embarrassed (she wouldn't say annoyed) by Prever's continual presence in her house, she bore it with resignation. Graziella had whispered to Silvia that madama tolerated his presence out of the fear that he, too, Monsù Martino—if she ever tried to distance him from her a little—might do, God forbid, what his younger brother had done. Yes, yes, because . . . You laugh? Well, there's nothing to laugh about. Those Prevers must be touched by a little madness, everyone in Cargiore said it, a little strain of madness. You should hear how monsù talks out loud to himself for hours and hours. . . . And perhaps it would be better if her uncle, Signor Ippolito, didn't tease him so unmercifully about wanting to marry madama. Graziella had advised Silvia to persuade her uncle to tease Don Buti instead, the priest who also came to the house occasionally.

Oh, that Don Buti, what a disappointment! In that white rectory with the garden, Silvia had imagined quite a different man of God. Instead she had found a tall, thin, bent priest, his nose, cheeks, chin all sharply angular, and a pair of tiny round eyes always staring and alarmed. Disappointment on the one hand, but on the other, what pleasure she had felt on hearing that good man speak about the marvels of an old telescope he used as a very efficacious instrument of religion, nearly as sacred to him as the chalice of the main altar.

Don Buti thought that men were sinners because they see things up close, the things of the earth, all too well, as if enlarged, but the heavenly things that they should think about most of all, the stars, they see poorly and in miniature, because God put them too high and far away. Uneducated people look at them and say, sure they're beautiful, but they seem so tiny that people can't appreciate them, and don't know how to appreciate them, so a great part of God's power remains unknown to them. The uninstructed need to see that the real greatness is up there. Hence, the telescope.

On clear nights Don Buti would set up his telescope in the church-yard and call all his parishioners to gather around. They even came down from Rufinera and Pian del Viermo, the young people singing, the old leaning on sticks, the children dragged along by their mothers, to see the "great mountains" on the Moon. How the frogs at the bottom of the streams laughed about it! And it seemed that even the stars had flashes of hilarity in the sky. Lengthening or shortening the instrument to adapt it to the sight of the person bending to look, Don Buti took charge of turns, and out of the confusion his shouts could be heard in the distance: "With only one eye! With only one eye!"

Of course! The women and children particularly would open their mouths wide, twisting their lips to keep their left eye closed and their right eye open, huffing and puffing so that they clouded the telescope lens. Don Buti, in the meantime, thinking they were already seeing something, would shake his hands in the air with thumb and index finger joined and exclaim: "The great power of Our Lord, eh? The great power of Our Lord!"

What delightful little scenes when he came to talk about it with Uncle Ippolito and Monsù Martino in that dear warm nest in the mountains, full of the secure familial comfort that breathed from all the objects, almost animated now by old memories in the house, sanctified by religious, honest, loving care; what scenes especially on rainy days when it was impossible to go outside even for a moment!

But just when Silvia was beginning to savor the peace of domestic life, here would come the postman with the mail, and the wind of glory would sweep in, upsetting everything with those bundles of newspapers from one city or another that her husband sent her.

The New Colony was a success everywhere. And its author, cheered by all the audiences, was there, in that little house lost on that green plateau of the Piedmont.

Was it really she? Or was it not a moment of her life that had been? A sudden mental flash, a vision, that surprised even her. . . .

Now she really couldn't imagine how or why that *New Colony*, that island with those sailors, had come to her mind. . . . What a laugh! She didn't know, but they all knew, all the drama and nondrama critics of all the daily and nondaily newspapers of Italy. How much they talked about it! How many things they discovered in that play of hers, things she had never dreamed of thinking! Oh, but all those things, let's admit it, were the source of great pleasure, because they were precisely what brought her the greatest praise, praise that actually belonged to the critics who had discovered those things she had never thought, rather than to her. But maybe, who knows! those things were really there if those top-notch critics had found them. . . .

In his hastily written letters Giustino let her read between the lines his satisfaction, or rather his great happiness. He portrayed himself, it is true, as someone caught in a whirlwind, and he never finished complaining about his extreme fatigue and his struggles with the administrators of the companies and the impresarios, and about his anger with the actors and journalists. But then he would write about the big theaters bursting with spectators and of the losses that the directors would voluntarily take upon themselves when they stayed weeks beyond the limits of their contracts in one place or another to satisfy the request for additional performances by a public that never tired of applauding deliriously.

While reading those newspapers and letters, the fascinating vision of those theaters, of the multitudes that applauded her—applauded her, the author—flashed before her eyes. Silvia felt relief from those stinging chills she had experienced in the waiting room of the Rome train station, when, unprepared, prostrate, lost, she was faced with her success for the first time.

Removed from that onslaught and now alive and energetic, she asked herself why she shouldn't be where they applauded her with such enthusiasm, instead of here, hidden, set apart, secluded, as if she were not the one they were calling for!

But yes, if Giustino hadn't said it outright, he let it be clearly understood that she wasn't important, that he had to do everything, since he was the one who knew how to do everything.

Oh, yes, him . . . Silvia pictured him in her mind. She saw him sometimes working excitedly, other times in a fury, still other times exultant among the actors and journalists, and a feeling came over her—not of envy or jealousy, but rather an anxious annoyance, an irritation still not well defined, somewhere between anguish, pain, and spite.

What must all those people think of her and of him? Of him especially, seeing him like that? But also of her? That she was stupid perhaps? Stupid, no, if she had written that play . . . Anyway, someone who didn't know how to act or talk. Unpresentable?

Yes, it was true: without him *The New Colony* might never have reached the stage. He had taken care of everything, and she had to be grateful. But it would have been all right if his great flurry of activity just hadn't been so blatant while her name and fame were still not widespread, and she could have stayed in the shadows, retiring, aloof. Now that success had come to crown all his frantic work, what impression was he making, alone there, in the midst of it? Would she be able to keep standing aside, leaving him there by himself, exposed, as the creator of everything, without making them both look ridiculous? Now that success had come, now that he had finally—in spite of her reluctance—accomplished his purpose of pushing her, launching her toward the blinding light of glory, she—against her will—yes, even against her will, and harming herself, had to step out and be seen; and he—against his will—had to withdraw now and stop being so dogged, so preoccupied, always in the middle, always focused on himself!

Silvia got the first inkling of the ridicule she was beginning to see with her own eyes in a letter from Signora Barmis. In it she spoke of Gueli and of Giustino's rash visit to get him to write the preface for the publication of *The New Colony*. Giustino hadn't even hinted about such a visit in his letters. Some of Signora Barmis's vague insinuations about Gueli had made her tear up the letter in disgust.

A few days later an equally ambiguous letter arrived from Gueli that only increased her bad humor and agitation. Gueli begged to be excused for not being able to write the preface for the publication of her play, along with puzzling hints about personal reasons that had kept him from staying to the end on opening night. He also spoke of certain tragic and at the same time ridiculous concerns (without saying what they were) that entangle the spirit and block the way when they don't actually do one in. The letter ended with a request that she address her letter (if she wanted to reply to him) not to his house, but to the office of the director of *Vita Italiana,* where he went to talk to Borghi from time to time. Silvia ripped up this letter also in exasperation. That request at the end had offended her. But the whole letter was offensive. The tragic and at the same time ridiculous concerns he wrote about could only be related to Signora Frezzi, but he spoke as if it were something she should understand and know well from her own experience. In short, it was a clear allusion to her husband. And the offensiveness of that allusion grew proportionately as she began to realize her husband's absurdity.

In the meantime winter had settled in, terrible at that elevation. Continual rain and wind, snow and fog. A suffocating fog. If she hadn't already had so many reasons for feeling anxious and oppressed, that weather would have given them to her. She would have run away, alone, to join her husband, if the thought of leaving her baby before it was time hadn't stopped her.

She had moments of anxious tenderness for the little creature, feeling unable to be the mother she would have wished. And even the anxiety that thoughts of her son caused her she blamed, with dull rancor, on her husband, who with that stubborn mania of his had pushed her so far from normal affectionate relationships and cares.

Perhaps he had plotted all this: to make her write there, like a machine, and to keep all glitches out of the machinery, to keep her away with the child, isolate her, then do all the rest himself, manage that great new literary enterprise. Oh, no! Oh, no! If she could no longer be a mother . . .

But perhaps she was being unfair. In his most recent letters her husband spoke of the new house they would get in Rome soon, in the spring, and he told her to prepare to come out of her shell, meaning that her salon would soon be the gathering place for the cream of art, literature, journalism. This idea, however, of having to play a part, the part of the "grande dame" amid the silly vanity of so many literati and journalists and so-called intellectuals disconcerted, depressed, and nauseated her.

Perhaps it was better to stay hidden there, in that nest in the mountains, with Signor Prever and Uncle Ippolito. Even her uncle had said he never wanted to leave, never—and he had slyly winked at Monsù Martino, who was eaten up inside when he heard him talk like that.

Her poor uncle! . . . Never again, really never again, poor uncle! He really had to stay there in Cargiore forever!

One evening, while he was complaining loudly about Giustino after his letter arrived with the news that, back against the wall, he had been dismissed from his job, and while arguing with Signor Prever, who kept insisting that in the long run it wouldn't be a great loss, because . . . some day . . . who knows! (doubtless alluding to his will)— suddenly Uncle Ippolito had rolled his eyes and twisted his mouth as if attempting to yawn. A great shudder of his powerful shoulders and head made the ribbon on his hat fall across his face, then down on his chest as his whole body collapsed.

Struck down!

In that bad weather it took a lot of time and effort for Signor Prever to find the local doctor, who, all out of breath, came to tell them what they already knew, and it took poor Graziella forever to bring the priest with holy oil!

"Careful! Careful! Don't muss his beautiful beard!" Silvia wanted to tell everyone, moving them aside to stand there and look at her poor uncle a little longer, still and severe, his arms crossed.

"What was Signor Ippolito's profession?"

"Gardener."

And as she looked at him she couldn't take her eyes off the ribbon that with that horrible shudder had fallen across his face. Poor uncle! Poor uncle! He thought it all madness—Giustino's stubborn efforts, literature, books, the theater. . . . Oh, yes. But perhaps all life was madness, all efforts, all cares, poor uncle!

He never wanted to leave? Now he would stay there forever. There, in the little cemetery near the white rectory. His rival, Signor Prever, who couldn't forgive himself for having been so exasperated by his presence, had given him space in his tomb, which was the most beautiful in Cargiore.

The days that followed Uncle Ippolito's sudden death were for Silvia full of a hard, dull, bleak gloom, which more than ever crudely typified the stupidity of everything and of life itself.

Giustino continued to send, first from Genoa, then from Milan, then from Venice, packets and packets of newspapers and letters. She didn't open them—she didn't even touch them.

The violence of that death had broken the easy, superficial rapport between her and the people and things around her there, a rapport that she could have maintained, but only briefly, on the condition that nothing serious and unexpected might come to reveal their real selves and the differences of their concerns and natures.

With the sudden disappearance of someone who comforted her by his presence, someone who had the same blood in his veins and represented her family, she felt alone and exiled in that house and those places—if not exactly among enemies, among strangers who couldn't understand her or directly share in her sorrow, and who looked at her in a certain way and silently watched all her actions and the way she expressed her mourning, as though they were waiting for something. They made her better understand, almost see and touch, her solitude, exacerbating the feeling. She felt excluded on all sides. Her mother-in-law and the wet nurse, since her baby had to remain there entrusted to their care, excluded her from her maternal cares. Her husband, running from city to city, from theater to theater, excluded her from his triumph. And so everyone tore the most precious things from her, and no one cared about her, left there in that void, alone. What should she do? No one was left in her family after her father's death, and now the death of her uncle, so far from her hometown, uprooted from everything familiar, flung onto a path she shrank from, not moving freely at her own pace, but almost as though pushed from behind by others. . . . And perhaps her mother-in-law inwardly accused her of having led her husband astray, filling his head with idle dreams and exciting him even to the point of making him lose his job. Yes, of course! She had already noticed this accusation in sidelong glances caught on the sly. Those vivid expressions in her pale face that she always kept turned away, as though to hide her thoughts; they demonstrated so clearly a certain distrustful prejudice, a regret she wanted to hide, full of anxiety and fear for her son.

However, rather than turning her against that ignorant old woman, Silvia's sense of injustice turned her against her absent husband. He was the reason for that injustice. He, so blinded by his frenzy that he no longer saw what he was doing to himself or to her. She had to stop him, to tell him to quit. But how? Was it possible now that things had gotten so out of hand, now that that play, composed in silence, in solitude, and in secret had become such a hit and put her name in lights? How could she judge from that corner of the world, without having seen anything yet, what she could or should do? She realized confusedly that she couldn't and shouldn't be more than she had been up to now; that she had to rid herself forever of what she had wanted to preserve in her life that was limiting and primitive, and instead give herself up to the secret power she had in herself, and which up to now she hadn't wanted to recognize. Just thinking about it made her feel the agitation seethe deep within her. This only affirmed the obvious: she had changed. Her husband could no longer remain in charge, riding *her* fame, blowing *his* trumpet.

Into what weird shapes the skeleton trees were twisted, sunk in the snow, with scraps, strips, tatters of fog caught in the distorted limbs! Looking at them from the window she mechanically brushed a hand over her forehead and eyes, almost as though to remove those scraps of fog from her distorted thoughts, shaped weirdly in her frozen soul like those trees. She stared at the drops of rain lining the moldy, damp wooden porch railing, shining against the leaden sky. A breeze struck the quivering drops, one flowed into another, and together they ran in a rivulet down the railing post. From the posts she looked as far as the priest's house next to the church; she saw the five green windows overlooking the lonely snow-covered garden hung with curtains that declared in their gleaming whiteness that they had been washed and ironed along with the altar cloths. What a peaceful sweetness in that white house! There, next to the cemetery . . .

Suddenly Silvia stood up, put her shawl over her head, and went out into the snow, heading straight for the cemetery to visit her uncle. Her gloomy spirit was as hard and cold as death.

The coming of spring began to break this gloom, when her mother-in-law, who had so often begged her not to go to the cemetery every day in that snow, wind, and rain, began to beg her, now that the weather was good, to go down Via Giaveno in the sun with the nurse and the little one.

So she had begun to go out with the baby. Sending the nurse ahead on that road, telling her to wait at the first shrine, she would go to the cemetery for the customary visit with her uncle.

One morning, in front of the first shrine, she found with the nurse a young journalist with a camera. He had come up from Turin just to see her, or, as he put it: "on the trail of Silvia Roncella and her hermitage."

How that goofy charmer had made her talk and laugh. He wanted to know everything, see everything, and photograph everything, especially her, in all sorts of poses, with the nurse and without, with her baby and without. He said he was really happy to have discovered a mine, a mine completely unexplored, a virgin mine, a gold mine.

After he left, Silvia remained astonished at herself for some time. She, too, had discovered someone new, with that journalist. She had even felt happy to talk and talk. . . . And now she couldn't even remember what she had said. So many things! Foolish things? Perhaps . . . But she had talked—finally! She had been what she should have been before now.

The next day she immensely enjoyed seeing her image reproduced in so many different poses in the newspaper he sent her, and reading all the things he had her saying. But above all she enjoyed the journalist's profuse expressions of surprise and enthusiasm, more for her as a *woman* still unknown to everyone than for a now famous artist.

It was Silvia's turn. She wanted to send a copy of that newspaper to her husband right away to show him that when she put her mind to it, *she* could do things well, too. He wasn't the only one.

5 ✱ THE CHRYSALIS AND THE CATERPILLAR

1

Disappointed, always. But on top of everything, to be discouraged after you put all your efforts into something from which you expected praise and gratitude seemed too much. And yet . . .

Giustino wanted the two carriages to fly, fly home quickly from the train station where he had gone to meet Silvia, along with Dora Barmis and Attilio Raceni.

His wife's appearance on her arrival had disconcerted him, even more so her few words and looks during the short walk to the station exit, where she got into a carriage with Signora Barmis and he jumped into another with Raceni.

"The trip . . . She's probably tired. . . . Then, so alone . . ." Raceni said to Giustino, also disturbed by Signora Roncella's glum expression and icy demeanor.

"Ah, yes . . ." Giustino agreed at once. "I see now. I should have gone up there to get her. But how could I have? Here, with the house to take care of, everything topsy-turvy. And then there was her uncle's death. That, too. She felt it. Yes, she took that death very hard. . . ."

This time Raceni agreed at once: "Yes . . . yes."

"See?" Giustino went on. "She was with him on the trip up—now she's come back alone. . . . She left him there. . . . But it's not just her uncle! Of course! I most certainly should have gone to get her at Cargiore. . . . There's also the separation from her child, for heaven's sake! You see, don't you?"

And Raceni again: "Yes. Yes. Certainly. Certainly."

How many things had slipped their minds, the three of them working so hard to get the new house ready!

They had gone to the station in a festive mood, with the satisfaction of having managed, with incredible effort, to get everything in order for her, only to realize suddenly that not only did they not deserve any thanks or gratitude, but they had to regret not only having forgot about the mourning of that recent death, but also about the mother's torment at leaving her baby.

Every moment seemed an hour to Giustino. He hoped that as soon as Silvia saw her new house, the surprise would make her forget everything. . . . He had deliberately not mentioned it in his letters.

Miracles—that was the right word—he had performed miracles, with the assiduous advice and help of Signora Barmis and . . . yes, also of Raceni, poor man!

He had said *house*, but just as a manner of speaking. House? It wasn't a house. It was . . . "But hush, for heaven's sake, because Silvia doesn't know yet!" It was a small villa—sshh! A small villa on that new street lined with other villas, beyond Margherita Bridge, at the Prati, on Via Plinio. One of the first, with a little yard around it, gate, and everything. Out of the way? What do you mean out of the way! A short walk and you're on the Corso, Rome's main street. A high-class neighborhood, quiet; it couldn't be better for a writer! But there's more. He wasn't renting that little villa. "Hush, for heaven's sake!" He had bought it. Yes, sir, bought it, for ninety thousand lire. Sixty thousand down, the other thirty to pay in three years. And—hush!—about another twenty thousand spent on furniture. Wonderful! With Signora Barmis's expertise . . . All new, stylish furniture: simple, sober, delicate, and solid: furniture by Ducrot! You should see the parlor at the left of the entrance, and then the other one next to it, and then the dining room that opened onto the garden. The study was upstairs, on the top floor, reached by way of a wide, beautiful marble stairway with a pillared banister that began just beyond the parlor door. Upstairs the study and two beautiful twin bedrooms next to it. Giustino didn't know what Silvia would think about this, but as far as he was concerned, he wanted a room to himself.

Dora Barmis had seemed indignant, horrified: "For heaven's sake! Don't even say it. . . . Do you want to ruin everything? Separate rooms! . . . Learn to live, darling! Remember you told me that from now on you would always take tea. . . ."

Two bedrooms. And then the little bathroom, and the washstand, and the clothes closet . . . Marvels! Or insanities? To tell the truth, it seemed like Boggiolo had lost his famous notebook on this occasion. He had gone berserk, and how! But he had so much money at his disposal! And the temptation . . . Of all the objects shown him, he had only been interested in the few most expensive models, in order to select the most beautiful. Yes, sir, when all those very few were finally added up, it had rounded out to a string of nice fat zeros for the furnishings.

On the other hand, he had no regrets about buying the little villa. Why should he! Since he could afford it, since he had enough money on hand to avoid the high interest rates, it would have been crazy not to buy, and to keep on throwing away two to three hundred lire a month for a barely decent apartment. The house was theirs, and that rent money would have flown into the landlord's pocket. True, if he hadn't bought the villino, they would still have the capital. All right! Now he needed to figure out if with the profit from ninety thousand he could have paid a monthly rent of three hundred lire. It wouldn't have paid it! And in the meanwhile, instead of a barely decent apartment, with ninety thousand lire he had that villino, that palace! But the expenses? Yes, it's true, the taxes, and then so many other additional expenses. Maintenance, lights, servants . . . With a house like that, one maid from the south would certainly not be enough. It would take three servants at least. For the time being, Giustino had hired two on trial, or rather one and a half, or rather two halves: that is, half a cook and half a servant (*valet de chambre,* as Signora Barmis had suggested he be called): a bright boy in a nice livery for cleaning, waiting on the table, and opening the door.

Now, right away . . . as soon as the two carriages arrived at the gate, Èmere (his name was Èmere) . . .

"Hey, Èmere! . . . Èmere! . . ." shouted Giustino into the night, stepping down. Then, turning to Raceni: "You see? . . . He's not in his
place. . . . What did I tell him?"

Oh, here he is. He's turning on the lights, first upstairs, then down.
There. The entire villino looks splendid with its windows illuminated,
under the starry sky. It's enchanting! But Silvia, already out of the
carriage with Signora Barmis, is waiting behind the closed gate, waiting for Raceni to take down the suitcases, while a dog barks from the
neighboring house. Giustino hurriedly pays the drivers and runs at
once to his wife to show her on one of the gate pillars the marble plaque
with the inscription: *Villa Silvia.*

First he looked into her eyes. During the drive he had supposed that
while talking to Signora Barmis in the other carriage about her uncle's
death and having to leave her son, she would have cried. Unfortunately,
no, she hadn't cried. She had the same appearance as before: glum,
stiff, cold.

"See? Ours!" he said to her. "Yours . . . yours . . . Villa Silvia, see?
Yours . . . I bought it!"

Silvia frowned. She looked first at her husband, then at the bright
windows. "A villa?"

"You'll see how beautiful it is, Signora Silvia!" Raceni exclaimed.

Èmere ran to open the gate and took his place, flourishing his striped
hat in the air without the slightest concern about the reprimand Giustino was shouting in his face: "Thanks a lot for having everything so
nice and ready!"

Giustino's vexation grew on seeing Signora Barmis's long face.
Without a doubt Silvia hadn't been nice to her in the carriage. And the
poor woman had worked so hard with him, exhausting herself! A nice
way to thank people!

"See?" he tried again, turning to his wife, as soon as they entered the
vestibule. "See? I didn't come to Cargiore to get you, because . . . See?
In order to get this surprise ready for you! With the help of . . . What
do you say, eh? What a vestibule! With the help of this dear friend of
ours and Raceni . . ."

"No! What are you saying! Be quiet!" Signora Barmis quickly tried to interrupt him.

Raceni also protested.

"Not at all!" Giustino insisted. "If it hadn't been for you two! Yes, in fact . . . alone, I . . . Now—this is nothing! You'll see. . . . We have good reason not only to thank you both, but to remain eternally grateful. . . ."

"Dear me, how you exaggerate!" smiled Signora Barmis. "Stop it. Look after your wife. She must be very tired. . . ."

"Yes, really very tired . . ." Silvia said, with a smile at once sweet and cold. "And please excuse me if I don't thank you as I should. . . . The long trip . . ."

"Yes, supper must be ready," Raceni hastened to say, moved by that smile (finally!) and by those nice words (what a voice Silvia Roncella had! What sweetness! A different voice . . . Yes, it seemed completely different!). "A little refreshment, then off to rest!"

"But first," said Giustino, opening the parlor door, "first you have to see the upstairs. . . . Go ahead. . . . Or better, I'll lead the way. . . ."

And he began his explanation, interrupted from time to time by Signora Barmis with words such as "of course . . . go on . . . but she can see this later" for every detail on which he lingered, repeating awkwardly, in jarring tones, everything he had already told her about the property, the refinements, the comfort, the taste.

"See? Porcelain . . . They are by . . . Who are they by, Signora? Oh, yes, by Lerche . . . Lerche, Norwegian . . . They seem like nothing, yet my dear . . . they're expensive! Expensive! But how refined, eh? . . . This little cat, eh? How lovely! Yes, let's proceed, let's proceed. . . . All by Ducrot! . . . He's number one, you know? These days he's number one, isn't he, Signora? There's nothing better. . . . Ducrot furniture! All Ducrot furniture! . . . This, too . . . Look here at this armchair. . . . What do they call it? All fine leather . . . I don't know what kind of leather. . . . You have two of them upstairs in your study. . . . Ducrot! Wait till you see your study!"

If Silvia had said one word, or had shown by the slightest gesture any curiosity, pleasure, or surprise, Dora Barmis would have taken over to show her with the proper tact, the proper remarks, the proper delicacy, all those exquisite things; she felt extremely uncomfortable because it seemed that Boggiolo's grotesque explanations crumpled, crippled, ruined everything.

But Silvia was more uncomfortable than Signora Barmis by seeing and hearing her husband ramble on like that. She was uncomfortable for herself and for him; and right now she was imagining how much enjoyment that woman, if not Raceni, must have had decorating that house in her way with his money. The disdain, spite, shame she was feeling made her stiffer than ever. And yet she didn't break off that torture, restrained by the curiosity (that she forced herself not to show) of seeing that house that did not seem like hers, but alien, made not for living as she had lived up till now, but like a place in which to perform an obligatory play from now on; even for herself. She would be obliged to treat with due regard all those objects of exquisite elegance that would keep her in continual subjection, obliged always to remember her part to recite among them. And she was thinking that just as she no longer had her baby, so she also no longer had the house she knew and loved. But it had to be like this, unfortunately. And so soon, like a good actress, she would take possession of those rooms, of that stage furniture from which all familial intimacy would be banished.

When, upstairs, she saw the separate bedrooms: "Ah, yes," she said. "Good, good."

And it was the only sound of approval that came from her mouth that evening.

The thought that Silvia might not appreciate this arrangement had been like a heavy weight on Giustino's chest. He had racked his brain for the most convincing way to present this novelty without offending his wife on the one hand, and without moving Signora Barmis to laughter on the other. He suddenly felt relieved and happy, completely misunderstanding the reason for his wife's delight.

"And I'm here, see? Next to you," he hurriedly explained. "Here, right here . . . What kind of bedrooms are they called? Ah, twins, yes . . . twin bedrooms, because see? they're just alike . . . This is mine! And what do you have there? My picture. And what do I have here? Your picture. See? Twin bedrooms. You like them, don't you? Everyone does it like this now. All right! I'm glad. . . ."

Signora Barmis and Raceni exchanged looks and smiles of amazement at the sight of him following his wife around like a puppy that evening.

But Giustino was so subdued and anxious for Silvia's approval that evening, not just because the successful tour of *The New Colony* through the big cities of the peninsula had increased his regard for her and this now obliged him to show her greater respect and consideration; nor was it because he guessed from her appearance, or at least sensed, his wife's change of heart toward him. His esteem was the same as before. He had never actually considered himself a good judge of her artistic merit, and now he could not care less, happy if this merit was recognized by others and really convinced that it was because of the extraordinary work that he had done and continued to do. Of course that recognition was entirely due to his work. As for her, how could she doubt his admiration and gratitude? Now more than ever.

And so what was the problem? There had to be other reasons that neither Signora Barmis nor Raceni could imagine.

Giustino regretted spending so much money on the furnishings, and while he feared this could make him lose out on some admiration and gratitude, at the same time he needed her approval like a balm to soothe this regret. Also, he was really sorry he had made his wife travel alone for the first time without thinking about the separation from her son and her uncle's death (the only reasons for Silvia's stiff behavior as far as he could tell). And finally . . . there was another private, very particular reason for wanting her approval, founded on the most rigorous, most scrupulous observance of his conjugal duties for nearly six very long months. At least Dora Barmis would be able to surmise this last reason. She was smiling to herself. But of course! Without a doubt she had guessed it. . . .

However, that wasn't the only reason she would not acquiesce in

Giustino's insistent pleas when it was time for supper (which had been ordered for four people before they went to the station), and she left. Raceni realized that it was only right that he should follow Signora Barmis, but the fact remained that he had been dazzled by Silvia Roncella from the first moment he saw her, and was unable to say no when she had said with a smile:

"You'll stay at least."

Silvia continued to dazzle him during the supper that evening, much to Giustino's astonishment. At a certain point he felt so spiteful that he couldn't contain himself and snorted: "I'm so sorry about Signora Barmis!"

"My goodness!" Silvia exclaimed. "If she didn't want to stay . . . You begged her enough!"

"You could have begged her, too!" Giustino retorted.

And Silvia, coldly: "It seems to me I did tell her, just as I told Raceni . . ."

"But you didn't insist at all! You could have insisted. . . ."

"I never insist," said Silvia, and she added, turning to smile at Raceni: "Did I insist with you? I don't think so. If Signora Barmis had wanted the pleasure of our company . . ."

"Pleasure! Pleasure! And what if she left," Giustino interrupted, unable to contain his irritation, "so's not to bother you after your trip?"

"Giustino!" Silvia responded at once in a tone of rebuke, but then smiled. "Now you're being rude to Raceni who stayed with us. Poor Raceni!"

"Not at all! Not at all!" Giustino rebelled. "I'm defending Signora Barmis from your suspicions. Raceni knows we want the pleasure of his company, if we asked him to stay!"

Raceni didn't believe he really brought all that much pleasure to him, but to her, yes, a lot. The young man could hardly sit still. He was as red as a poppy and could feel his blood running like liquid fire through his veins, so strongly it practically stunned him.

Giustino, who saw what a state he was in, and heard him smilingly repeat Silvia's words from time to time—"*Poor Raceni! . . . Poor Ra-*

ceni!"—felt a different fire blaze up in him: the fire of irritation, or rather anger, fomented also by annoyance with his wife for not giving a single sign of pleasure, or surprise, or admiration for that dining room, for the table settings, for that splendid array of flowers in the middle of the table, full of fragrant white carnations, for Èmere's impeccable service in that nice uniform, and the cook's work. Nothing! Not the least sign. As though she had always lived amid such splendor, used to such service, to eating that way, to having guests at the table; or as though she had already known about everything ahead of time and had expected to find their own home, furnished like it was; or rather, as though not he, but she, she alone had thought of everything and had done everything.

But why? Was she doing it to him on purpose? And why? What was it? Just because he hadn't gone to get her at Carigiore? Because he hadn't thought of her missing her baby? But if she didn't seem the slightest bit upset? Look at her there, laughing. . . . But what sort of laugh was that? And still going on with that *"poor Raceni!"*

Giustino was shaken and felt himself inwardly ripped apart from his toes to the roots of his hair when Silvia announced a great bit of news to Raceni: she had written some poetry at Cargiore, a lot of poetry, and promised to give him a sample for *The Muses.*

"Poems? What poems? You've been writing poetry?" he exploded. "Please!"

Silvia looked at him as if she didn't understand. "Why," she asked, "can't I write poetry? It's true I've never written any before. But the poems wrote themselves, believe me, Raceni. I'm not sure if they're any good. They could even be bad. . . ."

"And you want to publish them in *The Muses?*" asked Giustino, his eyes glaring more furiously than ever.

"And why not, Boggiolo?" Raceni spoke up. "Do you really think they could be bad? Just imagine how popular they'll be with readers as a new, unexpected manifestation of Silvia Roncella's talent!"

"No, no, for heaven's sake, don't talk like that, Raceni," Silvia protested at once. "Otherwise I won't give them to you. They're little ditties you can't give any importance to. I'll give them to you on this condition, and only as a favor."

"All right, all right," Giustino chewed it over. "But . . . may I . . . remind you . . . not for Raceni who . . . all right, you've already promised him, so that's that. You promised Senator Borghi a short story first, and you haven't done it!"

"My goodness, I'll do it, if it comes to me." Silvia replied.

"I'm saying . . . instead of poems . . . you could at least have written this short story at Cargiore!" Giustino couldn't restrain himself. "And now . . . if you can't give these poems to the senator after promising them to Raceni . . . I would say . . . at least wait until Borghi's short story is ready."

Absolutely everything was ruining his celebration of the new house this evening, the reward for all his hard work! So now his wife wanted to return to those wonderful days when she gave her work away to everyone? Did she also want to start doing everything herself, taking advantage of the fact that this evening he wouldn't want to be discourteous to her?

Dear me, he realized he was losing all semblance of manners, and he could feel his agitation growing. Of course! Certainly! Disappointment over the lack of praise, over the lack of surprise, her whole manner, the unnecessary snub to Signora Barmis, now this promise to Raceni . . .

To vent his feelings, to make the furies evaporate, Giustino hurled a string of abuse and insults after Raceni as soon as he left: "Stupid! Imbecile! Clown!"

But here was Silvia defending him, smiling: "And your gratitude, Giustino? When he's been such a help to you?"

"He? He's been in my way!" Giustino broke out furiously. "Only in the way! As he was this evening! As he always is! Signora Barmis really helped me, don't you see? She, yes! Signora Barmis, who you made leave like that. And to that man, smiles, compliments, *poor Raceni, poor Raceni,* and even . . . even giving him poems, by heaven!"

"But don't the two of them work together?" Silvia asked. "He, the director; she, the editor? Don't you think it would be better from now

135

on to compensate them every once in a while for all the help they've given you, until they no longer want to help us for . . . I don't really know why. . . ."

"Oh, no, dear, no, dear . . . listen, dear . . ." Giustino started babbling, losing all control, wounded to the quick. "You mustn't get mixed up in things that are my business! But have you looked around, tell me, have you looked around carefully? All these things here . . . All ours! And it's the fruit, I say, of my work and worry! Now do *you* want to teach me what I should do and what I should say?"

Silvia broke off the argument at once, saying she was dead tired after the long trip and needed to rest.

She realized he would never give in on that point and that any attempt to stop him in the exercise of what he now considered his duty, his profession, would inevitably cause a rift between them, an incurable break.

She understood him better when, rejected, undressing in the adjoining room, he began wholeheartedly to give vent to his disappointment, his bitter irritation and rage, with curses and rebukes, reprimands and regrets, and outbursts of nasty laughter. The more these provoked and wounded her, the more his now exposed and flagrant absurdity grew before her eyes.

"But yes! She was right! *Help her, Boggiolo, help her avenge herself!* I was an idiot not to do it! This is my reward! This is my compensation! Stupid . . . stupid . . . stupid . . . A hundred thousand occasions . . . Well, all right! This is nothing, gentlemen! We haven't even started yet! Just wait and see! . . . We give them away, we give them away. . . . We write poems and we give them away. . . . Poetry, now! Poetry's popping out. . . . Of course! Let's start living in the clouds, shutting our eyes to all these expenses here. . . . All too boringly prosaic . . . So much pain, so much work, so much money: that's the thanks I get! We knew it . . . But such unimportant things . . . A little villa? Bah! What's that? Ducrot furniture? Bah! Nothing special . . . Oh, here's the bed! What a nice bed of roses! . . . What a nice way to inaugurate it, my dear Signor Ducrot! Hurry here, stupid! Run there! Break your neck! Get out of breath! Lose your job! Beg, threaten, pull strings! This is my reward, gentlemen! This is my reward!"

And he went on like this in the dark for more than an hour, tossing and turning wildly on the bed, coughing, snorting, scornfully laughing. In the meantime, in the other room, curled up under the blankets, with her head buried in the pillows to shut him out, she cursed her fame that had escalated with his help, but at the price of so much laughter and derision from others. She now felt attacked, whipped, enveloped by all that laughter, all that mockery, with the roar of the train still in her ears. Why hadn't she noticed it before? Only now all the times he had made a spectacle of himself, each more ridiculous than the other, rose before her eyes, tormenting her with such cruel clarity: all the times beginning with the banquet, when he stood up with her at Borghi's toast as if it was for his benefit also as her husband, up to the scene at the station before her departure for Cargiore when he, leading the way, had bowed as applause broke out in the waiting room.

Oh, to be able to turn back, to crawl into her shell to work quietly and unknown! But he would never allow her work of so many years, from which he now drew all his satisfaction, to be stymied like that. With that villino that he, with good reason, considered entirely the fruit of his labor, he had intended to construct a kind of temple to Fame where he could officiate and pontificate! It was madness to hope he might give it up now! It was fixed in his mind, and there it would stay forever as part of that fame that he knew he had made! And that he would keep trying to make greater so he could stay in the middle and keep looking more ridiculous.

It was her fate, and it was inevitable.

But how could she bear that torture, now that the blindfold had fallen from her eyes?

2

A few days later, Giustino wanted to solemnly institute the first of a series of "Literary Mondays at Villa Silvia," as Signora Barmis had suggested.

For the housewarming he invited all the best-known musicians and music critics of Rome for a piano recital of music from the opera *The New Colony*, composed by the young Maestro Aldo di Marco.

The composer's name drew a blank with everyone. All anyone knew was that this di Marco was a very rich Venetian Jew and that in order to set *The New Colony* to music, he had made such offers that Boggiolo had hurriedly broken off negotiations with one of the more distinguished composers.

Although Giustino didn't expect much to come of this work, and in fact he hoped it had only modest success so it wouldn't cast a shadow over the play, nevertheless he had his journalist friends announce that the composition would soon be introduced in Italy, etc., etc., and he had a picture printed in the newspapers of the slender, not too well-groomed young Venetian maestro, who . . . etc., etc.

The announcement had seemed to him necessary and opportune, not only considering the enormous amount of money the composer spent to set the successful play to music (with lyrics by Cosimo Zago), but also to enhance the solemnity of the inaugural evening.

That was the least he could do.

That piano recital, and the young, unknown composer, who looked so unpromising, was an annoyance to everyone. On the other hand, the curiosity to see Signora Roncella, in person, in her house after her triumph, was very lively.

Silvia expected it. Nervous about having to face that curiosity shortly, seeing her husband so frantically getting things set up but acting like someone who knows everything and needs no one, she would have liked to cry out: "Stop! Let it all go. Don't trouble yourself anymore! They are coming for me, just for me! You have nothing to do with it anymore; you don't have to do anything except sit quietly in a corner!"

Her nervousness was not only because of the expected curiosity; it was also because of him—in fact, primarily because of him.

She even went so far as to pretend to be jealous of Signora Barmis, to keep him from running to her for help with the preparations, hoping that without her he wouldn't take so much trouble and would think he had done all that was necessary.

The idea that his wife, who had become such a celebrity (even though it was through him), was beginning to be a little jealous (however wrongly) gave Giustino a certain pleasure. The irritation that this jealousy caused him at that moment manifested itself in a smug little smile. Signora Barmis's help was indispensable. But Silvia stood her ground.

"No, not her, no! Not her!"

"But, heavens . . . Silvia, are you serious? If I . . ."

Silvia shook her head angrily and hid her face in her hands to interrupt him.

Her deceitfulness made her suddenly ashamed and disgusted, seeing that deep down he was enjoying it: ashamed and disgusted, because it seemed to her that she was making fun of him for his silly spectacle, too.

Suddenly, wanting to give him a hard shake to save him and save herself, to make the blindfold fall from his eyes, too, she burst out: "Why, why do you want to make them laugh? At you and at me? Haven't you noticed Signora Barmis is laughing at you, has always laughed at you? And everyone with her, everyone! Haven't you noticed?"

Giustino wasn't the slightest bit shaken by his wife's angry outburst. He gave her an almost compassionate smile and raised his hand in a gesture more of philosophical indifference than derision.

"They're laughing? Yes, for some time now . . ." he said. "But add it up, my dear, and you'll see if those who laugh are the fools or I who . . . Look here . . . who did all this and put you on top! Let them laugh. See? They laugh and I take advantage of it and get everything I want from them. Look around you, here's all their laughter. . . ."

And he waved his hands while looking around the room, as though to say: "See what fine things they changed into?"

Silvia's arms dropped to her sides. She stood looking at him open-mouthed.

Then he knew? He had noticed? And he had gone ahead without

caring, and had wanted to keep on going? It didn't matter that everyone was laughing at him and at her? Oh, dear, but then . . . If he was
sure, very sure, that her fame was solely his work, and that all his work
consisted of basically nothing more important than letting them laugh
at him, and then converting this laughter into large earnings, into that
little villa, into the nice furniture in it — what did it mean? Did it mean
that for him literature was something to laugh at, something a man
of good judgment, wise, and discerning, wouldn't become involved in
except to take advantage of the laughter of fools who took it seriously?
That's what it meant? Oh, no!

As Silvia continued to look at her husband, she suddenly realized
these presumptions painted the wrong picture of him. No, no! He
couldn't have wanted to be considered a laughing stock. From the time
those three hundred marks arrived down there in Taranto for the translation of *Stormy Petrel,* he had begun to take literature seriously. The
only foolishness for him was her indifference toward the profit it could
make if administered well, like any other work. . . . And he had set
about to supervise it with such fervor, or rather with such fury, as
to provoke everyone's laughter. He hadn't intentionally provoked that
laughter to sell her work, but he had been forced to endure it, and now
he considered it the laughter of fools because he had succeeded in spite
of it. No matter what he did now, people would laugh at him! The more
serious he wanted to appear now, the more ridiculous he would seem.

Ah, that inaugural evening! Silvia seemed to detect mockery in every
sound, in the rustle of dresses, in the light squeak of shoes muffled in
the thick rugs, when a chair moved, a door opened, or a spoon stirred
in a cup. And then the sound of the piano when di Marco began to play,
and little smiles, titters, looks, gales of loud laughter, words blurted
and babbled. Every smile of deference or sympathy seemed mockery.
She sensed mockery in every look, in every gesture, behind every word
of the many guests.

She tried to ignore her husband, but how could she if he was always
there in front of her, small, all dressed up, restless, beaming, and be-
lieving that everyone in every part of the room wanted him? Now

Luna took him by the arm, and another four or five journalists flocked around him, then Signora Lampugnani called to him from a group of the liveliest women.

She would have liked to have been more receptive and sociable, but being incapable of this and boiling with scorn, she had been tempted from time to time to say or do something outlandish, unheard of, to make the desire to laugh pass from everyone who had come there to mock her husband, and consequently her, too.

Instead, she had to put up with the almost insolent flirting that those young literati and journalists felt free to engage in. As though she, fortunate enough to have a husband like that so willing to show her off to everyone, a husband who did so much to make everyone like her, a husband surely not even she could take seriously, she couldn't, indeed she shouldn't, refuse their attention, in order not to displease him.

And in fact, didn't he come up to her from time to time to suggest that she do what she could with one person or another, and particularly with the most shameless, with those she tried to keep at a distance with hard and cold contempt? Betti, that Betti who up to now had taken every occasion to write ill of her in several newspapers, and that Paolo Baldani recently come from Bologna, a very handsome young man and very erudite critic, writer of verses and journalist, who with incredible arrogance had whispered a declaration of love as though it were quite normal?

So it wasn't just the laughter and mockery she had to put up with, but this, too? Silvia asked herself in regard to her husband's brief, furtive recommendations that didn't seem innocent to her, as they apparently did to him. This, too?

She was freezing with disgust and burning with indignation.

The strangest thoughts darted through her mind, arousing dismay in her, since they went ever deeper into the unexplored parts of herself, uncovering things she hadn't wanted to know about herself. She had a premonition that if her demon should ever take possession of her, it would drag her who knows where.

Every concept that she had tried to hold firmly decomposed in her mind and, abandoned to her new destiny, or rather to chance, she saw that without wanting to, her soul could change in a minute, revealing itself capable of anything, of the most unthinkable, unexpected resolutions from one instant to another.

"It seems to me that . . . I say . . . it seems to me that . . . everything went well, eh? Very well, it seems to me." Giustino hurriedly said to her when the last guest had left, in order to shake her out of her mood: stiff, eyes intense and staring, mouth clamped shut.

Her cold hands could still feel the fiery clasp Baldani had given her just before he left.

"Everything was just fine, wasn't it?" Giustino repeated. "And, you know, walking around I heard them say so many . . . good things about you . . . very good things . . ."

Silvia shook herself and gave him such a look that he stopped a moment, as though lost, with an empty smile on his lips like someone who doesn't quite know what face to put on.

"Don't you think so?" he then asked. "Everything fine, I say . . . Only di Marco's music seems . . . did you listen? Scholarly, yes . . . It's scholarly music, but . . ."

"Do we have to go on like this?" Silvia suddenly asked in a strange voice, as if only her voice were there and she herself were miles away. "I'm warning you that I won't be able to write any more like this."

"How . . . Why? . . . In fact, now that . . . but what!" Giustino stammered, shocked by this unexpected blow. "With that study upstairs . . ."

Silvia blinked, made a face, shook her head violently.

"What?" Giustino repeated. "You can close the door. . . . Who will disturb you? . . . With so much silence . . . What I meant . . . Everyone asks what you are preparing. I answered: nothing, for now. No one believes it. Certainly a new play, they say. They would pay anything for a hint, some news, a title. . . . You have to think about it, get back to work now. . . ."

"How? How? How?" shouted Silvia, shaking her fist in frustration. "I can't think, I can't do it anymore! It's over for me! I was able to work when I was unknown, when I didn't even know myself! Now I can't anymore! It's over! I'm not that person anymore. I'm a different person! It's over! It's over!"

Giustino watched her in her frenzy. Then, with a shake of his head: "We are doing so well!" he exclaimed. "Now, that it's beginning, it's over? What are you talking about? Look here, why does anyone work? To reach a goal, I think! You want to work and stay unknown? Work, then, for what? For nothing?"

"For nothing! For nothing! For nothing!" Silvia responded passionately. "That's just it, for nothing! To work for work's sake and nothing else! Without knowing how or when, hidden away from everyone and almost hidden from myself!"

"But this is insane!" shouted Giustino, beginning to get worked up, too. "Well, what have I done? Was it wrong of me to make your work pay, is that it? Is that what you mean?"

With her face in her hands, Silvia shook her head yes several times.

"Really?" Giustino continued. "Then why did you let me do it for so long? This is how you thank me now that you are reaping the rewards so many yearn for who work like you: glory and ease? You're complaining about it . . . And that's not crazy? Come on, my dear, it's just nerves! Besides, what do you have to do with it? Who tells you to bother with things that don't concern you?"

Silvia looked at him dumbfounded. "They don't concern me?"

"No, dear, they don't concern you!" Giustino answered immediately. "You go on working for nothing, just as you did before. Go back to work when you like and let me worry about the rest. Of course, I understand . . . such a novelty! . . . I understand that if it was up to you . . . But look, if I milk it with my work, what do you have to do? Do I burden you with this, too? This is my business! You give me the written work, write for nothing, as you please, throw it away. I'll take it and change it into hard cash for you. Can you stop me? It's my business, and you have nothing to do with it. Work like you've worked up to now; work for work's sake . . . but work! Because if you don't work anymore, I . . . I . . . what will I do? Can you tell me? I lost my job, my dear, by looking after your work. You need to think about this! Now the responsibility is mine . . . I say, for your work. We've earned a lot, it's true, and there will be more with *The New Colony*. But you see here how the expenses have increased. . . . Now with the house we have another style of life. There are still thirty thousand lire to be paid for the house. I could have paid it, but I wanted to keep something aside so you could have a breather. . . . Now you'll get yourself together. It's been a big shock — the change was too sudden. You'll get used to it quickly, you'll calm down. The biggest part has been done, my dear. We have the house. . . . I wanted it like this. I spent a lot, but . . . for the sake of appearances, you know? Every little bit counts! Your name is worth something now, worth a lot in itself. . . . Without giving anything to anyone! If Raceni expects those poems you promised him for his magazine, he'll be in for a surprise! I won't let him have them. *Poor Raceni, poor Raceni,* you'll see how much those poems will earn now. . . . Leave it to me! You just get back to your writing. Write and don't think about anything else. Upstairs, by heaven, in that magnificent study."

In Giustino's long discourse Silvia saw no well-meaning intention to restore her to a calm and reasonable state, to the recognition and gratitude for what he had done and still wanted to do for her; she only saw, in that moment of exasperation, what she was supposed to do for the enemy and tyrant: that is, now that he had lost his job, he made it absolutely imperative that she work so he could have employment — a job that would seem odious to anyone, never mind how ridiculous. Didn't he want to live on her work and for her work, then take credit for the earnings himself? As long as the work hadn't cost her great effort, she could recognize that the credit for those unexpected earnings were all or almost all due to him, but no longer, now that he had so expressly and clearly made it her obligation to work. Now her work was an agony, just thinking how she had to turn everything over to him, unable to do as she pleased with it. She had to give him everything, everything, because in spite of the scorn and now also with the contempt of others, he wanted to make money out of it. That was it, make everything profitable, even those poor, private, shy little poems. . . . A business, even at the cost of her own dignity! Did he realize this? Was

144

it possible that the furor blinded him to the point where he couldn't see it?

Sleepless all night long, Silvia lay thinking, and at a certain point, with the help of the darkness and silence, she was surprised by a strange and unusual mixture of feelings that brought an unexpected anguish, almost like nostalgia, from the depths of her being up to her throat. She could clearly see the houses of her Taranto. Inside them she saw her good, meek fellow townswomen, who were used to being jealously protected by their husbands with the most scrupulous rigor so that no suspicion might come their way, used to seeing their men reenter their own home as in a temple closed to all strangers, even distant relatives. They would be upset, offended, as though their modesty were violated, if their husbands started opening the door of that temple, almost as if their good reputation was of no importance.

No, no. She had never had these feelings. Her father, down there, had always been hospitable, especially toward his underlings and outsiders. In fact she had scorned these feelings, knowing that many talked about her father's hospitality, which without a doubt would have made it difficult to marry anyone from her town. Rather, it seemed to her that the women should be offended by their husbands' possessive concern, as though it showed lack of esteem and trust.

Why was she now offended by the opposite, having discovered in herself those unexpected feelings, just like those women down there?

Suddenly, the reason was clear.

Almost every woman down there had not married for love, but for convenience, to achieve a certain status. She entered the home of her husband, the master, dependent and obedient. This obedience and devotion was not moved by affection, but only by respect for the man who worked and maintained her, a respect that she could feel only on the condition that this man, with his hard work (if not by his good behavior), knew in every way how to preserve the respect due the master. On the other hand, a man who relaxed his rigorous hold and opened his home to others lost the respect even of his guests, and his wife's modesty was injured because she felt exposed in her loveless private life, in her state of subjection to a man who no longer deserved it, for the sole reason that he permitted something that no other man would ever have permitted.

Yes, of course. She, too, had married without love, moved by the desire to achieve a status, and persuaded by a feeling of respect for and gratitude to the man who was willing to take her as his wife without getting skittish about another serious defect that would have turned away the men in her town, in addition to her father's hospitality—her writing. But look at him now trying to make a business of that secret on which her esteem and gratitude were based; he had set about to sell and tout the merchandise so loudly, so that everyone could be in on her secret, to see and touch it. What respect could others have for such a man? Everyone laughed at him, and he didn't care! What esteem and gratitude could she have now if he, reversing their roles, made her work and wanted to live off it?

More than anything else at that moment, it offended her that the others could think that she might still love such a man or, what's more, that she was devoted to him.

Did he perhaps believe this also? Or did his certainty lie in his faith in her integrity? Ah, yes; but integrity for herself, not for him! His certainty could have no other effect on her than to provoke her like a challenge, and offend and fill her with scorn.

No, no: she couldn't continue to live like this—that was clear.

3

Two days later, as was to be expected after that handshake, Paolo Baldani returned to the little villa.

Giustino Boggiolo welcomed him with open arms. "Disturb her? What an idea! On my honor, it's a pleasure. . . ."

"Shhh . . ." Baldani said, smiling, putting a finger to his lips. "Your wife is upstairs? I don't want her to hear me. It's you I need."

"Me? Here I am. . . . What can I do? Let's go to the living room . . . or, if you wish, let's go to the garden . . . or in the parlor in the next room. Silvia is upstairs in her study."

"Thanks, this will be fine," said Baldani, sitting in the parlor; then, leaning toward Boggiolo, he added softly: "I have to be indiscreet."

"You? But no . . . Why? Not at all . . ."

"It's necessary, my friend. But when the indiscretion is for a good end, a gentleman must not hold back. Here, I'll tell you. I have prepared an exhaustive study about the artistic personality of Silvia Roncella . . ."

"Oh, tha . . ."

"Easy, wait a minute! I've come to ask some questions. . . . I would say very personal, very particular questions that only you are in a position to answer. I would like from you, dear Boggiolo, a certain, I would say . . . physiological enlightenment."

By the low, mysterious tone with which Baldani continued to speak, Giustino was almost tugged by the tip of his nose to listen, with head bowed, eyes intent and mouth open.

"Physio?"

" —logical. Let me explain. A critic today, my friend, has other research aids that were unheard of previously. For the complete understanding of a personality a deep and precise knowledge is necessary, even of the most obscure needs, of the most secret and hidden needs of the organism. These are very delicate investigations. A man, you'll understand, submits to them without so many scruples; but a woman . . . eh, a woman . . . I say, a woman like your wife, let's be clear! I know a lot of women who would submit to these investigations without any scruples, even more openly than men. For example . . . no, let's not mention names! Now to make a rash judgment, as so many do, based solely on obvious physical characteristics is for charlatans. The shape of a nose, my God, can very possibly not correspond to the true nature of the one who wears it on his face. Your wife's dainty little nose, for example, has all the characteristics of sensuality. . . ."

"Really?" Giustino asked, surprised.

"Yes, yes, certainly," Baldani confirmed with great seriousness. "And yet, perhaps . . . To finish my study I need some information from you, dear Boggiolo. . . . I repeat, intimate, indispensable for the complete understanding of Roncella's personality. If you don't mind, I'll ask you one or two questions, no more. I would like to know if your wife . . ."

And coming still closer, still more quietly, Baldani, polite and serious, asked the first question. Giustino, leaning over with his eyes more intent than ever, turned deep red as he listened. In the end, placing his hands on his chest and straightening up: "Oh, no sir! No, sir!" he denied strongly. "This I can swear to!"

"Really?" Baldani said, searching his eyes.

"I can swear to it!" Giustino repeated solemnly.

"And now," continued Baldani, "be kind enough to tell me if . . ."

And very quietly, as before, still polite and serious, he asked the second question. This time Giustino's brow furrowed a bit as he listened. Then, expressing great surprise, he asked: "Why?"

"How naive you are!" Baldani smiled; and he explained why.

Then Giustino, again becoming red as a poppy, first pursed his lips as if he were ready to whistle, then he closed them with an empty little smile and answered hesitantly: "This . . . well . . . yes, sometimes . . . but you mustn't think that . . ."

"For heaven's sake!" Baldani interrupted. "You don't have to tell me. Who could ever think that Silvia Roncella . . . for heaven's sake! That's enough. Those were the two points I needed to clear up. Thank you so much, dear Boggiolo, thank you!"

A little disconcerted, but smiling, Giustino scratched an ear and asked: "Excuse me, perhaps in the article? . . ."

Paolo Baldani interrupted him with a wag of a finger; then he said: "First of all, it's not an article. I told you, its a study. You'll see! The research remains secret; it will help me shed light on the criticism. Later you'll see. Later. If you'll be good enough to tell your wife I'm here . . ."

"At once!" said Giustino. "Please wait just a moment. . . ."

He ran up to Silvia's study to announce Baldani. He was very sure of having swayed her recently and so didn't expect her furious refusal to see him.

"But why?" he asked, stopped in his tracks.

Silvia was tempted to hurl the truth in his face, to alter his demeanor of stunned, sorrowful surprise, but she feared he might resort to a show of philosophical indifference, as he had when she had thrown the laughter and mockery of people in his face.

"Because I don't want to!" she told him. "Because he irritates me! You can see I'm knocking my brains out!"

"Oh, come on, five minutes . . ." Giustino insisted. "He's making a study of all your works, you know! Today a critic like Baldani, look . . . He's a fashionable critic . . . a critic—wait! What are they called? I don't know . . . a new criticism that is talked about so much now, my dear! Five minutes . . . He's studying you, that's all. May I let him come up?"

"A wonderful thing, wonderful thing," Paolo Baldani said a little afterward in the study, lightly tapping his feminine hand on the arm of the chair and winking at Giustino Boggiolo. "A wonderful thing to see a man so solicitous about your fame and your work, so entirely devoted to you. I can just imagine how happy that must make you!"

"But you know? . . . because . . . if I . . ." Giustino tried immediately to butt in, fearing Silvia didn't want to answer him.

Baldani stopped him with a hand. He hadn't finished.

"May I?" he said, and continued: "I imagine so much solicitude and devotion must carry their weight in the importance of your writings, as far as selling them; you certainly can, without any extraneous cares, abandon yourself entirely to the divine joy of creating."

He seemed to be talking that way now in jest, as though he was aware of his affected way of speaking and accompanied it with a slight, barely perceptible ironic smile. Not to modify it, however, but to arm it with the fascination of disturbing ambiguity. "Only I know what I have in mind," he seemed to say. "For you, for everyone, I have this profusion of words, and I cloak myself in them with lordly indifference; but when necessary I can also throw them off and suddenly reveal myself strong and handsome in my bare animal nature."

Silvia had clearly made out that animal nature in the depths of his eyes. She'd had proof of it in the brazen declaration the other evening. If her husband left the room for a minute, she was certain she would be subjected to a new and more brazen assault. In the meanwhile—oh, how irksome!—he was praising and admiring Giustino to her face, to make friends with him, and after looking at him, he turned to her with unbelievable impudence. In fact, Baldani's look said: "You couldn't dream or even guess what I know about you. . . ."

"The joy of creating?" Silvia broke out. "I've never felt it. I'm really sorry I can't now, as before, attend to what you call 'extraneous cares.' They were the only things that put me at ease and gave some security. All my wisdom was in them! Because I don't know anything. I don't understand anything. If you speak to me about art, I won't understand anything at all."

Giustino squirmed nervously in his chair. Baldani noticed, turned to look at him, smiled and said: "But this is a priceless confession . . . priceless."

"Would you like to know, if it will help you, what I was doing, put here for the purpose of writing?" continued Silvia. "I have counted the black and white stripes on the sleeve of my mourning dress. One hundred and seventy-two white stripes from my wrist to the length of the sleeve. Therefore all I know is that I have an arm and this dress. Other than that I know nothing; nothing, nothing, nothing at all."

"That explains everything!" Baldani exclaimed then, as if that was what he expected. "All your art is here, my dear lady."

"In the black and white stripes?" Silvia asked, pretending to be amazed.

"No," smiled Baldani. "In your marvelous unconscious that explains the no-less marvelous spontaneous naturalness of your work. You are a real force of nature. More than that. You are nature itself, which uses the instrument of your imagination to create works above the common run. Your logic is that of life, and you can't be aware of it because it's an inborn logic, a mobile and complex logic. You see, my dear lady: the elements that make up your spirit are extraordinarily numerous, and you are ignorant of them. They join and separate with ease, with a prodigious speed, and this doesn't depend on your will. They don't let you fix them in any stable form. They keep themselves, I might say, in a state of perpetual melding, without ever congealing, malleable, plastic, fluid. And you can assume all shapes without knowing it, without your consciously willing it."

"Look! Look! Look!" Giustino began to babble, jumping about overjoyed. "That's it! That's it! Tell her, repeat it, make it stick in her mind, dear Baldani! She is writing something very nice at this moment. She's a little confused, you see . . . a little uncertain, after the triumph."

"Not at all!" shouted Silvia heatedly, in an effort to stop him.

"Yes, yes, yes!" Giustino urged, on his feet, standing between them, almost as though to keep the propitious occasion from slipping away now that he had it in his grasp. "You explained it so well, Baldani! It's just like you said, Baldani! She can't find a theme for the new play, and . . ."

"She can't find it? But she already has it!" Baldani exclaimed, smiling. "May I make a suggestion out of the affection I hold for you? You already have the play! Fools believe (and they go around saying) that it's easier to create outside daily experience, putting people and things in imaginary places, in unspecified times, almost as if art didn't mix with so-called common reality, and it didn't create its own superior reality. But I know your strengths, and I know you can confound these idiots and reduce them to silence and force them to admiration, facing up to and dominating a material much different from that of *The New Colony*. A play about people around us in a city. In your book *Stormy Petrels* you have a short story, the third, if I remember correctly, entitled "If Not This Way." . . . That's the new play! Think about it. I will consider myself fortunate to have pointed it out if someday I can say: This play she wrote for me; it was I who planted this vital new seed for fertilization in the womb of her imagination!"

He rose and said almost severely to Giustino: "Let's leave her alone."

Baldani went over, took her hand, with a bow deposited a kiss on it, and left.

As soon as Silvia was alone she was assaulted by that fierce anger that we feel when, buffeted in a storm in which we can't see our salvation or almost have no hope for it, suddenly and calmly it is offered to us by someone from whom we would least have wanted it—here it is,

151

a plank, a rope. We would rather drown than use it so as not to owe our salvation to the one who offered it to us so effortlessly. This ease, which almost makes our previous desperation silly and vain, seems insulting, and we want to make it clear that the help so effortlessly offered is silly and vain instead. But in the meanwhile we realize we have already grabbed it against our will.

Silvia yearned to get back to work, to a project that would captivate her and keep her from seeing, thinking of herself, and feeling. But she was seeking and not finding. The desire consumed her as she became more and more convinced that she really couldn't do anything anymore.

Now she didn't want to go to the bookshelf and take down *Stormy Petrel*, but the idea had taken root—she was already trying to visualize the play in the story Baldani had pointed out.

Was it there? Yes, it really was. The drama of a sterile wife. Ersilia Groa, a rich provincial, not beautiful, with a deep, passionate heart, but rigid and hard in aspect and manner, married for six years to Leonardo Arciani, a writer with no desire—after the wedding—either to write or to care about publishing books after he had aroused great public interest and expectation with one of his novels. Those years of marriage have gone by in apparent tranquillity. Ersilia doesn't know how to offer that treasure of affection she locks in her heart; perhaps she fears it might have no value to her husband. He asks little of her and she gives him little. She would give him everything if he desired it. So there is a void beneath that apparent tranquillity. Only a child could fill it, but now after six years she despairs of having one. One day a letter arrives for her husband. Leonardo has no secrets from her: they read this letter together. It's from his cousin, Elena Orgera, who was once engaged to him: her husband has died; she is left poor and without any income, with a son she wants to put in an orphanage. She asks for his help. Leonardo is indignant, but Ersilia persuades him to send her help. Soon after that he suddenly goes back to work. Ersilia had never seen her husband work. Completely ignorant of literature, she doesn't understand her husband's sudden new enthusiasm. She watches him waste away day after day, afraid he will become ill. If only he would not tire himself out so. But he tells her that his inspiration has revived and that she couldn't understand what it is. Thus he manages to fool her for nearly a year. When Ersilia finally discovers her husband's infidelity, he already has had a baby girl with Elena Orgera. Double betrayal: and Ersilia doesn't know if her heart bleeds more for the husband that woman took from her or for the child she was able to give him. Conscience certainly has a curious sense of shame: Leonardo Arciani breaks his wife's heart, steals her love, her peace, but he has scruples about money. Of course! But not scruples about his wife's money. As a gentleman he doesn't like having a love nest outside his house. But the rare and uncertain earnings of his stressful work aren't enough to provide for the needs that soon begin to fill that nest with thorns. As soon as she discovers the betrayal, Ersilia seals herself up hermetically without letting either scorn or sorrow leak out on her husband: she only expects him to continue living at home in order not to cause a scandal, but completely separate from her. She never favors him with a look or a word. Leonardo, oppressed by an unbearable weight, profoundly admires the dignified, austere behavior of his wife, who perhaps understands that, above and beyond all her rights, there is a more imperious duty now for him: his duty toward his child. Yes, in fact, Ersilia understands this duty: she understands it because she knows what she lacks; she understands it so well that if he, worn out now and discouraged, should return to her, abandoning the child with his lover, she would be horrified. He has proof of her tacit, sublime compassion in her silence, in her peace, in the many modestly concealed considerations he finds at home. And his admiration gradually becomes gratitude; and from gratitude, love. He no longer goes into that nest of thorns now except to see his daughter. And Ersilia knows it. What is she waiting for? She herself doesn't know; and in the meanwhile the love she feels growing in him is nurtured in secret. Her father appears to break up this state of affairs. Guglielmo Groa is a big country merchant, rough, uncultured, but full of sharp good sense.

The play could begin here, with the arrival of her father. Ersilia, who has not spoken a word to her husband in three years, goes to find him at the daily newspaper where he works as arts editor, to warn him that her father, from whom she has hidden everything, is suspicious and will come that very morning looking for an explanation. She wants him to put on an act in order to save her father from this unhappiness. It's an excuse. She is really afraid that her father, in an effort to reach an impossible solution, might forever break that tacit rapprochement that she has worked so hard to establish between her and her husband, which for her is the cause of indescribable secret pain as well as indescribable secret sweetness. Ersilia doesn't find her husband in the editorial office and leaves him a note, promising she'll soon return to help him with the pretense when her father, who has gone to attend a morning session of the Chamber, comes there to talk to him. Leonardo finds his wife's note and learns from the receptionist that another woman had just been looking for him. She is Signora Orgera, whom he has not seen in a week while feeling the suspicious eyes of his father-in-law spying on him. In fact, soon afterward she returns at that particularly inopportune moment, and Leonardo unsuccessfully tries to explain why he hasn't come and lets her read his wife's note as proof. She ridicules Ersilia's sacrificing herself to save her husband trouble and suffering, while she . . . yes, she represents the need, the rawness, of a no longer tenable reality: suppliers who want to be paid, landlords who threaten eviction. Better to end it! Everything is already over between them. He loves his wife, that sublime silent woman: well, then, go back to her, that's enough! Leonardo tells her that if the answer were so simple, he would have gone long ago, but unfortunately that can't be the solution, tied as they are to one another. He asks her to please leave, promising he'll visit her as soon as he can. To add to Leonardo's miseries, his father-in-law, bored with the parliamentary proceedings, chooses this moment to turn up. Guglielmo Groa doesn't know he is confronting another father in his son-in-law, who, like him, must protect his daughter. He believes his son-in-law has gone down a wrong path and can be steered back with a little tact and cash, and he offers to help and invites his confidence. Leonardo is tired of lying and confesses his guilt but says he has already been punished enough and refuses as unnecessary his father-in-law's help, as well as his preaching. Groa believes the punishment Leonardo speaks of is the work he is condemned to, and he rebukes him harshly. When Ersilia arrives, too late, her husband and father are about to come to blows. At Ersilia's appearance, Leonardo, overexcited and trembling, hurriedly gathers up papers from his desk and takes off. Groa is about to leap on him, roaring: "Well, now, you don't want to be reasonable?" But Ersilia stops him with the cry: "He has a daughter, Papa, he has a daughter! How can he be reasonable?"

The first act could end with this cry. At the beginning of the second act, a scene between the father and daughter. Both have been waiting in vain for Leonardo to come home that evening. Ersilia then reveals to her father all she has suffered and how she was deceived, how and why she silently adjusted to that pain. She almost defends her husband because, when he had to choose between her and his daughter, he ran to his daughter. Home is where the children are! Her father becomes indignant; he rages; he wants to leave at once, and when Leonardo turns up to get his books and papers, he asks him to stay; he himself will go away at once. Leonardo is confused, not knowing how to interpret his father-in-law's sudden invitation to stay. Ersilia comes in to say she has nothing to do with that invitation and he can leave if he wants. Then Leonardo cries and tells his wife about his torment and regret and his admiration and gratitude for her. Ersilia asks why he is suffering when he is with his daughter, and Leonardo answers that that woman wants to take her from him because he doesn't earn enough and she doesn't want to see him anymore in that upset condition. "Oh, yes?" shouts Ersilia. "She would like that? Well, then . . ." Her plan takes shape. She understands that she can have her husband back *only this way,* that is, on the condition that he can have his daughter with him. She keeps quiet about it, and when he begs her forgiveness, she assents, but at the same time pulls free of his grasp and makes him leave. "No, no," she says to him. "You can't stay here now! Two houses, no. With me here and your daughter there, no! Go, go! I know what you want. Go!" And she makes him leave, and as he goes out she breaks into tears of joy.

The third act should take place in the nest of thorns, in Elena Orgera's house. Leonardo has come to visit his daughter, but has forgotten to bring the present he promised her. The little girl, Dinuccia, has cried herself to sleep waiting for him. Leonardo says he will come back soon with the toy and goes away. The girl, now five years old, wakes up; she comes onstage and asks about her papa and wants her mother to tell her about the present he will bring: a farm with little trees, sheep, a dog, and shepherd. The doorbell rings. "Here he is!" her mother says. And the little girl runs to open the door. She soon returns in confusion with a veiled signora. It is Ersilia Arciani, who saw her husband leave the house and doesn't realize he will be back shortly. Elena, however, suspects a plot between the two to nab the girl. She shouts, threatens to call for help, curses, becomes frantic. In vain Ersilia tries to calm her, to show her that her suspicion is unfounded, and that she neither wants nor is capable of violence; that she came to have a heart-to-heart talk, for the good of her child who, if adopted, would be free of the shadow of guilt and would become rich and happy. Therefore it was pointless for her to pretend he would abandon his child if she didn't want to give her up. The little girl left the door open in her confusion at seeing a woman standing there instead of her father, and at that point Leonardo enters, stunned by the sight of his wife there, and finds himself in the midst of the quarrel between the two women. The child hears her father's voice and knocks on the door of the bedroom where Elena had run as soon as Ersilia Arciani took off her veil. Now Elena furiously throws open the door, takes the little one in her arms, and screams at the two to get out immediately, get out! At this outburst, a shaken Leonardo turns to his wife and urges her to forget that inhuman attempt and leave. Ersilia goes away. By this time Elena, who has seen him chase his wife out, is overcome by confusion and dismay and would like Leonardo to run after his wife at once and stay with her forever. But Leonardo, at the end of his rope, yells "No!" and takes the little one on his lap, gives her the gift, and begins to set up in the box the farm, the little trees, the sheep, the shepherd, the dog, amid Dinuccia's laughter, shouts of joy, and happy, childish questions. Hearing the child's questions and the anguished father's answers, Elena thinks over everything the woman had said about the future of her little girl, and in tears begins to ask Leonardo, absorbed in his daughter's joy, some questions: "She talked about adoption . . . but is it possible?" Leonardo doesn't answer but continues to talk to the child about the sheep and dog. After a few minutes Elena asks another question, or makes a bitter reflection about herself or Dinuccia, if ever she . . . Leonardo can't take anymore. He jumps to his feet, snatches up his daughter, and shouts: "You're giving her to me?"

"No! No! No!" Elena cries abruptly, tearing her from him and falling on her knees before the child: "It's impossible, no! I can't now. I can't now! Get out! Get out! Maybe later . . . who knows! If I have the strength. For her sake! But now get out! Get out! Get out!"

Yes, this could be the play. She saw everything clearly, every detail in the construction of the scenes. But it irked her that it was at Baldani's suggestion. And she didn't feel the least bit drawn to it.

She had never worked like this, constructing her work by will. Instead, barely intuited, the work had always imposed its will on her, without her having to provoke her spirit to move. Each work had always moved of its own accord, because it wanted to, and all she had ever done was docilely obey and lovingly follow this will of life at its every spontaneous turn. Now that she wanted to do it, and had to get it to move, she didn't know where to begin. She felt dry and empty, and in that aridity and emptiness she was miserable.

Every time she looked at Giustino (who didn't dare ask how her work was going, pretending he knew she was back at it and doing everything possible to make her think he was certain of it, keeping out of her way, keeping Èmere quiet, keeping her free of household concerns) she became so exasperated that she would have blown her top if her nausea over his other vulgar ways hadn't prevented it. She would have liked to tell him off:

"Stop it! Stop all this pretending! I'm not doing a thing and you know it! I can't do it, and I don't know how to do it. I've already told you! Èmere can whistle in his shirtsleeves while he works, overturn the chairs, and break all this famous Ducrot furniture: that would suit me fine, my dear boy! If I could, I would break up everything, everything, everything in this house and even tear down the walls!"

So many years ago in Taranto she had noticed something when her father had wanted to have her first short stories published. For a much less serious reason—that is, the thought of the praise she would receive for those stories—had blocked her from writing anything new, upsetting her so much that for nearly a year she couldn't put pen to paper. Now she sensed the same confusion, the same anxiety, the same consternation, but a hundred times worse. Instead of spurring her on, the recent success had numbed her; instead of raising her spirits, it had crushed and prostrated her. And when she tried to work up some enthusiasm, she immediately felt that the warmth generated was artificial, and when she tried to get rid of that sense of discouragement and prostration, she felt herself grow stiff with the effort, shallow and ineffectual. As could be expected, that success had encouraged her to redouble her efforts. But now, so as not to overdo it, its opposite appears: the arid grind, the skeletal bareness and rigidity.

And so, like a skeleton, with that arid, forced exertion, the new play came out painfully stiff and lifeless.

"But you're wrong. It's going beautifully!" Baldani told her when she read him the first act and part of the second, just to keep her husband quiet. "It's the character of this stupendous creature of yours, of Ersilia Arciani. It's her austere reserve that makes the play seem stiff to you. It's going very well, believe me. Ersilia Arciani's personality and ways have to control every aspect of a work like that. You're on the right track. Keep it up."

4

To make up for her lack of inspiration, Silvia felt she needed another guide and other advice.

Everyone had noticed the absence of Maurizio Gueli that inaugural evening. Many—and certainly not without malicious intent—had asked Giustino that evening: "And Gueli? Isn't he coming?"

Giustino in reply: "Oh, is he in Rome? I heard he was at his villa in Monteporzio."

Silvia was asked about Gueli, too, particularly by a few women feigning nonchalance. Silvia knew that out of jealously or envy, or, in any event, to wound her, the women and literati would sooner or later begin to speak ill of her. Besides, her own husband was the first to give them the excuse and material for malicious talk. She realized by now that with such a husband it would be nearly impossible to remain free of suspicion. Her own pride would eventually cause her to arouse suspicion, because she could no longer submit to the ridicule he heaped on her in front of everyone and keep pretending not to notice it. Somehow she had to show she felt either pain or spite (which perhaps might even make things worse because it would be too disheartening, and then everyone would take the opportunity to make her feel even worse). Or she had to show the same pleasure as the others, but then, even if she were partially saved from humiliation, she couldn't expect to be free from their harshest criticism. Can a woman openly mock her husband with impunity? Anyway, she couldn't do it intentionally or hypocritically. But she was afraid her own pride might make her do it against her will, by some unavoidable reaction. No, no. Really, there was no way she could go on being frank and honest under these conditions.

She was happy about Gueli's absence that evening of the inauguration. Happy—not because it gave the backbiters less to talk about, everyone having already noticed Gueli's interest in her, but because she didn't want to see him after that letter he had sent her in Cargiore. She still wasn't sure why. But the thought that Gueli's interest, obvious even to her and for a reason that had angered her from the beginning, had given rise to the gossip wounded her more than any other suspicion about Betti or Luna or Baldani, or anyone else.

She would never deceive her husband with anyone. As much as her composure had been shattered by the tumult of so many new thoughts and feelings, and as angry as she was, her disrespect for her husband's

159

behavior could never incite her to revenge. This she could still believe of herself: that no passion, no rebellious impulse, would ever overwhelm her to the point of being unfaithful. If tomorrow she could not continue living with her husband under these conditions; if, not defenseless, but almost goaded and pushed into it, with her heart not only void of affection for him but disgusted and drowning in nausea and sorrow; if she felt overcome by some desperate passion, she would not deceive him, ever. She would tell her husband and preserve her loyalty at whatever cost.

Unfortunately nothing in that house had the power to hold her with the murmur of old memories. The house had almost nothing to do with her and would be easy to leave. Everything around her constantly aroused images of a false, artificial, vacuous, fatuous life to which, unpersuaded by any affectionate feelings, she had not become accustomed, and which the absolute necessity of her work made odious. She was not even allowed the satisfaction of having her hard work at least serve to please someone else, if not her, who would be grateful. But on top of that, it was she who had to be grateful to her husband, who treated her as a farmer treats his ox that pulls the plow, as the driver treats the horse that pulls the wagon, both taking credit for the good plowing and the nice trip and then wanting to be thanked for the hay and stall.

Now she could take no notice of or worry about the more or less sincere interest that Baldani, Luna, and even Betti showed her—all those long-haired, ultramodish young writers and journalists; however, she was afraid of the interest shown by Gueli, who like herself was wrapped in a misery that was tragic and ridiculous at the same time, that took his breath away (so he had written). She was afraid of Gueli because more than the others he could read what was in her heart, and because in this woeful time, offended by Baldani's cold and arrogant conceit, she felt such acute and urgent need for his presence and advice.

Closed there in her study, wide-eyed and in a state of agitation, she caught herself following thoughts that made her shudder with horror.

These thoughts were like an easy staircase on which she could descend to her ruin; they were a sequence of justifications to calm her old conscience, to hide what her old conscience still represented to her as guilt, and to attenuate the condemnation of others.

Gueli's austere gravity and age wouldn't arouse suspicions that she, out of some perversion, saw a lover in him instead of a worthy and almost paternal guide, a noble, ideal companion. And perhaps Gueli looked for the same in her, and through her would find the strength to break the sorry bond with that woman who had oppressed him for years.

And her son?

This word intruding itself on her turbid musings scattered them for a moment. But the thought of her son anxiously brought back memories of an orderly life, chaste duties, a holy intimacy that not she but others had wanted to shatter violently.

If she could have clung to her son who had been torn away from her, and not think about or expect anything else, she would undoubtedly have found in her child the strength to involve herself entirely in her maternal role and be nothing but a mother. Then she would have found the strength to resist the temptation of art, and her husband would have had no excuse to offend her and reduce her to desperation with that passion for making money and that show of bravura.

She could continue to live with her husband only under one condition, that is, by giving up her writing. But was that possible now? Not any longer. Since he had no other employment except as agent for her work, she was forced to work, but she couldn't go on like this. She could be neither a mother nor work anymore. Work was mandatory? Well, then, get away from there! Get away from him! He could have the house and all the rest. She couldn't go on like this. But what would become of her?

This question threw her into confusion, and she drew back in horror. But what joy could come from realizing it was all in her imagination? Soon after, she fell back into those turbid thoughts, but, unfortunately, with less guilt because of her husband's stupid arrogance, which continued to importune her whenever he saw her restlessly slacking off work.

That is why, when finally Maurizio Gueli appeared suddenly and unexpectedly at the little villa with a strange, resolute expression and behaving strangely, looking into her eyes and treating Giustino's bows, ceremony, and hearty welcome with obvious disdain, she suddenly saw she was lost. Fortunately, while listening to her husband chatter on with Gueli without understanding a thing, she, at a certain point, had the strong and vivid impression of almost being pushed and shoved and pulled by her hair to do something mad. She was so ashamed of her state of mind, and felt so dishonored by it, that she was able to react fiercely against Gueli, who, emboldened by her disturbed manner, turned bitterly against her husband and in her presence nearly treated him like a common exploiter.

After his unexpected outburst, Gueli seemed dazed.

"I understand . . . I understand . . . I understand . . ." he said, closing his eyes, with a tone and air of such intense, profound, desperate bitterness that it suddenly became clear to Silvia what he had understood without scorn or offense.

And then he abruptly left.

Giustino, on the one hand confused and resentful, and on the other mortified by the way Gueli had gone away, and unwilling to defend himself or criticize Gueli, decided to rid himself of this perplexity by scolding his wife for the violent manner in which . . . But before he could reproach her, Silvia faced up to him, trembling and profoundly disturbed, shouting: "Go away! Shut up! Or I'll jump out the window!"

The order and threat were so ferocious and peremptory, her expression and voice so changed, that Giustino hunched his shoulders and slunk out of the study.

He thought his wife had gone insane. What in the world had happened to her? He didn't know her anymore! "*I'll jump out the window.* . . . *Shut up! . . . go away!*" She had never talked to him like that. . . . Women! Do too much for them . . . And look what happens! "*Go away! Shut up! . . .*" As if she didn't get where she was because of him! If it wasn't insanity, it was something much worse—ingratitude.

162

With his narrow, turned-up nose, Giustino, wounded to the quick, tried to make sense of it all. But yes, of course, yes! Now she selfishly wanted to make him feel the necessity of her work, when for her—he —without ever complaining, without ever giving himself a moment's rest, had taken on so much, and for her, so he could devote himself entirely to her, he had given up his job without hesitation! That was it: she no longer thought she owed everything to him. The way she saw it, he was unemployed and waiting for her work, and she took advantage of it by treating him like a servant: *"Go away! Shut up!"*

Well, for less than a year . . . no, what was he saying? He'd like to see her without him for less than a month, with a play to produce or with a contract to settle with some publisher! Then she'd find out if she needed him. . . .

But no! She had to know this. . . . It must be something else! The change since she came back from Cargiore, the discontent, the restlessness, the tantrums, all that bitterness toward him . . . Or did she perhaps seriously entertain the thought that he and Signora Barmis . . . ?

Giustino stretched his neck and screwed the corners of his mouth down to express his amazement at that doubt, shrugged, and continued thinking.

The fact was that just after she returned from Cargiore and saw those two damned twin bedrooms Signora Barmis had wanted, she seemed to turn away from him, as if she had suspected it was Signora Barmis's idea to keep them separated. Maybe her pride and jealousy wouldn't let her show this rancorous feeling openly, and that was the way she vented her feelings.

But good heavens, how could she imagine him capable of such a thing? If at the table he had seemed displeased by Signora Barmis's brusque departure, this displeasure—she should have understood— was only because she would be missing the wise advice and useful instruction a woman of such taste and experience could have given her. Because he understood that she couldn't remain so stubbornly withdrawn, so alone, without friends. She didn't want to work, she didn't like the house, she probably had unworthy suspicions about him: she didn't want to see anyone or go out for a little fun. . . . What kind of life was that? The other day when a letter came from Cargiore in which his mother spoke of her grandchild with such tenderness, she had burst into tears, into tears. . . .

After several days of his wife's sulking, Giustino mulled over the idea of bringing the baby to Rome with a wet nurse. It was hard on him, too, to keep the baby so far away, but not for the baby, who couldn't be in better hands. He thought that her child would certainly fill the emptiness she was feeling in that house and even in her soul at that moment. But he also had other things to think about, other compelling necessities, many undertakings contracted in view of the new works that she would have to do. Now, if it was so hard for her to work with her hands free, imagine how it would be with the baby there, who would absorb all her time with maternal cares. . . .

Suddenly a long-awaited notice came to distract Giustino from this and every other thought. In Paris *The New Colony*, translated by Desroches, would be performed early next month. In Paris! In Paris! He had to go.

Giving himself over to the frenzy of preparation, armed with that telegram from Desroches calling him to Paris, he started off on his rounds from one newspaper office to the other. And every morning on the desk in the study and at noon on the dining room table and at night on the nightstand in the bedroom Silvia found three or four newspapers at a time, not only from Rome, but also from Milan, Turin, Naples, Florence, Bologna, where those Parisian performances were announced as a new and grand event, a new triumph for Italian creativity.

Silvia pretended not to notice them. But he didn't have the slightest doubt that this new preparatory work of his had had a big effect on her when one night he heard his wife in the next room suddenly get out of bed and dress to go shut herself in the study. At first, to tell the truth, he was a bit apprehensive. But after peeking through the keyhole and seeing that she was sitting at the desk in the attitude she usually struck when she was inspired to start writing, he managed, by some miracle, to contain his overwhelming joy, just as he was in his nightshirt and barefoot in the dark. There she was! There she was! Back to work! As before! At work! At work!

And in his fever of anticipation he didn't sleep that night either; and when day came he ran with outstretched hands to Èmere to keep him absolutely quiet, and immediately sent him to the kitchen to order the cook to prepare coffee and breakfast for the signora, immediately! As soon as it was ready: "Pst! Listen . . . Knock, but softly, softly, and ask if she wants . . . but softly, eh? Softly, please!"

Èmere returned shortly with the tray in hand, saying the signora didn't want anything.

"Well, all right! Quiet . . . let . . . the signora work . . . quiet everyone!"

He was a little concerned when even at noon Èmere, sent with the same orders to announce that it was time to eat, returned to say the signora didn't want anything.

"What's she doing? Writing?"

"She's writing, yes, sir."

"What did she say to you?"

"I don't want anything, go away!"

"And she's still writing?"

"She's writing, yes, sir."

"All right, all right; we'll let her write. . . . Quiet everyone!"

"Will the signore have something at the table in the meanwhile?" Èmere asked in a whisper.

Giustino was very hungry after a sleepless night, but to sit at the table alone while his wife was working on an empty stomach didn't seem right. He was dying to know what she was working on with such fervor. On the play? Certainly on the play. But did she want to finish it all in one sitting? Did she want to wait until she was finished to eat? Even this was crazy. . . .

Toward three in the afternoon, Silvia left her study exhausted and groggy and threw herself on her bed in the darkened room. Giustino ran to the desk to look: he was disappointed. What he found was a short story. A long short story. On the last page, under the signature, was written: *For Senator Borghi*. Without any pleasure he started reading it, but after the first few lines he began to get interested. . . . So that's what it's about! Cargiore . . . Don Buti with his telescope . . . Signor Martino . . . Mamma's history . . . the suicide of Prever's brother . . . A strange short story, fantastical, full of bitterness and sweetness at the same time, pulsing with all the impressions that she had had during that unforgettable sojourn up there. She must have had the vision suddenly in the middle of the night. . . .

Never mind if it wasn't the play! It was something, anyway. And now it was up to him! He would show her what could be done with what little he had in hand. The senator should pay at least five hundred lire for that short story: five hundred lire immediately or nothing.

That evening he went to see Borghi at the editorial office of *Vita Italiana*.

Perhaps Maurizio Gueli had been there earlier and had spoken ill of him to Romualdo Borghi. Giustino wasn't bothered by the fastidious coldness of his reception. In fact he was pleased because this way, with all former debts of gratitude removed, he could be equally cold and clearly dictate the terms. Borghi could think whatever he pleased about him; his only interest was in showing his wife what she owed to him alone.

A few days after the publication of the short story in *Vita Italiana*, Silvia received a note of enthusiastic admiration and heartfelt congratulations from Gueli.

Victory! Victory! Victory! As soon as Giustino glanced at the note, frantic with joy, he ran to get his hat and cane: "I'm going to his home to thank him! You see? Self-invited."

Silvia came up to him. "Where? When?" she fumed. "This is nothing but a note of congratulations. I forbid you to . . ."

"Good heavens!" he interrupted her. "Is it so hard to understand? After the scene he made, he writes you a note like this. . . . Let me do it, my dear! Let me do it! I understood that Baldani was a bother. I understood that, didn't I? And you see I didn't let him come again. But Gueli is something else! Gueli is a maestro, a real maestro! You will read him your play, you will follow his advice, you'll both closet yourselves here, you'll work together. . . . Tomorrow I have to leave; let me leave in peace! A short story, all right; but I'm worried about the play, my dear! Right now we need a play, a play, a play! Leave this to me, please!"

And he took off for Gueli's house.

Silvia didn't try to detain him any longer. She screwed her face into a grimace of nausea and hate, wringing her hands.

Ah, he wanted a play? Well, then, after so much comedy, he would have his drama.

6 ✸ THE FLIGHT

1

Maurizio Gueli was going through one of the cruelest moments of his miserable life. For the ninth or tenth time, at the end of his patience, he had found the strength in his desperation to wrench his head out of the halter. This animal comparison was of his own making, and he repeated it to himself with pleasure. For two weeks Livia Frezzi had been in the villa at Monteporzio, alone, and he in Rome, alone.

He said "alone," but not free, knowing from sorry experience that the more strongly he insisted he was through with that woman forever, the sooner came the day of reconciliation. Because if it was true that he could no longer live with her, it was also true he couldn't live without her.

Gueli had come from Genoa to Rome some twenty years ago at a judicious moment, right after the publication of his *Demented Socrates,* when his fame as a strange and profound writer was indisputably established in Italy and elsewhere. As a writer of inventive brilliance he juggled the most weighty ideas and erudite knowledge with the graceful agility of an acrobat. He had been welcomed into the home of his old friend Angelo Frezzi, a mediocre historian, who had recently married his second wife, Livia Maduri. At that time Gueli was thirty-five, and Livia little more than twenty.

However, Livia Frezzi had not fallen in love with Gueli's fame, as so many believed. In fact, from the beginning she had shown herself to be so coldly disdainful of his fame and his euphoria over it at that time that out of spite he immediately got it into his head to conquer her. This forced him to close his eyes to his obligations toward his friend and host with the same hardness with which she belligerently and openly faced her husband, without taking into account his old friendship for him, and without any regard for his hospitality.

In his defense, Maurizio Gueli remembered that in the beginning he had really tried to leave in order not to betray the friendship and hospitality. But by now his vexation with himself and everyone else, his disgust with his cowardice toward that woman, and the shame of his slavery had filled his soul with such bitterness, and had made him so cruelly merciless with himself, that he could no longer allow himself this hypocrisy. Even though he remembered his attempt to flee, deep down he knew it didn't really count in his favor, because if he really had wanted to save himself and not betray his friend, he would undoubtedly have turned his back and left that hospitable house.

But instead . . . Of course! That farce involving the four or five or ten or twenty conflicting personalities that he believed each man harbors in himself, distinct and alterable, according to his own capacity, had played itself out in him for the thousandth time. With marvelous clarity he had always been able to pinpoint the varied, simultaneous play of characters going on inside himself and other people.

We assume one of those many personalities, often unconsciously, as a pretense suggested by the advantage or imposed by the spontaneous need of wanting to be one way instead of another, of appearing to ourselves to be different from what we are. And in pursuing this personality we accept the most favorable fictional interpretation of all our acts that, hidden from our consciousness, slyly works on the others. We tend to marry ourselves for a lifetime to one personality, the most comfortable, the one that brings as a dowry the characteristic most suited to attaining our goal. But outside the honest conjugal roof of our conscious mind we are apt to have affairs and encounters with the other rejected personalities, who give birth to bastard actions and thoughts that we quickly try to legitimize.

Didn't his old friend Angelo Frezzi notice that it didn't take much to persuade Gueli to stay, after he had expressed his wish to leave, a wish doubly and astutely fabricated, since he wanted to stay, and had disguised it as regret for being unable to please his wife? If Angelo Frezzi had noticed the fabrication, then why had he gone to such lengths to make him stay? No doubt he had performed a farce, too! Two personalities, the social and the moral: the first made him go around in a frock coat, putting his friendliest smile on his thick pale lips strung with saliva, while the second often made him lower his watery, anguished eyelids over his bluish, egg-shaped, veined, impudent eyes with languid dignity. The two had flaunted their virtue in him, maintaining with frowning firmness that his friend, come worthily into such fame, would never stoop to betray his friend and host. At the same time a third little character, shrewd and derisive, whispered to the old man so softly that he could very well pretend not to listen:

"Bravo, old boy, make him stay! You know very well how lucky you would be if he would take away this second wife, so wrong for you, so stuck up, bitter, hard, and stubborn—even against you, poor man, too old, oh, too old for her! Keep insisting, and the more you pretend to believe him incapable of betraying you, the more trusting you show yourself to be, the easier it will be to make a trifle into a scandal."

In fact, Angelo Frezzi, although without the slightest reason, at least as far as his wife was concerned, had immediately made accusations of betrayal. A year had to pass before Livia, who had gone to live alone, gave herself to Gueli.

Over that year he became bound in such a way as never to be free again, capitulating entirely, committing himself to accepting and following her every thought and feeling without any compromise.

Now he pretended to believe that this bond was forged by the unshakable duty assumed toward this woman who had lost her status and reputation for him, driven out by her husband while still blameless. Without a doubt he felt this responsibility; yet deep down he knew that it was not the only reason for his enslavement. Then what was the real reason? Perhaps the pity that he, sound of mind, and with a clear conscience that he had never given her any reason for jealousy, had

170

to feel for that woman of doubtful mental stability? Oh, yes, the pity was real, just as the sense of duty was real. But more than a reason for his enslavement, wasn't this pity perhaps an excuse, a noble excuse, to camouflage the burning need that dragged him back to that woman after a month or two of separation, during which time he had even pretended to believe that, at his age, after having given his best to her for so many years, he would no longer be able to take up life with any other woman? These considerations also were true, yes, very well founded, these considerations, but, weighing them on the scales buried in his innermost consciousness, he knew that his age and dignity were also excuses and not reasons. In fact, if another woman, unsought, had had the power to attract him, liberating him from his subjection to the one who had inspired such a deep and invincible loathing of every other embrace and had kept him in such a reclusive state that not only could he have no contact with another woman, but he couldn't even think about it—then, yes, he certainly would have cared nothing about age, dignity, duty, pity, or anything else. So it came down to that—the real reason for his enslavement was this reclusive timidity brought about by Livia Frezzi's bewitching power.

No one was able to understand how or why that woman had been able to exercise such a continuous, powerful fascination over Gueli, or rather such a fatal spell. Granted, Livia Frezzi was a beautiful woman, but her rigid bearing, her severe, hostile, incurious expression, her almost ostentatious disregard for any common courtesy, detracted from any natural grace and charm. It seemed, or rather it was obvious, that everything she did was calculated to displease. This was precisely the source of her fascination; and the only one who could understand it was the only one she wanted to please.

That which other beautiful women give to a man in private is so little compared to what they lavish on other men all day long, and this little is given with the same grace and pleasantries they shower on so many others; therefore these others, though not sharing in that intimacy, can easily imagine it. Thus, just by thinking about it, the joy of possessing those women vanishes.

Livia Frezzi had given Maurizio Gueli the joy of sole and total possession. No one could know her or imagine her the way he knew and saw her in moments of abandon. She belonged entirely to one man — was unapproachable to all men except one.

However, at the same time she wanted this one man to be everything for her: wrapped up in her forever, exclusively hers, not just sensually, but with his heart and mind — even his eyes. To look at another woman, even without the slightest ulterior motive, was almost a crime as far as she was concerned. She didn't look at anyone, ever. Going beyond the bounds of the coolest courtesy was a crime. *Displiceas aliis, sic ego tutus ero.*[2]

Jealousy? What jealousy! Seriousness of purpose demanded such behavior, just as honesty did. She was serious and honest, not jealous. Everyone should behave as she did.

To make her happy, he had to force himself to live only for her, excluding himself entirely from the company of others. And even this wasn't enough: if the others, though ignored and unseen — or perhaps because of it — showed the slightest interest or curiosity in a life so set apart, for a demeanor so unfriendly and haughty, she would be critical just of him, as if it were his fault when other people paid any kind of attention to him.

Maurizio Gueli was helpless to prevent this. No matter what he did, he was so well known that he could not pass unnoticed. The most he could do was not look, but how could he keep others from looking at him? He received invitations, letters, tributes from everywhere. He could never accept any of those invitations, and he never responded to the letters and tributes; but he also had to give an accounting to her of everything he received.

She realized that all this interest and curiosity was due to his fame as a writer; however, it was at this fame and at literature itself that her anger was most fiercely aimed, armed with bristling mockery. She harbored the most morbid and bitter hatred for it.

2 A line from the *Elegies* of Tibullus (IV, XIII, 6): "Displeasing to others, so I will be safe and secure."

Livia Frezzi was firmly convinced that the literary profession was not a serious or honest business; that it was indeed the most ridiculous and dishonest of professions, as it consisted of always being in the limelight, trading on one's vanity, begging for fatuous gratifications, yearning for the praise and delight of others. According to the way she saw it, only a foolish woman could take pride in the fame of the man she lived with, or would feel happy thinking that with all the admired and desired women available this man belonged, or was said to belong, to her alone. How could this man belong to just one woman if he wanted to please all men and women, if day and night he knocked himself out to be praised and admired, mixing with people to get as much pleasure as he could, continually calling attention to himself so he would be pointed out and talked about? If he continually exposed himself to temptation? With that irresistible desire to please others, how could he possibly resist those temptations?

Many times—in vain—Gueli had tried to convince her that a true artist (as he was or at least thought himself to be) didn't go looking for silly satisfactions, nor did he yearn to receive pleasure from others, that he was not a clown bent on entertaining people and being admired by women, and that he only enjoyed the praise of the select few he recognized as capable of understanding him. However, overcome with enthusiasm for his defense, he often lost his case by just one point. As, for example, if he happened to add, as a general consideration, that it was only human (and anyway, there was nothing wrong with it) for anyone—not just a writer—to feel a certain satisfaction when his work was well received and valued by other people, whatever it might be. Oh, yes, other people! Other people! Other people! She had never had such a thought! He saw nothing wrong with this? Well, just what was wrongdoing, according to him? Who could ever see clearly into a literary man's conscience, a man whose profession was a continual game of make-believe? Pretending, always pretending, to give the appearance of reality to unreal things! And all that austerity was undoubtedly a facade, all that dignified honesty he affected. Who knows how many skipped heartbeats and inner quaking thrills, shivers of excitement there were because of a mysterious glance, a tiny little laugh from a woman passing on the street! Age? Age has nothing to do with it! Does the heart of a literary man grow older? The older he gets, the more ridiculous he becomes.

At her incessant scorn and fierce denigration, Maurizio Gueli felt his guts twist and his heart turn over. Because at the same time he sensed the awful ridiculousness of his tragedy: to be the victim of a real madness, to suffer martyrdom for imaginary wrongs, for what were not wrongs at all and which, besides, he had been careful not to commit, even at the cost of seeming impolite, proud, and bad-tempered, in order not to arouse her slightest suspicion. Nevertheless it seemed that he committed them unknowingly, who knows when or where.

Obviously he was two people: one for himself, another for her. And this other person that she saw, slyly catching every look, every smile, every gesture, the sound of his voice itself, not just the meaning of his words, twisting and falsifying everything about him, in her own eyes this person came to life as a miserable phantom, the only one she knew. Gueli himself no longer existed. He existed only for the unworthy, inhuman torment of seeing himself living in that phantom, and only in it; he racked his brains without success for ways to destroy it. She no longer believed in him; she saw him only as that phantom and, as was reasonable, showed her hate and scorn for it.

So alive was this imaginary figure she had created, assuming such a solid, obvious substance in her sick imagination, that he could almost see it living his life, but undeservedly distorted. It had his thoughts, but they were twisted. It had his every expression, word, every gesture. It was so alive for him that he almost reached the point of doubting himself, of thinking perhaps he really was that man. And by now he was so conscious of the alteration that his slightest movement would have undergone immediate appropriation by that other self, so that he almost seemed to be living with two souls, to be thinking with two heads at the same time, in one sense for himself and in another sense for that other being.

"Now, then," he would suddenly realize, "if I say such and such, my words will assume another meaning for her."

He was never wrong, because he knew perfectly well that the other self that lived in her and for her was as alive as he himself was alive. Perhaps it was even more alive, because whereas he lived only to suffer, that other lived in her mind to enjoy itself, to deceive, to pretend, to do all sorts of things, each more despicable than the other. He repressed every action, stifled even the most innocent desires, forbade himself everything, even smiling at a vision of art that might pass through his mind, even speaking or looking. But the other one (who knows how or when) found a way, with the insane inconsistency of an illusory phantom, to escape from that jail and run around the world making all kinds of trouble.

Maurizio Gueli could do no more than he already had done to keep the peace: he had retired from life and had even renounced his art, not writing a line in more than ten years. But his sacrifice had been made for nothing. She couldn't appreciate it. To her, art was a dishonest game, no activity for a responsible man. She hadn't read even one page of his books, and she bragged about it. She was totally unaware of his mind's life or his finer attributes. In him she only saw the man, a man so violated, so excluded from any other life, so deprived of any other satisfaction—because of all his renunciations, deprivations, and sacrifices—he was forced to seek in her that single compensation, that single outlet she alone could give. And this was the reason for that unhappy concept she had formed of him, that phantom that she had created out of him and that only she saw, not realizing in the least that he was that way just for her, because it was the only way he had found to be with her. Nor could Gueli point this out to her for fear of offending her by his too meticulous honesty. Often besieged and made indignant by her own continual suspicions, she denied him even that compensation; and then he would become even more exasperated at the cowardice of his slavery. At other times, when she became more pliable and he took advantage of it, a greater irritation would seize him, a shiver of indignation would shake him from the grim weariness of satiated sensual pleasure. He would see at what cost he obtained those sensual satisfactions from a woman who opposed all sensuality, and who brutalized him besides, not allowing him to live the life of the mind, and who condemned him to the perversity of that lascivious union. And if at those times she was so obtuse as to begin her mockery again, a fierce rebellion would break out.

It was precisely in these moments of weariness that the temporary separations would take place. Either he would go to Monteporzia and she would remain in Rome, or the other way around, both of them very resolved never to get back together again. But in Rome or away from it, he always provided for her, as she had no other means of support. Even though no longer as wealthy as his father had left him (he had been a senior partner in one of the biggest transoceanic travel agencies), Maurizio Gueli was still very well off.

Nevertheless, as soon as he was alone he felt disoriented in the life he had been excluded from for such a long time. He immediately felt his lack of roots and could in no way replant them, and not just because of his age. The idea that others had formed of him after so many years of Spartan seclusion weighed on him heavily, and vigilantly affected his behavior and habitual reserve. It condemned him to be what others believed and wanted him to be. The surprise he read in so many faces whenever he appeared in a place unusual for him, the sight of other people accustomed to living freely, and the notice covertly taken of his embarrassment and discomfort in facing the insolence of those fortunate people who never had to give an accounting of their time and actions, bothered him, disheartened and exasperated him. And he observed something else with a shudder, something downright monstrous: as soon as he was alone, he seemed to discover the other *him* in himself, truly alive in every step, every glance, every smile, every gesture, the one who lived in Livia Frezzi's morbid imagination, that miserable, detested phantom making fun of him, saying:

"Look at you. Now you go where you want, now you look where you please, even at women. Now you smile and move and you think you are doing it innocently? Don't you know that all of this is wicked, wicked, wicked? If she only knew! If she could see you now! You who have always denied it, you who have always told her you didn't want to go anywhere, to any public gathering, you didn't want to look at women, to smile. . . . But even if you don't do it, she'll always think you did. Well, then, you might as well do it. Go ahead and do it. It's all the same!"

No, he couldn't do it anymore; he didn't know how, he felt blocked, exasperated, by the unfairness of that woman's judgment. He saw the wrong in what he did—not for itself, but for her because she had for so many years accustomed him to thinking it wrong, things he had attributed to that other *him*, who, according to her, did it continually, even when he didn't do it, even when he forbade himself to do it in order to keep peace, as though it were truly wrong.

All this profusion of private admonitions generated such disgust and revulsion, such spiteful cowardice, and such dull, sour, black sadness that he immediately withdrew from the contact and sight of others and, again excluded and insignificant, terribly alone, he fell into thinking that his misery was both tragic and ridiculous, with no hope of relief. He didn't have the strength to lose himself in his work, the only thing that could save him. And then all those pretenses he used to rationalize his slavery would begin to resurface. They would come forward primarily because of instinctive need, made more and more urgent by his still strong virility, by the bewitching memory of her embraces.

And he would return to his chains.

2

He was just on the point of returning to her when Giustino Boggiolo came to invite him to their home, where Silvia—according to him— was anxiously waiting.

Maurizio Gueli lived in an old building on Via Ripetta, with a view of the river that he remembered flowing along its natural, steep banks, between oak trees; he also remembered the old wooden bridge thundering with every passing vehicle and, near the house, the wide stairs of the port and the Sicilian fishing boats full of wine that came to moor, and the songs that rose in the evenings from the floating taverns with lowered sails, the reflections of their long, red lights snaking through the black water. Now the steps and the wooden bridge, the

177

natural banks, and those majestic oaks had disappeared: a large new neighborhood stood there alongside the river enclosed within gray embankments. And like the river within those embankments, like the area itself with those straight, long streets, still unhallowed by time, over twenty years his life had become constricted, colorless, impoverished, and turbid.

Through the two large windows of his spartan study, which seemed like a room in a library, without pictures or artifacts, the walls covered with tall bookshelves crammed with books, came the last dazzling violet of twilight, flaming behind the cypresses on Monte Mario.

Sunk into a large leather armchair next to the large, heavy old desk, Maurizio Gueli frowned glumly for some time as he studied the little man who nearly evaporated before him in the violet splendor, the little man who came so smiling and confident to hound the destiny of two lives.

Already on two occasions Gueli had shown Silvia Roncella his esteem and his interest in her work and talent, by participating in the banquet in her honor soon after her arrival in Rome and going to greet her at the station after the success of her play. He had written to her the first time at Cargiore and had visited her recently at her home on Via Plinio. All these displays of esteem and interest had to take place during one separation or another from Livia Frezzi, and because of these expressions of regard he had more strongly felt his anxiety and impression of transgression and wrongdoing, for he had glimpsed in that young woman's spirit (so like his, though still wild and uncultivated), something that could free him from Livia Frezzi's influence. That is, if the wide age difference and her sense of duty—if not toward that unworthy husband, then certainly toward her son—hadn't made him consider it a crime just to think about it. And yet, in that letter sent to her at Cargiore, he had allowed himself to say more than he should have, and recently, during his visit to her home, he had let her know more than he had said. He had read in her eyes the same horror that he had of his own situation, along with the same terror of getting away from it, and he had admired the strength with which she had suddenly managed to get a hold of herself in his presence, almost turning him

178

out. Should he now believe what her husband was saying—that she was anxiously waiting for him? That meant, without a doubt, that she had made a violent, desperate resolution that she couldn't go back on. And had she really sent her husband to invite him? No. That was too out of character. The invitation undoubtedly followed the note of congratulations that he had written after reading her story in *Vita Italiana;* and that impatience to see him was perhaps her husband's invention.

Maurizio Gueli didn't want to admit it, but he clearly recognized that he had been the initiator, twice: the first time with his visit and then with that note. And as she had dismissed the first encouragement, almost offending him, it was natural that now, after the note, she would invite him.

Should he go? He could refuse. He could make up an excuse. Oh, the continuous violence that gripped his life for twenty years and the continuous exasperation of his soul urged him, as soon as he was left on his own, to commit excessive, heedless acts, to compromise—and to compromise himself.

In fact, what was for him an excessive and heedless act, a serious compromise, would have been an innocuous, a very ordinary and inconsequential act for anyone else: a visit, a note of congratulations. He had to consider them crimes and, as such, to keep them deep in the monstrous conscience that that woman had made for him, for which even the simplest and most innocent acts weighed like lead: a look, a smile, a word. . . .

Maurizio Gueli felt himself overcome by a rebellious impulse, a powerful rush of pride. At that moment his irritation focused on Livia Frezzi, the irritation for the wrong he believed he really had committed—first by his visit and then by the note. To get rid of that man waiting for an answer, he promised he would come.

"You have to encourage her!" Giustino now said to him as he was leaving. "Urge her, urge her, even force her . . . This blessed play! She's finished the second act; she just needs to finish the third, but she has it all thought out, and, believe me, it seems good. Even . . . even Baldani heard it and says it's. . . ."

"Baldani?"

By the tone in which Gueli asked this Giustino realized he had touched a nerve. Giustino didn't know that Paolo Baldani had recently unleashed a scathing series of articles in a Florentine newspaper about Gueli's entire literary and philosophical works, from the *Demented Socrates* to the *Roman Fables.*

"Yes . . . Yes, he came to see Silvia, and . . ." he acknowledged awkwardly, hesitantly, "Silvia really didn't want to see him. It was my idea, you know? To . . . to give her a nudge."

"Tell Signora Roncella that I will come this evening," Gueli broke in, seeing him out the door with a hard look.

Giustino was lavish with his bows and thanks.

"Because I'm leaving tomorrow for Paris," he wanted to add, already on the first landing, "to attend the . . ."

But Gueli didn't give him time to finish. He bowed his head slightly and closed the door.

That evening he went to Villa Silvia. He returned the next day after Giustino Boggiolo had left for Paris, and after that every day, either in the morning or afternoon.

They were both aware that the slightest act, the slightest concession, the slightest relaxation of scruple would turn their lives upside down.

But how long could they keep their resolve if they both felt so exasperated in their souls and each observed it so clearly in the other? If their eyes locked on contact, and their hands trembled at the thought of a fortuitous touch? If restraint kept them in such a state of anxious, unbearable suspense as to make them consider what they most feared and most wanted to avoid as a relief and liberation?

The mere fact that he came and she received him, and that they both stayed there together alone, though almost without looking at each other and without ever touching, was already a sinful concession for both of them, a compromise they came to feel was without remedy.

They both realized they were gradually, inevitably, giving in not to the passion they had for each other, but to a united effort to resist it and to keep each other at a distance, both feeling that their union would not really be what either wanted.

Oh, to be able to release one another from the odious conditions without having to do what struck her with disgust and horror and him with fear and remorse!

These emotional upheavals were caused by their having to commit a serious transgression more powerful than they, but essential, unavoidable, if they wanted to free each other. And they were put there to do it, trembling, ready, and reluctant.

Looming over him was the fierce shadow of that stiff, angry, harsh woman. Her words were already ringing in his ears: he "could never return to her, could never again lie or deny he had taken advantage of his freedom to get close to another woman: that woman there! Honest, isn't she? As honest as he, like him in every way. Oh, yes, that woman! That one, by taking his hand, could lead him back to art, to live in poetry, and his sluggish blood would be rekindled with the fire of youth. Well, then, why so timid? Come on! Ah, perhaps love . . . Yes! Love had stunned him. . . . Isn't that a lovely little hand, with those little blue veins branching out. . . . To put it on his forehead, to pass that little hand over his eyes . . . and kiss it, kiss it there on her pink nails . . . Those nails don't scratch, no. Nice little kitten, nice little kitten . . . Go on, just try to stroke her! Mew or bleat? Poor little lamb that a dreadful husband wanted to shear . . ." How could he face such mockery again? He heard those words as if Livia were standing behind him.

And behind her, nudging her on, Silvia felt her husband who had left her alone with Gueli and had gone off to Paris to make a spectacle of himself there, too, to turn into money the entertainment he offered the French actors, actresses, writers, and journalists there, too—certain that she would be writing a new play with Gueli's help. She wanted to write it! She wanted nothing more! And just as he was impervious to all the laughter, so he didn't care now if the gossips were suspicious of his wife, whom they would see Gueli visit during his absence. Gueli, now free of Livia Frezzi, Gueli whose interest in Silvia had already been such a topic of discussion.

Sticking to the task at hand, they both kept their tempest pent up inside, keeping a prudent distance from each other, concentrating on that new play whose title seemed to mock and goad them: *If Not This Way. . . .*

Was that why he suggested a change of title? The act of the protagonist, Ersilia Arciani, when she went to the house of her husband's lover to get his little girl, made him think of a hawk swooping down on a nest of baby birds. So perhaps the play could be called *The Hawk*.

But did the image of cruel greed that the hawk invoked suit the character of Ersilia Arciani, or the reasons and feelings that motivated her action? It wasn't suitable, according to Silvia. But she understood why he, with his suggestion for changing the title, wanted to alter the protagonist's character to suggest vengeance and an aggressive purpose in her action: he undoubtedly saw in the closed, austere character of Ersilia Arciani something of Livia Frezzi, and since he couldn't stand her having noble, blameless motives, he wanted to change her nature. However, if her entire nature were transformed, wouldn't that be another play? She would have to rewrite it, rethink it from the beginning.

He paid close attention to those sage explanations she made in a tone that clearly let him know she understood and didn't want to touch a still painful wound.

Newspapers from Rome, Milan, Turin had already published her husband's long conversations with correspondents from Paris, who, though commenting seriously on the play and on the Parisian public's avid interest in seeing it, worded it in a way that left no doubt as to the underlying mockery; they reveled in the prodigious activity, the zeal, the admirable fervor of that little man "who considered his wife's work so much his that it was only proper he receive some of her glory." Finally, Giustino's telegram came announcing the triumph, and following the telegram he sent one newspaper after another with the most influential critics' judgments, which were for the most part favorable.

Silvia kept Gueli from reading those newspapers in her presence, for both their sakes.

"No, no, please! I can't stand to hear any more about it! I swear I would give . . . I don't know, it all seems like such a small thing. I would give anything not to have written that play!"

In the meanwhile, Èmere came almost every hour to announce a new visitor. Silvia would have liked to have him tell everyone she wasn't home. But Gueli convinced her that would not look good. She would go down to the living room, and he would stay there, hidden in the study waiting for her, scanning those newspapers, or rather, thinking. In the meanwhile she would be downstairs with Baldani or Luni or Betti.

"Ah, youth!" Gueli once sighed at seeing her return to the study with a flushed face.

"No! What are you saying?" she erupted promptly and fiercely. "I'm fed up! I'm fed up! This has to stop. If you only knew how I treat them!"

Already enormous, heavy silences in which they felt their blood tremble and tingle and their souls fret in anxious expectation had fallen on their tired, forced conversation. He only needed to put a hand on hers: she would have left it there and leaned her head on his chest, hiding her face, and their destiny, by now inevitable, would have been sealed. So why delay it any longer? Ah, why indeed! Because each one could still think him- or herself to blame. The self-restraint continued, although privately they had hopelessly surrendered to each other.

The unthinkable moment had yet to arrive!

They could see themselves coming up to the outer edge of an act that would signal the end of their former life without having spoken a word of love, merely while discussing art like a student with her teacher. They would suddenly be at the beginning of a new life, lost, anxious, bewildered, not knowing which road to take at once so she, at least, could get far away from there.

They felt such an absolute need to get away, more out of self-pity than love, that their disgust with the dillydallying over details constrained them even more.

Of course, he too would have to leave a house that was chock-full of memories of that woman. Where to go? Some refuge had to be found, at least in the beginning, a haven in which to hide from the explosion of the inevitable scandal. The situation disheartened and disgusted them profoundly.

Didn't they have the right to live in peace, humanely, in the uncorrupted fullness of their dignity? Why lose heart? Why hide? Because neither her husband nor that woman would have accepted in silence the reasons they could have flung in their faces even before the betrayal, the assertion of their rights trampled on so long and in so many ways. Giustino and Livia would have argued, tried to stop them. . . . Another revulsion, stronger than before.

They were suspended and tethered in these thoughts, when Gueli — on the eve of Giustino's return from Paris — began a discussion that Silvia at once understood as a scheme to end their painful state.

That difficult play she had started and couldn't finish weighed on them like a curse. Up to this time the anxiety of their indecision had been entangled in discussions about its characters and scenes. Now, his suggestion that they put that play aside and write another one together — a play based on a vision that he had had many years ago of the Roman countryside, near Ostia, among the Sabine people, who come there to spend the winter in miserable huts — clearly signified the end of the indecision. And still more clearly she found him ready to put an end to all delay and face their new noble and industrious life when he invited her the next day, the very day her husband was to arrive, to go with him to see those places near Ostia. Those foreboding places toward the sea, where a solitary tower looms, Tor Bovacciana, beside the river crossed by a cable along which passes a service boat for ferrying some silent fisherman or hunter . . .

"Tomorrow?" she asked, her manner and voice expressing total acquiescence.

"Yes, tomorrow, tomorrow. When will he arrive?"

She knew at once who "he" was and responded: "At nine."

"Fine. I'll be here at nine-thirty. You don't need to say anything. I'll do the talking. We'll leave right after that."

No more was said. He rushed off; she was left shaking under the dark mystery of her new destiny.

The tower . . . the river crossed by a cable . . . the boat carrying the rare passerby through those menacing places . . .

Had she dreamed it?

Was that the haven, then? At Ostia . . . She didn't have to say any-thing. . . . Tomorrow!

She would leave everything here. Yes, everything, everything. She would write him. She wouldn't have to tell any lies. For this more than anything she was grateful to Gueli. Even when she left tomorrow she wouldn't have to lie. In that play, with that play he suggested, she would enter a noble new life, with art and in art. It was the way. It wasn't a means or a pretext for deceit. It was the way to get out, with-out lying and without shame, away from that hateful house no longer hers.

3

"Hurry, hurry, quickly, quickly: you won't get there on time!"

From the gate Giustino shouted this last recommendation to the two driving off in a carriage, expecting that Silvia at least, if not Gueli, would turn to wave at him. She didn't.

Exasperated by his wife's persistently haughty attitude, Giustino shrugged and went up to his room to wait for Èmere to tell him when his bath was ready.

"What a woman!" he was thinking. "To make that disgusted face even at such a kind invitation. The cathedral at Orvieto: wonderful! Old art . . . a subject for study."

To tell the truth, he really wasn't so very glad, because on that very day, in fact almost the moment he had come back from Paris, Gueli had come to invite his wife on that artistic excursion. But if Gueli hadn't known he was arriving that morning! Gueli had been out of sorts be-cause he had to go to Milan the next day and wouldn't have much time to show Silvia all the marvelous art there—in the cathedral at Orvieto.

Beautiful, beautiful was the Orvieto cathedral: or so he had heard . . . But of course it wouldn't have made a big impression on him, since he'd just come from Paris, but . . . old art, a subject for study . . .

How irritating that disgusted face. All the more because, confound it, Gueli had been kind enough to keep her company these past few days, and he had encouraged her so charmingly not to worry about her

185

husband's arrival just then. No doubt he had had a good time in Paris and so wouldn't mind if his wife had some recreation for a few hours, until evening. . . .

Giustino himself had even said: "I'll be happy for you to go!"

Giustino tapped his forehead with a finger, made a face, and crooned: "I don't waaant to. . . . I don't waaant to. . . ."

Èmere came to announce that his bath was ready.

"Good. I'm ready, too!"

In a short time he was delightfully stretched out in the white enamel tub, the water taking on a soft bluish tint. Thinking back over the sensational whirl of Parisian splendors in the clean quiet of his bright bathroom, he felt lucky. He felt this really was the reward of the victor.

Delightful also there in that warm bath was the sensation of tiredness reminding him how hard he had worked to earn that triumph.

Ah, that Parisian victory, that Parisian victory had been the crowning glory of all his work! Now he could say he was thoroughly satisfied, even happy.

All told, it was also a good thing that Silvia had gone on that trip. Considering how tired he was, and in the excitement of his arrival, he might have ruined the effect of all that he wanted to tell her.

Later, after his bath, he would have some refreshment and take a nap. Then, rested, in the evening he would make a complete report to his wife and Gueli of the "great things" in Paris. It would have been nice to have some journalists present so they could report it to the public in the form of an interview. But tomorrow, just wait! He'd find one, he'd find a hundred, very happy to oblige him.

He woke up toward eight in the evening and for the first time thought about the gifts he had brought his wife from Paris: a wonderful dressing gown, all frilly with lace; a very elegant traveling bag of the latest fashion; three combs and a hair clip of clear, very fine tortoise shell; and then a silver set for her desk, very artfully decorated. He wanted to get them out of his suitcase so his wife's eyes would fill with surprise and pleasure the minute she walked in: the combs and the bag on the dressing table, the gown on the bed. He had Èmere help carry the pieces of the other gift to the desk. After putting them down, he remained in the study to see what his wife had done in his absence. What? What? Nothing! Could it be possible? The play . . . oh, no! Still at the end of the second act . . . On the top sheet of paper the title had been struck out and next to it, between parentheses, *The Hawk* was written, followed by a question mark.

What did this mean? How could that be! Nothing at all? Not even a line after so many days! Was it possible?

He rummaged through the desk drawers: nothing!

From the play manuscript a small piece of paper fell out. He picked it up. Some words were scribbled here and there in a tiny handwriting: *fleeting lucidity* . . . then, underneath: *cold impediments to loving* . . . then further down: *in such prosperity lies abound* . . . and then: *Many steady ideas staggering like a drunk* . . . and finally: *bells, drops of water lining the balcony railing* . . . *crazy trees and crazy thoughts* . . . *white curtains of the parish house, ragged dress over shabby shoe* . . .

Hum! Giustino made a long face. He turned the paper over. Nothing. There was nothing else.

This was all his wife had written in nearly twenty days! It wasn't worth a thing, then, not even Gueli's advice. . . . What did those broken phrases mean?

He rested his hands on his cheeks for a while. His eyes returned to the second phrase: *impediments to loving* . . .

"But why?" he said out loud, shrugging his shoulders.

He began to pace the study, his face still in his hands. Why and what impediments, now that everything, thanks to him, was smooth and easy? The road was open and what a road! A wide, unobstructed road for running from triumph to triumph!

"Impediments to loving . . . Cold impediments to loving . . . *Cold* and to *loving* . . . Hum! What impediments? Why?"

And with his hands behind his back now, he continued to pace. Suddenly he stopped, deeply absorbed, started walking, stopped again, repeating at every pause now, pulling a long face:

"*Crazy trees and crazy thoughts* . . ."

He had expected the play to be finished, and he had counted on working it into the conversation the next day when he talked to the journalists about the triumph in Paris!

Èmere came in to bring him the evening newspapers.

"How come?" Giustino asked him. "Is it already so late?"

"It's after ten," Èmere answered.

"Really? How come?" Giustino repeated, having slept so late he lost all track of time. "What are they doing? They were supposed to be here at nine-thirty at the latest. The train arrives at eight-fifty."

Èmere stood stock-still, waiting for his employer to finish his comments, and then he said: "Giovanna wants to know if we should wait for the signora."

"Of course we should wait!" Giustino answered irritably. "And we'll wait for Signor Gueli, who will also have supper with us. Maybe there was some delay. If . . . if . . . but no! If they had missed the train they'd have sent a telegram. It's already ten?"

"After," Èmere repeated in his stiff and impassive manner.

At the sight of him, Giustino felt his irritation growing. He checked the newspaper to see if by chance there was some change in the train schedule.

"Arrivals . . . arrivals . . . arrivals . . . Here it is: from Chiusi, eight-fifty."

"Yes, sir," said Èmere. "The train has already arrived."

"How do you know that, imbecile?"

"I know because the gentleman next door who goes back and forth to Chiusi arrived forty-five minutes ago."

"Oh, really?"

"Yes, sir. In fact, when I heard the carriage I thought it was the signora, and I went to open the gate. Instead, I saw the gentleman next door who'd come from Chiusi. If the signora had gone to Chiusi . . ."

"She went to Orvieto!" shouted Giustino. "But it's the same line. It means they missed the train!"

"If you would like, sir, I'll go next door to ask . . ."

"You'll ask what?"

"If the gentleman really came from Chiusi."

"Yes, yes, go, and tell Giovanna to wait."

"They missed the train . . . they missed the train . . . they missed the train . . ." he began to chant, with angry gestures. "Orvieto! . . . The trip to Orvieto! . . . The cathedral in Orvieto! . . . This very day, the cathedral in Orvieto! Why that? If they get it into their heads! . . . Certain sudden, irresistible needs! . . . Certain ideas! . . . Then they get mad if they hear from that man . . . what's his name? that they're all a bunch of nuts! The Orvieto cathedral . . . If she'd done any work I'd understand the need for diversion! She didn't do anything, confound it! *Crazy trees and crazy thoughts* . . . That's it, she said it herself. . . ."

Èmere returned to say that the gentleman in the house next door had indeed come from Chiusi.

"Oh, all right!" Giustino yelled at him. "Put something on the table just for me! They could have at least sent a telegram, it seems to me."

At the table, the sight of the two settings for his wife and Gueli, to whom he had promised himself the pleasure of recounting the "great things" of Paris, increased his spite, and he told Èmere to remove them.

Perhaps Èmere was standing there looking at him as he always had, but to Giustino it seemed like he was looking at him differently that evening, and this was another annoyance, so he sent him to the kitchen.

"I'll call you when I need you."

The sight of a husband whose wife by some unforeseen circumstance was sleeping away from home in the company of another man must be very amusing for one who has no wife, especially if this husband arrived home that very day after twenty days of absence and had brought his wife so many beautiful gifts. A nice gift in return!

Giustino would never have dreamed that the austere, the more than mature Gueli would take advantage of a situation like that. . . . Hardly imaginable! And then, Silvia was restraint and honesty personified! But a telegram, by heaven—they could have, should have sent a telegram. No, they really should have sent a telegram.

This missing telegram grew progressively more serious in Giustino's eyes, because he grew progressively more congested with all the irritation he was feeling: for that trip smack-dab on the very day of his arrival, for all those "great things" of Paris that had stuck in his throat and kept him from eating, for the gifts that his wife hadn't seen, and for the consideration he had every right to expect after twenty days of absence, confound it! Not even to send a telegram . . .

Suddenly the silence in the house seemed sinister, perhaps because he kept waiting for the telegraph messenger's ring. He got up from the table, looked again at the train schedule in the newspaper to see what time next day his wife might return, and saw nothing before one in the afternoon. There was another train in the morning, but too early for a lady. In the meantime it was possible that if the telegram didn't arrive during the night, it might arrive in time in the morning. He went upstairs to read the newspaper in bed and wait for sleep that would be late coming for many reasons.

He looked into his wife's empty bedroom. How disappointing! Waiting on the bed was the beautiful lace dressing gown. In the reflection from the electric-lamp shade, the white of the lace was tinted a very soft pale pink. It made Giustino feel upset and anxious, and he turned to look at the dressing table to see the combs and the bag hanging on one of the mirror braces. He noticed a certain disorder on top of the dressing table, probably because of Silvia's hurry to fix her hair and get ready in the morning after Gueli's importunate invitation. He was thinking that it must be sad for his wife, by now accustomed to sleeping in a nice room like this, to have to spend the night in some miserable little hotel in Orvieto.

4

He woke up late the next morning, and the first thing he did was ask Èmere if a telegram had arrived. It had not.

An accident? An accident? No, of course not! Gueli and Silvia Roncella weren't two ordinary travelers. If something had happened to them he would have been informed at once. And, in addition, if something had come up, Gueli or someone else would have telegraphed him so he wouldn't be kept in painful suspense by the silence. He thought of telegraphing him at Orvieto, but where to send it? No, nothing to do. Better just to wait patiently until the train arrived. While waiting he could spend the time putting his accounts straight, the income and outgo for so many days. A big job!

For about three hours he was immersed in the small details of his accounts, forgetting his worries about his wife, when Èmere came to announce that there was a lady downstairs wanting to speak to him.

"A lady? Who?"

"She wanted to see Signora Roncella. I told her the signora was not here."

"But who is she?" Giustino shouted. "Signora . . . Signora . . . Signora . . . Has she ever been here before?"

"No, sir, never."

"A foreigner?"

"No, sir, I don't think so."

"Who can it be?" Giustino asked himself. "I'm coming."

He went down to the living room and stood in the doorway as though paralyzed at the sight of Livia Frezzi, who, with her face horribly deformed, pinched here and there with rapid nervous tics, attacked him with teeth clenched, lips snarling, green eyes fixed and bloodshot.

"She hasn't come back? They haven't come back yet?"

At the sight of her leaping at him, bristling with demonic fury, Giustino felt fear, compassion, and contempt at the same time.

"So, you know too?" he began. "Last evening . . . last evening no doubt . . . they missed the . . . the train . . . but . . . but . . . perhaps any minute . . ."

Signora Frezzi came at him again, almost on the attack: "Then you know? You allowed them to go off together? You!"

"What . . . my dear lady . . . but why?" he equivocated, moving backward. "You . . . wait a minute . . . I'm sorry . . . but . . ."

"You?" Signora Frezzi insisted.

Then Giustino, joining his hands in an imploring gesture, almost as though to scoop up and offer reason to that poor woman: "But how does this hurt us? Please believe that my wife . . ."

Livia Frezzi didn't let him finish: she clapped her clawlike hands to her contorted, squeezed face, to let the gall-soaked insult and contempt escape through her clamped teeth. She erupted: "Imbecile!"

"Oh, for heaven's sakes!" Giustino lost his temper. "You insult me in my house! Insult me and my wife with your sordid suspicions!"

"But if you had seen them," she went on, her face in his, her lips twisted into a horrible sneer. "Together, arm in arm, in the ruins at Ostia . . . Like this!" As she grabbed for his arm, Giustino took a step back.

"Ostia? What do you mean, Ostia! You're mistaken! Who told you that? How could they if they went to Orvieto!"

"To Orvieto, is it?" Signora Frezzi sneered again. "Is that what they told you?"

"Yes, indeed, Signora! Signor Gueli!" Giustino asserted firmly. "An artistic excursion, a visit to the cathedral at Orvieto. Old art . . . something to . . ."

"Imbecile! Imbecile! Imbecile!" Signora Frezzi exploded again. "And so you were in cahoots with him?"

A very pale Giustino raised his hand and, holding himself back with difficulty, he trembled: "You can thank God you're a woman, otherwise . . ."

Wilder than ever, Signora Frezzi gave him no slack, interrupting him with: "You, you're the one who can thank God I didn't find her here! But I know where to find him, and you'll be hearing from me!"

With this threat she ran off, and Giustino stood looking around him, shaking and stunned, working his ten fingers in the air as though unsure what to do with them.

"She's crazy . . . crazy . . . crazy . . ." he whispered. "Capable of violence . . ."

What should he do? Run after her? A scandal in the street . . . But in the meantime?

He felt he was being pulled along by her fury, and he leaned forward as though about to throw himself into the race. Immediately he straightened up, checked by the thought that he didn't have the time or the means of confirming anything in the bewildering confusion, the perplexity amid so many conflicting uncertainties. He could only rave: "Ostia . . . Ostia? . . . They would be back by now. Arm in arm . . . among the ruins . . . She's crazy. . . . Someone saw them. . . . Who could have seen them? . . . And they went to tell her? . . . Someone who knows she's jealous, just for the fun of it. . . . And in the meantime? . . . She's capable of going to the station and doing who knows what. . . ."

He looked at his watch, without realizing that Signora Frezzi had no reason to go to the station at that hour if she thought Gueli and Silvia had gone to Ostia and not to Orvieto; and he called Èmere to bring down his hat and cane. It was twelve-thirty. He had just enough time to get there for the one-o'clock train.

"To the station, hurry!" he shouted, getting into the first carriage he saw near Margherita Bridge.

But he arrived a few minutes after the train came in from Chiusi. The last passengers were still getting off. He looked them over. They weren't there! He ran to the exit, looking here and there at everyone who was leaving. He didn't see them! Was it possible they hadn't arrived even on that train? Perhaps they had already gone out and were in a carriage. But then wouldn't he have run into them as he entered the station?

"I could have missed them!"

And he jumped into another carriage to rush back home. By the time he got there he was almost sure that Èmere would tell him no one had arrived.

There was no doubt in his mind that something serious must have happened. He was struck by the strangeness of that trip (which now seemed fishy), undertaken just at the moment of his arrival, followed by the long, unexplainable silence when they didn't return, and that crazy woman's outrageous suspicion. He wanted to stop that outrageous suspicion before it filled the emptiness and silence and even took possession of him, and he tried to ward off the enormity of the trick those two had played on him. It was incompatible with his conscience as an exemplary husband, and inconsistent with Gueli's reputation for austerity, and the honesty, the glum and stubborn honesty of Silvia. He had always put himself out wholeheartedly for his wife, to the extent

193

of obtaining all those triumphs and a comfortable life for her. Strange, yes: she had been strange lately, after the success of her play, but only because of that glum and stubborn honesty of hers. Loving simplicity and dreading the limelight, she didn't know how to adapt to the pomp and splendor of fame. No, no, stop it! How could he doubt her honesty and the loyalty of Gueli, who was already an old man, and for so many years tied to that woman, her slave?

A sudden thought . . . One of Gueli's servants might have sent a telegram to him at Orvieto to alert him of Signora Frezzi's sudden return from Monteporzio, and now he didn't dare return to Rome? And, for goodness sake, he had to keep Silvia with him there, because of his fear of returning? And Silvia was accommodating him without realizing the harm to her dignity? Not at all! It wasn't possible! They knew the longer they delayed their return, the greater would be the suspicions and fury of that crazy woman. . . . Except that Gueli, conquered by fear, persecuted by suspicion, and now out of Signora Frezzi's clutches, should not have included Silvia. . . .

That infernal silence was worse than anything!

Should he go to Orvieto? And what if they weren't there anymore? What if they had never gone there? Now he was beginning to doubt it. . . . Maybe they went someplace else. . . . It suddenly occurred to him that Gueli had said something about having to go to Milan. And what if he had taken Silvia there with him? How could he? Without telling anyone? If they had in all honesty felt like visiting some other place, they would have found a way to let him know. No, no . . . Where did they go?

Ah, the doorbell! He jumped at the ring and, not waiting for Èmere, he ran to the gate himself. The mailman with a letter from Silvia! Ah, at last . . . But what? A local postmark on the envelope. She was writing him from Rome?

"Never mind!" he shouted when Èmere came rushing out, indicating that he had taken the letter himself. And he tore open the envelope right there in the yard, by the gate.

The letter—very short, about twenty lines at the most—was without a provenance, date, or greeting. Reading the first words, as though transfixed, he twice tried to take a breath. His face turned white, his eyes grew glazed, he passed a hand over them, and then rubbed his hands together, crumpling the letter.

What? . . . Going away? . . . Just like that? . . . In order not to deceive him? And he looked fiercely at the placid little terra-cotta lion beside the gate, with his head lying on his front paws, sleeping. What was this? And hadn't she deceived him with that old man? . . . Hadn't she gone away with him? . . . And she was leaving him everything? . . . What did that mean—everything? What was everything anymore, what was he anymore, if she . . . But what? Why? Not an explanation! Nothing . . . She went away just like that, without saying why. . . . Because he had done so much, too much, for her? This was his reward? She threw everything in his face. As if he had worked only for himself and not for her, too! Could he stay there anymore without her? It was the ruin . . . the ruin of his whole life . . . his destruction. But why? She gave no details in that letter. She said nothing at all about Gueli. She said she didn't want to deceive him and was definite only about wanting to break up their life together. And it came from Rome! So she was in Rome? Where? Not at Gueli's. No, that was impossible—Signora Frezzi was there and had come to him that same morning. Perhaps Silvia wasn't in Rome and had sent that letter to someone else to mail it. Who? Maybe Raceni . . . maybe Signora Ely Faciolli . . . She must have written to one or the other in Rome; otherwise he would know where it came from by the envelope. He had to go find her at any cost, make her talk, explain why she couldn't live with him any longer, and make her listen to reason. She must have gone mad! Perhaps Gueli . . . No, he still couldn't believe she'd leave him for Gueli! But maybe Gueli induced her to leave him, vexed as he was by Signora Frezzi, insane himself. . . . So everyone was crazy! How blind he had been to invite him into their home against her will. . . . Who knows what Gueli thought of him! That he persecuted his wife as Signora Frezzi persecuted him, perhaps? Yes, that must be what got this dreadful business started. . . . Why had he urged her to work, anyway? For her own sake, of course! To keep alive her fame that he had worked so hard to produce! Everything, everything for her! Hadn't he even lost his job for her? When he lived only for her, how could he see such a disaster coming? If anything, it was she, she, Silvia, who had taken advantage of him, had taken all his work, all his time, his entire soul, and now she was deserting him, tossing him away like a worthless rag. Out! Could he keep their home, the money made from her work? Impossible! Don't even think about it! Now here he was, out in the street, with no status, no profession, like an empty sack. . . . No, no, for heaven's sake! Before a scandal broke, he would find her! He would find her!

He rushed to the gate with the idea of running to Signora Ely Faciolli's house, but he hadn't even opened it before two reporters and then a third and a fourth appeared before him with faces flushed from their exertion and excitement.

"What happened?"

"Gueli . . ." one of them panted. "Gueli has been wounded—"

"And Silvia?" shouted Giustino.

"No, nothing!" answered another who had barely caught his breath. "Don't worry, she wasn't there!"

"Where is she? Where is she?" asked Giustino, burning to escape.

"She's not in Rome! She's not in Rome!" they yelled in chorus to keep him there.

"If she was with Gueli!" exclaimed Giustino, trembling convulsively. "And her letter . . . her letter's from Rome!"

"A letter, ah . . . you got a letter from your wife?"

"Yes! Here it is. . . . About fifteen minutes ago . . . With a local postmark."

"May I see it?" one of them asked tentatively.

But another was in a hurry to get things straight: "No! That's impossible! Your wife's in Ostia."

"In Ostia? You're sure?"

"Yes, yes, in Ostia. Ostia without a doubt."

Giustino, trembling, covered his face with his hands: "Then it's true! It's true! It's true!"

The four stood looking at him, moved with pity. One of them asked: "Did you think your wife was in Rome?"

"No, yesterday," Giustino snapped, "with Gueli. They told me they were going to Orvieto. . . ."

"To Orvieto? No, how could they!"

"A pretext!"

"To put you on a false trail . . ."

"Look, if Gueli came back from Ostia . . ."

"Excuse me," repeated the reporter, holding out his hand. "May I see the letter?"

Giustino pulled back his hand. "No, it's nothing . . . she says that . . . never mind! But where, where was Gueli wounded?"

"Two very serious wounds!"

"In his stomach and right arm."

Giustino shook his head: "No! I mean, where? At home? On the street?"

"At home, at home . . . Frezzi did it. . . . He was coming back from Ostia and . . . as soon as he walked in . . ."

"From Ostia? Then he could have mailed the letter."

"Oh, yes . . . That's likely. . . ."

Giustino covered his face with his hands again, groaning: "It's over! It's over! It's over!"

Then he asked angrily: "Has Signora Frezzi been arrested?"

"Yes, immediately!"

"I knew she could do something crazy! She was here this morning!"

"Signora Frezzi?"

"Yes, here looking for my wife! And I didn't run after her! Ah, my friends! My friends! My friends!" he went on without a break, holding out his arms to Dora Barmis, Raceni, Lampini, Centanni, Mola, Federici, who, as soon as they heard, had run to Gueli's house. They still had on their faces the horror of the blood splattered in the rooms and on the stairs invaded by curiosity seekers, and the fever of the enormous scandal.

Dora Barmis, breaking into tears, threw her arms around him. All the others gathered around, solicitous and distressed, and as a group they entered the living room. Once there, Dora Barmis, an arm still around him, nearly had him sitting on her lap. While shedding copious tears she kept sighing: "Poor dear . . . poor dear . . . poor dear . . ."

Softened by this sympathy and feeling somewhat consoled, his heart was gradually warmed by the display of esteem and affection of all those literary and journalist friends.

"What a disgrace!" Giustino said, looking each in the face piteously. "Ah, my friends, what a disgrace! This betrayal to me, to me! You are all witnesses to what I've done for this woman! Here, here, all around us, even the things talk! I did everything for her! And look at the reward I get! Yesterday I came back from Paris . . . glory there, too, in one of France's greatest theaters . . . parties, banquets, receptions . . . everyone gathering around me to hear news about her, about her life, her work . . . and then I come back here! Ah, what a disgrace, my friend, my friend, dear Baldani, thank you! What a disgrace! What an indignity! Thank you! Dear Luna, you, too! Thank you. Dear Betti, thank you. Thanks to all of you, my friends. You, too, Jacono? Yes, real treachery, thank you! Oh, dear Zago, poor Zago . . . see? see? No!" he suddenly shouted, noticing the four reporters intent on copying his wife's letter that must have fallen from his hand. "No! Let them tell everyone! Let the press have it and let all Italy hear! All of you might as well know and all my friends in France, too. Here, in this letter, she says she leaves me everything! But I'm leaving everything to her. I'm sick of it! I've given her everything . . . and I'm ruined! I'll leave everything here . . . house, money . . . everything, everything . . . and I'll go back to my son, with nothing, ruined. To my son . . . I hadn't even thought of my son . . . it's all been for her! For her!"

At this point Barmis couldn't stand it anymore. She jumped on her feet and frantically embraced him. To everyone's amazement, Giustino burst into a flood of tears and buried his face on the shoulder of his consoler.

"Sublime, sublime," Luna whispered to Baldani as they left the room. "Sublime! Ah, it's absolutely essential that some other woman writer take that poor man as a secretary! Too bad Signora Barmis doesn't know how to write. . . . He's just sublime, poor man!"

7 ✳ A LIGHT GONE OUT

1

"And your common sense? Where's your common sense, little dummy?"

The little boy, astride old man Prever's legs, looked at him with big, intent, laughing eyes; then he stopped, raised his tiny hand, and with his index finger touched his forehead.

"Right here."

"Not true!" the old man yelled, grabbing him with his thick hands, playfully poking him in the stomach: "It's here, here, here."

The boy collapsed with laughter at this often repeated joke.

At that explosion of fresh, ingenuous, childish laughter, his grandmother turned to look at the inverted curly head of the little boy. Didn't he laugh too much? And there was a pesky fly buzzing so annoyingly in the room. A bad omen. No use trying to find it. Sadly, she turned to look at her son standing by the window, head on his chest, hands in his pockets, glum and taciturn.

It was nearly nine months since he had come back from Rome with nothing much but those clothes on his back. Would that he had lost just his clothes and job! He had lost everything—his heart, his mind, his whole life—all because of that woman, who must be wicked. In Signora Velia's more than sixty years she had never seen a man reduced to such a state by a good and honest woman.

For goodness' sake, not even a smidgen of love for that little boy anymore, or her! Look at him there. He didn't want to think anymore.

He stared and didn't seem to see or hear anything, cut off from every sensation, empty, destroyed, lifeless.

He seemed to come alive only at some reminder of her presence left in the house, like a dog that lies on his dead master's things, brooding over the lingering odors as if to preserve them. Giustino just stayed there, hanging around. There was no way to send him out for a little distraction.

Many times Prever had suggested he go with Graziella for several months, for a week, for a day anyway, to his villa on Braida hill. Besides, he was old now and Giustino could help a little with the administration of his estate. This last suggestion had some effect, but it was like the weight of an obligation and made him even more cruelly despondent. So much so that Prever immediately excused him, even though the priest, Don Buti, thought he should have insisted, letting him believe it was a coldhearted obligation.

"It's good medicine," he said. "Don't worry if he finds it a little bitter."

Signor Prever didn't want to be medicine—or anyway, not bitter medicine.

"Fine thing," Prever said to Madama Velia as soon as Don Buti went on his way. "He comes here with his telescope for medicine, and I should come here with my bookkeeping."

In fact, when Don Buti saw that Giustino would never visit the parish house a few steps away, he brought his famous old telescope under his cloak one evening to let him admire *the great power of Our Lord*, as he did as a child, when in order to keep his left eye closed he screwed up his mouth:

"Like this, little mouse!"

But Giustino was not moved by the sight of the old telescope. Just to please the good man, he had looked at "the great mountain" of the moon and had frowned and shaken his head slightly when Don Buti repeated the customary refrain with the customary gestures:

"*The great power of Our Lord, eh? The great power of Our Lord!*"

The refrain was followed by a long lecture full of *ohs!* and *ahs!* because that nodding head and frown made Don Buti think that the great power of God, if not exactly doubted, was recognized as capable of allowing much evil to be done to a poor innocent man. However, Giustino listened impassively to the talking-to, accepting it as something Don Buti had to do as a priest, which had nothing to do with him, so removed from priestly obligation as he was, and able to think TO EACH HIS OWN, as was written on the church tower.

Giustino had been shaken somewhat from his grim spiritual torpor by the new doctor recently arrived in Cargiore with a woman who no one knew whether she was his wife or not. She must have been a rich *madama*, because Dr. Lais had rented a beautiful villa from some people in Turin and said he wanted to buy it. Tall, thin, stiff, and precise as an Englishman, with a still-blond mustache and with thick, very short, already graying hair, he gave the impression of practicing his profession just to have something to do. He dressed with expensive and simple elegance and always wore a pair of splendid leather leggings that he seemed purposely to forget to hook in the house, so as to have to finish the job outside on the street in order to call attention to them. Literature was of special interest to Dr. Lais. Called to the house because of a slight upset of the boy, and learning that Boggiolo was the husband of the famous writer Silvia Roncella, who had also been involved with literature for years, the doctor bombarded him with questions and invited him to his villa, where his signora would certainly be pleased to hear him talk, passionate lover of literature and insatiable reader that she was.

"If you don't come, watch out!" he had said. "I'm just apt to bring her here."

In fact, he did bring her. And the two of them—he who seemed so English, and she who seemed Spanish (she was from Venice), all ribbons and bows, mincing, dark, with two very dark, dancing eyes and two very red fleshy lips, her little nose proudly straight and impertinent—made Giustino talk the entire evening. They were both amazed and irritated by certain details, certain opinions contrary to their passionate impressions as provincial amateurs. "That's too much!" she protested. "You say Signora Morlacchi . . . Flavia Morlacchi! Really, no one appreciated her in Rome? But her novel, *The Victim* . . . so wonderful! . . . But *Snow Flakes* . . . marvelous poems! . . . And the play. What was it called? *Conflict*, yes, yes, no, *The Conflict* . . . My goodness, so well received at Como four years ago!"

Signor Martino and Don Buti listened and looked, wide-eyed and open-mouthed, and Signora Velia grew concerned about her Giustino, who, however unwittingly, was so stimulated by those two that he started talking about those things again, growing more and more heated. . . . Oh, dear, no. Signora Velia preferred to see him glum, taciturn, sunk in mourning rather than animated like that. Away with that temptation! She was relieved a few days later when those two had the effrontery to send a maid to ask for a certain book of his wife's and to invite him to lunch and Giustino replied that he didn't have the book and was unable to attend the luncheon.

In this way he got free of them.

"What can be wrong with him today?" little Signora Velia wondered as she watched her son at the window while Vittorino was cutting up on Prever's knees.

He might be more preoccupied than usual that day because in the morning—owing to a foolish oversight on Graziella's part—he had discovered a letter that had arrived a few days earlier and that had not been destroyed like all the others had been, whenever possible, without his knowledge.

So many letters still arrived for him, forwarded from Rome, even from France and Germany. When they arrived Signora Velia shook her head, as if the extent of the harm that woman had done to her son could be measured by the distance from which the letters came.

He would throw himself on those letters like a starving man, close himself up in his room, and begin to reply. However, he didn't send those letters with the replies directly to his wife. Signora Velia learned by way of Signor Martino, who heard from Monsù Gariola, owner of the post office building, that her son sent them to a certain Raceni in Rome. Perhaps through this friend he would suggest to his wife how she ought to be behaving.

And such was the case.

After he returned to Cargiore, and until a few months ago, Giustino had frequently received letters from Barmis and Raceni, from which he learned with indescribable torment what a disorderly life his wife was living in Rome.

Now he was more than ever convinced that nothing had happened between Silvia and Gueli, and he believed the proof was the fact that Gueli, almost miraculously healed from the two wounds, even with his right arm amputated, had returned to live with Signora Frezzi, who had been released by the court as mentally incompetent, after five months of preventive detention, precisely because of the support of Gueli himself and at his insistence.

If only he hadn't let himself be overcome by the scandal in the beginning and had run to Ostia to get his wife, who was still blameless except for wanting to escape from him! No, no, no: he couldn't believe, in spite of that deception of the trip to Orvieto—he couldn't believe she could stay with Gueli. He should have run to Ostia and brought his wife back himself, who then certainly wouldn't be so lost. Who was she living with now? Signora Barmis said with Baldani; Raceni suspected a relationship with Luna. Apparently she was living alone. The villino and all the furniture sold. In his last letters Raceni implied that she was in some financial straits. Of course! Without him . . . Who knows how badly they were cheating her! Maybe now she knew what it meant to have a man like him beside her! Everything sold . . . What a shame! That villino . . . that Ducrot furniture . . .

For about two months neither Signora Barmis nor Raceni, nor any other friend from Rome, had written. What had happened? Perhaps they saw no reason to keep corresponding with someone who had by now almost disappeared from life. Signora Barmis had tired first. Now not even Raceni wrote.

But he was not more sullen than usual that day because of their silence nor for the reason his mother supposed.

From the time of his return no newspapers had entered the house because of the promise he made his mother not to read them anymore. How he regretted that promise now! But he didn't dare show how much he wanted to read those from Turin at least, for fear his mother would think he was still obsessed with that woman. As long as Signora Barmis and Raceni had written, he hadn't suffered that privation so much, but now . . .

Well, then, that morning, in a twenty-day-old newspaper, in which Graziella had wrapped the freshly ironed collars and cuffs she brought to his room, under the rubric of theaters he had read two notices that had upset him.

One was from Rome: the coming performance at the Argentina Theater of his wife's new play, the same one he had left before his job was finished, *If Not This Way.* . . . The other notice was that the Carmi-Revelli Company was performing at the Alfieri Theater in Turin.

Devoured by the wish to know how that new play fared in Rome and perhaps in other cities as well, maybe even in Turin if the Carmi-Revelli Company was there, and by the wish to talk to Signora Laura or Grimi, or to anyone, he didn't know how to tell his mother he wanted to go to Turin the next morning. Also, he was afraid Signor Prever would want to go with him. He knew how anxious his mother was for him. To tell her he wanted to go alone so far so suddenly, when he had refused to take two steps outside the house up to that day, would worry her. And then, he didn't have much money left over from what he had earned in Paris. He was almost ashamed to say it to himself—just imagine then asking his mother for money. She had only a little pension from her husband, and now with the added burden of him it was a struggle for the poor thing. Signor Prever, of course, helped out from time to time, with one excuse or another. But if his mother was now down to nothing and had to ask Signor Martino for help, he would learn of his plan and certainly offer to go with him.

He waited for Prever to go home after supper, and to provoke a new and more urgent suggestion from his mother that he find some kind of distraction, he complained about a terrible mental weariness. Her concern, as he expected, brought the suggestion: "Go to Braida tomorrow."

"No, I would rather . . . I'd rather see people. Maybe this solitude is not good for me. . . ."

"You want to go to Turin?"

"Yes, I'd rather."

"Of course, immediately, tomorrow!" his mother hastened to say. "I'll send Graziella to reserve a seat for you in Monsù Gariola's carriage."

"No, no," Giustino said. "Don't. I'll go by foot to Giaveno."

"But why?"

"Because . . . Never mind! It'll do me good to walk. I've been in the house too long. Instead . . . for the tram from Giaveno . . . Mamma, I . . ."

Signora Velia understood at once and brought a hand to her forehead and closed her eyes, as if to say: "Don't even say it!"

When he went to his room, accompanied by his mother, who brought the lamp, he noticed she had put three ten-lire bills on the dresser.

"No, no!" he exclaimed. "What do you want me to do with so much? Take them, take them. One's enough for me!"

His old mother moved away, parrying with her hands, with a sad, and at the same time a little mischievious, smile on her lips and in her eyes.

"Do you really think your life is finished, my son?" she said. "You're still practically a boy. Go on!"

And she closed the door.

2

Stepping off the tram, the first impression that came to him as he put his feet down in the city again after nine months of deep, dark inner silence, of entombment and sadness, was that of no longer knowing how to walk amid noise and confusion. He was immediately deafened, almost as if in a heavy, hollow drunkenness—like the irritation, distaste, resentment of a sick person who is forced to go around with the buzz of medication in his ears among active and indifferent healthy people.

He looked rapidly sideways this way and that for fear that one of his old nonliterary acquaintances might recognize him, and for another, opposite fear, that one of his new acquaintances might pretend not to recognize him. More cruel than the mocking commiseration of the former would have been the scornful snub of the latter, now that he was not even a shadow of what he had been.

If a journalist friend passing by had put an arm under his, cheerfully, as in the good old days, he might have said: "Dear Boggiolo, what's new?"

And Giustino would have told him about the Parisian success he hadn't been able to tell anyone about and that had left an anguished knot in his throat that would never go away!

"And your wife? What work can we expect? A new play, eh? Come on, tell me something. . . ."

He didn't even know if the new play had been performed, or what reception it had had.

He went to the newsstand and bought newspapers from Rome, Milan, and the smaller cities.

No mention of it.

But in the announcements of plays in Rome, there it was, at the Argentina Theater: *If Not This Way.*

So it had been performed! It was successful! If it was still playing . . . Who knows how many nights? Very successful . . .

He imagined that this time Silvia must have been in charge. In his mind's eye he saw the stage during the rehearsal. He imagined the impression it must have made on Silvia, who had never done this before, and he saw himself there with her, her guide with the actors; she uncertain, lost. He, on the other hand, experienced, sure of himself. And he displayed all his certainty, his command over everything, and he encouraged her not to despair at the actors' laziness and indifference, at cuts made in the script, at the director's angry outbursts. It sure wasn't easy to work with those temperaments! You had to go along with them and be patient even if they didn't seem to know their parts up to the last moment.

Suddenly his face darkened. Perhaps she had been assisted, escorted to those rehearsals by someone, perhaps by Baldani, or Luna, or Betti. . . . Who was her lover now? And with this thought it suddenly became much easier to imagine her staging that play, attending the rehearsals, fighting with the actors. But yes, certainly, much easier now that she, thanks to him, had made such a name for herself and all doors were open to her and all the actors hung on her words with admiration and smiles. Much easier for her!

"It's the accounts, however, that matter! The accounts! The accounts!" he exclaimed to himself. "Admiration, smiles . . . What are they worth! A woman . . . and after all, now . . . without a husband . . . But who's taking care of the accounts? Will she do it? With all her fine experience! He'll look after them, her lover. . . . They'll eat her alive! Yes, yes, just see if you can get another villino now like that one! Just wait. . . ."

He opened a Turin newspaper and saw that the Carmi-Revelli Company was giving its final performances at the Alfieri Theater.

He stood there for a bit with that paper open before him, wondering whether or not to go. The desire to know about the play, to talk about it, to hear it talked about was urging him to go. The thought of facing all those actors and their questions was holding him back. How would they receive him? At one time they had made fun of him, but he held the rope then, and after letting them show off for a while like so many ponies frolicking around him, he could give the rope a tug and hook them up, tamed, to the triumphant cart. But now . . .

He kept walking, absorbed in the memories that were now all he had, and after a long time, unconsciously led by those memories, he found himself at the Alfieri Theater.

Maybe there was a rehearsal going on now. He stopped hesitantly at the entrance and pretended to be reading a poster about the play to be given that evening, the title, the list of characters. Finally, getting up his nerve, as though he were an inexperienced writer, he respectfully asked a guard who didn't know him if Signora Carmi was in the theater.

"Not yet," the man answered.

Giustino continued to stand in front of the poster without daring to ask anything else. In the past he would have entered like the lord of the theater, without even deigning to glance at that watchdog!

"And Revelli?" he asked after a bit.

"He came in just now."

"It's a rehearsal, isn't it?"

"A rehearsal, a rehearsal."

He knew that Revelli was very strict about outsiders at the rehearsals. If he gave that man a calling card to take to Revelli, he certainly would let him in. But then he would be exposed to everyone's indiscreet and insolent curiosity. He didn't want that. Better to stay there like a beggar waiting for Signora Carmi, who couldn't be much later, if the others had already come.

In fact, Signora Carmi arrived shortly in a carriage. She wasn't expecting to see him by the door and at his greeting she bowed slightly and went on without recognizing him.

"Signora . . ." Giustino called after her, transfixed.

Signora Carmi turned, blinking her myopic eyes, and suddenly her face lengthened into an *oooh* of surprise.

"You, Boggiolo? Why are you here? Why?"

"Well . . ." Giustino said, barely opening his arms.

"I heard, I heard," continued Signora Carmi with compassionate concern. "My poor friend! What an awful thing to do! Believe me, I never would have expected it. I don't mean I wouldn't have expected it from her. Ah, I know something about that woman's ingratitude! But awful for you, dear. Come along, come with me. I'm late!"

Giustino hesitated, then said in a trembling voice, his eyes glassy with tears: "Please, Signora, I don't want . . . I don't want them to see me."

"You're right," Signora Carmi realized. "Wait. Let's go this way."

They entered the nearly dark theater, crossed the hallway of the first row of boxes. Signora Carmi opened the little door of the last box and said to Boggiolo in a whisper:

"Wait for me here. I'm going to the stage and I'll be right back."

Giustino crouched down at the back in the dark, his shoulders against the wall adjacent to the stage in order not to be seen by the actors whose voices echoed in the empty theater.

"*Oh, Signora, oh, Signora,*" Grimi intoned in his usual baritone, over-riding the prompter's irritating voice. "*Does she seem too lovely to you?*"

"*But no, not lovely, my dear sir,*" little Signora Grassi smiled, her tiny voice tender.

And Revelli shouted: "More drawn out! More drawn out! *But nooo, but not at all lovely, friend—*"

"The second *but*'s not there!"

"Just put it in, for heaven's sake! It sounds more natural!"

Giustino listened to those familiar voices that unconsciously changed as they gave life to the characters of the scene, he looked at the vast resonant emptiness of the dark theater, and he breathed in that particular mixture of dampness, dust, and stagnant human breath. He could feel his anguish growing, as if his throat were seized by the vivid memory of a life that could no longer be his, which he could never be part of again, except like this, hidden, almost furtive, or pitied just as he was a few moments ago. Signora Carmi had recognized, and everyone would certainly have recognized along with her, that he didn't deserve to be treated that way. The pity of others, though it made him feel his misery more deeply and bitterly, was also a precious reminder of what he had been.

He waited some time for Signora Carmi to rehearse a long scene with Revelli. When it was finished, she returned to find him weeping, sitting with his elbows on his knees and his face in his hands. He wept silently, but with an abundance of hot tears and restrained sobs.

"Now, now," she said, putting a hand on his shoulder. "Yes, I under-stand, poor friend, but come on now! This isn't like you, dear Bog-giolo! I know, devoting everything, body and soul, to that woman; and now . . ."

"It's the ruin, don't you see?" Giustino burst out, stifling his tears. "The ruin, the ruin of all I built, Signora, stone by stone. Built by me, by me alone! When everything was in place and it was time to enjoy what I had made, a blast of traitorous wind blew over it, a blast of in-sanity, believe me, of insanity with that old man, with that cowardly old lunatic, who, maybe out of revenge, offered to destroy another life as his had been destroyed. Everything collapsed, everything!"

"Quiet, yes, quiet, calm down!" Signora Carmi urged him with words and gestures.

"Let me get it off my chest, for heaven's sake! I haven't talked or cried for nine months! They've destroyed me, my dear lady! I'm not anything now! I put everything into that work that only I could do, only I. I say that with pride, my dear lady. I alone because I paid no attention to all the foolishness, to all the whims, to all the strange ideas these literary types get in their heads. I never let it get to me and I let them laugh, if they wanted to. You laughed at me, too, didn't you? Everyone laughed at me. What did I care? I had something to build! And I did it! And now . . . now do you understand?"

While Boggiolo talked and wept in the dark box, choked by anguish, he was following the rehearsal taking place there on the stage. Signora Carmi suddenly noticed, with a shiver, the strange contemporaneity of those two dramas—one real, here, of a man consumed with tears, with his back against the wall facing the stage, where the voices of the other fictional drama sounded false. The direct comparison wearied and nauseated her, as if the play was a pointless, impudent, disrespectful game. She was tempted to lean out of the box and motion for the actors to stop and come here. Here to see, to witness this other real drama. Instead, she went over to Boggiolo again and with kind words and pats on his back, begged him to calm down.

"Yes, yes, thank you, Signora . . . I'm calm, I'm calm," Giustino said, swallowing his tears and drying his eyes. "Excuse me, Signora. I really needed this. Excuse me. Now I'm calm. Tell me something about this play . . . this new play, *If Not This Way*. It's going well, isn't it? How's it doing?"

"Ah, don't talk to me about it!" Signora Carmi protested. "It's the same business, darling, the same ugly business she did to you! Don't talk to me about it. Let's drop it."

"I just wanted to know the end result. . . ." Giustino insisted timidly, humiliated by his own suffering.

"Silvia Roncella, my dear friend, is ingratitude personified!" Signora Carmi pronounced. "Who made her a success? Say it, Boggiolo! Didn't I, I alone, believe in the power of her talent and her work while everyone else laughed or doubted it? Well, then: she thought of everyone but me for the new play! Listen, I'm telling you this because I know what happened to you, too. I told the others—oh, thank heavens I keep my dignity—I told the others that I didn't want to do it. And I don't even act in *The New Colony* anymore. Thank goodness people come to the theater for me, to hear me, whatever I do: I don't need her! I mention it only because no one likes ingratitude, and you will understand."

Giustino remained silent for some time, shaking his head. Then he said: "Everyone, you know? She treated all the friends who helped me the same. I remember Signora Barmis, too. . . . Well, then, this new play . . . how is it going?"

"Oh!" Signora Carmi said. "It seems . . . nothing out of the ordinary . . . It's what is called a critical success. Some scenes here and there seem good . . . the last scene of the last act, especially. Yes, that one has saved the work. Haven't you read the papers?"

"No, Signora. For nine months I've been shut up in the house. This is the first time I've come down to Turin. I'm staying up there above Giaveno, in my little village, with my mother and my son. . . ."

"Ah, you've kept your son with you?"

"Certainly! With me . . . He's always been there, really, with my mother."

"Bravo, bravo," Signora Carmi approved. "And so you haven't had any more news?"

"No, nothing at all. By chance I learned a new play was being performed. I bought the newspapers today, and I saw that it was being performed in Rome. . . ."

"Also in Milan," Signora Carmi said.

"Ah, it's playing in Milan, too?"

"Yes, yes, with the same success."

"At the Manzoni Theater?"

"Yes, at the Manzoni. And soon . . . wait, in three days the Fresi Company will come from Milan to put it on here, in this theater. Roncella is in Milan now and will be here for the opening."

At this news Giustino jumped to his feet, breathless. "You know that for certain?"

"Yes, that's how I understood it. What? Has it . . . has it upset you? I understand. . . ."

Signora Carmi also stood up and looked at him compassionately.

"She'll come?"

"That's what they say! And I believe it. After all the stir created around her, her presence can help a lot, as the play isn't all that good. And then the public doesn't know her yet, and wants to know her."

"Yes, yes," Giustino said eagerly. "It's natural . . . this is like the first work for her. . . . Maybe they even insisted she come. . . . The Fresi Company will be here in three days?"

"Yes, in three days. The poster is in the lobby. Didn't you see it?"

Giustino couldn't stay still any longer. He thanked Signora Carmi for her warm welcome and went away feeling suffocated in the heavy darkness of the theater, agitated as he was by the tremendous news she had given him.

Silvia in Turin! They might call her out, there, in the theater, and he could see her again!

He felt weak in the knees as he went outside. Feeling a sort of vertigo, he put his hand to his face. The blood had all run to his head and his heart was pounding. He would see her again! Ah, who knows what she was like now, after the storm she had lived through! Who knows how she had changed! Perhaps nothing of the Silvia he had known existed any longer!

But no: maybe she wouldn't come, knowing that he could come to Turin from Cargiore, and . . . And if she came just for this? To make up with him? Oh, God, oh, God . . . How could he forgive her after such a scandal? How could he begin living with her again? No, no . . . He had no status anymore. He would be covered with shame, and everyone would think he got back with her just to live off her again, shamefully. No, no! Now it was no longer possible. . . . She would understand that.

But hadn't he left her everything? That showed he wasn't a contemptible exploiter. He had given everyone proof that he wasn't capable of living with shame, with money that still was largely his, fruit of his work, his blood, and he had left it! Who could blame him?

This proud protest he dwelled on with growing satisfaction was the excuse with which, hemming and hawing, his conscience harbored the secret hope that Silvia might come to Turin to get him back.

But what if she was coming because she had to, as contracted with the Fresi Company? And maybe . . . who knows? . . . she wasn't alone. Maybe someone would be with her, to assist her on that tiresome journey. . . .

No, no. He couldn't, he mustn't do anything. But he had to return to Turin in a few days to attend, in hiding, the opening of the play, to see her again from a distance one last time. . . .

3

Hidden! From a distance!

On that sweet May evening a river of people were flowing into the theater, bright with festive lights. Carriages thundered up to crowd around the doors in the confusion of lights and the hum of the excited crowd.

Hidden, from a distance, he watched that spectacle. Wasn't that still his work, which had taken shape and now ran by itself, no longer concerned with him?

Yes, it was his work, the work that had absorbed, drained all his life to the point of leaving him like this, empty, spent. And it was up to him to see it through there, in that river of anxious people that he could not even go near or mingle with. Expelled, repelled, he himself who had moved that stream of people the first time, who first had put it together and guided it on that memorable evening at the Valle Theater in Rome!

Now he had to wait like this, hidden, from a distance, while that river invaded and filled the whole theater where he would be the last to plunge furtively and shamefully.

Tormented by this exile, so near and yet so infinitely far from his own life, which lived here, outside of himself, in front of him, and left him an inert spectator of his own present unhappiness, of his nothingness, Giustino had a surge of pride and thought that—yes—his work would keep going on by itself. But how? Certainly not as if he were still the one directing it, overseeing it, controlling it, supporting it in every way! He would have liked to see firsthand how it took shape without him! What preparation could the play's first night have had? Last night's newspapers and that morning's had barely mentioned it. Now if he had been there! Yes, people were still flowing in. But why were they? Because of the memory of *The New Colony*, of the success he made of it, and to see, to know the playwright, that timid, morose, inexperienced young woman from Taranto that he, by his effort, had made famous. He who stood there abandoned, hidden in the dark, while she stood in the light of glory, surrounded by admiration.

She certainly had to be backstage now. Who knows what she was like! What was she saying? Could she possibly think he wouldn't come from Cargiore, so near, to attend the performance? Oh, God, oh, God . . . He trembled when he remembered his thoughts at learning she would be coming to Turin, that she might be coming just to get back with him, that she would be waiting, after the first applause, for him to erupt furiously upon the stage and passionately embrace her in front of all the astonished actors, and then, and then . . . Oh, God—he couldn't stop shaking. There, in his mind's eye, the curtain was opening, and both of them, he and she, hand in hand, were bowing, reconciled and happy before the delirious audience.

Madness! Madness! But, on the other hand, didn't it go beyond the bounds of discretion for her to come to Turin, before his very eyes?

He was frantic to know, to see. . . . But how could he, from the back of that center box he had managed to get the day before? He had just now come into the box, hurriedly taking the steps two at a time. To keep from being seen he stayed far back. Above his head the gallery was making a racket; from below, from the orchestra seats came the din and ferment of grand evenings. The theater must be full and splendid.

Still breathless—more from emotion than from exertion—he looked at the curtain and wished his eyes could bore through it. Ah, what he would have paid to hear the sound of her voice again! He didn't think he could remember it any longer. How did she speak? How was she dressed? What was she saying?

He jumped at the prolonged ringing of the bell that was answering the growing din in the gallery. And now the curtain was rising!

In the sudden silence, he instinctively leaned forward, looking at the scene that simulated a newsroom. He knew the first and second act of the play, and he knew she hadn't been happy with them. Maybe she had rewritten them, or perhaps, if the play had a moderate success, she left them just as they were, forced to put the work on stage because of financial difficulties.

The first scene, between Ersilia Arciani and the editor of the newspaper, Cesare D'Albis, was the same. But Signora Fresi did not play the part of Ersilia with the severity that Silvia had given her character. Perhaps she herself, Silvia, had softened that severity to make the character less hard and more sympathetic. But evidently it wasn't enough. From the first lines a chill of disappointment spread over the theater.

Giustino noticed it, and he felt his head growing hot from that chill, making him perspire and wriggle restlessly. For God's sake! To expose oneself like this to the terrible trial of a new play, after the clamorous success of the first one, without adequately preparing the press, without informing the public that this new play would be totally different from the first one, revealing a new aspect of Silvia Roncella's talent. This was the result: the audience expected the savage poetry of *The New Colony* and expected to see strange costumes and unusual characters; instead it found itself facing ordinary, prosaic, everyday life and remained cold, disenchanted, unhappy.

He should be enjoying it, but he couldn't! Because what was still alive in him was all involved in that work failing before his very eyes, and he felt it a shame he couldn't get his hands on it, to prop it up, lift it up to make it into another triumph. A shame for the work and a ferocious cruelty to himself!

He jumped to his feet at a prolonged hissing that suddenly rose out of the orchestra like a wind to shake the whole theater, and he shrank to the back of the box with his hands on his flaming face, almost as if he had been whipped.

Leonardo Arciani's stubborn refusal to reason with his father-in-law had offended the spectators. But perhaps in the end Ersilia's cry that explained that stubbornness—"Papa, he has a daughter, a daughter: he can't reason anymore!"—would save the act. Signora Fresi entered. Everyone grew silent. Guglielmo Groa and his son-in-law almost came to blows. The audience didn't understand yet and became even more restless. Giustino wanted to shout from his box in the last row: "Idiots, he can't reason! He has a daughter!"

But there, there, Signora Fresi shouted it. Brava! Loudly, with her whole soul, like a whip. The audience broke into a lengthy *aaahhh*. Why? . . . Didn't they like it? . . . Wait. . . . Many were applauding. . . . There, the curtain fell during the applause, but it was scattered applause, many were hissing also. . . . Oh, God, a sharp, lacerating whistle from the gallery . . . damned, damned whistle! In reaction, the applause picked up in the boxes and orchestra seats. With his face bathed in tears, Giustino convulsively twisted his hands trying to applaud furiously, impeded by his anxious concentration on the stage. The actors came out. . . . No, she wasn't there. . . . Silvia wasn't there. . . . Another curtain call! Oh, God . . . Was she there? . . . The applause tapered off, and with the applause Giustino also fell on a chair in the box, worn out, gasping for breath as though he had been running for an hour. Large, tearlike drops of perspiration appeared on his burning forehead. He tried to relax his contracted muscles, his pounding heart, and a moan came out of his labored breathing as from intolerable suffering. But he couldn't remain still an instant. He stood up, leaned on the box railing with his arms limp, handkerchief in hand, head dangling . . . he looked at the exit . . . brought the handkerchief to his mouth and tore it. . . . He was a prisoner there. . . . He couldn't let himself be seen. . . . He would at least have liked to hear the comments about the first act, to go near the stage, to see those who were going there to comfort the writer. . . . Ah, at that moment she certainly was not thinking of him. He didn't exist for her: he was one of the crowd, mixed in with everyone else. No, no, no, not even that—he couldn't even be part of the crowd. He couldn't be and in fact he wasn't: closed up, hidden there in a box that everyone had to think was empty, the only empty one, because someone wasn't able to come. . . . What a temptation, now, to run to the stage, to push through the crowd as if he owned the place, to take his rightful position again, as the one who gave the orders! A heroic furor stirred him to do things unheard of and never before seen, to change the destiny of that evening point-blank, before the amazed eyes of the entire audience, to show that he was there, he who had staged the triumph of *The New Colony*. . . .

Now the bells rang for the second act. The battle began again. Oh, God, how could he watch, exhausted as he was?

The restless audience entered the theater noisily. If they didn't like the first scene of the second act, between the father and daughter, the play would have failed completely.

The curtain rose.

This scene represented Leonardo Arciani's study. It was daylight and the lamp still burned on the desk. Guglielmo Groa was sleeping in an armchair with a newspaper over his face. Ersilia entered, put out the lamp, woke her father, and told him her husband had not yet come home. At his stern, blunt questions, like a hammer pounding rocks, Ersilia's hardness broke, and her repressed emotions began to flow. With a languid, sorrowful calmness she spoke in defense of her husband, who, having to choose between her and his daughter, had chosen his daughter: "*Home is where the children are!*"

Giustino, enthralled, fascinated by the profound beauty of that scene played admirably by Signora Fresi, didn't notice that the audience had now become very attentive. At the end, when a warm, long, unanimous applause broke out, he felt his blood rush to his heart and then suddenly rise to his head. The battle was won, but he was lost. If Silvia had appeared with that applause to thank the audience, he wouldn't have seen her: a veil had fallen over his eyes. No, no, thank goodness! The play went on. He, however, could no longer pay attention. The anxiety, the heartache, the excitement grew as the act progressed, approaching the end, the marvelous scene between the husband and wife when Ersilia, pardoning Leonardo, sends him away: "*You can no longer stay here now. Two houses, no; I here and your daughter there, no. It's not possible, go away! I know what you want!*" Oh, how Signora Fresi told him! Now Leonardo was going away. She breaks into tears of joy, and the curtain fell amid loud applause.

"Author! Author!"

With arms tightly crossed over his chest and his hands gripping his shoulders, almost as if to stop his heart from leaping out, Giustino groaned and waited for Silvia to appear at the footlights. The torture of waiting made his face look almost ferocious.

There she was! No. Those were actors. The applause continued to thunder.

"Author! We want the author!"

There she was! There she was! That one? Yes, there she was between two actors. But she was barely discernible from such a height: the distance was too great and too great the commotion clouding his vision! Now they were calling her out again. There she was, there she was again. The two actors stepped back and let her go to the footlights alone, exposed for such a long time to the powerful response of the audience, on its feet clapping. This time Giustino could see her better: standing straight, pale, and unsmiling. She barely bowed her head, with a dignity not cold but full of unconquerable sadness.

Giustino thought no more about hiding. As soon as she left the footlights he dashed out of the box like a madman, threw himself down the stairs along with the crowd leaving the theater and filling the hallways, pushed his way through with furious gestures, to the surprise of those he knocked out of the way. He heard shouts and laughter behind his back as he found the theater exit. In the murky dizziness filling his head, pierced by flashes of light, he felt nothing but the fire that devoured him and made his throat burn atrociously.

Like a beaten dog he took off down the first long, straight, deserted street that opened off the piazza. He kept going without knowing where, eyes closed, scratching his head at both temples and repeating voicelessly, his mouth dry as cork:

"It's over . . . it's over . . . it's over. . . ."

This certainty had penetrated his being at the sight of her and was fixed like an absolute conviction: everything was finished, because that was no longer Silvia. No, no, that was no longer Silvia. It was someone else he could never approach. Someone distant, unreachably distant, above him, above everyone because of that sadness enveloping her: isolated, elevated, so stiff and severe, as if she had survived a calamity. She was another person for whom he no longer existed.

Where was he going? Where had he gone? Lost, he looked around at the quiet, dark houses. He looked at the street lamps, watchful in the sad silence. He stopped, about to fall, and leaned against a wall with his eyes on a lamp, staring at the motionless light like an idiot, then down at the circle of light on the sidewalk. He looked farther down the street. But why try to sort it out if everything was finished? Where should he go? Home? Why? He had to go on living, didn't he? Why? There in Cargiore, in a vacuum, in idleness, for years and years and years . . . What was left for him, what could give some sense, some value to his life? No affection that didn't represent an intolerable duty: for his son, for his mother. He no longer felt the need for those affections. They, his son and his mother, needed him, but what could he do for them? Live, right? Live to keep his old mother from dying of sorrow . . . After he and his grandmother died, his son would have his mother and they would both be better off. With the boy she would have to think about him, the boy's father, the man who had been her husband, and so he would go on existing for her, with her son, in her son.

How could he get back to Cargiore from Giaveno on foot, so exhausted? His mother was certainly waiting up for him, sad about his leaving. . . . For days he had behaved like a lunatic after learning that Silvia would be coming to Turin. His mother had found out through Prever, who had probably heard it in town. Perhaps Dr. Lais had read it in the newspaper. His mother had come to his room to beg him not to go to town at this time. Poor woman! Poor woman! What a spectacle he had made of himself! He had begun to shout like a madman that he wanted to be left alone, that he didn't need anyone's protection, that he didn't want to be smothered by all those concerns and fears, or done in by all that advice. For three days he didn't even go down at mealtimes, staying in his room, not wanting to see anyone or to hear anything.

Now he was through. He had seen her and lost all hope. What was left for him to do? Return to his son and his mother, that was it . . . that was it forever!

He took off for the station to get a tram to Giaveno and arrived just in time for the last one.

After reaching Giaveno around midnight, he started off for Cargiore. All was silent under the moon on the sweet cool May night. More than surprise at the amazing and nearly stunning solitude in the soft moonlight, he felt almost brokenhearted over the mysterious, fascinating beauty of the night, all dappled with shadows from the moon and resonant with silvery trills. At intervals murmurs of unseen water and leafy branches made the heartache more intense. It seemed like that murmuring didn't want to be heard, nor did it want to hear his footsteps, and so he walked more softly. Suddenly from behind a gate a ferociously barking dog made him jump and tremble and grow cold with fright. Other dogs began to bark from near and far, protesting his passing at that hour. When he stopped trembling, he noticed how extremely tired his legs felt. He thought about how he came to be so tired. He thought about the interminable road he had ahead of him, and suddenly the beauty of the night dimmed for him, its fascination vanished, and he sank into the somber darkness of his pain. He walked on for more than an hour without wanting to stop a moment to catch his breath. Finally, he couldn't take anymore and sat on the edge of the road: he just collapsed, without the strength to hold up his head. Gradually the deep roar of the Sangone down in the valley became more distinct, then the rustle of the new chestnut leaves and the thick coolness of the wooded valley, and finally the laugh of a little brook down there. And he felt the burning in his mouth again. He moaned in pity for himself, for his grim and harshly treated soul, and tired and desperate, he felt a scorching need for comfort. He stood up again to go quickly to the only one who could give it to him. But he had to walk another half hour before seeing the octagonal cusp of the church, pointing like a threatening finger toward the sky. When he got there and looked in the direction of his house, he was surprised to see lights in three windows. He had expected one, but why so many?

In the dark, sitting on the steps in front of the door, he found Prever weeping.

"Mamma?" Giustino shouted.

Prever stood up, and with head down he held out his arms:

"Rino . . . Rino . . ." he groaned between sobs in his long beard.

"Rino? But how? What's wrong?" Shaking himself angrily from the old man's arms, Giustino ran to his son's room, still shouting, "What's wrong? What's wrong?"

The little boy was being bathed in cold water, and his grandmother held him on her knees, wrapped in a sheet. Dr. Lais was there. Graziella and the nurse were crying. The little boy wasn't crying; he was shaking all over, with his curly little head soaked with water, his eyes closed, his little face red, almost purple, swollen.

His mother barely looked up, and Giustino felt pierced by her glance.

"What's wrong? What's wrong?" he asked the doctor in a trembling voice. "What happened? So . . . suddenly."

"Well, for two days," the doctor said.

"Two days?"

His mother turned to stare at him.

"I didn't know . . . I didn't know anything," Giustino stammered to the doctor, as if to excuse himself. "But how? What's wrong, Doctor? Tell me! What happened? What happened?"

Doctor Lais took him by an arm and motioned with his head, taking him into the next room.

"You came from Turin, didn't you? You were at the theater?"

"Yes," whispered Giustino, looking at him, dazed.

"Well, then," Dr. Lais continued hesitantly. "If his mother could come . . ."

"What?"

"I think that . . . it would be a good thing, perhaps, to advise her to . . ."

"Then," shouted Giustino, "then Rino . . . my little boy . . ."

Three sobs answered him from the next room, and a fourth behind him from Prever, who had come back up. Giustino turned, threw himself into the old man's arms, and broke into tears himself.

Dr. Lais returned to the room of the boy, who had been put back into bed. Although sunk into lethargy, he jerked convulsively. He was burning again. Breaking free from Prever, Giustino went back into the room.

"I want to know what's wrong with him! I want to know what's wrong with him!" he shouted at the doctor, seized by uncontrollable anger.

Dr. Lais was irritated with him and shouted back: "What's wrong with him? He has tertian fever!"

His tone and scowl said: "You go to the theater and have the gall to ask me in this way what's wrong with your son!"

"But how? In three days!"

"Certainly in three days! Why the surprise? That's what tertian fever means! Everything has been done. . . . I've tried . . ."

"My Rino . . . My Rino . . . Oh, God, Doctor . . . My little Rirì!"

Giustino threw himself down on his knees next to the bed to touch the boy's burning hand with his forehead, and sobbing, he thought he had never given all his heart to that little being who was going away, who had lived for nearly two years away from his love, away from his mother's, poor boy, and who had found refuge only in his grandmother's love. . . . And only that evening he had thought of giving him to his mother! But she didn't deserve him, either, just as he didn't! And so the little boy was going away. . . . Neither of them deserved him.

Dr. Lais had him get up and with gentle insistence took him into the next room again.

"I'll be back as soon as it's daylight," he told him. "If you want to send a telegram to his mother . . . It seems the right thing to do. . . . I can, if you wish, take care of it before coming back. Here, write on this."

He took a piece of paper from his notebook, and a pen. He wrote: "Come at once. Your son is dying. Giustino."

4

The little room was full of flowers; the bed on which the little corpse lay under a blue veil was full of flowers. Four candles sputtered at each corner, as if the flames were laboring to breathe in that air too heavily laden with sweet perfumes. Even the little dead child seemed oppressed by them: ashen, eyes hardened under livid eyelids.

All those collective flowers no longer gave off a single odor: they polluted the closed air of that little room; they dazed and nauseated. And the child under the blue veil, abandoned to that nauseating smell, sunk into it, prisoner of it, could be looked at only from a distance, in the light of those four candles whose yellow heat made the stagnating stench of all those odors almost visible and impenetrable.

Only Graziella, her eyes red with weeping, was staying by the door to watch the little body when, toward eleven, like a sudden wind on the stairs, among moans, the rustling of clothes, and renewed sobbing down on the ground floor, Silvia, supported by Dr. Lais, started to rush into the little room. Suddenly she stopped just outside the door, lifting her hands as if to protect herself from the sight, and opening her mouth for one cry after another that would not erupt from her throat. Dr. Lais felt her faint in his arms; he shouted: "Get a chair!"

Graziella pulled one over, and they both helped her sit down, and suddenly Dr. Lais ran to the window, exclaiming: "But how can you stand this? You can't breathe in here! Air! Air!"

And he quickly returned to Silvia, who now sat with her hands over her face, her head bowed as though under a sentence. Besides the weight of sorrow, she carried the weight of remorse and shame, and was weeping, shaken with violent sobs. She wept like this for a while. Then she raised her head, propping it with her fingers splayed over her eyes, and looked at the little bed. She got up and went to it, saying to the doctor who wanted to stop her: "No . . . no . . . let me . . . let me see him."

First she looked at him through the veil, then without the veil, stifling her sobs, holding her breath to feel deeply within herself the death of her son, whom she no longer recognized. As though unable to bear the lifelessness she had taken into herself, she bent to kiss the forehead of the poor little body and moaned: "Oh, how cold you are . . . how cold you are."

And she wept inwardly: "Because my love couldn't keep you warm. . . ."

"Cold . . . cold . . ." And she lightly caressed his head, his blond curls.

Dr. Lais persuaded her to leave the bedside. She looked at Graziella, who was crying, but she noticed behind her tears for the boy a hostile look for her. She didn't feel indignant, but instead loved that old woman's hate, which was an act of love for her child. And she turned to the doctor.

"What happened? What happened?"

Dr. Lais led her to the next room, to the same room where she had slept during the months of her stay there. The tears that had come to her eyes and that had been restrained and nearly dissolved by the emotional tumult of what she saw, now flowed freely and spontaneously. Here she felt her heart lacerated by live memories of that little creature, here she felt herself really a mother, with the heart of that earlier time, when every morning the nurse brought to her bed the little naked pink being fresh from his bath, and she, holding him to her breast, thought that soon she would have to leave him. . . .

In the meantime, Dr. Lais told her about his sudden illness, what he had done to save him, and he told her that even for the father that misfortune had been an unexpected agony, because the evening before he had been at the theater to see her play, without knowing that the boy was so seriously ill.

Silvia looked up with a shudder at this news: "Last night? At the theater? But how could he not know?"

"Signora," Dr. Lais replied, "when he heard that you would be in Turin . . ." And he made a gesture with his hand that meant: he seemed to have gone out of his mind.

"His mother didn't tell him anything, seeing him like that," he added. "She didn't think it was really so serious. It's sad, believe me, sad! As soon as he arrived last night, around two, on foot from Giaveno, he found his boy dying. It was I who suggested notifying you by telegram. In fact, I took it myself, when the boy already, unfortunately . . . He died around six. . . . Listen! Do you hear him?"

Suddenly on the stairs Giustino's sobs were heard among the confused shuffling and shouts of the others who perhaps were trying to hold him back.

Silvia jumped to her feet in distress and drew back in a corner as if trying to hide.

Assisted by Don Buti, Prever, and his mother, Giustino appeared in the doorway as though on the verge of collapse, his clothes and hair in disarray, his face bathed in tears. He looked fiercely at Dr. Lais and said: "Where is she?"

As soon as he saw her, his body gave a start, his legs and chin began to tremble, until tears, gradually distorting his features, gurgled in his convulsed throat, but as Prever and Don Buti tried to drag him out, he broke away furiously:

"No, here!" he shouted.

He stood there like that for an instant, unrestrained, perplexed. Then, gasping, he threw himself on Silvia and embraced her wildly.

Silvia didn't move, but stiffened to withstand that desperate impulse. She closed her eyes in pity, then opened them again to reassure his mother she need have no fear. She let herself be embraced out of pity and she knew how to control that pity.

"Did you see? Did you see?" Giustino sobbed on her breast, grasping her harder. "He's gone. . . . Rirì's gone because we weren't here. . . . You weren't here . . . and I wasn't even here anymore . . . and so the little one said: 'What am I doing here?' and he went away. If he could see you here now . . . Come! Come! If he could see you here . . ."

He pulled her by the hand to the boy's room, as if the joy of her coming could perform the miracle of bringing the boy back to life.

"Rirì! . . . Oh, Rirì . . . oh, my Rirì . . ." He fell on his knees again at the bedside, burying his face in the flowers.

Silvia felt faint. Dr. Lais ran to support her, taking her to the next room. Giustino was also pulled away from the bedside by Don Buti and Prever and led downstairs.

"Silvia! Silvia!" he kept calling, overpowered by those two, and without the strength to rebel now that he had seen his dead son again.

At the sound of her name fading in the distance, Silvia felt as though called from the depths of the life spent there a year ago: an obscure premonition of this tragedy had existed in the happiness of that time, and that premonition now called to her in the distant cry: *Silvia! . . . Silvia! . . .* Oh, if she had been able to hear her name called out like that, she would have found the strength to resist every temptation. She would have stayed here with her little one, in this peaceful nest in the mountains, and her little one wouldn't be dead, and none of the horrible things that happened would have happened. The most horrible thing of all . . . Oh, that! Among the flashes of smothering images, she still felt her flesh burn with shame for the single embrace, attempted almost coldly, out of a terrible, inevitable necessity there in Ostia, and left desperately incomplete. She would feel sullied by it forever, more than if she had sinned thousands of times with all those young men rumored to have been her lovers. The cloying memory of that single inconclusive embrace had aroused an invincible nausea, a loathing, in which every desire for love would be forever drowned. She was sure that Giustino, if that were her wish, could be torn from his mother's arms and from every shred of self-respect to return to her. But no, she didn't want that, and she shouldn't for both their sakes! Now the last bond between them had been broken by the death. And he was struggling down there in vain against the arms trying to hold him. Dr. Lais had been called to help. In there her dead son lay among the flowers. People were coming up to see him: women from the town, old people, children, and they all brought more flowers, more flowers. . . .

A short time later Dr. Lais, hot and panting, came back to her with a sheet of paper in his hand, the draft of a telegram that her husband down below, shouting and struggling, had thought necessary to write. He wanted Dr. Lais to send it as soon as he showed it to her.

"A telegram?" Silvia asked, surprised.

"Yes. Here it is." Dr. Lais handed it to her.

It was a telegram to the Fresi Company. Several words were made almost illegible by the tears that had fallen on it. It announced the death of the boy, asking that the play performances be suspended, after announcing to the public the author's grave loss. It was signed *Boggiolo*.

Silvia read it and remained, under the eyes of the waiting doctor, absorbed, confused, and bewildered. "Does it have to be sent?"

She knew it! After the embrace, he felt he had already become her husband again.

"No, not like that," she said to the doctor. "Remove the announcement to the public, and if you don't mind the bother, go ahead and send it, but under my name, please."

Dr. Lais bowed. "I understand perfectly," he said. "Don't worry, it will be done." And he went out.

But after about half an hour, Giustino came up again with a foolish expression on his face, along with a journalist, the same young journalist who came from Turin a year ago looking for the writer of *The New Colony*.

"Here she is! Her she is!" he said, bringing him in the room, and turning to Silvia: "You know him, don't you?"

Embarrassed by Boggiolo's unseemly, almost jocular anxiety intruding on that tragic moment (although the poor man's face was burned by tears), the young man bowed and shook Silvia's hand, saying: "I am sorry, Signora, to find you here in such different circumstances from our first meeting. I learned at the theater that you had rushed here. I didn't think that already . . ."

Giustino interrupted him, taking him by the arm: "While the play was being performed last night in Turin," he began telling him, with a great tremor in his voice and hands, yet with his eyes fixed on his, as if he were lecturing him, "the boy was dying here, and we didn't know it, neither she nor I, you see? And she," he continued, pointing to Silvia, "do you know why she came here the first time? Because our baby was born! And do you know when our baby was born? The same evening as *The New Colony*'s success the very same evening, which is why we named him Vittorio, Vittorino. . . . Now she has returned for his death! And when did this death happen? Just while her new play was being performed in Turin! Just think about it! What destiny . . . He is born and dies like that. . . . Come here, come here, I'll show him to you. . . ."

So taken up was he by the excitement of his endeavors, it was almost frightening. The young man looked at him, appalled.

"Here he is! Here he is! Our little angel! See how beautiful he is among all those flowers? These are the tragedies of life, my dear sir, the tragedies that grip us. . . . There's no need to go looking for tragedies on faraway islands, among savage people! I am telling you this for your readers, you know? The public doesn't want to know some things. . . . You journalists must explain to them that if today a writer can get a tragedy out of . . . of her head, a savage tragedy, that everyone likes immediately for its novelty, tomorrow she herself, the writer, can be seized by one of these tragedies of life, that crushes a poor little boy and the hearts of a father and mother, understand? This, this is what you should explain to the public, those people who feel nothing when faced with the tragedy of a father who has a daughter living apart from him, of a wife who knows she cannot have her husband back except by taking in his child, and she goes there, she goes to her husband's lover to get the child! These are tragedies . . . the tragedies . . . the tragedies of life, my dear sir. This poor woman here, believe me, can do nothing . . . she doesn't . . . she doesn't know how to get the most out of her work. . . . I, I want, I who know these things so well . . . but right now my head hurts . . . it hurts so much. Too much emotion . . . too much, too much . . . and I need to sleep. It's the weariness, you know? that makes me talk like this. I need to sleep. . . . I can't take any more. . . . I can't take any more."

He went out, his head in his hands, repeating: "I can't take any more . . . can't take any more. . . ."

"The poor man!" sighed the journalist, going into the other room with Silvia. "What a state he's in!"   •

"For heaven's sake," Silvia quickly begged, "don't say anything, don't refer to any of this in the paper. . . ."

"My dear signora! What are you thinking?" he interrupted, fending off the idea with his hands.

"It's a double torment for me!" Silvia continued, almost suffocated. "It's like being struck by lightning! And now . . . this other torment."

"It really makes you pity him!"

"Yes, and just because of the pity I feel, I want to go away, I want to leave."

"If you want, Signora, I have here with me . . ."

"No, no: tomorrow, tomorrow. As long my little boy is here, I'll stay here. My uncle is buried here also. And the thought of my dear old uncle being in a stranger's tomb makes me feel so sad. The dead, I understand, are neither friends nor enemies to each other. But I think of him among the dead who aren't friends. Now he'll have his little nephew with him and won't be alone anymore. I'll give him my little one tomorrow, and when everything is done I'll leave."

"Do you want me to come tomorrow to take you back? I would be very happy to do it."

"Thank you," Silvia replied, "but I still don't know when."

"I'll find out, don't worry. Until tomorrow!"

The young journalist left, very pleased. Silvia closed her eyes, with her lips in an expression more of bitterness than disdain, and shook her head. A little later, without looking at her, Graziella brought her something to drink. But she didn't want to put it to her lips. Later she had the torment of a visitor: the doctor's wife, more than ever over-flowing with affectations. But fortunately, in her weariness and dazed condition, while the woman foolishly tried to comfort her, she found a new well of tears and turned her eyes to a corner of the room.

On the dresser, as if conversing with one another, were Rirì's toys: a papier-mâché horse attached to a four-wheeled cart, a tin horn, a boat, a little clown with a tambourine. The little horse, with a threadbare tail, a crushed ear, and a missing wheel on the cart was the saddest of all.

The little sailboat with its prow turned toward the horse seemed far, far away, a large boat in a dream sea far, far away, and it was sailing along in that dream sea with Rirì's little soul amazed and lost. . . . But of course not! The little clown, smiling, told her it wasn' true, that the top of the dresser wasn't the sea at all, and that Rirì's little soul could sail no more on it.

Rirì had left them there to do something very important, something that seemed unusual for a little boy: to die! The little horse, although lame and threadbare, as is the destiny of all toys, seemed to bob its head, almost as if it couldn't understand. If only the horn could call him back from that sleep amid all those flowers there! But the horn was broken, too—it didn't play anymore. Rirì's mouth spoke no more . . . his little hands moved no more . . . his eyes opened no more . . . himself a broken toy, Rirì!

What had those little two-year-old eyes seen, open to the spectacle of a world so big? Who keeps memories of things seen with two-year-old eyes? And now those little eyes that looked without keeping memories of the things seen were closed forever. Outside there were so many things to see: the meadows, the mountains, the sky, the church. Rirì had left that big world that had never been his, except in that little papier-mâché horse that smelled of glue, in that little boat with its sails spread, in that tin horn, in that little clown that laughed and beat his tambourine. And he hadn't known his mother's heart. Rirì . . .

Evening came. The doctor's wife went away; Silvia remained alone, in the enormous, total silence.

She looked into the little mortuary room. There was Graziella saying her rosary and the nurse napping in a chair. Silvia was suddenly tempted to send them both to bed and stay alone with her little boy, to bar the window and door and lie down next to her little one, to let herself be absorbed by his cold death, killed by all those flowers. Dazed by their perfume that had made her head leaden, she felt suddenly overcome by a desperate weariness of everything in life, in the gloomy silence of that house crushed by death's nightmare. However, looking out the window, she had the strange feeling that her soul had remained outside there all this time, and that she had just found it now with an infinite wonder and relief. It was that same soul that had looked up at the sight of another moonlit night like this one. But in the sweetness of the relief there was now a more intense heartache, a more urgent need to be free of everything. And with the wonder, a more eager awakening to new revelations, vaster revelations of eternal dreams. She looked at the moon hanging over one of the big mountains, and in the placid pure light that spread over the sky, she gazed at, drank in, the few stars that were appearing like pools of more vivid light. She lowered her eyes to the earth and saw again the mountains in the distance with their blue brows lifted to breathe in the light. She saw again the amazed trees, the meadows resounding with water under the limpid silence of the moon. Everything seemed so unreal that her soul, suffused in that unreality, became tree and silence and dew.

From the depths of her spirit an immense darkness rose to join that limpid, dreamlike unreality: a vague, deep feeling for life, made up of so many inexpressible, whirling, gusting, overlapping impressions from the deepest darkness. Outside of all the things that gave meaning to our lives there was another meaning in the life of things that we couldn't understand: those stars said it with their light, those grasses with their odors, that water with its murmur. A mysterious meaning that was bewildering. We had to go beyond the things that give meaning to our lives, to penetrate this mysterious meaning of the life of things. Beyond the petty necessities that we create for ourselves, there were other obscure, gigantic necessities taking shape in the fascinating flow of time, like those great mountains there, in the enchantment of the very silent lunar dawn. From now on she had to keep her mind fixed on them, to face them with the mind's rigorous eyes, to give voice to all the unexpressed things of her spirit, to those things that until now had caused distress, and leave the miserable absurdities of daily existence, the absurdities of humans, who, without realizing it, stumble around immersed in the immense vortex of life.

She stood at the window all night long until the cold dawn slowly came to change and solidify the appearances of her earlier vaporous dream. In this cold solidity of things touched by the light of day she also felt the divine fluidity of her own being almost congeal, and come up against the cruel reality, the brutal, hard dreadfulness of matter, that powerful, greedy, ferocious destroyer, nature, under the implacable eye of the rising sun. That dreadfulness and ferocity would now put her poor little boy underground and make him earth again.

There, they were bringing the casket. The church bell rang gloriously in the light of the new day.

How long is a day for a little dead body lying on his bed waiting to be buried? How long is the return of light not seen since the previous day? The light already finds him further away in the shadows of death, already further away in the survivors' grief. Soon now grief will draw closer and howl at the horrible spectacle of enclosing the little body in the waiting casket. Then, immediately after the burial, this grief will go away again, to remake itself hurriedly in that brief, cruel return, until it slowly disappears in time where only occasionally will memory struggle to rejoin it, to recognize it, and then, oppressed and tired, it will retreat, called back by a sigh of resignation.

What did Giustino, who had slept heavily, read in Silvia's face, which seemed to have absorbed the pallor of the moon she had watched from the window all night long? He looked dazed as he stood before her. He was again racked by tears, but no longer dared embrace her as before. Instead, he dropped down next to the little body already lying in the flower-covered casket. Prever dragged him away. Graziella and the nurse dragged the grandmother away. No one troubled with Silvia, who hoped to have the strength to stay there until the end, after having kissed death on the little boy's small, hard, cold brow. After the cover of the casket had been soldered, the young journalist came, and though his concern touched her, she didn't want to leave.

"Now . . . now it's done," she said to him. "Thank you. Leave me alone! Now I've seen everything. . . . There is nothing more to see. A casket and my love as a mother, there . . ."

A flood of tears leapt to her throat, gushed from her eyes. She restrained them almost angrily with her handkerchief.

As soon as Giustino, supported by Prever, in the middle of those come to the funeral procession, saw the young journalist walking behind the casket next to Silvia, he realized that after the burial she would never come home again. Then he said to Prever and to the people standing around him: "Wait, wait . . ."

He ran upstairs. For him death was not in that little casket as much as it was in Silvia's appearance, in her definite departure. His child's death was nothing compared to what was dying with his wife's desertion. The two sorrows for him were one and inseparable. In putting the boy in the tomb, he was putting something else in her hands: nothing less than the rest of his life.

A short time later he was seen coming down with a sheaf of papers under his arm. Leaning on Prever, he followed the funeral procession to the church graveyard while holding on to these papers. When the service was over, he let go of Prever's arm and went unsteadily to Silvia, who was ready to leave in the journalist's car.

"Here," he said, handing her the papers. "Take them. . . . Now I . . . what . . . what can I do with them? They might be useful to you. . . . They are . . . they are from translators . . . my notes . . . calculations . . . contracts . . . letters. . . . They might be useful to . . . to keep you from getting cheated. . . . Who knows . . . who knows how badly they'll cheat you. . . . Take them . . . and . . . good-bye! Good-bye! Good-bye! . . ."

Sobbing, he threw himself into the arms of Prever, who had come to his side.

AFTERWORD

Known almost exclusively in the United States for his great contributions to modern European theater, especially *Six Characters in Search of an Author* and *Henry IV,* Luigi Pirandello began his literary career as a novelist and writer of short stories. While these works are still widely read and studied in Italy, they have received little attention abroad. Although it is true that his innovations in fiction never made the startling impact of those in *Six Characters* when that play first appeared on the stage, they nonetheless deserve a place in the canon of early twentieth-century European fiction evolving from naturalism to modernism.

A Sicilian by birth and by formation, Pirandello began to write under the influence of two prominent fellow countrymen, Luigi Capuana and Giovanni Verga, leaders of the Italian school of naturalism known as *verismo.* His first novel, *L'Esclusa* (*The Outcast*), written in 1893 and published in 1901, realistically portrays aspects of contemporary Sicilian life and mores while recounting the story of a woman banished from her home because of unfounded rumors of her adultery, which threatened her husband's honor. With the ironic conclusion, however, when the protagonist, Marta, is deemed innocent and allowed to return home (although she has in fact by then committed adultery), Pirandello begins to find new artistic means for depicting the relation between being and seeming, and between illusion and reality, for which he will become famous. This theme, and the fictional innovations it requires, will be more fully developed in his best-known novel, *Il fu Mattia Pascal* (*The Late Mattia Pascal*), published in 1904. In this novel, Pirandello experiments with free indirect discourse, restricted points of view, and interior monologues in telling the story of a man who, finding that he has been reported to be dead in his native town, creates for himself a new personage under a new name in Rome, only to discover the impossibility of living out the fiction. Pirandello here reveals the fictional or "constructed" basis of all social existence, a theme he will develop more fully in his theater.

Her Husband (*Suo marito*), Pirandello's fifth novel, has its roots in the "veristic" observation of society, appearances, mores, and character, but betrays a peculiarly Pirandellian modernism in the dialectic between subjectivity and objectivity, the metafictional reflections on language and literature, the use of cinematic close-ups, and especially the portrayal of the evanescent and illusory nature of the self. In 1908, three years before the publication of *Suo marito*, Pirandello published his most famous treatise on poetics, *Umorismo* (*On Humor*), where he studies the process of "decomposition" that certain authors exert on conventional literary forms and expectations. The greatest novelists, in his view, combine comic distance and tragic pathos—thereby revealing the contradictions of existence—by creating characters at whom we laugh and with whom we sympathize at the same time. Pirandello clearly applies his "humoristic" theories to the creation of the character Ely Faciolli in *Her Husband*, and even to some extent to the title character, Giustino Boggiolo. But the author's voice becomes heavily satirical, even sarcastic rather than humoristic, in its portrayal of certain elements of contemporary society in what was then known as "the third Rome."

The first and the second Rome refer to the hegemonies of the ancient Roman empire and of the papacy. Although Italy was unified in 1861, with its capital first in Turin and then in Florence, the nation only wrested Rome from papal control in 1870. The next year, in an attempt to revive the nation's past glory and grandeur, as well as to found a new society based on the ideals of Italy's national movement, the risorgimento, the capital was moved to Rome. Given these expectations, it is hardly surprising that disillusionment would set in. The difficulties of governing a country with regional traditions ranging from the Sicilian to the Milanese and political allegiances from socialist/anarchist to Catholic/royalist did not coincide with romantic aspirations to unity.

The early twentieth-century Rome in which Pirandello lived was the seat of the government of Giovanni Giolitti, the prime minister who did his best to bring together the divergent economic and political interests of the new nation. Intellectuals, however, considered Giolitti the embodiment of bureaucratic mediocrity, and his efforts at democratization and liberalization evidence of the flaws inherent in parliamentary democracy itself. They accused the liberal state of betraying the glorious ideals of the risorgimento. Pirandello, who subscribed to these criticisms of Giolitti, never wavered in his conviction that democracy, "the tyranny of the crowd," was not a viable form of government for Italy. Along with mediocrity in government, democracy—and *fin de siècle* decadence—bred mediocrity in society, individuals, and art. The aristocracy, who no longer exercised any real function in the society of the "third Rome," took refuge in a kind of sterile aestheticism and preservation of forms without substance, while the bourgeoisie, who did hold power, pretentiously mimicked aristocratic taste.

One of the major accomplishments of the Giolitti government was a significant rise of literacy in Italy. With this came a surge in publications, primarily journals and magazines, but also popular novels. Thus writers of popular literature, literary bohemians with avant-garde pretensions, would-be aristocratic aesthetes, and serious writers mingled in the society of the new Rome, aware of the newly acquired power of journalists and the publishing establishment to make or break their careers. It is this literary scene that Pirandello satirizes mercilessly in the first part of his novel. At the beginning, where he depicts the encounter of a literary-magazine publisher with a riotous proletarian crowd, he also evokes the reality of the often violent strikes, which were organized frequently by socialist labor unions at the time. Attilo

Raceni, however, representative of the new bourgeoisie, understands even less of the significance of the demonstration he witnesses than Stendhal's Fabrizio del Dongo understood the battle of Waterloo.

Raceni is not just a literary publisher, but a specialist. Pirandello describes his publication as "la rassegna femminile (non femminista) *Le Muse*," which we translated as "the women's (not the feminist) magazine *The Muses*." The brief sentence reflects the facts that early twentieth-century Italy, with a surge in the number of literate women, witnessed not only a proliferation of women's magazines and fiction, poetry, and drama written by and for women, but also the rise of a small but vocal and influential feminist movement. The distinction between "feminine" and "feminist," which is still being made today, was even then probably not as clear as it seems to have been in Attilo Raceni's mind. Pirandello, if we can judge from his satirical attitude toward Raceni's journal and his remarks elsewhere on feminism, had no particular respect either for the new social movement or for the "feminine" literature then being produced for women readers. Why then did he choose to write a novel centered on a sympathetic and penetrating portrayal of a woman writer of great talent?

While it is by no means primarily a roman à clef, *Her Husband* was clearly based on Pirandello's acquaintance with the Sardinian writer Grazia Deledda (winner of the Nobel Prize in 1926) and her husband Palmiro Madesani. Analogies between Deledda and Pirandello's fictional woman writer Silvia Roncella and between Mandesani and her husband Giustino Boggiolo are evident throughout the novel. Although Silvia is from Taranto, in Apulia, rather than from Sardinia, she, like Deledda, left her provincial southern hometown to come to Rome with her husband to continue the writing she began almost as a child. Grazia Deledda's lifelong dream had been to live in Rome, a place where she imagined her writing, also begun at an early age, would be better appreciated than in Sardinia. Like Silvia, she published her first stories in a women's magazine. However, one difference between the real writer and the fictional one becomes immediately apparent. Deledda had the nineteenth-century woman's determination to achieve what she set out to do through her heavily disguised manipulative skills, and even before Deledda and Palmiro Madesani were married in Sardinia in 1900, she importuned important friends to find her husband work in Rome. Silvia, on the other hand, is brought to Rome rather reluctantly by her husband's job and wants no part in the marketing of her work. Both the fictional and the real husband hail from northern Italy, and they take upon themselves the business affairs and social contacts necessary for promoting their wives' work; both women are unusually shy, sometimes morose or sullen, in social gatherings.

One evening shortly after their arrival in Rome Deledda and her husband, just like the fictional Silvia and her husband, were honored at a dinner hosted by Giovanni Cena, editor of the prestigious *Nuova Antologia*. One of the guests there was Senator Ruggero Bonghi, another literary editor, who helped to launch Deledda's career by writing a preface to her novel *Anime oneste* (*Honest Souls*) in 1895. He is represented, not particularly kindly, by the character Romualdo Borghi. Another guest at the event was Luigi Pirandello, at that time a comparatively lesser known writer of poetry, short stories, plays, and novels than she, but important enough for Deledda to have included him in her list of those to receive a copy of her novel *Nostalgie* when it first came out in 1905.[1] In 1906 Deledda's husband referred to Pirandello as a "friend" in a letter to her French translator.[2] But at this particular gathering of writers and editors, Pirandello's disparaging attitude toward the celebrity's husband had been embarrassingly apparent. All evening Pirandello referred to Palmiro Madesani as "Grazio Deleddo." By making the final vowels of her names masculine, apparently to show his low regard for Madesani's supporting role, he succeeded in discomforting everyone present.[3]

Used as a vehicle to satirize what he felt was the insensitivity, pretentiousness, and materialism of Roman literati, as well as to express his own particular concerns, Pirandello's portrayal of the Deledda-Madesani couple is not entirely accurate. He does reflect the fact that "her husband" helped Deledda with the business end of her work.

Deledda wrote to an old friend: "I have had many requests for translations, and Madesani is studying English and German and Spanish to keep up with the correspondence."[4] However, a truer picture of Palmiro Madesani would show him as someone who supported her efforts, and who was in no way jealous of or threatened by the public acclaim she attracted. Perhaps it would be fair to say that Madesani, too, like Silvia's husband, saw there was gold to be mined from his wife's output, but this did not seem to bother Deledda. She was happy to give him credit for his work on her/their behalf. On one occasion she jokingly referred to their mutual enterprise as the Madesani-Deledda Company.[5]

Pirandello had expected that the distinguished Florentine publisher Treves would publish *Suo marito*, not taking into account the embarrassment it would cause an important author on the publisher's list—Deledda herself. In a letter to his editor friend Ugo Ojetti, Pirandello wrote: "I will send my novel, *Suo marito*, to Treves, I hope in April. It's a takeoff on the husband of Grazia Deledda. Do you know him? What a masterpiece, Ugo—Grazia Deledda's husband, I mean. . . ."[6] After Treves rejected it out of "delicacy,"[7] and probably because of Deledda's objections, Pirandello blamed the writer. In another letter to Ugo Ojetti (to whom the novel is dedicated), he explains the situation, claiming that he was being persecuted unjustly. Far from writing a novel about the couple, he claimed, he had taken from their reality only a cue (*spunto*), working freely with his imagination to create a work of art. Deledda's actions had only made the situation worse. "What spiritual poverty, what narrow-mindedness in that Deledda! Not to understand that acting in this way, she only incites the morbid curiosity of that filthy, petty barnyard of gossips that is our modern literary world!"[8] Here Pirandello seems to imply that as an artist, Deledda should be on *his* side. Perhaps she has been corrupted by her husband? In any case, he delineates in no uncertain terms his opinion of the milieu that is the object of his satire in the novel.

Suo marito was finally published in 1911 by Quattrini of Florence, a much smaller, less prestigious publishing house. Pirandello would not allow the novel to be reprinted after the first printing sold out. He seems to have eventually regretted his quarrel with Deledda. In his later years, he expressed on numerous occasions his admiration for her work. Yet his views on the business of literature did not change. In 1934, after Deledda's death and two years before his own, he began to work on a revision of the novel, of which he completed four chapters. In 1941, his son Stefano published the four revised chapters, along with the three unrevised ones, under the new title chosen by his father, *Giustino Roncella nato Boggiòlo,* thus continuing the name play he started when he called Deledda's husband Grazio Deleddo. Although the satire seems somewhat attenuated in this new version, the differences are not on the whole significant. Italian publishers have in recent years preferred to reprint Pirandello's original novel, *Suo marito,* the text we have translated here.

It could be argued that one of the sources of Pirandello's portrayal of Silvia Roncella was his sense of a "feminine" side of his own creativity, or perhaps of all literary creation. Certainly, he put into Silvia's character important aspects of his own biography and writing. Just a year before the publication of the novel, Pirandello's first works for the stage, *The Vise* and *Sicilian Limes,* based, like many of his one-act plays, on two of his short stories, were performed in Rome. Silvia's perceptions of the contemporary theater and the effect of writing for the stage are his own; Deledda was not a playwright. Furthermore, the plots of Silvia's plays, *The New Colony* and *If Not This Way* . . . , recounted in some detail in the novel, are those of Pirandello. Although he did not write *The New Colony* until 1928, the story line, except for a significant change in the ending, is almost the same. Pirandello published *Se non così* (If Not This Way) in 1915, rewriting it later as *La Ragione degli altri* (The Reason of Others). Other Pirandellian texts attributed to Silvia include a page of his treatise on poetics, *On Humor,* published in 1908, in an interior monologue in which Silvia "sees herself living," and one of Pirandello's poems, written by Silvia during her sojourn in Piedmont.

Pirandello was undoubtedly right when he said that his original interests in satirizing Grazia Deledda's husband along with the literary scene of the new Rome were only points of departure. His real interest lies in exploring the relationship between femininity and creativity, an interest that takes his artistry far beyond his own time and his own prejudices to chart new territory. His intricate and subtle explorations of the mind of the woman writer, of the relations between creation and procreation, and the contradictions inherent in literature as art and literature as business, speak to the preoccupations of the twenty-first century as they did to those of the first years of the 1900s.

NOTES

1 Grazia Deledda to Antonio Scano, 25 April 1905, *Studi sardi*, vol. 19 (Sassari: Gallizzi, 1966). Four unpublished letters from Grazia Deledda to Antonio Scano.

2 Palmiro Madesani to Georges Hérelle, 5 February 1906. Transcribed by Rosaria Taglialatela from the collection in the Bibliothèque nationale in Troyes for her unpublished dissertation.

3 Remo Branca, *Il segreto di Grazia Deledda* (Cagliari: Editrice Sarda Fossataro, 1971), 111.

4 Grazia Deledda to Antonio Scano, from Rome, 12 November 1902.

5 Grazia Deledda to Madesani, 13 July 1910, *Onoranze a Grazia Deledda*, ed. Mario Ciusa Romagna, Nuoro, Sardinia, 1959.

6 Luigi Pirandello to Ugo Ojetti, 18 December 1908, in *Carteggi inediti* (Rome: Bulzoni, 1980), 28.

7 M. Grillandi, *Emilio Treves* (Torino: UTET, 1977), 590–91.

8 Letter of 3 August 1911, in *Carteggi inediti* (Rome: Bulzoni, 1980), 62. Reprinted in *Suo Marito*, ed. Rita Guerricchio (Florence: Giunti, 1994), 236.

Like many of Italy's greatest modern writers, Luigi Pirandello was a Sicilian. He was born in a community called "Caos," near Agrigento, where his father owned sulphur mines, in 1867. He studied in Rome and in Bonn, Germany, then married and settled in Rome. His wife's life-long mental illness had a deep effect on his writing. He began his career as a poet, novelist, and short story writer, also publishing an important essay, *On Humor*, in 1908. His best-known novel is *The Late Mattia Pascal*, 1904. His earliest plays, such as *The Vise* (1912) and *Sicilian Limes* (1913), were one-act adaptations of his stories. Pirandello became best known as a dramatist, rising to international fame with the production of *Six Characters in Search of an Author* in Paris in 1923. This was followed by the success of the play many consider his greatest, *Henry IV*. Other representative plays by Pirandello include *Liolà, It is so! (If You Think So)*, and *Each in His Own Way*. These five plays were translated by Eric Bentley and published under the title *Naked Masks* in 1952. *Maschere nude (Naked Masks)* is the title given to the entire corpus of Pirandello's plays in Italy. Pirandello received the Nobel Prize for Literature in 1934. He died in 1936.

Mary Ann Frese Witt is Professor of French and Italian at North Carolina State University. She is the author of *Existential Prisons: Confinement in Mid-Twentieth-Century French Literature* (1985); *The Humanities: Cultural Roots and Continuities* (1980; rev. ed. 1985, 1989, 1993, 1997, 2001), and of the forthcoming *Aesthetic Fascism and the Search for Modern Tragedy* (2001).

Martha King is the translator of Grazia Deledda, *Reeds in the Wind* (1998); Grazia Deledda, *Cosima* (1988) and *Elias Portolu* (1995). She is also the editor of *New Italian Women: A Collection of Short Fiction* (1989). A selection of stories by Anna Banti, with introduction, in collaboration with Carol Lazzaro-Weis, will be published in 2001 in the Modern Language Association translation series.

Library of Congress Cataloging-in-Publication Data
Pirandello, Luigi, 1867–1936.
[Suo marito. English]
Her husband / by Luigi Pirandello ; translated from the Italian
by Martha King and Mary Ann Frese Witt.
ISBN 0-8223-2600-0 (cloth : alk. paper)
I. King, Martha, 1928–   II. Witt, Mary Ann Frese.   III. Title.
PQ4835.I7 S7713 2000   853'.912—dc21   00-030868